Scarlet Wilson wrote her first story aged eight and has never stopped. She's worked in the health service for twenty years, having trained as a nurse and a health visitor. Scarlet now works in public health and lives on the West Coast of Scotland with her fiancé and their two sons. Writing medical romances and contemporary romances is a dream come true for her.

HEALING THE
SINGLE DAD'S
HEART

&

JUST FRIENDS
TO JUST MARRIED?

SCARLET WILSON

MILLS & BOON

First Published in Great Britain 2019
by Mills & Boon, an imprint of HarperCollins*Publishers*
1 London Bridge Street, London, SE1 9GF

© 2019 Scarlet Wilson

ISBN: 978-0-263-26988-8

MIX
Paper from
responsible sources
FSC
www.fsc.org
FSC™ C007454

This book is produced from independently certified FSC™ paper
to ensure responsible forest management.
For more information visit www.harpercollins.co.uk/green.

Printed and bound in Spain
by CPI, Barcelona

HEALING THE SINGLE DAD'S HEART

SCARLET WILSON

MILLS & BOON

To Auntie Margaret who, thirty-six books in,
is still reading and recommending
every one of my books to her friends!

CHAPTER ONE

ON PAPER, THE journey had seemed so long. But for Joe it had been a blink-and-you've-missed-it kind of day. *Go and show your little boy a part of the world where you can make some new memories.* That was what his mother had said to him as she'd handed him the plane tickets to Vietnam.

She had been right. He'd known she was right. And that she was finally giving him the push he needed.

After that, everything had passed in a blur. Getting all their vaccinations, finishing up at work, packing, handing over his house keys to a letting agency and making sure all his mail was redirected to his mother's house.

By the time he'd sat down on the plane he had been well and truly ready for a rest. But his stomach had had other ideas. It had fluttered in a weird kind of way. It had been so long since he'd felt excitement about something he almost hadn't recognised the sensation.

Regan had loved the journey. Between watching movies, eating snacks, sleeping and asking questions he'd been a great travelling companion. And now, as they came in to land at Hanoi airport Regan stared in wonder at the green landscape. 'It's just like home!' he said with a smile.

Joe couldn't stop the ache in his heart. This whole trip was about moving on. He got that. Inside he was ready—up until now he just hadn't quite managed to take the steps. But every now and then Regan did something—it could be a wave of his hand or a look in his eye—that reminded him of Esther. He'd never push away the ache that came from knowing she couldn't see this—couldn't share this moment and be proud of their son and the bright, brave little boy he was becoming.

Joe leaned over and stared out of the window too. He'd half expected to see a city landscape but it seemed Hanoi landing strips were just as green as Glasgow's. Maybe this place would be more familiar than he expected.

The airport was filled with a melee of people. Joe held tightly to Regan's hand as they navigated through passport control and collected their luggage. A guy dressed in a white shirt and casual trousers was leaning against a pillar, holding a piece of paper with their names hastily scrawled in black on it.

Dr Joe Lennox and son

He juggled pulling the cases while still keeping hold of Regan as he gave the guy a nod. Around him a dozen languages were being spoken. He just prayed this guy spoke a little English.

'Dr Joe?' the guy asked.

He nodded again. The guy held out his hand. 'Rudi. I'm your ride to the May Mắn Hospital.' He grabbed hold of the two cases and started walking quickly to the exit. 'From Scotland?' he said over his shoulder.

Joe nodded again and bent to pick up Regan, lengthening his strides to keep up.

'I know all the football teams. Which is your favourite?'

Joe laughed. It didn't matter where he went on the planet, Scotland was known for its football and most conversations started off this way.

It didn't take them long to hit hectic traffic. It seemed the whole world travelled by scooter or motorbike in Hanoi. Regan was tired and tucked in under Joe's arm, snuggling against his chest.

For the briefest of seconds Joe had a moment of doubt. What if Regan didn't like it here? He didn't have his grandparents for reassurance. This was completely different from anything Regan had experienced before. As he brushed his hand over his son's soft hair, he had a flashback to Esther. Regan shared his mother's adventurous spirit. No matter what they tried, Regan tended to jump in with both feet. Like most young boys he was fearless. And that made Joe's heart swell. He didn't ever want his son to lose that element.

After half an hour Joe couldn't resist winding down the window in the car to let the sounds and smells of the city surround them. The first thing that struck him was how busy the place was, how packed in everything looked, from people to shops to transport to homes.

Colour was everywhere. They drove by a row of shops with red, blue and yellow awnings, while packed above, almost squashed together, were flats.

One was in pink brick, with a balcony on each level, next door was white, with plants trailing down towards the awning beneath, next was the thinnest block of flats he'd ever seen, its first balcony entirely taken up with a dining table and chairs. Next came a pale blue block, littered with children's toys, then a flat of unknown colour because green foliage completely covered the roof and the outside walls.

It was like a higgledy-piggledy town constructed from a kid's set of building blocks, and it was utterly charming. The area in front of the shops was packed with street vendors, food carts, a variety of tourist souvenirs and brightly coloured long-sleeved shirts. A tiny part of the chaos of the stalls reminded him of the Barrowlands back home in Glasgow. He smiled as he wondered if the street vendors here used as colourful language as the guys back home.

The driver pointed out places as they drove into the Ba Dinh district—then into the French quarter. The French Colonial architecture was evident all around them, but as they passed through, it was clear they were moving further away from the more tourist-oriented areas and out towards the suburbs. It was denser here, street vendors everywhere, but poverty was evident at every turn. A little prickle ran down his spine. Again, it reminded him of home. His GP surgery served one of the most deprived areas of Glasgow.

Children were running happily through the streets, and even though they were still in the city, strips of green occasionally showed. The taxi turned down a slightly wider street. The houses were different here, not as packed in as before. These looked like private residences, each with a little more ground around them.

The taxi driver pulled up in front of a large, pale yellow two-storey French colonial-style house that was a little shabby around the edges. There was a sign just above the door: 'May Mắn Hospital'. The driver turned and smiled, gesturing at the sign and getting out to open the door for them. Joe lifted Regan into his arms and stepped out, letting the close, warm air surround him. 'Bit of a temperature change from Scotland,' he said quietly to himself, turning his head from side to side to take in his surroundings.

There were several similar-style buildings. What once must have been residences seemed to have been converted. Two appeared to be restaurants, another a hotel. It was clear that once the houses had been very grand, though now they all looked a bit run-down. Paintwork was a little faded, some shutters on the windows slightly crooked, and most of the houses gave a general air of tiredness. The only thing that seemed bright was the sign above the door: May Mắn Hospital.

The driver collected their cases from the boot and followed him up the steps to the hospital entrance. He walked through the wide double doors and stopped.

A wave of familiarity swept over him. The smell, the buzz—something he hadn't felt in six months, maybe even longer. Working as a GP wasn't the same as working in a hospital, and the crazy thing about hospitals the world over was that, in some respects, they were all the same.

It didn't matter about the facilities, the climate or the time. The smell of disinfectant, the quiet hum of voices and brisk footsteps made him take a deep breath and let the edges of his mouth turn upwards.

He had missed this. No matter how much he tried to pretend he hadn't. Joe had wanted to be a doctor since he was a kid, and for the last six months...

He swallowed. He'd been working. But he hadn't

been enjoying it. He hadn't loved the job the way he'd once done.

And even though he knew nothing about this place or these people, this felt right.

There was a noise to his right. 'Can I help you?'

He turned to see a woman at his side. She'd spoken English to him. She could obviously tell he wasn't from around here. 'I'm supposed to meet Nguyen Van Khiem, or Nguyen Van Hoa,' he said, trying to say the names in the right order. 'The two doctors that run this place.'

As he spun around to face her, she caught sight of the bundle in his arms. 'Oh,' she said, taking a step back in surprise. She blinked then took a breath.

For a second the air was still between them. He could see the surprise on her pretty face. He obviously wasn't quite what she'd expected. But as his eyes took in her dark hair and eyes, the barest hint of make-up and straight white teeth, he realised that this wasn't quite what he'd expected either. His mother had told him the hospital was run by an older couple with fifty years of experience between them.

The woman spoke. 'You must be the new doctor. Khiem and Hoa told me you should arrive today.' She tilted her head as she tried to catch a look at Regan, who was snuggled into his father's shoulder. 'This must be... Regan, isn't it?'

Now he was intrigued. Who was this woman who'd obviously paid attention to the new arrival?

She was a little shorter than him, with shiny dark brown hair tied back with a clip at her neck. She was wearing a pink shirt and black trousers that showed off her neat waist.

She held out her hand towards him. 'I'm Lien—one

of the other doctors that works here.' Her smile was broad and reached her dark eyes. He must have been looking at her curiously because she filled in the blanks. 'Dang Van Lien,' she said, giving her name in full. 'But the people around here just call me Dr Lien.'

He gave a nod, trying to familiarise himself with saying the family name first. Her handshake was warm and firm. He liked that. She was still holding his hand while she spoke.

'Khiem and Hoa have been called away. They're sorry they couldn't be here to meet you. Come with me. I guess you'll want to put the little guy down.' She reached over and grabbed the handle of both suitcases before he had a chance to stop her and tugged them along behind her.

'Is everything okay?' he asked as he followed her down the corridor, wondering if everything was going to stop before it even started. He was surprised the doctors who had employed him weren't here. 'Where did they have to go?'

She nodded her head. 'They've had to go to one of the other hospitals. It's a few hundred kilometres away, and some of the staff have taken ill. They'll probably be away for the next few weeks.' For a small woman, she had surprisingly long strides. He didn't even get a chance to really see the facilities before she'd led him out the back of the building and pointed to one of three smaller houses set in the grounds at the back. She shot him a smile. 'We're lucky. Good staff facilities here.'

It seemed that the slightly shabby colonial-style house had been hiding some secrets. The grounds at the back were bigger than he would have expected. He hid a smile, likening it to walking into the Tardis in *Dr Who*. There were green bushes, some trees and the three individual white houses set just far enough away from each other to give some privacy. Each of the houses had a different coloured front door, one yellow, one blue and one lilac.

She led him over to the house with the blue door, swinging it open and flicking a switch. She picked up the key that was hanging on a hook behind the door. 'Here you go,' she said as she handed it over.

A warm glow filled the small space. It was cosy. Nowhere near as big as his house back home. There was a small red sofa in the main room and a table with two chairs, then a neat kitchen set in the back. With a smile Lien showed him the two compact bedrooms, both beds covered with mosquito nets, and bathroom.

It didn't matter that the space was small. There was something about the furnishings and decor that made it welcoming. He laid Regan carefully down on the white bedspread, ensured the mosquito net was in place, then paused for a second and pulled something from Regan's small backpack. He didn't want Regan to wake up with nothing familiar around him.

The picture frame held two pictures of Esther. In one, shortly after delivery, she was pale, holding Regan wrapped in a white blanket, and in the other Esther was much brighter—it was taken a year before her diagnosis with acute myeloid leukaemia and Regan said it was his favourite picture of his mum. In it she was laughing on a beach as her blonde hair blew in her eyes. Joe's fingers hovered over the photo as he placed it on the bed next to Regan's head and backed out of the room, leaving the door open.

'I need a story,' Regan whispered with his eyes still closed.

Joe looked at the stuffed-full cases and Lien caught his gaze. She gave a little shrug. 'I have a never-ending stack of stories. Why don't you let me tell him one while you try to get yourself settled?'

Something inside him twinged. Telling Regan a bed-time story had been part of their bedtime routine for the last four years. He was tired himself, though, his brain not really computing what time of day it was. Fatigue told him that it might be nice for Regan to hear a story that wasn't one of those he'd repeated time and time again over the years. New stories were in short supply. 'That's really kind of you,' he said. 'Thank you.'

'No problem,' said Lien as she sat at the edge of Regan's bed and launched into a story about dragons.

Joe was actually sad that Regan was so sleepy. He would relish a story like this. Still, it gave him time to open their cases and find their toiletries and some clothes for the next day, along with their mosquito repellent. Everything else could wait.

Lien appeared next to him just as he was trying to shake the creases out of a shirt. 'He's gone,' she said quietly. 'I think he was halfway there when I started.'

Lien moved over to the kitchen. 'Tea?' she asked, holding up a pair of cups. She opened the fridge and a few cupboards. 'Don't worry, Hoa has filled the fridge and cupboards with some staples for you.'

'She has? That was kind of her.'

Lien gestured to the red sofa. 'Sit down. You must be tired.' She gave him a curious look. 'Scotland? Isn't it? You've come along way.'

Joe relaxed down onto the sofa. It was just as comfortable as it looked. He watched as Lien moved easily around the kitchen, boiling water and preparing the tea. The smell drifting towards him was distinctly floral. This wasn't the strong black tea he was used to in Scotland.

A few minutes later Lien handed him the steaming cup of pale yellow liquid. He tried to give an unobtrusive sniff. 'What kind of tea is this?'

She settled next to him, her leg brushing against his jeans. 'The best kind, jasmine. Haven't you tried it before?'

It smelled like perfume, but he wasn't going to say that out loud, so he balanced the cup on his lap and turned a little to face her. 'Thanks for this. You didn't need to.'

'I did.' She grinned, eyes glinting as she sipped her own tea. 'It's bribery. I'm just trying to make sure you'll be fit to work tomorrow. The jasmine tea should relax you a little, and hopefully you'll get some sleep and your body clock will adjust.'

He nodded. 'Ah, bribery. Now I understand.'

She gestured with her hand to the window in front of them. It looked back over to the main building. 'Tomorrow will be busy, a baptism of fire.' She pulled a face and gave a shrug. 'There's some kind of norovirus bug out there right now. We're getting lots of dehydrated kids and adults.'

Joe shuddered. 'Norovirus. Perfect.'

He waited a second then gave her another curious look. 'How long have you been here?'

'All my life,' she replied simply. 'Born and brought up in Hanoi. Trained here, then spent a year in Washington and another in Dublin.' She gave him a smile. 'I wanted to see the world.'

'But you came back?'

She hesitated for a second. 'Of course. I trained with Duc. He's Khiem and Hoa's son. This local hospital has been here since I was kid. They opened it with some money they inherited, and have kept it running ever since.'

'The government doesn't pay?'

She pulled a face. 'They make a contribution. Hanoi has a population of over six million...' she let out a laugh '...with nearly as many motorbikes. The government is trying to get a handle on our health system, but it's nowhere near as robust as the system in the UK. In most circumstances, you still have to pay to see a doctor in Vietnam.'

'And can the people around here pay?'

She shook her head and held out both hands. 'That's why we're here. We offer free healthcare to anyone who attends. Immunisations for kids. Prenatal health care for mothers. And anything else too.'

Now he'd sat down he realised his bones were actually aching, along with every muscle in his shoulders. Travelling did that to you. The aroma from the tea was strong, vibrant. He took a sip of the hot liquid and tried to let his taste buds acclimatise. He was conscious of the fact that Lien's dark eyes were watching him carefully.

He held up the cup. 'Not too bad.'

She shot him a suspicious glance. 'Well, get used to it. Jasmine tea and iced coffee are the norm around here.'

He lifted one hand to give his tired eyes a rub. 'Your English is great. I'm a bit worried about tomorrow.

Let's just say I'm not entirely fluent in Vietnamese. I've learned a few words, but I couldn't hold a proper conversation.'

She shook her head and waved a hand. 'Don't worry. We have a full-time interpreter in the hospital. She'll normally be around to help you. A number of our nurses are bilingual too. You should manage fine.'

She nodded towards the bedroom. 'Have you made arrangements for your son?'

He glanced to the little sleeping figure on the bed. 'Yes, I've registered him at the international school just a few streets over. Khiem had sent me details about it. I've to take him there tomorrow—just before eight.'

'Perfect, it has a good reputation. I'm sure he'll like it.'

She paused once more. 'Khiem said you're here for six months.'

It was a statement, but she said the words like a question. He tried not to let his doubt show on his face. 'That's how long I've taken time off work back home. We needed...' he hesitated, trying to find the right words '...a change of scene. Regan is due to start school back home in six months, so I plan on taking him back for that.' He looked around, realising he hadn't set eyes on any other staff members. 'Does Khiem and Hoa's son work here too?'

Lien laughed. 'Not if he can help it. No, Duc has been lured to the dark side.' She said the words with good humour.

'What do you mean?'

She gave a small shrug. 'He's still doing his round-the-world tour. Getting experience wherever he can. He's a surgeon. This place wouldn't be for him.'

Now Joe was curious at the first part of her answer. 'You said you did the same.'

She put her hand to her chest. 'I just went to two places. That was enough. Got the experience I needed then brought it back here.'

There was something about the way she said those words. He got the impression she was either slightly exasperated by her friend's continued travels, or that she didn't quite approve, but was far too polite to say those words out loud.

'You always wanted to work back here?'

She met his gaze, her brown eyes sincere. 'This is home. I trained to be a doctor to take care of the people that I love.' She held out her hands and gave a soft smile. 'And the people I love are here.'

Something twisted inside his chest. She was talking about herself. He knew that. He understood it. Though he couldn't help but feel the imaginary punch to the guts. He hadn't been able to help the one he loved. There wasn't anything he could have done to save Esther. He'd picked apart every element of her diagnosis and treatment a million times in the long sleepless nights after her death.

As his stomach twisted, Lien gave him a look. She glanced between him and the sleeping form of Regan. 'Why Vietnam?'

Two words. But he knew she was asking so much more.

He swallowed, wishing the tea wasn't quite so scalding so he could gulp it down.

He took a deep breath. He hated it that he'd got used to telling people that Esther had died, seeing their pitying glances or slight discomfort.

'My mother chose it for us,' he said with a rueful smile.

Her brow wrinkled. 'What?'

He lifted one hand and ran it through his hair. A wave of tiredness had just hit him, and he really hoped that bathroom had a shower that he could hit soon. He relaxed back against the sofa. He was too tired for anything but honesty. He didn't have the energy to dress things up.

'My wife died three years ago. It had always been our intention to travel, to show Regan the world, and my mother...' he gave a slow nod of his head '...decided we both needed a change of scene.' He held up one hand. 'Vietnam was one of the places on the wish list.'

'Your wish list, or your wife's?' She hadn't rushed in with an immediate offer of condolence, instead she'd asked an unexpected question.

He shifted a little on the sofa and gave her an interested look. 'It was mine actually. I always wanted to come and work here at some point, it just kind of...fell off my radar.' He paused for a second. 'A lot of things did,' he added quietly.

Lien fixed her eyes back towards the bedroom. 'That's understandable. You had to change your priorities. Becoming mum and dad to a little boy can't have been easy.'

He turned to face her again. He liked this woman. She was direct. They'd only just met but she seemed to read him well. For the last few years people had tiptoed around him instead of having actual conversations with him, just giving him sympathetic glances or a squeeze of an arm.

He closed his eyes for a second and breathed in the warm air of Vietnam. He'd had doubts the whole way here, but now, for the first time, this actually felt like the right move. He smiled.

'Regan makes it easy,' he said. 'I'm lucky.' He shot her a sideways glance. 'I know what happened wasn't lucky, but I still have a part of her. I can see her every day in our son. From a gesture, a look, even his laugh. And I know she would be proud of the little guy.' He let out a deep breath. 'I just hope that this was the right move, at the right time, and Regan will love it here.'

Lien gave an understanding nod as she took a final sip of her tea. 'There's lots to love here, it's a great hospital, and great staff. If you need a hand from any of your colleagues, all you have to do is ask.'

He gave a nod of thanks. The words were reassuring. This was the first time he and Regan had been away from their extended family, and the added complication of Khiem and Hoa not being here when they'd arrived had given him a moment of concern.

He looked back at Lien. 'At the entrance...' he gave a little smile '...you were expecting someone...different?'

Her smile was gentle in return. She knew she'd been caught out. She gave a nod. 'From the description Khiem gave me I was expecting someone...older.' He could see the compassion and warmth in her eyes. 'But you'll do, Dr Joe. You'll do.' She patted him on the shoulder as she stood up and pointed to the fridge.

There was something about the way she said those words that sent a little buzz through his body. The nod of approval meant everything to him and he couldn't quite work out why. Maybe it was the journey, the distance, the unknown. Whatever it was, he could already tell that Lien was someone he could work with. She'd asked a lot of questions tonight and he hadn't really had the opportunity to ask much in return. He was intrigued. He already wanted to know more about his colleague but Lien was talking again.

'There are noodles, vegetables and pork in there. The wok is in the cupboard to the side of the cooker. If you're hungry, you should be able to rustle something up.' She lifted her cup and walked over with it to the sink. 'I can show you where the market is tomorrow if you need to get some other things. It's not too far.'

He stood up quickly, remembering his manners.

'If you need anything, I'm just in the house next door.'

'You are? Which one is yours?'

'Khiem and Hoa stay in the one with the yellow door, and I'm in the lilac one.'

He gave a nod as she opened the door, then realised something. 'Darn it, I haven't even looked around the hospital properly yet.'

Lien waved her hand as she strolled away. 'Plenty of time for that tomorrow. I'll see you in the morning.' She gave him a bright smile as she headed towards the house with the lilac door, her hair bouncing as she walked.

He gave a little shake of his head. He'd been worried. Maybe even a tiny bit scared. But Lien seemed like she could be a good colleague. He looked around the house. It was compact but had everything they needed. Six months.

Six months of something completely and utterly different. And for the second time since his mother had handed him the tickets, he felt a wave of emotion that this time he could recognise. Excitement.

Lien closed the door behind her. Maybe she'd been too direct—too forward. Truth was, she was a little on edge. Khiem and Hoa had expected to be here, but the phone call from the other hospital had meant they'd had to leave at short notice. Joe didn't realise it yet, but it actually meant that they'd be two doctors down for the next few weeks. Lien hadn't been joking about the bribery.

She pulled the clip from her hair and gave her head a shake. She couldn't pretend she wasn't a bit intrigued by the new Scottish doctor. She'd had to concentrate hard at some points when he'd been speaking. Did he realise just how quickly he sometimes spoke, and how the words just seemed to all run into one?

She'd noticed his fingers hovering near the picture he'd placed next to Regan. It was clear it was pictures of his wife. Was he really ready to be here?

She sighed. They'd had doctors here for six months at a time before. The last doctor from Germany had been suffering from mental health problems that had come to a head while he'd been here. A female doctor had come to Vietnam without declaring her drug addiction—something that had quickly become evident. Another colleague had appeared from the US, romanced his way around the staff in the hospital, then left abruptly after three months. Turned out he'd left a wife back home he'd forgotten to tell anyone about.

All three of those doctors had been escaping something, running away from something. It sounded very much like Joe Lennox was doing something similar. Would he really last six months? Because she needed him to. The hospital needed some stability. Sad as his story was, the last thing they needed was another doctor with problems of his own who would leave because he discovered the experience in Vietnam wasn't what he wanted.

She started stripping off her clothes as she headed to the shower. She'd have to help him out as much as she could—particularly until his little boy was settled in the international school. If Joe got cold feet he might decide to get on the first plane home to Scotland. She believed him when he said he'd needed a change. But the fact he'd been honest enough to say his mother had pushed him in this direction bothered her. Was he really ready for this? She hadn't seen his CV. She had no idea what his previous experience was. Khiem and Hoa did all the recruitment and she trusted their judgement. If they thought he'd fit in, then she had to believe that.

But the truth was, it wasn't his skills she was worried about. It was more his heart and his head. If his head was somewhere else he could make mistakes, and if his heart wasn't in it, he wouldn't want to stay.

Something twisted in her chest.

This place meant everything to her.

For lots of the residents in Hanoi, this was their only accessible healthcare. Yes, services were pushed. Yes, they didn't always have all the supplies that they needed. But she was determined that this place would always serve the population that needed it.

People like her, and her family.

This was her city, her people.

And no matter how much empathy she had for the new doctor's circumstances, he had better be prepared to pull his weight around here.

CHAPTER TWO

Lien was waiting for him when he arrived back after dropping Regan at the school. He'd obviously been nervous about leaving his son at the strange school in an unfamiliar city, but the place had given him good vibes. The nursery teacher had shown them into a bright, welcoming environment filled with a host of happy-looking children chattering in different languages.

Regan had tugged at his hand after a few minutes, anxious to go and join in the fun, so Joe had left with reassurances that they would call the hospital if there were any concerns.

By the time he got back to the hospital it was a few minutes before eight o'clock. Already the place was a hive of activity. The waiting room had only a few seats left. Lien was wearing a pale blue shirt and navy trousers, and her hair was in a ponytail again. There was no sign of the traditional white coat.

He'd swithered for a few moments this morning over what to wear, before settling on a pair of dark trousers and a simple short-sleeved white shirt. The temperature here was much warmer than he was used to, and he wasn't sure if the hospital had air-conditioning or not. He hadn't noticed last night. He gave a sniff. He wasn't quite used to the aroma of the insect repellent he'd covered both himself and Regan in this morning. Maybe he should have tried to drown it out with more aftershave?

Lien gave him a brief nod as he walked back through the main entrance. 'Good. Is Regan settled?'

He gave a brief nod and she started speaking again straight away. 'Come with me, and I'll give you a walk around. I'll show you our systems and our supplies and when Mai Ahn, our translator, gets here, I'll assign her to you for the rest of the day.' She walked him over to a sink and started washing her hands. He quickly followed suit. She'd already mentioned norovirus problems. Hand washing was one of the key practices to help prevent the spread.

Joe barely had time to draw breath. 'First thing,' Lien said as she kept scrubbing her hands, 'you should really wear long sleeves. If your shirts are too warm, I'll show you a place where you can buy some lighter weight clothing. Do you have your insect repellent on?'

He nodded and she kept talking. 'With Khiem and Hoa away, we're two doctors down. I can't afford for our latest recruit to pick up something from a mosquito bite.'

It felt like a bit of a reprimand and he wasn't quite sure how to react, but Lien was already talking again. 'Hoa covered antenatal and maternity care, so we'll all have to pick up her role while she's gone.'

Joe didn't miss the way that she'd phrased that. She hadn't asked him about his experience, or if he was happy to cover this area. She was letting him know what was expected of him. It seemed her directness last night hadn't been unusual but the norm.

As they finished scrubbing their hands she kept talking while she dried hers. 'Okay, I'm sure you've done some general reading on the health issues in Vietnam.' She shot him a sideways glance. 'Or at least I hope you have.'

He nodded quickly. 'Of course. Main issues are malaria, tuberculosis, HIV and AIDS, with some cases of dengue fever and ongoing issues with Agent Orange.'

She gave an appreciative nod and held out her hands. 'Biggest killer of kids in our area is malnutrition, coupled with diarrhoea and vomiting. They have no extra fat layers to fall back on. It hits hard and fast.'

'So a norovirus outbreak is your worst nightmare?'

'Pretty much.'

She led him down one corridor and then up a set of stairs. 'Okay, downstairs is basically our clinic area. Upstairs we have six four-bed rooms with a variety of patients. Children and adults.' He could see how the layout of the traditional colonial house had been adapted to work as a hospital. There were a number of nursing staff upstairs to whom she introduced him quickly. The staff seemed friendly, and the patients well-cared-for. Most were on IVs. Lien caught his gaze.

'We have a mixture of dehydration in both the young and the elderly. Lots of chest complaints too. Anyone suffering from diarrhoea is cared for separately in one of the single rooms at the other end of the corridor.'

Joe nodded. He'd known whole hospital wards closed because of winter vomiting bugs. They couldn't ignore, or not treat, people affected, but, because it was infectious, it had a real chance of being passed to other patients or staff. Hygiene issues had to be the top priority.

'Anyone today that you're worried about?'

She gave him a half-smile. 'I've already done a ward round this morning, but we'll do another one later so you can familiarise yourself with the patients. Today we start downstairs at the clinic.'

They washed their hands again, and moved back down the stairs.

Downstairs was separated into four areas. One was a general waiting room, one was for children, one for pregnant women and a fourth for X-rays, with a plaster room next door. It was a real mixed bag. A kind of cross between a GP surgery and community hospital back in Scotland.

Lien gave a little sigh as she showed him into an office and gestured for him to sit in the chair opposite her. 'We have a real mixture of antenatal care. Only around sixty per cent of women in Vietnam attend antenatal care. Some women don't present until late in pregnancy. Others present early, requesting their pregnancy be monitored all the way through for birth defects. It's not unheard of for a pregnant woman in Vietnam to have up to twenty scans.'

Joe's eyebrows shot upwards. The norm for the UK was two, unless there were any concerns. Something clicked in his brain. 'Agent Orange?'

She nodded.

'How often nowadays do women present with birth defects?'

Lien's face was serious. 'It's more prevalent now in the south of Vietnam, but forty years on there are still children affected here. The spray that was used to destroy the crops obviously went into the soil. Poverty is a major issue in Vietnam and some families are solely reliant on growing their own foods. They have no other option but to eat the food they grow—whether the soil is damaged or not.'

She shook her head. 'We have two other hospitals. One is in the outskirts of the city of Uông Bí city, in northeast Vietnam, and the other—the one Duc's parents have just gone to—is in Trà Bồng District in the south of the country. At that one, we also take care of the kids in the nearby orphanage. A lot of them are affected. There's poverty across Vietnam, just like there's poverty in every country in the world, but it's worse down in the south. Down there, families are reliant on farming. If their crops fail, it's disaster for them. A lot of them rely on their kids to work alongside them. If their kids are affected by Agent Orange, or any other genetic or medical condition, often the family can't afford to keep them.'

'So they end up in the orphanage?' Joe asked.

'Exactly. We offer free medical care to the orphanage. Things have improved in the last few years, but we still aren't where we should be.'

'Sometimes I forget how lucky we are in the UK. Yes, things aren't perfect. But the healthcare part of the job generally always gets done.' He gave a slow nod. 'And the first hospital you mentioned?'

'The other is in Uông Bí in Quang Ninh province, in northeast Vietnam, more towards the coast. We'll cover both hospitals at some point in the next six months—generally just for a week or two to cover holidays.'

'Okay.' He was beginning to get a general feel for the place, for the sort of patients he'd be seeing, and the kind of responsibilities he'd have here. None of it seemed beyond his ability, though he'd have to do a bit more background reading on some treatments.

Lien ran through the paperwork they used, how to order tests and their prescribing arrangements. She handed him a pre-printed list with Vietnamese names for some of the more commonly used drugs. It was clear she'd familiarised foreign doctors with the clinic workings before.

Joe leaned on one hand. Everything seemed straightforward enough. 'This place,' he said, 'it's like a cross between a community clinic, a cottage hospital and an ER.'

Lien was watching him with careful eyes. He couldn't quite work out what was going on in her mind. He was sure she was part vetting him, part examining his motives. It was only natural. She was looking for someone she could rely on. Having to check another doctor's practices would be almost as bad as not having a colleague at all. 'Let's hope you don't have to cover it all at once,' she said softly.

He could see the flash of worry in her eyes. But the only way to earn the trust of a colleague was to prove himself. Joe was willing to do that. Back home everyone trusted him in his current role, but he wasn't back home any more. He was in an entirely different country, and while some health needs would be the same, there were others he'd need to query, and Joe wasn't too proud to do that. He would never put patients at risk.

'Where do you want me?'

Lien's eyes brightened at the question. Was that relief he'd just spotted? 'What do you prefer?' she asked. 'I need someone to cover the children's clinic, and someone to cover the adult clinic.'

He gave a nod. The clinic work, whether it was for children or adults, would be very much like his GP role back home. He shot her a smile. 'Happy to do either.' Then met her gaze. 'Put me wherever I can be of most use.'

She shifted a little in her chair, caught off guard at his words. He almost let his smile broaden. She liked being straightforward and so did he. 'I'm not here to be a hindrance, Lien, I'm here to be a help.'

She reached up and brushed an errant strand of brown hair behind her ear that had escaped her pony-tail. She was close enough that he could see just how smooth her skin was. She wore very little make-up. But she didn't need any, her dark hair and eyes comple-mented her appearance beautifully. In another life, in another place, he would definitely have looked twice.

It had been so long since a thought like that had even entered his head that he automatically frowned. What was wrong with him? Where had that come from?

Lien tilted her head. 'Something wrong?'

He shook his head too quickly. 'No, nothing.' He pushed himself up from the chair. 'Where do you want me?' He was anxious to get this day started.

The few seconds of silence was slightly uncomfort-able. He flashed back to being a junior doctor and the nurse in charge of the ward shooting him a glance to say she doubted he should even actually touch a patient.

A figure appeared in the doorway and Lien stood up. 'Perfect. Mai Ahn, this is Joe. Joe, this is Mai Ahn, your interpreter. She'll help you with the children's clinic.'

'Children's clinic it is,' he said with a nod, before reaching out to shake hands with Mai Ahn. 'Lead the way.'

She was unsure of him. Of course she was. Did he even notice he occasionally glanced at his mobile clipped onto his belt? It was only natural that he was worried about how his son was settling in on his first day of nursery, she only hoped it wouldn't distract him from the job he had to do.

The children's clinic wasn't for the faint-hearted.

She couldn't help but be automatically protective of the place she loved working in. At least he'd been honest last night. He'd told her that he and his son needed a change after losing his wife. He'd said it had been three years. But she'd seen the glint of pain in his eyes. Was he really ready to move on?

She still had doubts.

It was a shame. Because he was undoubtedly handsome. The burr of the Scots accent was almost melodic—even though she had to concentrate hard. And it was clear that he doted on his son. Just as she'd expect him to.

She gave herself a shake. It was a ridiculous observation. She was used to doctors coming here on short-term contracts, and she'd never considered any kind of relationship. She was too busy. Too dedicated to her work. She'd had her heart broken once, and that was enough for her.

Too poor. Not the words he'd used, but those were the words he'd meant. Lien had never pretended to be anything she wasn't. As a child she'd always been well mannered and as well presented as she could be. She'd been bright, and her teachers had noticed. They'd encouraged her to study hard, and eventually helped her to seek out scholarships so she could attend medical school.

At medical school she'd got along with most of her classmates. Reuben had come from a rich family in another city. He'd never asked her where she lived—he'd just made assumptions. Then, when he'd found out, after two years, she'd been dumped quicker than a hot brick.

Her family was proud of her, and she was of them. She'd hated the way it had made her feel. Not good enough. Not rich enough.

She came from one of the poorest areas in the city. Her family still lived there—no matter how much she'd tried to assist them since she'd qualified as a doctor. But even now they wouldn't accept any financial help from her.

They liked where they lived. They still worked hard. They didn't want change, in any form.

Lien lifted the pile of patient notes from the desk. They were all people who were due back at the clinic today to be reviewed.

One of the nurses gave her a smile as she walked into the waiting room. There were already ten people waiting. She gave a nod of her head and smiled, speaking in Vietnamese. 'Okay, who is first?'

The only person having trouble concentrating today was her. She kept casting her eyes through to the other waiting room. She knew that Mai Ahn, the interpreter, would come and find her if he had any concerns. But she didn't. Instead, she saw an occasional glance of Joe carrying babies and toddlers through to the examination room for assessment or vaccinations. Through Mai Ahn, he chatted to the mothers. Most of them seemed happy to talk to him and from the looks on their faces the Scottish doctor was proving a hit.

After a few hours he came through and knocked on her door.

'Lien, can we have a chat about a child?'

She nodded, pleased that he'd come to talk to her.

'I think I've got a little one with complications of tuberculosis. I can't find any previous notes, and there's no X-ray.' His brow wrinkled. 'Don't most babies get immunised against tuberculosis shortly after birth?'

'They should. Unfortunately, tuberculosis is common around here. If babies are born in hospital they are immunised if the parents consent. But not all babies are born in hospitals. What do you think are the complications?'

He ran his hands through his hair. 'She's losing weight, even though she's feeding. Her colour is poor, she's tachycardic, and I suspect her oxygen saturation isn't what it should be. Her lungs don't sound as if they are filling properly. She has a temperature and a cough. I suspect a pleural effusion. Do you have a paediatric monitor I could use while I order a chest X-ray?'

Lien stood quickly and gave him a serious kind of smile. 'Let's do this together.'

He raised one eyebrow. 'Don't you trust me?' He didn't seem annoyed by the fact she was effectively second-guessing him. He might even have looked a little amused.

'You asked for a second opinion, Dr Lennox. I'm going to give you one.'

The amused look stayed on his face. 'Absolutely. I haven't seen many kids with tuberculosis in Scotland.'

She gave a nod as they walked through to the paediatric treatment room. As soon as they reached the door, Lien could almost verify his diagnosis. She switched to Vietnamese and introduced herself to the mother and her five-year-old daughter, who was clearly sick.

Joe's notes were thorough. Three other members of

the family had active tuberculosis. Only one complied with their treatment. It was no wonder the little girl was affected.

Five minutes later they were looking at a chest X-ray. Joe was right at her shoulder. She held her breath and caught a slight whiff of the aftershave he was wearing, even though it was overshadowed by his insect repellent. She wanted to know if he'd recognise what she needed him to on the X-ray.

She needn't have worried. He lifted one finger and pointed to the film. 'Pleural effusion without any parenchymal lesion.' He didn't finish there. 'I know there's some mixed feelings, but because of how this little girl has presented, I would be inclined to drain the effusion rather than leaving it.'

She took a few minutes to recheck things. This was the first time he'd seen a child with tuberculosis, never mind the added complications, and he'd picked it up straight away. She couldn't help but be impressed.

She turned to face him. 'I think you're right. Let's put our public health heads on and try to persuade the rest of the family to comply with their medications. We can use a sample of the effusion to diagnose the tuberculosis. A pleural biopsy would likely be too traumatic right now.'

He nodded in agreement. She paused for a moment, wondering whether she should question his skill set any further.

'Any experience of doing a pleural effusion in a five-year-old?'

He nodded. 'I specialised in paediatrics before training as a GP.' He gave her a steady look. 'I've got this. But I'm happy for you to stay if you'd like.'

He didn't seem defensive or annoyed, but it felt like a bit of a line in the sand. He already knew she'd questioned his diagnosis. Now she'd asked about his experience. Lots of other clinicians that she knew might have been annoyed by this, but Joe just seemed to have accepted her actions without any discomfort. Still, the tone in his voice had changed a little, as if he was getting a bit tired of her.

She pressed her lips together. If he'd expressed any anxiety about the situation she would have been happy to take over. But he hadn't, and she knew it was time to step back. She had enough patients of her own to see still in the waiting room.

She glanced at the nurse and interpreter. She had confidence in both of them. Either of them would come and find her if they were worried. She tried her best to look casual. 'I'll leave it with you. Shout if you need anything.'

Joe watched her retreat, knowing exactly how hard it was for her. Was his counterpart a bit of a control freak? Or maybe she just second-guessed everyone she worked with?

He tried to understand, even though he couldn't help but feel a little insulted by her lack of faith in him. It's not like he hadn't experienced this himself. He'd worked with plenty of other doctors, in a variety of settings over the years, and it always took a bit of time to reassure himself about a colleague's skills and competencies.

It was clear she loved this place. She'd more or less told him that already. There was also the added responsibility of her employers not being here right now, so the well-being of May Mǎn hospital was really in her hands.

He gave some instructions to the nurse, who seemed to understand his English, then knelt down beside the little girl and her mother with Mai Ahn, the interpreter, to explain what would happen next.

Thirty minutes later the procedure was complete, with some hazy yellow fluid in a specimen bottle for the lab. The little girl's cheeks and lips had lost their duskiness, the oxygen saturation monitor showed improvement, and when he listened to her chest he could hear the improved inflation of her lung. He gave instructions to the nurse for another X-ray, and to further monitor for the next few hours.

'I'll come back and have a follow-up chat about the medicines,' he said. Something came into his head. 'Do doctors make home visits here?'

The nurse frowned for a second as if she didn't quite understand what he'd said, then shook her head. 'No. Never.'

Joe sat back in his chair for a moment. He didn't want to send this child home with just a prescription in her hand. The rest of the family were important too. The mother had already told him that both her husband and father-in-law kept forgetting to take their tuberculosis meds. Only her own mother remembered. If he could just see them, and persuade them how important it was, it might stop other family members being infected. He glanced out to the waiting room. He still had a whole host of patients to see, some of whom would need vaccinations, and some might need tuberculosis testing. He went to the waiting room with Mai Ahn to call the next patient, while his idea continued to grow in his head.

* * *

'He went where?'

Ping, one of the nurses, shrugged. 'He talked kind of strange. Something about a home visit. Apparently they do them in Scotland a lot. He persuaded Mai Ahn to go with him.'

Lien walked over and looked at the notes, checking the address on the file, then grabbed her jacket. She'd nearly made it to the front door, when her brain started to become a bit more logical. All she was feeling right now was rage. She went back and scanned the rest of the notes, checking to see what other family members were affected. 'Did he take prescriptions, or did he take the actual medicines?' she asked Ping.

Ping gave her a smile as she carried on with her work and brought a single finger to her lips. 'I couldn't possibly say.'

Lien nearly exploded. It was obvious that the Scottish charm was already working on her staff. What on earth was he thinking? They had to account for every dose they used. They weren't a dispensary. On a few occasions they gave out enough medicines to see a patient through the night, but they didn't give out medicines on a regular basis.

She snatched up her bag and made her way out into the streets. It was around six now, and the pavements were filled with people making their way home from work, the streets filled with traffic. She did her best to dodge her way through the crowds and cross the few streets. The home address wasn't too far away, but the walk did nothing to quell her temper.

By the time she'd reached the address her heart was thudding in her chest. This wasn't exactly the best part of town. She had no idea how he'd managed to persuade Mai Ahn to bring him here, but she would make sure it wouldn't happen again.

The house was on the second floor of an older block of flats, where each storey looked as if it squished the flats beneath it even more. She climbed the small stairwell and walked swiftly along, checking the number before she knocked on the door.

'It's Dr Lien, from the hospital,' she said.

She held her breath for a few moments, and then frowned. Was that laughter she heard inside? The door creaked open and the elderly grandmother of the household gave a little bow as she ushered Lien into the house.

Lien walked through to the main room, where the majority of the family was sitting on bamboo mats on the floor, Joe amongst them.

Mai Ahn was by his side, translating rapidly as he spoke. He had laid the complicated drugs for tuberculosis out in front of the elderly grandfather, instructing Mai Ahn to draw a paper chart with dates and times.

Lien stopped the angry words that were forming in her mouth. Back when she'd worked in the US, dispensary boxes had been commonplace for patients who were on several drugs. But they weren't widely used here at all. That was what he was doing. He was making a do-it-yourself chart and placing the individual tablets on it.

He looked up and caught her eye. 'Lien, oh, you're here.' His eyes shot protectively to Mai Ahn, whose face revealed she thought she was in trouble. The little girl from earlier was sitting curled into her mother's lap. She'd done well, had been sent home with a prescription for her own meds, and if they were administered to her, she should do well.

Joe stood up. 'I was just explaining to the family the problems with drug resistance and how important it is to keep taking their medicines.'

There was a shout behind Lien and she turned to see another two children playing in another room. She swallowed and took a deep breath. 'This might be common practice for Scotland, Dr Lennox, but it's pretty unconventional for Vietnam.'

He stood up casually and shook hands with the grandfather, and then the little girl's father, who also had a chart in front of him. He nodded towards Mai Ahn to get her to translate for him again. 'Thank you so much for seeing me.' He nodded to the little girl's mother. 'Make sure you collect that prescription tomorrow, and if you think there are any problems, feel free to come back to the clinic and see me again.' He gestured towards the kids in the other room. 'And remember to come in for the testing. Remember, we can vaccinate too.'

Lien didn't know whether to be angry or impressed. He hadn't just covered the delivery of the prescriptions, he'd covered the public health issues they'd talked about earlier, taking into account multi-resistant TB, contact tracing, further testing and immunisations.

She bowed in respect to the family and spoke a few extra words of reassurance before leading the way out of the house. She waited until the door had closed behind them, and Mai Ahn had hurried on ahead, before spinning around to face him. 'What on earth were you thinking?'

His brow creased. 'I was thinking about patients

and their medicines. I was thinking about stopping the spread of disease.'

'We don't do this.' She almost stamped her foot. 'We don't visit people at home.'

He held up his hands. 'Why not? Particularly when it's a public health issue? That mother told me back at the clinic that both the father and grandfather were struggling with their meds. You don't need to be a doctor to know that's how the little girl got infected. What about those other two kids? I didn't even know about them before I got here. Are we just supposed to sit at the clinic and wait another few months until they turn up sick too?'

She could see the passion on his face. It was the first time she'd seen him worked up about anything. 'Have you any idea about this area?' she shot back. 'Have you any idea about any of the areas around here—how safe they are?' She wrinkled her nose. 'Aren't there places in Glasgow city that you shouldn't really walk about alone?'

Now he frowned. 'But you walked here alone,' he said.

She threw up her hands. 'But I'm from here,' she emphasised. 'You,' she said, pointing at him, 'are clearly not.'

She was furious and he'd obviously played this wrong.

Joe looked down at his trousers and the long-sleeved shirt he'd changed into. He knew with his tall build, pale skin and light brown hair he must stand out like a sore thumb. But instead of venting more frustration on his new workmate, he took a different tack and gave her a cheeky smile. 'I don't know what you mean.'

He watched her erupt like a volcano. 'It's not funny!'

Maybe he should wind it back in. He leaned against the wall and folded his arms. 'No, you're right, it's not. But neither is the fact that there could be two more children in that household with tuberculosis and two adults risking developing drug-resistant tuberculosis.' He gave a sigh. 'I'm just trying to do my job, Lien. I know things are different here. I know the systems aren't the same as the UK. But I still want to treat patients to the best of my ability.'

There was a noise in the stairwell beneath them, and Mai Ahn rushed back up towards them with a stricken expression on her face. She muttered something to Lien, whose face became serious.

She turned swiftly. 'Other way,' she said quietly, pointing to the stairwell at the opposite end of the passage.

'Something wrong?' he asked, as the women hurried ahead of him.

Lien's expression was a mixture of worry and anger. 'You've made us a target, Joe. A Western doctor—rumoured to be carrying drugs in a poor area of town—is always going to cause problems.'

A cold shiver ran over his body. He hadn't thought about this at all. He tried to relate this to back home. Would he have gone out alone to one of the worst areas in Glasgow? He didn't even want to answer that question in his head, because the truth was that he had done it before, and would probably do it again. Some parts of Hanoi didn't seem that different from Glasgow. But he hadn't meant to put either of his new colleagues at risk. Anything he could say right now would just seem like a poor excuse. He followed them both, turning rapidly down a maze of side streets until they were back on one of the main roads.

Lien didn't say another word to him until they reached the hospital again. A reminder sounded on his phone and he pulled it from his pocket.

'Apologies, Lien, I need to collect Regan.' He hesitated for a second, knowing that things couldn't be ignored. 'Can we talk about this later?'

Lien's face remained stony. She gave a nod to Mai Ahn. 'Thanks so much, I'll see you tomorrow. Sorry about the extra work today.'

The words felt pointed. Part of him was cringing and the other part was annoyed.

Lien turned back to face him. 'I'll walk with you,' she said firmly.

It was clear he was about to be told off. First day on the job and he was already in her bad books. It wasn't the best start. He could easily defend his position, but did he really want to get onto the wrong side of his work colleague, who was also his next-door neighbour?

He decided to be direct, since Lien seemed to like that approach herself. 'I'm sorry about today. I wasn't aware there are areas in Hanoi that aren't particularly safe. I shouldn't have taken Mai Ahn with me. I'll get a better grasp of the language soon.'

He could see her grip tightening on the handle of her shoulder bag. 'You shouldn't have gone at all, Dr Lennox.' Her voice was clipped.

He took a deep breath, resisting the urge to snap back. 'You should let me know now—since we'll be working together for the next six months—are you always going to call me Dr Lennox when you're mad at me, and Joe all the other times?'

She must have been expecting some kind of argument, because his response made her stumble for just a second. She stopped walking and looked him in the eye. 'Why do you do that?'

'Do what?'

People were stepping around them in the busy street.

'Try and interrupt my train of thought.'

He gave a half-smile. 'Because your train of thought was going down an angry rail. Can we pause at a station and back up a bit?'

She shook her head at his analogy.

He shrugged and held up his hands. 'What can I say? I'm the father of a four-year-old. Train and spaceship examples are the ones that usually work.'

She closed her eyes for a second. Her grip on the bag was becoming less pinched. When she opened her eyes again, her pupils were wide. 'You don't get it,' she sighed. 'The staff and patients at the hospital are my responsibility. Mine.' She put her hand on her chest. 'Can you imagine if I had to phone Khiem and Hoa and tell them that our new doctor had been attacked on his first real day of work and now wanted to head back home to Scotland?'

His hands went to his hips. 'Do you really think I'm the kind of guy to leave at the first hurdle?'

Her gaze was steady but sympathetic, and he could tell from that glance alone that she *did* think that about him. Disappointment swelled in his chest. Her voice was hushed on the crowded street. 'What if that first hurdle results in Regan having no parents?'

He flinched as if she'd just thrown something at him. The words were harsh. They were also something that he hadn't even considered.

Ever. He'd spent the first year after Esther had died wrapping his son in cotton wool, worrying about every minor accident, rash or childhood sniffle. In every thought his worst-case scenario had always been about something happening to Regan—not about something happening to *him*.

He stood for a second, not quite sure how to respond, and then he just started walking, lengthening his strides as he hurried to reach the nursery.

All of a sudden he had to set eyes on his son again. He'd already paid a quick visit at lunchtime, spending his break time with his son and making sure he was settled and happy in his new nursery school. But that had been five hours ago.

Lien walked in short, brisk steps alongside him. If she was struggling to keep up she didn't complain.

'I'm sorry,' she muttered. 'That came out a bit...'

'Wrong?' He raised his eyebrows.

'Direct,' she countered.

'Is crime around here really that bad?' he asked. His brain was whirring. He'd read a lot about Vietnam before coming here—although most of what he'd read had been health related. He couldn't remember reading anything about crime.

'No,' she admitted. 'Hanoi isn't any worse than any other major city. But home visits by doctors are just not done here. Particularly when the doctor might be taking out medicines to patients. Surely you can see that if word got about, it could be dangerous for you, and for anyone around you.'

He wasn't happy. 'So you exaggerated?'

She pressed her lips together. 'I protected my staff,' she said.

'Then who was at the bottom of the stairs?'

'Some members of a local gang. Mai Ahn and I know them, they've attended the hospital before—usually for emergency treatment, you know, stitches for fighting or stab wounds.'

The flare of anger abated. Maybe she hadn't been exaggerating after all. 'Surely they wouldn't hurt you, then?' he asked carefully.

Her gaze met his. 'But they would probably hurt you,' was her reply.

He swallowed. It seemed he'd need to get to know this city a little better. In Glasgow even the worst kind of people would generally leave a doctor alone. Most people had a moral code when it came to healthcare professionals, knowing that they would likely need help from them one day. But there had been attacks. One of his good friends had been assaulted and his bag stolen when he'd been visiting a terminally ill patient, so it did happen.

She sighed and put her hand up, tugging her ponytail band from her hair and shaking it out. 'Sorry, headache,' she explained. 'They probably wouldn't hurt you. But the truth is I do know them, and they drink. Heavily. They're all fairly young, and some of them think they have something to prove.'

'So you were erring on the side of caution?'

She gave him the first smile he'd seen since she'd come looking for him. 'That's the polite way to say it.' She shook her head again as they approached the inter-national school. 'I'm not trying to scare you off. This is a fantastic city. But like all cities, there is good and bad, and until you familiarise yourself a little better, or at least get a hang of the language, can you try not to get into trouble? Believe me, I've got enough to worry about without having to check on you.'

She was trying to pretend the words were light-hearted but he could sense the sincerity behind them. They reached the door of the school. 'Can you give me five minutes?' he asked.

She nodded and waited outside as he went in to collect an excited but tired Regan, getting a full report from his teacher.

He walked back out with Regan in his arms. 'It seems nursery was a big success,' he said with a smile, conscious of how relieved he felt. Knowing that Regan had had a good day always made him happy. He'd be able to text his mum and dad tonight to tell them that things were good, and he knew they'd be relieved too.

'Tell you what, let me try and make amends. How about I buy you dinner?'

Lien looked a bit surprised. 'Dinner?' she repeated.

He nodded and looked around. 'You choose. Somehow I haven't managed to get to the market today, and we devoured the food in the fridge last night. Show us somewhere we can eat on a regular basis.' He raised one eyebrow. 'Familiarise me with the area.'

She let out a laugh and shook her head, looking at Regan. She moved closer to talk to him. 'Big day at nursery?'

Regan nodded in a tired kind of way. 'It's cool,' he whispered.

Joe gave his back a rub. 'I suspect Master Lennox is struggling with jet-lag. Once we've eaten I think I'll get him straight to bed.'

Lien looked up and down the street. 'What does

Regan like? Are there foods he doesn't eat? Or is he allergic to anything?'

Joe gave a brief shake of his head. 'Take us somewhere you like, somewhere good. The wee man will more or less try anything.'

Lien let out a laugh.

'What?' Joe's brow creased. 'What is it?'

Her eyes were gleaming. 'Have you any idea how Scottish you just sounded?'

She started walking down the street and he fell into step alongside her. 'Don't I always sound Scottish? I know my accent is a bit thick—'

'A bit?' Now it was her turn to raise her eyebrows.

He laughed now too. They crossed a few streets and she showed him into a small Vietnamese restaurant. By the way they greeted her it was clear she was a regular.

They sat in a booth and Regan settled next to his dad. He seemed to perk up a little. 'Are we getting food?'

'Yip,' said Joe, glancing at the menu. His smile broadened and he looked up at Lien.

She was leaning her head on one hand and watching them both. She too had a big smile on her face, and he knew exactly why.

'What's on the menu, Dad?' asked Regan.

'What's on the menu, Lien?' he asked. He nudged Regan. 'What do you want to eat tonight? I think we're going to get Lien to order for us.'

He slid the menu across the table towards Lien. It was entirely in Vietnamese. He was really going to have to get a handle on the language. He didn't even know how to order fries somewhere—the staple food of lots of kids.

'Rice and more pork,' said Regan brightly. 'And can it be a little bit spicy like the kind we had last night?'

Joe almost gave a sigh of relief. He was lucky Regan was such a great eater. With the exception of Brussels sprouts, there was very little his son would refuse.

Lien leaned across the table towards Regan. 'Oh, they do the best spicy pork in here. We can definitely get you that.' She looked up. 'What about you, Joe?'

'I'll just get the same as Regan.' He pulled a face. 'But can you order big? I'm famished—I skipped lunch.'

'You did?' She frowned and sat back. 'I thought you took a break today.'

He glanced down at his son, and mussed Regan's hair. 'I went to check on Regan. Didn't have time to eat.'

She gave him an appreciative glance, then turned to their waiter and ordered rapidly in Vietnamese for them all. As she did it, she flicked a bit of hair out of her face. He smiled. She did that often. There was always a strand that seemed to defy the ponytail band or clip she wore to tie her hair back. It was a habit, one he found endearing. He straightened in his chair. Where had that thought come from? He focused his thoughts back on his sleepy son.

She was right about the restaurant. It was a good choice. The food arrived quickly, and they chatted easily while they ate.

He could see Lien gradually beginning to relax further. The more she relaxed, the more animated she became. He started to realise just how stressed she must have been earlier by his actions. Trouble was, he really wanted to check on the family again at some point. He just wasn't sure how to do it without getting on her wrong side.

By the time they finished eating, Regan was sleepy again and Joe gathered him into his arms to carry him back to the house.

Lien smiled. 'It's getting to be a habit, isn't it? Don't worry. It takes some adults a whole week to adjust to jet-lag. Got to imagine it's worse for kids.'

They walked along the main road back to the hospital. 'Do we need to do anything when we get back?'

She shook her head. 'Dr Nguyen—Phan, you met him earlier—is on call tonight. You'll have that pleasure later in the week.'

He nodded. 'Well, since I'm only a few steps away, that seems fine.'

'There aren't many emergencies at night,' she said, her dark hair catching in the wind. 'An IV might need to be re-sited, but unless someone appears at the door, being on call is generally just about being available if needed.'

'So what do you do on your nights off, then—apart from show the best restaurants to your new colleagues?' He wasn't quite sure where that question had come from. It was out before he had much of a chance to think about it. But he was curious.

She gave him a half-smile. 'Are you being nosy, Joe?'

He dragged one hand across his brow. 'Phew. I must be at least half-forgiven. I didn't get *Dr Lennox*.'

She laughed. He could tell she was trying decide what to say. It had only been one day, but she appeared to live alone in the house next door. There had been no mention of another half. But that didn't mean she didn't have one.

'To be honest, I concentrate on work most of the time.'

There was something about the way she said those words. A hint of regret. A hint of something else.

'Not married?' What was wrong with him? His mouth seemed to be having a field day of talking before his brain could engage.

'Me? No way.' She held up one hand. 'When would I have time to be married? I spend just about every waking hour at the hospital.' Then she laughed. 'Plus the non-waking hours.' She wagged a finger at him. 'The only exception is when I have to chase after our international doctors who have crazy ideas.'

This time he made sure his brain engaged before he leapt to his own defence. 'Can we have a chat about that tomorrow? There are a few things I want to run past you.'

She rolled her eyes. 'Dr Lennox,' she said with a smile on her face, 'why do I get the impression you're going to be trouble?'

CHAPTER THREE

THEY'D FALLEN INTO an easy routine. Joe was keen and enthusiastic, and she couldn't fault his clinical skills for a second. Which was just as well as the place was even busier than usual. Khiem and Hoa had returned for a week, and then gone to the other hospital in Uông Bí in the northeast of Vietnam.

They'd quickly given their approval of the latest employee, loving his enthusiasm and listening to his wide range of ideas.

She couldn't help but admire the relationship Joe had with his son. When they weren't working, he devoted all his time to Regan. The little boy seemed to love his new environment. He'd even tried a few Vietnamese words on Lien that he'd learned at nursery. She was impressed.

Her fears had started to settle. Even after the awkward first day, Joe didn't seem inclined to jump on the first plane back home.

Dinner at her favourite restaurant had been…interesting. His dark green eyes often had a glint of cheekiness in them, and she liked that. She was beginning to believe that he really was looking for a fresh start—even if he was only here for six months. Apart from his mum and dad, he rarely mentioned home. It was almost as if he was putting things firmly behind him. He'd been learning the language basics from Mai Ahn, and had taken an interest in some of the wider public health issues in the area.

The biggest adult health problem in Hanoi was strokes. Joe had been keen to assess every adult who attended the clinic—with any condition—to see if they were at risk. Blood-pressure medications and dietary advice were at the top of his list of general patient care. She could be annoyed. He'd started something that was in her future plans. But sometimes new blood was needed to kick-start things, so she was happy to go along with his ideas.

He'd also followed up on the family with tuberculosis. The younger two children had tested negative and been vaccinated to protect them. The father and grandfather were being actively encouraged to keep taking their medications, and the other little girl was being regularly reviewed at the clinic.

Lien stretched her hands above her head to try and relieve her aching back.

'Whoops.' Joe put his hand up to his face as he walked in the door opposite.

Heat rushed into her cheeks as she pulled her shirt back down. He'd clearly got a flash of her abdomen.

'What do you have?' she asked quickly.

'Just an adult with what could be appendicitis.' He frowned. 'I know there's a theatre here, but I'm definitely no surgeon. What do we do with patients like this?'

Her hands gave her shirt another pull and she moved over to stand next to him. 'We generally monitor for a few hours, then, if we have to, we arrange an ambulance and admission to one of the bigger hospitals.'

'How does that work for payment?'

'It's an emergency surgery and should be covered. But things can be tricky. Sometimes patients get billed for the ambulance or for the nursing care. Sometimes they get billed for nothing at all.'

She pulled the notes towards her. 'Let's see. We have a few patients with grumbling appendices. They like to wait until they absolutely have to come out.'

Joe ran his fingers through his hair in frustration. 'This guy is obviously in pain. I'll go and give him something in the meantime.' He put his hands on his hips. 'Can't you persuade someone to do free surgery for your patients?'

She smiled. 'It's on our wish list, along with free hospital care, free rehab, addiction and mental health services.'

He nodded slowly. 'I guess it's a long list, then.'

'It is.' She could tell he was feeling a bit despondent. She reached up to put her hand on his arm. 'You'll get used to the differences here. We all want to do more than we actually can.'

His eyes went to her fingers resting on his arm. He didn't say anything or pull away. He just stayed still. His gaze made her self-conscious and she stepped back, feeling a bit flustered.

'What are your plans for tomorrow?'

Joe blinked. It was as if she'd lost him for a moment. 'What?' He shook his head. 'Nothing. Just spending some time with Regan.'

'Would you like me to show you some of the sights?'

His head tilted to one side, as if he was considering

the offer. She was still a little flustered and her mouth just kept talking. 'There are a few places not too far away that you might not have had a chance to visit yet. Have you been to Hoàn Kiếm Lake yet? Or Ngoc Son Temple?'

Joe shook his head. 'No. We haven't really had a chance to see much of the city. Is it something Joe would like?'

She nodded and smiled. 'Sure. It's a lake with boats and turtles. He's a kid. Of course he'll like it.'

She said it so matter-of-factly that Joe burst out laughing.

She nodded. 'Okay, then, let's finish up with this patient and see if he needs to be transferred, or if he just needs to be monitored overnight. Neither of us is on call tomorrow so we can take Regan out for the day.'

Her skin prickled. Joe was looking at her a little strangely. 'Thank you,' he said after a few seconds.

'What for?'

'For thinking about Regan.'

She shrugged. 'What are friends for?'

The next morning seemed to come around quickly. By nine o'clock they were walking to Hoàn Kiếm Lake. Even though it was a weekend morning, the lake seemed as popular with locals as it was with tourists. The large green lake was surrounded by grass and old trees. There was a whole variety of activities going on, from joggers circling the lake, to walking groups and people doing exercises beside the still water. Tourist groups with guides carrying bright umbrellas hurried around the lake shore, obviously anxious to complete this part of their tour before the sun rose too high in the sky.

Regan was excited and bounced on his toes. 'It's just like the one back home, Daddy,' he said.

Joe nodded thoughtfully. 'Maybe.' He glanced at Lien. 'There's a park we go to back home.' He paused. 'There are a lot of parks actually, but Regan's favourite is Rouken Glen. There's a lake and a gorgeous boathouse for food.' He smiled down affectionately at Regan and ruffled his hair. 'But it's not quite on this scale.' He held up one hand. 'This place seems more…elegant.'

He was struck by how many similarities he could see between Hanoi and Glasgow. It hadn't even occurred to him before he'd got here. He'd partly hoped that moving to a new place would flood him with a whole host of new emotions—leaving no time or space for new ones. It seemed he was going to have to work a little harder at leaving Glasgow behind.

'This is one of my favourite places for people-watching,' said Lien as she showed them around. 'Hoàn Kiếm Lake means "Lake of the Restored Sword".'

Regan's eyes went wide. 'Wow,' he said quickly.

She bent down next to him. 'The legend says that Emperor Lê Lợi had just won a great battle against the Ming dynasty. It was rumoured he had a magical sword that helped him win that battle. The sword was supposed to have great power and be inscribed with the words "Thuận Thiên", which means "The Will of Heaven".' She gave a broad smile. 'I think you have a similar story back in the UK about King Arthur and his sword Excalibur. Didn't he get his sword from the Lady of the Lake?'

Regan's eyes flitted to Joe's and back again. He tugged at Lien's sleeve. 'Tell me about this sword.'

She had an art for storytelling. She seemed able to

pull them into the stories she was telling, putting her own special spin on them so they were suitable for Regan. 'Well, one of Lê Lợi's fishermen had found this sword. He caught the blade in his net. It was thought it had come from the Dragon King's underwater palace. Once he had the blade, Lê Lợi found the hilt—the bottom of the sword—inside a banyan tree. His soldiers said that Lê Lợi grew very tall when he used the sword and that it gave him the strength of many men.'

'Is that how he won the battle?' asked Regan eagerly.

Lien smiled and nodded. 'Lê Lợi won the battle and the Chinese accepted Vietnam as a country in its own right. Shortly after, Lê Lợi was boating on this lake— it was called Luc Thuy then, the Green Water Lake— when a golden turtle appeared. The turtle told him he'd been given the sword to protect the country against the enemy, but now it was time to return it. The turtle took the sword from Lê Lợi's belt and dived back to the bottom of the lake with the glowing sword. At first, Lê Lợi tried to find the sword as he wanted it back, but then he realised it had gone back to its rightful owner, the Dragon King.'

Regan ran to the edge and peered into the green depths. 'Do you think the sword is still down there?'

Lien grabbed his hand. She could almost see the tiny mind working. 'I think it is, but it's back with its rightful owner.'

Regan's eyes remained wide. He was staring out across the expanse of the green lake when something else caught his eye. 'Look!' He pointed.

Joe and Lien followed his gaze and saw a wedding party gathered at the other side. She nodded. 'This is a popular place to get married or to take wedding pictures. There are a few temples around here.'

'What kind of temples?'

Joe had just opened his mouth to ask the same question but Regan got there first. Joe let out a laugh. It was almost as if Lien had his son under some kind of spell. He was literally hanging on her every word. And Joe could understand why.

She was animated when she talked to him, using her hands and gestures to draw him in. Her eyes were full of fire.

'Let's go to the Ngoc Son Temple. It's on an island in the middle of the lake. We have to walk around this way.'

She guided them around the lake. Every now and then they stopped at some other sight—people doing yoga on mats, another group practising tai chi. Every time Regan spotted a ripple on the lake surface he would yell, 'Is it a turtle?'

'I wish it was,' sighed Lien. 'There are only a few left. But keep a lookout, we might spot one.'

They reached a brightly painted ornate red bridge that had a stream of people walking across it. 'This is the Huc Bridge—that means "morning sunlight". It leads us to Jade Island.'

Lien bought some tickets from a booth and they joined the crowd of people filing across the bridge. Regan kept staring expectantly into the water of the lake, hoping to spot an elusive turtle. Lien pointed further down the lake to what looked like an abandoned building on another island. 'That's the Turtle Tower. It's the place where the turtles are supposed to live and breed.' She gave a sad kind of shrug. 'Here's hoping there are still some left.'

She turned back and continued across the bridge. Joe caught his breath as the temple emerged. It was beautiful. Built in traditional Vietnamese style, it was grey in colour with splashes of white and blue.

Lien gave a smile as the people in front of them stopped to take some photos. 'This was built in the eighteenth century and honours one of the military leaders. He fought against the Yuan Dynasty.'

Regan's brow furrowed. 'There was a lot of fighting.'

Lien knelt next to him. 'There's a lot of fighting all over the world. Thankfully this was all hundreds of years ago and we don't need to worry now.'

She turned back to the temple as they walked forward. 'It's still used—and it's been repaired a number of times over the years.' She lowered her voice as they walked through the main entrance. 'Monks pray here, and you can smell the burning incense.' She showed them around the various buildings on the small island, explaining them all. There were many antiques displayed with the temple, along with the preserved remains of a turtle that had been captured on the lake many years before.

Lien said, 'Some people think the last one died a few years ago.' She bent down and whispered in Regan's ear, 'But I live in hope that there are a few still in there, and they're hiding from all the people. I bet they come out at night.'

They spent a while on the island, taking pictures and looking at the displays. Joe could sense that Regan was starting to get distracted, and they led him back across the red bridge and back to the grounds around the lake.

They sat on the grass underneath one of the trees

for a while as the sun climbed in the sky. Joe reapplied Regan's insect repellent, then Lien took them to
a nearby store that sold ice cream.

They walked along the busy streets with their ice
creams dripping. It was only when they stopped at one
of the crossings that Joe sucked in a breath.

He hadn't thought about Esther today. Not at all.

Pain sliced through him. For a long, long time she'd
been the first thing he'd thought about in the morning
and the last thing he'd thought about at night.

This morning they'd just been so busy waking up and
getting ready that they really hadn't had a minute. All
Joe's thoughts had been on Regan and Lien.

He'd known this would happen at some point but
guilt still flooded through him. He'd promised Esther he
would keep her memory alive in his son, and how could
he do that if he hadn't even spared her a thought today?

'Joe? What's wrong?'

Lien was standing in front of him, her nose only
inches below his, chocolate ice cream dripping down
her hand.

He jerked back. 'What?' He felt a bit confused.

She gave him a curious smile and he noticed she
was holding Regan's hand. 'The lights changed for us
to cross, and you missed them. We had to come back
for you.'

He flinched. Had he really been so lost in his own
thoughts? Heat rushed into his cheeks. Not only was
he embarrassed, he was angry with himself. What if
something had happened to Regan?

He noticed the crossing lights change again behind
Lien's head. 'Let's go,' she said easily, as if nothing
had happened.

He sucked in a breath as he watched her slim figure in white loose trousers and a bright pink long-sleeved tunic walk in front of him. From the way the sun was striking her, he could see the outline of her body beneath the thin clothes.

They'd taken a hundred photos today. Some together, and some of just Regan and Lien.

He licked his lips as he tried to rationalise the blood racing around his body. She was good for him. She was good for them.

Of course, she was a colleague. It was quite likely she had a no-date rule for work. And that was fine. Because he had to deal with his feelings before he could even consider anything else.

This was the first time he'd felt this rush, this attraction, in for ever. At least it felt like for ever.

The only woman Regan had really had in his life since Esther had died had been Joe's mother, and while she was great, it was nice to see him interact so well with someone else. He watched as they stopped at the other side of the street and Lien pulled some tissues from her bag so they could all wipe their sticky fingers.

She looked over the top of Regan's head. 'You okay?' she asked softly.

It was almost like she knew. As if she'd read his mind.

His heart stuttered, partly because of the empathy she showed and partly from the thought that if she *could* read his mind, she might not be entirely happy with some of the thoughts he'd been having.

He gave a quick nod of his head. 'I'm fine.'

He sucked a deep breath in and closed his eyes for a second, inhaling the scent from the nearby street vendor carts. As he opened his eyes again he took in the bright splashes of colour all around them, and his ears adjusted to the constant buzz of noise. He smiled. Vietnam. Something about this city was giving him a new lease on life.

The next two days were busy. No time to sightsee or do anything other than work. Lien liked that. It was normal for her. But she was conscious of the fact that Joe was used to more support back home. She also wondered how well he was sleeping. She'd noticed some dark circles under his eyes today. Her hand paused at the blue door, wondering if she should knock or not. She wasn't being nosy but she hadn't seen Regan for a few days. From the smell wafting through the open window she could tell they'd already had dinner. Good. She wouldn't be interrupting. She knocked at the door and pushed it open when she heard the shout telling her to enter.

Joe waved her inside. Regan was perched on the edge of the sofa and she could see they had an electronic tablet in their hands. 'We're just video-calling back home with my mum and dad,' he explained. He moved over on the sofa. 'Come and say hello.'

She shook her head quickly and backed up. 'Sorry, I didn't mean to interrupt.'

'Don't go.' He smiled and waved his hand, beckoning her inside. 'Come. My mum and dad want to say hello.'

She smiled nervously. This definitely felt like an intrusion, but Regan waved her over too. 'Come on, Lien, say hi to my grandma.'

Lien took a few steps and sat down nervously next to Joe. There was an older couple on the screen, waving at her.

'Mum, Dad, this is Lien.'

Regan stuck his head across the screen. 'She works with Daddy.'

Joe nodded to the screen. 'Lien, this is Rob and Ann, my mum and dad.'

Lien laughed nervously and waved back.

The woman, Ann, stepped right up to the screen, obviously to get a better look at her. She clasped her hands together. 'Lien, it's so nice to meet you. Regan's been talking about you and how you live in the house next door.'

Lien nodded. 'Yes, that's right. I'm next door.'

She'd spent her life talking to patients and relatives—usually complete strangers—and managed perfectly well. But right now she'd never felt so awkward. She had the strangest sensation of meeting a boyfriend's mum when she was nineteen years old, and vowing not to set foot in that house again.

His mum had been nice, but it was clear she didn't think anyone would be good enough for her son.

Ann kept talking. 'How are they getting on? Regan says he likes the nursery, have you seen it? Does it have a good reputation? And Joe? Is he behaving? And how big is the laundry pile? Has he started wearing crumpled shirts yet?'

Lien's head was buzzing, not least with the speed of the barrage of questions, but also with the broad Scottish accents. She actually started laughing.

Joe gave a casual shrug and rolled his eyes. 'See, Regan? I told you. She doesn't believe a word we say.' He gave Lien a slight nudge. 'Go on, back me up here.'

She turned from Joe to Regan and back to Ann. Rob stood in the background with his arms folded and his head shaking in amusement. It was clear he was used to all this.

Lien started to brush off the nerves. She shook her head. 'Oh, no. I know how this works. I'm Team Ann.'

Joe's mother's face broke into a wide grin and the older woman held up her hand towards the screen. 'High five!' she said.

Lien returned the gesture. 'High five.' She shifted on the sofa. 'So, the real story is, yes, your boys are doing fine. The nursery is great and Regan...' she gave the boy an appreciative nod '...is mastering the language better than his dad.' She gave Joe a quick glance. 'As for Joe, well...' she put her hand to her face '...where do I start?'

Ann started laughing and Joe leaned forward. He gave Lien a pretend shocked look. 'What? No way?'

Lien shrugged. 'Well, he seems to be doing okay in the doctor department but sometimes...' she gave a slow nod and an amused grin '...he needs to be reined in.'

'Oh, don't I know it!' declared Ann.

Lien pretended to look over the back of the sofa. 'As for the laundry basket... I wouldn't like to comment.'

Regan was laughing so hard he fell off the edge of the sofa and jumped back up again almost instantaneously. All four adults let out a yelp at once, and then a sigh of relief.

This time Rob stepped forward. He exchanged glances with his wife and put an arm around her waist. 'We're so glad to meet you, Lien,' he said. She could see the genuine appreciation in his eyes. 'We're relieved there's someone to keep an eye on our boys.'

Something panged inside her. They missed Joe and Regan. It was obvious. But there was something else too. Joe had told her that his mother had pushed him in this direction. She could almost see the older couple reaching through the screen and making a grab for the hopefulness they could see. She suddenly realised how this must look.

'Everyone at the hospital is looking out for them,' she said quickly.

Ann still had her gaze fixed on Lien, who tried not to look nervous, or shift uncomfortably. She didn't want his mum and dad getting the wrong idea. She reached a hand out and patted Joe's leg. 'I'll leave you to it,' she said, as she stood up.

Joe gave her a strange look, his gaze fixing on her hand. Of course. She'd just touched his leg. It had been an unwitting move. There had been no intent. But she doubted she'd helped things.

She gave her head a tiny shake and shot him a look of apology. 'Nice to meet you, Rob and Ann.' She waved at the screen as Regan climbed onto her vacated spot on the sofa.

She reached the door and glanced back. Regan had started talking again quickly, regaling his grandparents with stories from the nursery. But Joe's eyes were fixed on hers.

She couldn't quite tell what the expression on his face meant. Was he angry at her? Annoyed? No.

It was almost like…something else. As if a veil had just lifted from his eyes and he was seeing her in a different light.

The tiny hairs on her arms stood on end as her skin prickled instantly. She lifted her hand in a silent wave and ducked out the door, crossing the ground to her own house in double quick time.

When she opened her own door she closed it firmly behind her and stood for a second, leaning against it. What was wrong with her? Nothing had happened. Nothing had been said. But every cell in her body was on red alert. Her heart was racing. And somehow she knew it wasn't from her burst of quick walking.

But there was something else. Something more subconscious. His parents were lovely, and clearly good fun. But she'd noticed something. It couldn't be helped. It was obvious.

They'd been in the garden of their home. Their very *large* home. She had no idea about how people lived in Scotland, but she could tell a very large home and beautiful gardens at first glance. It all meant money. Joe's family was rich. And she had experience of rich families.

Her stomach twisted uncomfortably. There was obviously something wrong with her. Why had those thoughts even come into her head? Joe was only a work colleague. Nothing else. She was merely being hospitable.

But if she was only being hospitable, why did the fact he had a rich family back in Scotland make her want to run in the opposite direction?

She closed her eyes for a second and leaned her head back. This was crazy. *She* was crazy. She just wasn't quite sure what came next.

Regan was oblivious to the subtleties of adults. He took every question about Lien at face value and blurted out answers left, right and centre.

Joe sat quietly cringing. The only thing was, he couldn't help but smile. He could read his mum and dad like a book and shook his head at a few of their more inquisitive comments, pretending he hadn't even heard them.

Eventually, he grabbed Regan and pulled him onto his lap. 'Say goodnight to Grandma and Papa. It's time for bed.'

His mother pulled a face and started to blow kisses. Then, just as they were about to disconnect, his father shot in a quick comment. 'Love to Lien!'

Joe was sure the second the connection ended they'd be hugging each other. He spent the next half-hour settling Regan into bed and making up some story about pirates, before making his way back to turn out the lights. 'Not as good as Lien,' Regan murmured in a sleepy voice.

Joe left the room smiling and glanced out of the window. The pale lilac door was taunting him. Begging him to knock on it.

None of this had been planned. When Lien had appeared at the door it had seemed only natural to call her over to say hello to his parents. He'd half hoped it might give them some reassurance that he and Regan had actually settled in.

Instead, it had opened a whole new can of worms.

He felt his phone buzz and pulled it from his pocket. A text from his mother. Three words.

We love her.

Nothing else.

Guilt swamped him. What was he doing? As soon as Lien had sat down she'd fallen into the family conversation with no problems and been an instant hit with his parents.

He couldn't pretend that hadn't pleased him. He'd liked the way they'd exchanged glances of approval and joked and laughed with her.

But it also—in a completely strange way—*didn't* please him.

Part of him still belonged to Esther. Always had. Always would.

He'd found love once. He'd been lucky. Some people would never have what he and Esther had.

How dared he even contemplate looking again?

His mother had pushed him here to start living again. Not to find a replacement for his wife.

The thought made his legs crumple and he slid down the wall, his hands going to his hair. For a few seconds he just breathed.

He was pulling himself one way and another. Guilt hung over him like a heavy cloud.

He knew why he was here. He knew he'd been living life back in Scotland in a protective bubble. It *was* time to get out there. That was why he'd accepted the tickets and climbed on that plane.

But what he hated most of all was that he did feel ready to move on. He was tired. He was tired of being Joe the widower. It had started to feel like a placard above his head.

But part of him hated the fact he wanted to move forward. He was tired of being alone. He was tired of feeling like there would never by anyone else in his and Regan's lives. He was tired of being tired. Of course, he had no idea about the kind of person he was interested in. The truth was, the few little moments that Lien had caused sparks in his brain had bothered him.

It had been so long and he couldn't quite work out

how he felt about everything yet. Of course he'd want someone who recognised that he and Regan were a package deal. He'd want someone who could understand his usual passion for this work. These last few weeks had mirrored how he'd been a few years before. Every day there was something new to learn. Someone new to help. It was what had always driven him, and he knew that, for a while, he'd lost that. But Vietnam was reawakening parts of him that had been sleeping for a while.

He lifted his head and peeled his damp shirt from his back and sighed. Too much thinking wasn't good for a man.

CHAPTER FOUR

LIEN FINISHED WRITING up the notes on her last patient just as one of the nurses stuck her head around the door. 'Lien? I know it's late, but Joe asked if you'd mind dropping in at his house on the way home. There's something he wants to talk to you about.'

She couldn't help the way her face automatically curved into a smile. It seemed the nurse noticed too as she gave Lien an amused glance. 'Okay, then, see you later.'

Lien glanced at her watch. It was late. Regan would likely be sleeping by now. She couldn't help but be curious. What did Joe want to talk to her about?

She washed her hands and pulled her shirt a little straighter, then walked across the grounds towards his blue door.

She knocked lightly, waiting for only a second before he pulled it open with a tired smile. 'Come in.'

He was wearing a white T-shirt and some lightweight jogging trousers. From the way he had papers scattered across the table he'd been working on this for some time.

He gestured towards the table, indicating she should sit next to him. In the last few weeks he'd made this place a bit homier. There were now a few pictures scattered around, and it looked like he'd finally got around to buying a laundry basket to get on top of the washing. She could see a haphazardly folded pile of clean clothes sitting on a chair in the corner of the room.

'Want something to eat?'

She shook her head. She'd been hungry a few hours ago, but the feeling had passed. He held up a tin that she knew was where he kept Regan's favourite biscuits. 'One of these?'

'Go on, then,' she said. 'But promise not to tell him.'

Joe smiled. 'Oh, too late, he has these counted. I'll need to account for the missing biscuit tomorrow.'

She bit into the chocolate-coated biscuit. It was one that Regan's grandparents sent every few weeks from Scotland and she was beginning to think she was getting quietly addicted to them.

There was a noise, a bit like a whimper, and Joe crossed to Regan's doorway. As she watched she could sense his breathing get heavier. It was clear he had something on his mind. She waited a few moments, and when he didn't move, she crossed over to stand just behind his shoulder.

Regan was curled into a little ball. His lips were moving, as if he were singing some song or nursery rhyme in his sleep.

Joe took a deep breath, his voice so low it was barely a whisper, his eyes fixed on Regan.

'Sometimes when I'm in my bed at night, I get up and watch Regan sleeping. Then I start to wonder, is there some horrible, secret gene that predisposes you to cancer?'

Lien's stomach gave an uncomfortable twist. He kept talking, his voice racked with emotion.

'Both of Esther's parents died of different types of cancer, and she died of leukaemia. So I look at my little boy and wonder if there's even a tiny possibility that he might have inherited something that I don't know about, can't see, and won't find out about until it smacks us in the face.' His voice was shaking now, as were his hands.

She slid her arm through his.

He shook his head. 'I know it's crazy. I know it's irrational. But I can't help it.'

Her voice was tinged with sadness because she got the impression he'd been hiding these feelings for a while, storing them up, letting them fester, and not sharing them with anyone else. 'But it's not irrational, and it's not crazy, Joe. It's the thoughts of a man who has already lost his wife, and is terrified he might lose his son.'

She hated the fact they were having this conversation. She could reach out and touch his pain. It was so visible in the air it was practically creating a cloud around his head.

There was also a tiny twinge in her that wondered if this was why he'd asked her here. She'd been bright and happy about the invitation, hoping that—just maybe— it was for something other than work.

But now he was talking to her about his dead wife, and his fears for his son. Her heart ached for him, but she was also trying hard to hide the tinge of disappointment she felt.

She should have been pleased that he felt he could reveal this part of himself to her. But somehow it also gave her the feeling that, no matter what Joe said out loud, his heart really wasn't ready to move on.

She ran her fingertips along his bare skin. 'I can't say much to help, because we do know some cancers seem to run in families. But think back. Think back to the random patients you've seen over the years that came in with symptoms. Symptoms that led to a diagnosis of…' she paused for a second, obviously recalling a few cases '…skin cancer, anal cancer, prostate cancer or renal cancer. People with no family history at all. It happens all the time.'

She stopped talking for a few minutes and just let him consider. 'Sometimes it's easier to see the things that worry us most.' She paused and gave him a sympathetic smile. 'The kinds of things that keep you awake in your bed at night.'

'What kind of doctor does that make me then?' He looked pained.

She shook her head. 'No kind of doctor. Just a worried parent. You don't have to be a doctor every moment of your life, Joe.' She looked up into his worried green eyes and gave him the softest smile. They were barely inches apart now. 'Make room for other things,' she whispered.

It was almost as if she'd touched a nerve. He jerked. He physically jerked at the impact of her words and she immediately averted her eyes, embarrassed for them both. She moved back quickly to the table and sat down, giving him a few moments to join her.

Her brain was whirring now. She shouldn't have touched him. How could she explain that it had been done in empathy for how he was feeling?

She wasn't really that surprised that he was feeling vulnerable right now. He was in a strange country with his son. Yes, they seemed to have settled well, but who really knew what went on inside someone else's mind?

Clearly not her. No matter how much she tried to deny it, she was beginning to feel a connection to this guy. But after that reaction she was apparently not reading things well. She'd just embarrassed them both. The easiest thing to do was try to pretend nothing had happened.

She shifted a little in the seat. The last thing she wanted to do was sit here in his company after that.

But she still had to work with this guy every day. So she took a deep breath and plastered an interested look on her face, ignoring the little strands of hurt she felt inside.

His phone buzzed with a text and when it flashed up, she saw the screenshot that lay behind it. It was the same photo that Regan had next to his bed. The picture of Esther on the beach, laughing.

Something twisted inside her. She had no reason to be jealous, absolutely none. Of course Regan should have a picture of his mum, but did Joe also need to have it on his phone?

She stared at the array of papers alongside a laptop on the table. 'What on earth have you been doing?'

As he sat down at the table and started organising his papers her eyes went to one of the pictures Joe had put on the wall. What drew her attention was a large, grand-looking house surrounded by an expanse of gardens. From the view and setting it seemed to be back in Scotland. Joe and Regan were standing in front of the property—it was clearly their family home. She had no idea what house prices were like over there, but one look at the obviously expensive property made her feel distinctly uncomfortable. She'd already seen the house belonging to Joe's mum and dad, but this must be the house that Joe and Regan lived in. She tried not to calculate in her head how many times this tiny two-bed bungalow could fit into that grand house. What was the English TV series set before the war, where they had staff? It was nearly as big as that.

'Is that a house or a castle?' she quipped. Unease spread across her. No, more than that. It was like every nerve in her body was on edge; she could sense the instant hostility and she couldn't do a darned thing about it. It was like every automatic defence system had just slid into place.

'It's not a castle,' he said with a wave of his hand, then peered back at the screen. 'At least, I don't think it was.'

Her skin prickled. She actually wasn't sure if he was joking or not. She licked her lips. It was funny how being uncomfortable made her mouth instantly dry. 'Bigger than the average house, I imagine.' She tried to make her voice sound casual.

He leaned back against the sofa and nodded towards the window and the hospital across from them. 'Not as big as this place.'

She folded her arms across her chest. 'I'm not so sure.'

He shook his head. 'Nah,' he said breezily. 'And anyway, didn't you know everyone lives in a castle in Scotland?'

Of course he was joking, but just the way he said those words tugged at something inside her, and not in a good way. History had taught her that only those

who had never had to worry about money would make
a quip like that.

'Here.' He turned a large piece of paper around to
face her. He hadn't thought twice about their conversation. He hadn't even noticed her reaction.

She bent forward. It was a map of the surrounding
areas. It was littered with red and blue dots.

'What is this?' She was confused.

'I decided to take a look at some of our patients,'
he said. His fingers traced across the paper. 'The ones
with the red dots are the patients currently attending
that have tuberculosis. The ones with blue dots are the
ones we know have multi-resistant tuberculosis.' He
leaned forward so his head was almost touching hers.
'Look here. This is the biggest cluster.'

She nodded slowly. The information wasn't a surprise to her, she'd just never seen it laid out this way. Her
skin prickled. The district with the biggest incidence of
tuberculosis was the one where her parents lived, and
in which she'd been brought up.

He kept talking as he moved some papers around
the desk. 'Okay, so you don't like me going out and
doing follow-ups…' he gave her a slightly teasing smile
'…but I got to thinking. I've checked up on some of
these patients. There's a low uptake of tuberculosis
vaccinations after birth. Not everyone is bringing their
children to the clinic. What about if we set up a kind
of pop-up clinic to try and screen some people for
TB, and immunise any kids that have been missed?'

He was clearly brimming with enthusiasm at the
prospect. 'Is this district one I should be worried about?
Are the crime rates high there?' He kept talking without waiting for a response. 'Because I've checked some

of the other stats. I know there's deprivation and poor health. I know one of the biggest issues for the kids in that area is malnutrition. Maybe we could try and do something to address that while we're there?'

Something swept over her. Resentment. A wave of anger. 'What, do you want to give them all money to feed their kids too?'

He pulled back, obviously surprised by her outburst. She ran her fingers through her hair. 'Do you think we haven't tried these things before?' she asked. 'Do you think we haven't tried to find new ways to help the people who need it most?' Her words came out more fiercely than she'd meant them to, but she couldn't hide how many buttons his ideas had just pushed.

Joe was looking at her with cautious eyes. He clasped both hands together and spoke carefully. 'Of course I think you've tried different things. But sometimes it's a timing issue. All I'm saying is maybe it's time to try again.' His voice was low. 'I don't know the people in these areas the way that the rest of the staff here do. I can only look from an outside point of view. My public health head tells me we have a current hotspot for tuberculosis, and potentially more cases of multi-resistance. Can't we take a look at this?'

He spoke so earnestly she knew he meant every word of this. She couldn't help but be oversensitive. She often felt like this when outsiders remarked on the area she'd been brought up in. People made so many judgements. Formed so many opinions.

She struggled to find the right words. 'Let me think about it. We can discuss it with Khiem and Hoa. Setting up pop-up clinics is more difficult than it sounds.'

Joe pressed his lips together and ran his fingers

through his hair. She could tell he was frustrated. He'd probably wanted her to jump all over his idea and tell him it was wonderful. And in some ways it probably was.

He leaned back and stretched his arms out. 'Regan is hankering after another bedtime story from you. He'll be sorry he missed you tonight.'

'Couldn't be helped,' she said as lightly as she could. 'We can catch up some other time.' She gave Joe a softer look. 'Are your stories really that bad?'

He smiled. 'Not bad. Just the same. I keep recycling, and Regan's now getting old enough to realise that.' He raised his eyebrows. 'Whereas you swept in here with your dragons, warriors and magic turtles and blew me out of the water.'

She raised her eyebrows in challenge. 'Time to up your game, then.'

He shook his head. 'Oh, no way. I'm not getting into that. You have an unfair advantage.'

'What's that?' The atmosphere between them was definitely mellowing. She was starting to calm down. Gain a bit of perspective. She'd had no reason to act so hurt about earlier. He'd clearly been sad, vulnerable and worried about his child. Over-reacting wouldn't do either of them any good.

He waved his hand. 'Untried and untested kids' stories.'

'Who says they're untried and untested? I've worked the children's clinic for a while now. It's amazing what you can learn when you start telling a chid a story.'

His face changed, becoming more serious, and he nodded. 'Yeah, sometimes they tell you a story back that makes you want to wrap your arms around them and hide them away.'

Their gazes clashed. Unspoken words. Joe had worked as a general practitioner in Scotland for years. Doubtless he'd encountered child protection issues just like she had here. It was a sobering thought, and she didn't want to go there.

'Have you and Regan video-called with your parents again?'

He nodded. 'Oh, yes. Every Tuesday and Friday. My parents are creatures of habit. If they don't get their Regan fix they get very testy.'

'They must miss him.'

He gave a little sigh. 'Yeah, they do. And he misses them. I don't think he quite understands the distance. He's asked a few times if we can go and see them. He was used to seeing them every day, so it's a big difference.'

'You must miss them too.'

Joe paused for a second. 'I do. They've been my biggest supporters for the last few years. I don't know what I would have done if they hadn't been there when...' His voice drifted off and she filled in the blanks by herself. She didn't need him to say any more. He looked up. 'They keep asking for you too. You'll need to come and say hello again sometime.'

She smiled nervously. Something in the air felt quite odd between them. They were working together so well, and she enjoyed his company. Maybe that was it? She was enjoying his company a bit more than any other colleague's. Maybe that was why she was being so defensive? Self-protect mode kicked in when anything felt remotely personal. She wanted to keep herself safe. And how did you keep your heart safe when there was already an adorable kid tugging away at it, and a guy with the sexiest accent in the world breathing the same air?

He reached over for the biscuit tin again, offering it to her. 'Hey, you've met my mum and dad now. When do we get to meet yours? I'm sure Regan would love to say hello.'

The words came like a bolt out of the blue. It felt like a tidal wave sweeping the ground from beneath her feet. She wasn't prepared. She wasn't ready. She swallowed. 'I…I…' Panic flooded her. This wasn't her. She was a professional. She'd had lots of questions or statements thrown at her over the years. None had made her as tongue-tied as this simple request.

She stood up quickly, scattering some of the papers that were on the table to the floor. 'Sorry,' she said. 'I've just remembered there's something I need to do.' She crossed the room quickly and opened the door, her mouth achingly dry. 'See you tomorrow.'

The thudding of her heart echoed in her ears as she hurried to her own front door. She'd seen the look on Joe's face. He'd been totally confused by her actions. But the thought of taking him to meet her parents made her stomach churn in a way she couldn't put into words.

She'd been down this road before. At medical school she'd known how to dress—designer classics bought from charity shops, clothes that had barely aged from season to season. She had been polite. She'd been able to talk about a vast range of international topics. She'd read widely. All things to hide her background from her fellow students. It had all gone so nicely. Until she'd started dating Reuben.

And he'd wanted to meet her parents. They hadn't

even got that far. As soon as he'd heard where she lived, she'd been dropped like a hot brick. The look of disdain and disappointment that he'd given her had seared into her heart, destroying a little part of her for ever. It seemed as if Joe, despite his humble nature, was from just as rich a family as Reuben had been.

The thought filled her with dread. They were just colleagues, that was all.

But how could Joe meet her parents without judging them? Wasn't that what everyone from wealth and privilege did? She didn't want that for her parents. She loved them dearly, and supported the fact they liked where they lived. But anyone walking into the neighbourhood could see the poverty there. It reached out and grabbed you from every faded awning and tumbled litter bin that was strewn across the streets. From the patched-up windows, along with the thin, angular frames of the people who lived there. Malnutrition was a big issue. Overcrowding another.

The area was home to her. Even if it wasn't the nicest area. She could name most of the families in the same street as her mother and father. Some of these people had cleaned up her grazed knees or wiped her nose when she'd been a tiny kid. She'd been invited to sit at the table of bigger families with a large bowl of food shared out between however many faces were round the table at the time. Sometimes it meant only a few spoonfuls each, but the laughter and chatter around the table had meant that bellies had felt a little less empty.

The thought of walking Joe—the man who practically lived in a castle back in Scotland—down those streets filled her with dread.

Her parents were every bit as polite and hospitable

as Joe's were, and Joe didn't seem like Reuben in any other way.

But she couldn't take that chance.

She wouldn't have her parents judged the way she had been.

Not ever.

CHAPTER FIVE

THEY SETTLED INTO an easy routine. Joe took Regan to
the international nursery every morning and was back
at the clinic to start at eight. Khiem and Hoa were back
from their other hospital, and they all split the hospital and clinic duties between them. Joe occasionally
helped out Hoa with the maternity side of things to try
and keep his skills up. He found the friendly doctor a
real pleasure to work with, particularly around maternal conditions and complications specific to Vietnam.

Khiem wore a different-coloured bow-tie every day
along with a long-sleeved shirt. At times Joe wondered
how he could stand the heat. After wearing shirts for
the first two months, he'd eventually adopted the same
clothing as Lien and started wearing the lightweight
long-sleeved loose tunic tops that she preferred. The
first time she'd spotted him wearing a yellow one she'd
laughed and taken him to the shop that she favoured
where he'd stocked up on white, beige and pale blue
versions.

He'd just finished covering the ward round when
Khiem called them all down to a staff meeting.

'How was it?' asked Lien, and he walked into the
room and sat down next to her.

'Not bad. Two chronic chests, one forty-five-year-old with a suspected stroke, and another young woman I think might have renal problems.' He shook his head. 'She hasn't admitted it but I suspect she might have tried some of the locally brewed alcohol.'

Lien screwed up her face. 'Oh, no.'

He smiled. He liked it when she did that. It was cute. Not a word he'd usually use to describe a colleague, but cute none the less. He still hadn't figured out what had made her virtually bolt from his room the other night.

But it had also been the first time since he'd arrived in Vietnam that he'd been feeling a bit worried, a bit sentimental. He had no idea why. But crazy thoughts about genetics and biology had blossomed in his mind like a tiny flower, and it hadn't helped that the flower had rapidly turned into an orchard with messy unknown things growing there. Then Lien had said a few things to reassure him he wasn't going mad.

Oh.

That.

Had she thought…? Was that why she'd seemed so off later?

Was he really so turned off to the feelings of those around him? It was hardly an admirable trait for a doctor.

'Joe?'

Lien was looking at him, and he realised he'd been part way through a conversation about a patient.

He nodded. 'Oh, yes. I've run some blood tests this morning, so when I get the results this afternoon I'll go back and ask her some more questions. I think she was being careful what she told me this morning. That, and she was just feeling so bad. She was really dehydrated so I've got her up on an IV at the moment.'

Lien sighed. 'Is she a tourist?'

He nodded. 'She's a student from Australia.'

Lien gave another sigh. 'What do you suspect—rice wine? People just don't realise how strong it is over here.' She rolled her eyes. 'The normal rice wine is bad enough, at twenty-nine per cent, but if she's drunk something unbranded…' She shook her head. 'The methanol levels can be so high they can be fatal.'

He nodded. 'I'm watching her. She's conscious. She does have abdominal pain and vomiting, but her co-ordination seems fine.'

'Any problems with her vision?'

'Not so far, but, like I said, I'm going to keep an eye on her. Right now I'll keep her hydrated and consider some bicarbonate, or maybe even some fomepizole if it's appropriate.'

She slid him a curious sideways glance. He smiled. 'Okay, you got me. I might have consulted with Khiem. It's my first potential methanol poisoning.'

She held out both hands. 'Hey, and you've been here, what, more than two months? That's almost unheard of.' She dropped her hands and gave a small shrug. 'I like it that you ask if you're not sure. She could easily have been misdiagnosed. Missing methanol poisoning can be the biggest error a physician makes around here.'

He leaned back in the chair. 'I just hope she's going to be okay. That this will just turn out to be rice wine that was too strong for her and it feels like the worst hangover in the world. Hopefully she'll recover and everything will be okay.'

Khiem hurried into the room. His wife, Hoa, came

in behind him, along with a few of the other staff members. They settled down and Khiem picked up a chart from his desk. 'Sorry to keep you all. I promise this won't take long. I just wanted to let you all know that we have another staff member joining us for a month. A volunteer.'

One of the nurses frowned. 'Who is it?'

Lien shot Joe a look. She'd told him that they occasionally had volunteer doctors—usually private, very well-paid consultants who wanted to say they had at least spent some time working in the underprivileged areas in the city.

Khiem smiled brightly. 'His name is Reuben Le Gran. His father is French, his mother Vietnamese, and even though he doesn't sound it, he's a local boy. Did his training in Hanoi, and has also worked in Paris and London. He specialises in plastic surgery, and works out of a private clinic in the Tay Ho district.'

The nurse next to Joe quipped, 'Just what we need— a plastic surgeon. Bet he lives in one of the gated communities in Tay Ho.'

Joe had learned a little more about the city. He knew Tay Ho was one of the richest areas, and he'd passed by the gated communities on more than one occasion. Saying that they were opulent didn't even come close to the truth. They had twenty-four-hour security guards, private schools, golf courses and the biggest houses he'd seen in a long time.

Khiem waved his hand. 'A plastic surgeon will be good. We have lots of patients on whom he might be able to do minor procedures. We've used the mini-theatre at the back on a number of occasions. This time will be no different.' He smiled. 'He'll only be here one day a week.'

Joe turned to his other side and jolted. Lien's face was frozen and her body stiff. He could see the tense muscles at the base of her throat. Her fingers were clenching her legs. He reached over to touch her to ask what was wrong, but she jumped up.

Khiem looked surprised but just continued speaking in his jovial manner. 'And you two, Lien and Joe, there's a special request for you to go to Uông Bí to cover holiday leave at the clinic there next week.'

For a few seconds Joe wondered if Lien had heard the words, but then her face changed and she gave the briefest of nods. 'Perfect,' she said as she walked out the door.

She couldn't hide her anger. Her skin had prickled, almost like a premonition before Khiem had said the name out loud. No one here knew about her previous relationship with Reuben. Once he'd found out where she lived he hadn't exactly wanted the world to know about their connection. Reuben was the type of guy who wanted to move in the right circles and be seen with the 'in' crowd. Lien would never be one of those people.

Even if the others had known about her past relationship, she wouldn't expect them to turn down the services of a free plastic surgeon. She could think of a few patients straight off the top of her head who could really benefit from seeing him. As angry as she was at him for turning up at *her* hospital, she could be rational enough to put the needs of the patients first.

She stalked down the corridor and into the nearest bathroom, closing the door behind her and splashing some water on her face, then she rested her hands at the side of the sink and just breathed.

This wasn't an accident. Reuben was far too calculating for that. She'd tried to ignore him over the last few years, but his reputation had grown and grown, and his publicity machine had been working overtime.

His beaming face had adorned countless magazine covers as he'd become known as the 'plastic surgeon to the stars'. There was much speculation about who he'd worked on. Hollywood film stars, a top British model, three Bollywood stars and numerous other celebrities had been seen on his arm, or in his company, over the last few years. It seemed deliberate. Every time things quietened down he would whirl along some pavement with some new star and the press would go mad again. The latest rumour involved politicians, a few of whom seemed to have reversed the aging process.

Then there had been the interview given by a co-worker that had been slightly malicious. Even Lien had felt uncomfortable at its contents. Sad thing was, the words the co-worker had used about Reuben's ego being larger than his clinic, his apparent self interest, and his lack of philanthropy, had caused Vietnam's golden boy to lose a little of his shine. And Lien knew it was all entirely true.

Helping at the hospital in one of the most deprived areas in Hanoi was a prediction she could have made herself. It had been inevitable. Reuben needed some good press again. She was sure he would sweep in here with a whole host of his own staff, plus camera crew, and perform a few minor surgeries to try to claw back some of his golden-boy image.

She stared at her reflection in the mirror for a few

seconds. Pressing her lips together, she straightened her shoulders.

Last time around he'd made her feel small and worthless, all because of her address. She was older now, wiser. She'd worked hard to serve the people who lived here. She'd done a good job.

The last thing she wanted was to come face to face with the smug surgeon again.

She dabbed her face dry with a paper towel and walked back to Khiem's office. Everyone else had already left. Khiem was sitting behind his desk.

'I've had some thoughts,' she said determinedly. 'Let's draw up a list of patients for our visiting surgeon.'

She didn't need to see him. She didn't need to be involved in anything that he did here. But she wanted to be sure she'd served the needs of her patients.

Khiem looked up and smiled, nodding his head. 'What a good idea.' He pulled his chair closer to Lien's. 'Let's make a start.'

CHAPTER SIX

JOE COULD TELL something was off. Lien had been stilted this week. Not her usual relaxed self. Even Regan had noticed. 'Where's Lien? I want another dragon story,' he'd said as Joe had tucked him into bed the night before.

'Sorry, pal,' he'd sighed. 'I guess she's just busy with work.'

But as he watched her the next day, it seemed like anything but work that was on her mind. She was distracted. Tense.

The nurses had to repeat things to her on a number of occasions, and her gaze kept wandering to the main door.

He couldn't pretend he hadn't noticed her reaction the other day. Did she know this other doctor? If she did, it was clear she wasn't enamoured with him.

He'd just finished up immunising a few children when the main door opened and a guy swept in wearing a white doctor's coat.

Joe frowned in confusion, then tried not to laugh out loud. Really? No one here wore a white coat, and yet this guy had walked in off the street in one?

The door was still open, and Joe could see the black limousine parked in the street outside.

The guy smiled. 'I'm here,' he said loudly to no one in particular. 'Reuben Le Gran, at your service.' He started striding through the clinic, his head flicking from side to side. 'Now, what do we have here?'

Joe stuck his hands in his pockets and wandered after the guy. A few people—obviously his staff—had followed him inside the clinic, most of them carrying large boxes.

Joe shook his head and walked over to the nearest woman and held out his arms. 'Let me help you.'

After a few moments Hoa appeared. Her smile was broad and she extended her hand towards the doctor. 'Reuben, it's a pleasure to meet you.'

Reuben Le Gran was taller than average for Vietnam, with broad shoulders, extremely straight white teeth and light brown skin. His thick dark hair was a slightly strange colour. Was it dyed?

Joe showed the staff through to the small theatre at the back of the hospital. He didn't even get a chance to make any introductions before the staff looked around and started speaking rapidly to each other. It seemed they were a finely honed and confident team. There was also a hint of arrogance about them that made him a bit uncomfortable. They didn't seem interested in any of the existing hospital staff, as they moved things around and set up their own equipment without a single question about whether it was convenient.

Joe could see the baffled expressions on a few of his colleagues' faces. Good. It wasn't just him. It struck him just how discourteous Reuben and his team were being. He watched the initial welcome from Hoa—one of the nicest women he'd ever met. Reuben wasn't particularly interested in her either, just immediately started talking about himself and his plans. He'd arranged to be interviewed by a TV journalist while he was working here. What was most interesting was that he seemed to favour talking in English rather than his native Vietnamese. Joe found it strange.

The dazzling white teeth were even stranger, faker than the latest TV pop star who was apparently plucked from a pavement, even though she'd clearly had every plastic surgery known to man.

Joe shook his head and took himself back off to the patients he was looking after. He wasn't interested in meeting Reuben, and it seemed Reuben wasn't interested in meeting him.

He'd only taken a few steps when he heard the words, 'Oh, you have a doctor here—Dang Van Lien. Is she on duty?'

Joe's footsteps seemed to freeze in mid-air. He sucked in a breath as he waited for Hoa's reply. 'Yes, Lien works here. Has for years. She's one of our finest doctors.'

'Yes, I'm sure she is. Can you tell her I'm looking for her?'

It was almost like a summons. Something flashed across Hoa's face. Joe had only ever seen her in friendly mode, but he had heard a few tales that she wasn't a woman to be messed with.

'Tell her yourself,' replied Hoa dryly. 'Now, take a seat please, Dr Le Gran, and we'll discuss the patients you will be seeing here.' It was as if a switch had been flicked. Ice dripped from her voice.

There was a pregnant pause.

Joe held his breath, waiting to see what the response would be. He heard the scraping of a chair. 'Of course.'

Hoa continued, 'And just so we're clear, Dr Le Gran, I make decisions about television crews in my hospital, and I will only allow them with patient permission. You might be offering your services free—and we're grateful to have you here—but patient confidentiality will not be breached.'

Joe felt a shiver down his spine and a smile came to his lips. He might just love this older woman. There was a clear line in the sand. If Lien didn't like this guy, she would love this. He glanced over his shoulder. She was strangely absent, though he was sure she'd been around a few minutes before.

Joe kept out of sight, still listening to Hoa. The older woman commanded respect, and yet he'd seen her on her hands and knees cleaning vomit from the floor, and watched her playing games with some of the babies in the clinic.

Reuben had already shown little respect for the hospital and its staff. It seemed Hoa had already determined that he might act the same way towards their patients. She wouldn't tolerate that for a second.

Joe heard one of the nurses mutter something under her breath. He turned his head as he hadn't quite picked it up. 'What was that?'

The nurse rolled her eyes before turning her eyes back on the open office containing Reuben and Hoa. 'We've had his type before. Better start digging the grave in the back. Hoa will chew him up and spit him out.'

Joe let out a laugh. He couldn't help it. 'Well, show

respect, get respect was what my old mentor taught me. For everyone—friends, colleagues and patients.'

The nurse smiled. 'Oh, don't worry, Joe, you're safe. We like you.' She gave him a strange knowing glance. 'In fact, we might have big plans for you.'

He put one hand on his hip as she started to walk away. 'Wait a minute, what does that mean?'

The nurse laughed and waved her hand as she kept walking. 'I'll let you know!'

Lien felt as if she were dancing some kind of complicated choreography. Every time she knew Reuben was in the clinic she made herself scarce. He hadn't deigned to give them his schedule to begin with, and just turned up whenever he saw fit. But Khiem took him aside and discussed with him the problems of co-ordinating patient care if they didn't know in advance that he was coming. Some of the patients that they wanted him to see lived far outside the city limits. It wasn't easy for them to reach the free clinic.

What complicated things more was the fact that the patients seemed to love the idea of being treated by the celebrity doctor, and all of them agreed to being filmed. This meant that the rest of the staff had to put up with film crews trailing through the hospital at inopportune times.

She could sense Joe standing at the door of one of the rooms in the ward today where she was sitting talking to a young mum. The woman was sick. Her blood tests and chest X-ray had revealed she was HIV-positive and had tuberculosis. Her lungs were under severe attack, and she'd only just been diagnosed; Lien was currently trying to balance a drug regime for both illnesses, alongside the pregnancy.

She held the young mum's hand and explained to her what her diagnosis meant.

This young woman had had no idea she'd even been sick. She'd been tired, and had a severe night-time cough. She'd presented late into the pregnancy and been automatically brighter as soon as she knew she was pregnant—she seemed to think both of her other ailments were down to the pregnancy. Hoa had done the initial pregnancy booking, and a few simple tests had revealed the results that all the doctors had expected, with each disease speeding up the progress of the other.

Now the woman had developed a high temperature and breathing difficulties. She was thirty-six weeks pregnant, and both she and the baby were currently at risk.

Lien reached out and took the young woman's hand and spoke quietly and steadily, pausing to make sure she understood what Lien was saying and comforting her when it seemed appropriate. By the time she was finished she felt positively drained.

The young woman would be in hospital for the next few days. Hoa might even decide she needed a caesarean section if either the baby or the mum's condition deteriorated rapidly.

As Lien walked through to the office, she could feel tears brimming in her eyes. Some patients just got to her.

She walked in and closed the door behind her, expecting the office to be empty, then jumped when she realised Joe was sitting in a chair to her left.

'Sorry,' he said. 'I was just waiting until you'd finished.' He took one look at the expression on her face and jumped up. 'Lien. What's wrong?'

He didn't wait for her to reply, he just put his arms around her and pulled her into his chest.

She burrowed her head in his shoulder and just started to sob. Once she started she couldn't stop. 'I'm sorry,' she breathed. 'I don't know what's wrong.'

His grip was firm and comforting. She could feel the planes of his chest against hers. His voice was husky. 'You've got a really sick girl who should be celebrating her pregnancy. Instead, you've had to give her bad news. We both know she might not live to see this baby grow up, Lien. You wouldn't be human if you weren't upset.'

She sniffed and tried to wipe some of the tears away. 'But I know all this. I've dealt with it before. I should be stronger.'

He slid his hands to the tops of her shoulders and stepped back a little. He was still close enough that his breath warmed her forehead. She could see every little line around the corners of his eyes. 'You're strong. You're still here, Lien. You work in one of the most challenging places in the world and you love it.' He took a deep breath and gave her a sympathetic smile. 'There's always one that gets to you.'

She was still trembling. 'Who was yours?'

'What?'

'Who was the last patient that got to you?'

He closed his eyes. She actually felt him shiver as his expression grew dark. 'That's easy. A baby. A six-week-old baby with a spiral fracture in his forearm. Apparently he rolled off the bed and Dad reached out to grab him.'

Lien held her breath. She knew how rare spiral fractures were, and what caused them. 'A six-week-old baby doesn't roll,' she whispered.

He opened his eyes. 'No,' he breathed. 'I could have lost my job over that one. I put Dad up against the wall when he tried to grab the baby and leave.'

She shivered. 'What's wrong with some people?' She moved forward. This time it was her that wrapped her arms around him, hugging him tight.

His muscles were tense and it took a few moments for him to relax. After a second his hand went up to the back of her head, resting against her hair. It felt more personal.

She felt herself relax even more. She liked being in his arms. She could smell his woody aftershave at the nape of his neck. She could feel the muscles that lay underneath his lightweight top. It awakened senses in her that had been dormant for a while. One of her hands started running up the length of his back. As soon as she realised what she was doing, she froze.

He moved his head. And she lifted hers.

They were inches from each other. If either made the slightest movement their lips could connect.

It was unnervingly intimate. She was currently at work, standing in the arms of a colleague. She'd never done this in her life before. When she'd dated Reuben, they'd still been students at uni. Since then she'd only dated a few guys with other occupations. Never anybody related to her workplace environment. It was like her own little rule.

He blinked, and it broke the haze that felt as if it had descended between them. She couldn't help but feel bereft.

He gave a nervous smile and dropped his hands from

her, stepping back. 'Sorry, you just looked like a colleague in need of a hug.'

'I was,' she said quickly. Then she took another breath and met his gaze again. 'And so did you.'

He broke their gaze and glanced towards the floor.

The silence seemed to last for ever. Did he want to say something else?

After a moment he lifted his head and cleared his throat. 'I came to speak to you about the prescribing regime for your patient. I'm unfamiliar with what can be prescribed for a pregnant woman with TB and HIV. I thought I should find out what protocols you have.'

Work. He'd turned this back to work. Her stomach flipped. She was uncomfortable. For a moment there she'd thought he might kiss her. She'd thought he might just lean forward an inch and let his lips connect with hers. She'd felt it. She'd almost tasted it.

What would she have done if he'd made that move? Would she have pulled back, or would she have responded?

Did she really want to admit the answer to that question?

She licked her lips and nodded. Work. This was work. 'Of course,' she said, her voice tight. 'Let's sit down. Hoa has made a flow chart for some of the protocols for pregnant women. There is a prescribing regime, but I actually planned to check with her once I got the results of some of the blood tests.'

Talking about work was easy. She knew she'd been tense this last week. Turning every corner in her workplace—her safe place—and wondering if she might see the man who'd told her she wasn't good enough was unnerving.

She'd no wish or desire to speak to Reuben again. But she'd heard he'd asked after her. How much could she realistically avoid him?

She stared at the paperwork in front of her, trying not to focus on Joe's strong hands as his fingers curved around the pen. What was wrong with her?

Concentrate.

Her brain was going places it shouldn't.

It had only been a hug, and she'd do well to remember that.

She held in a sigh and stared back at the protocol in front of her. For the first time in her life, she was tempted to mix work with pleasure. No matter how hard she tried, it seemed the logical part of her brain could only hear the pitter-patter of her heart.

This had disaster stamped all over it. Having Reuben around reminded her just how far apart her world was from Joe's.

What was that children's story—*The Prince and the Pauper*? That was how far apart they felt to her. No matter what his eyes had told her in that hug earlier. If he knew the truth about her, and her poor background, he would start to look at her differently, more coolly.

She remembered how that felt. How belittling. How sad it had made her.

And even though her brain told her all this, she could tell that her heart wasn't listening.

CHAPTER SEVEN

THE TELEVISION CREW was like a virus. They seemed to spread everywhere, particularly into parts of the hospital they'd been explicitly told they weren't allowed.

On the other hand, the surgeries that Reuben had performed over the last few weeks were proving to be a miracle for some of the patients.

He didn't just do the showbiz plastic surgery. He'd performed a skin graft on a child who'd had her face scarred by boiling water. The early results were good. He'd also performed surgery on a woman with contracture of her fingers. For the first time in years she was virtually pain-free and had a hand she could actually use. He'd reset a woman's nose and fixed her shattered cheekbone after she'd been attacked by her ex-husband and had thought she'd be disfigured for life. Even from the sidelines, Lien's heart had tugged as the woman had seen her reflection once the bruising had subsided and had then flung her arms around Reuben in complete gratitude.

These were the moments for which Lien had become a doctor and, a long time ago, Reuben had made her believe this was also his reason for being a surgeon.

The cynical part of her knew that when the moment had been captured by the film crew, Reuben had achieved the best publicity he could possibly hope for. It wasn't a mistake. There was obviously another reason for all this, but so far Lien had managed to avoid him completely and now her curious brain wanted to know what he was really up to.

She and Khiem had been discussing two other potential patients for Reuben. One was a maternity patient who'd had an emergency section in an outlying village and had been left with a persistently leaking wound. They'd spent the last few weeks treating her underlying infection with IV antibiotics, and were hopeful that Reuben could use his skills on the scar and they could finally get the wound to heal.

The second was a child with a congenital condition who required facial surgery to assist his breathing. The surgeries were vastly different—but already the TV team were asking for permission regarding filming and publicity. It made Lien feel distinctly uncomfortable, but there was nothing she could do about it. Reuben was offering his time and services free, the hospital was picking up the aftercare. In any other set of circumstances these patients would never get the opportunity for surgery.

She'd just finished a ward round and was writing up a treatment regime for a TB patient when she sensed someone walk into the room behind her.

She hadn't even turned before every cell in her body froze. The confidence of the footsteps followed by the waft of familiar cologne was all it took.

'Why, there she is, the mystery doctor!' Reuben exclaimed.

She kept working. 'I'm busy,' was her brisk reply.

'Aren't we all?' He swept over to her with a swish of the white coat he persisted in wearing.

'What do you want, Reuben?' she sighed, still refusing to look up.

'Why, Lien? What's wrong? Anyone would think you weren't pleased to see me.'

'Anyone would be right.'

His hand closed over hers, and she was so shocked it took a second for her to snatch it away.

'Lien, why be like this? We were such good friends.' She couldn't quite work out if he was being deliberately sarcastic or if he really was so wrapped up in himself he couldn't see further than the end of his own nose.

'What are you doing here, Reuben?'

Now she did look up. He pretended to look hurt. 'Why do you think I'm here? I want to give a little back to the people of Hanoi.'

'And yet it's taken you six years to realise that is your calling.' The sarcastic words shot out before she had a chance to soften and rephrase them. She mentally cursed herself. It didn't matter how she felt about him, she still wanted him to do the surgeries on the two other patients.

It was so weird, staring into the face again of the man she'd thought she might have loved. It had been so long. His light brown skin had a strange sheen, his hair much darker than before. In fact, it looked a bit odd around his hairline. Years ago, Reuben's hair had been a bit thinner and he'd been paranoid about it. Had he had a hair transplant?

He'd always been good looking, but his face seemed different. Maybe he'd had some work done. She couldn't quite tell. The skin on his forehead and around his eyes was unusually smooth. Maybe some Botox? One thing was for certain, he'd had every single one of his teeth veneered. They'd been reasonably straight before, but now they were sparkling white and uniformly sized.

She laughed out loud. 'You look quite different.'

'I'm in the business,' he said quickly. 'When people come to see a plastic surgeon, they expect perfection. I try my best.'

'There was nothing wrong with the way you looked before,' she said quietly, and a little sadly.

His green eyes met hers. Even they looked different—a bit more startling. Was he wearing green contacts?

She sighed. How could she ever have thought they were on the same wavelength? She had no problem with anyone trying to improve their appearance if they chose to. But Reuben seemed to be trying to achieve an unrealistic perfection. That couldn't be healthy.

He waved his hand. 'Anyway…' his eyes swept up and down her body '…pleased to see you haven't let yourself go.'

She blinked, temporarily incensed at the entirely unprofessional comment. Her body was rigid and she struggled to keep her voice steady. 'Well, obviously my whole life depends on your approval of how I look, Reuben.'

One of his eyebrows cocked. She was surprised the Botox allowed it. They hadn't seen in each other in a long time and her obvious indifferent attitude to him wasn't sitting well.

She really didn't care. She was holding back—really she was. If she truly engaged her brain and her mouth he would doubtless walk out of here and never come back.

She took a breath. 'Tell the truth. What's going on—why are you really here?'

He leaned against the worktop, moving slightly closer to her. He seemed to be under the illusion that she might welcome this.

'You know me, I'm just being civic-minded.'

She finished her chart. 'You're right. I do know you. At least, I do now. So, spill, Reuben. What gives?'

He looked down towards his handmade shoes for a second. 'I might need a little help.'

'Help with what?'

He straightened his back. 'It seems I might have some bad publicity heading my way. My publicist said that I should—'

'Your what?' She couldn't help but interrupt. She'd heard everything now.

'My publicist. She said that I should look a bit more civic-minded. It seems that some of the activity at the clinic has been examined. It was granted a licence on the grounds it would also see some local patients for free, but it's been so busy there just hasn't been time.'

She smiled. 'Ah, now we're getting to the real news.'

He lifted his hand to run his fingers through his hair, but they kind of got stuck.

'She asked me about my past, and if I knew anyone, and if there was some place I could think of to see some local patients.' He shrugged awkwardly. 'And your name came up.'

It was like a cold breeze sweeping over her skin. 'What do you mean, my name came up?'

He couldn't look her in the eye. 'Well, when she asked me if I knew anyone...'

'What, I was the one person who came from the

worst district in Hanoi that you knew—the token person from the slum?' She couldn't stop the rage that surged through her veins.

The eyebrow remained raised. He seemed surprised by the passion behind her words. 'I know that you are familiar with the area, with the people—and their health needs.' He looked as if he was trying to find the right words, but there was an inherent smugness in how he sounded. He waved his hand dismissively. 'We know the stats. The people.' He glanced at her. 'The most deprived populations have the worst health.'

She put a hand to her chest. 'You mean *my* people?'

The words just came out. She hated the fact that her stomach almost curled in embarrassment or that she could feel tears prickling at the sides of her eyes.

'Well…yes,' he said simply.

She tried to push all her emotional and irrational thoughts to the back of her mind. She had to be professional. This was her workplace.

His hand swept past her again. 'I'm not all bad, Lien. You just think I am.' He put his hand to his chest and stepped a little closer, letting her inhale his cloying aftershave. 'I'm me. And you're you. We can't change that. But…' he took a deep breath '…I would rather fulfil the terms of my licence here than anywhere else.' His eyes rested on the stack of patient files on the desk. 'That tiny part of me that wanted to do well as a doctor? It is still there.' He shrugged. 'It just got lost in the hype. I know you have more patients for me. People I can help, who would never get these surgeries otherwise. People like you, Lien. I can be here once a week for the next four months. Will you let me help them, or should I go somewhere else?'

She hated him. She hated him for being so factual, and reasonable, but continuing to throw in subtle digs about their different backgrounds.

It was quite extraordinary. When she'd started dating Reuben at university, he'd been a little pompous perhaps, but he had at least tried to fit in with all the other students. It had only been as they'd got further along in their studies that his entitled persona had appeared.

For a time Lien hadn't told anyone where she was from. Maybe she had felt a bit ashamed at the time— fitting in had been hard enough. It had been clear that most of the students who had been studying medicine came from well-to-do families. No one had known about her scholarship, and for that she'd been glad.

She'd been so focused on her studies that when Reuben had started to show an interest in her, and invite her on dates, she'd been quietly flattered.

After a few months of his endless attention she'd started to believe it was real. He'd invited her to his home and she'd been dazzled. When he'd asked about her family she'd made excuses.

It shamed her now to think about it, but she'd felt pressurised to fit in. She'd got along with the rest of her colleagues. Duc, Khiem and Hoa's son, had also been in her class. He'd been great, and he'd seemed to understand that she was trying to keep things quiet about her background. He'd never judged, or commented. Just kept gracefully silent. For that, she'd been eternally grateful.

Two years along it had been inevitable things would come to a head.

She'd noticed that Rueben had started to attend more

and more events within his mother's elite circle—where Lien had felt distinctly uncomfortable. One night they'd been socialising with colleagues and he'd made some comments about those born in the 'wrong places', and she'd asked him to define exactly where he meant.

He named a few districts with a gesture of his hand—one of those districts had been hers. She hadn't waited. She'd exploded then and there, asking him what exactly was wrong with people from that district and not waiting for his answer before she'd told him that was where she had been born, and where her parents still lived.

The table had been shocked into stunned silence.

She'd realised what she'd done by the looks on some faces, but she hadn't been sorry. When she'd grabbed her bag to leave, Duc had joined her, along with a few other colleagues.

Two hours later she'd received a text from Reuben saying it might be better to break up. Even though she couldn't have agreed more, it hadn't stopped angry tears from spilling down her cheeks. The next day she'd discovered he'd transferred out of some of her classes.

She hadn't needed any more messages. He'd been embarrassed by her, and she'd been furious with him. She'd avoided him ever since.

He gave her an amiable smile. 'How about we look at these files together? You can fill me in on some of these patients.' He gestured towards the chairs.

Lien pressed her lips together. She should do this. She should do this for her patients. They had to come first, no matter how much she didn't want to be in his company. That was her problem—not theirs.

Once a week for the next four months wasn't actually

enough. But it was more than he'd originally promised and it was a start. For now, she'd take it.

As she sat stiffly in the chair next to him, he gave her another half-smile. 'Oh, don't think I haven't noticed. The other doctor, the Scot…is there something going on between you two?'

Her breath caught somewhere in her throat. She wasn't quite sure how to answer that question—she was caught totally off guard. But his words made old memories and feelings flood to the surface.

Feelings of how inadequate Reuben had made her feel. Would she feel that way around Joe too?

'Nothing's going on,' she said quickly. 'We're colleagues. I've been showing him around, helping him get settled in. That's all.'

Reuben gave her a knowing nod. It was clear from his expression he wasn't buying anything she was saying. 'Okay,' he replied simply as he pushed the first set of case notes towards her. 'Let's start here.'

CHAPTER EIGHT

TWO WEEKS LATER, Joe and Lien headed to Uông Bí hospital to provide some holiday cover.

The car journey only took a few hours, with them mainly entertained by Regan singing at the top of his voice to the selection of songs he'd picked for the trip.

As they passed lush green hills with gorgeous scenery, Joe let out a sigh. 'This place is more like Scotland than I ever imagined possible.' He smiled and turned his head towards Lien, who was concentrating on the road ahead. 'I think it would surprise you. You should come and see it sometime.'

There was an odd silence for a few seconds. One that he wanted to fill. 'Ever thought about coming to Scotland to work for a while? You tried Dublin, didn't you? I bet we can be more hospitable. You should give us a try.'

Her jaw tightened, as did her hands on the steering wheel. 'I've done my travelling,' she said. 'I'm happy just to stay here now.'

Joe leaned towards her, his enthusiasm catching fire as he started to imagine showing Lien around the sights back home. 'You would love it. There are a few islands with cottage hospitals that you might like, or you could come and work in Glasgow with me. There are always positions for doctors.' He shot her another sideways glance. 'And we have plenty of space. You could stay with me and Regan.'

She shook her head as she drove. 'Nice offer, but I'm happy here. I don't want to work anywhere else. This is where my heart is.'

She said the words with an edge of determination. His stomach flipped. *Where her heart was.* Did that mean there wasn't room for anything else?

The thought was probably ridiculous, but as the seed grew in his mind he became even more enthusiastic about Lien coming to Scotland. He was sure she could love it just as much as he loved Vietnam. With Regan due to start school in a few months, he had to return. Was it possible he might be able to persuade Lien to join them?

'Glasgow and Hanoi aren't that different.' He gestured towards Regan in the back seat. 'Our life here isn't that different.'

Lien looked surprised. 'You're on a totally different continent, treating people with conditions you've never came across before, and speak a totally different language. How on earth can you find anything the same?'

He stared ahead and shrugged casually. He understood her points, but still felt the same. 'Patients are patients, no matter where in the world you treat them. They have the same expectations of you—that you treat them competently, and fairly, without judging them. For me, the hours are more or less the same, I have somewhere for Regan that I trust, and I'm getting to do the job that I love. The same as you.' He gave her a smile. 'We're not that different, you know.'

Her eyebrows shot upwards. 'We're a world apart,

Joe. You just don't see it yet,' she added with a hint of sadness in her voice.

He wasn't quite sure what she meant. In his mind, Lien was one of the most dedicated doctors he'd worked with. He'd hoped that she felt the same about him. Maybe he wasn't convincing her he was as dedicated to his work as he'd hoped. But he could work at that.

He shifted in the passenger seat. And he would.

She gave him a sideways glance and her lips hinted at a smile. 'Wait and see where we're going next, then tell me it's just like Scotland.'

He bit his bottom lip as he glanced at her again. Every day he spent around Lien he found himself more and more attracted to her—even though he hadn't acted on it. They worked so well together. He loved being around her. When ideas sprang into his head, she was the first person he wanted to talk to.

He smiled to himself. Lien had no aspirations to come to Scotland, but maybe he could persuade her. He kept smiling and settled back in the seat.

When they arrived in Uông Bí Lien took them for a quick drive around a few parts of the city, before driving out towards the hospital and giving Joe some background on the people who lived here.

By the time they finally pulled up in front of the hospital they were all ready to get out and stretch their legs.

The hospital was a more traditional building for Vietnam, made from wood, bamboo and cane, and set on stilts. Lien smiled as Regan and Joe looked up in wonder. 'Many homes in Vietnam are like this. Vietnam can be prone to flooding, so lots of houses built on flood-prone plains or in mountains are set on stilts.'

'Has this place been here a while?' Joe asked as he climbed the steps.

Lien smiled and nodded. 'We're like magpies. We tend to take over places that are a little run-down and neglected and take them over for ourselves.'

Joe's eyebrows shot up in surprise, but she laughed and shook her head. 'I'm kidding. The building in Hanoi was bought by Khiem and Hoa. This place was taken over and renovated by us after it fell into disrepair and the local community was requesting health care facilities. It does actually belong to us now.'

Joe grabbed the replenished medical supplies that she tossed to him and helped carry them up to the hospital. Her smile had got brighter with every mile of the journey and he could see the tension leaving her shoulders.

Lien opened the door to the hospital and showed Joe around. Even though it was set in a city, this hospital was very much on the outskirts and had a much more rural feel.

She showed them into a wide waiting room at the front of the building, with the back of the building divided into separate rooms. 'We have three consulting rooms, and six beds for patients if required. There is permanent staff here, so we generally only come down to cover holidays, or if there's some kind of outbreak.'

Two nurses came over to meet them and Joe quickly shook their hands and familiarised himself with the hospital setting and clinic arrangements. Lien appeared with a whole host of things she seemed to conjure up out of thin air. A pile of flat smooth rocks, along with some half-used bottles of paint for Regan. 'You paint these while your dad and I work, and once they are dry we can varnish them. You could send one of them back home to your grandma and papa as a present.'

'Wow, thanks, Lien,' murmured Regan. She'd also found some snacks and set Regan up in one part of the clinic where Joe could keep a close eye on him. Her thoughtfulness impressed him. She never forgot Regan, and it was clear that he appreciated the attention.

'We're ready.' She smiled as she moved over to the other treatment room with her nurse. 'Let's get started.'

Joe glanced outside. People were already forming a queue outside the main door. He smiled. It didn't matter where you were in the world—whether that was a GP practice in Glasgow or an outlying hospital in Vietnam—come opening time, there was always a queue of people waiting.

He nodded. 'Looking forward to it,' he said, and he meant it. The drive inside him that had disappeared these last few years had seemed to magically reignite the longer he stayed in Vietnam. It was good to feel this way again. He'd forgotten just how much it invigorated him.

He glanced around at the people. Lien was chatting away with one of the nurses, her dark hair swept up in a clip. Regan was engrossed in the corner of one room with his stones. Another nurse was setting out vaccinations on a metal trolley in the next-door room. He licked his lips, feeling the buzz deep down inside. Part of his interest was in the place and the people. His eyes went first to Regan; his son was happy here. He'd been happy in Scotland too, but somehow, now Joe could see new sparkle in his son's eyes. He was excited by the changes around him and seeing his son happy was feeding Joe's soul.

But there was something else. Something he couldn't ignore.

They'd been here three months, and the longer he was here, the more he was drawn to Lien. Everything about her pulled him in. Her work ethic, her passion, her drive, her sense of humour, and the electricity between them.

As he watched Lien, he couldn't stop the smile that had seemed permanently etched on his face since they'd all left Hanoi together. He hadn't felt this alive or happy in years.

A new determination spread through him. One thing was clear—now he'd found it again, he didn't want to lose it. When he and Regan boarded that plane back to Scotland, he wanted Lien to be sitting next to them.

Lien was happy to be busy. She always liked covering in the other areas because it gave her a wider feel for the health of the population. Sometimes it was nice to get away from the hustle and bustle of her own city.

Had Joe really invited her to Scotland, and to stay with him in his house/castle? She'd struggled to find words as the offer had seemed to come out of nowhere.

She couldn't deny the blossoming attraction, but he'd seemed to think the plan was easy. Did he really think she would just pack up and go with them back to Glasgow—to a country she literally knew nothing about? As for his house...

She shook her head at the thought. Her parents' house could probably fit forty times over into the place that Joe called home. She couldn't even imagine herself somewhere like that. The more she thought about it, the more she realised they were worlds apart. Just like she and Reuben had been.

She pushed all stray thoughts from her mind. The queue outside the hospital was getting longer. She was here to do a job and she had patients to see.

Halfway through the morning, things started to go downhill. The young man in front of her had muscle and joint pains, a headache and a fever. When Lien examined him he also had a widespread rash. He was clearly exhausted and going downhill fast. She asked if he had anyone with him and he nodded and pointed to the waiting room. 'My wife and son, they both feel the same,' he added.

Her stomach flipped. Her brain was already computing what was wrong and it wasn't good news, but from the look in the man's eyes he knew already what she would tell him.

She swallowed and put a hand on his arm. 'Give me a few minutes, Tadeus,' she said. She needed to chat with Joe. If she'd found one with this disease, it was likely there could be others. But Joe was just coming out of his own door to find her. 'I need to chat,' he said quickly. 'I think I've got two cases of dengue fever. It's most common in the rainy season here, isn't it?'

She nodded quickly, glanced in his room at the two patients, and at his notes. Dengue fever was spread by mosquitoes and was more common in the south of Vietnam, and in the wet season. Her eyes couldn't help but glance towards Regan. These people weren't infectious. The disease could only be spread by mosquito bite, but it still made her feel a little anxious.

'It does look like dengue fever. We don't wait, or rely on, the blood test for antibodies, we just go with the clinical symptoms.'

He nodded. 'But why here? Why now? Isn't it more common in the south?'

'Usually, but there can be lots of different factors. Just because it's more common in south—and in the rainy season—it doesn't mean that we don't see it at other times too. We'll need to ask about water storage, particularly if they store water in containers at their house—that can play a part in hosting mosquitoes.'

He scribbled some notes on the papers he had.

'How are your patients?' she asked.

'The mother has clinical signs and is tired, but I'm more concerned about the ten-year-old. He's clinically dehydrated and looks as if he could do with some IV fluids for a short spell.'

'Have they been anywhere unusual in the last ten days?'

Joe shook his head. 'Just at home.'

'Okay, I've got the dad. He's exhausted too, and a bit dehydrated. How about we hook up the father and child to IV fluids and some antipyretics for a few hours and assess them again. There's no widely available vaccine for this, no cure. We just have to treat the symptoms and hope they don't progress.'

He nodded seriously. 'Leave it with me. I'll take them all through to the ward and get things organised.'

Most international doctors would have left this to her, and it was nice to have someone want to truly share the load. It was like he could read her mind. He gave her a smile. 'My nurse, Eartha, will help me with the translations.'

He was trying to reassure her. 'I'll give you a shout if I have any questions.'

She was tempted to add more. To tell him about the one or two per cent who developed complications. But somehow she had faith he'd already looked that up himself. She needed to let him run with this—he was more than competent.

Four hours later she'd seen a steady stream of patients. She kept being tempted to go and find Joe and catch up with him, but she knew that would look as if she was checking up on him. So instead she busied herself with putting a temporary cast on a broken wrist, prescribed antibiotics for everything from a severe chest infection, pneumonia and a kidney infection to an infected insect bite that really needed attention on a daily basis.

She also had a chance to catch up with a few long-term patients of the hospital who had tuberculosis, and a few with HIV. She always did her best to try and review the long-term patients to make sure they were keeping up with their treatment regimes and not suffering from any complications.

By the time she'd finished, Joe was waiting for her at the door, holding Regan's hand.

'How are things?' she asked.

'Both patients seem quite stable. They're going to stay in the hospital overnight and Terry will keep an eye on them.'

Lien nodded. Terry was one of the other local doctors and she trusted him completely.

'Let's wash up and we can go and find some dinner, then,' she sighed. 'Let's grab the car. There's a place just down the road that I like.'

They drove a little closer to the city and settled into a local restaurant half an hour later, but not before she'd made both Joe and Regan reapply their mosquito repellent. It hadn't taken them long to adjust to wearing long sleeves and trousers on a daily basis. Today's cases of dengue fever hadn't been unusual, but it still made her nervous.

Joe was surprised by her choice of restaurant. It was styled like an old American diner and even had a play area in the corner for kids. He glanced around at the street. It was dotted with a variety of international restaurants—some of them chains—but this one seemed a little more unusual. It was already crowded, with a host of locals and tourists.

'What?' she asked as she slid into one of the booths.

He shrugged as he slid in on the other side. 'I'm surprised this is one of your favourites.'

'Ah.' She nodded as she perused the menu. 'When I worked in Washington there was a diner that I loved. I swear they've stolen the chef's recipes and just transported him over here, because the burgers in here taste exactly like my favourite over there.'

He eyed the menu with caution. 'Okay, which one of these is your favourite?'

She pointed. 'The barbeque grand. Double stack with cheese, pickle, onion rings and fries.'

He laughed and she pointed to something else. 'If you're not that hungry you can always have the southern fried chicken burger. I like that too.' She paused a second. 'But if you're having that one, have it with the curly fries with cheese sauce and bacon.'

He shook his head. 'Where on earth do you put it all?'

'Hollow legs.' She smiled. 'It's a family secret.'

The waitress came over a few moments later and they ordered quickly. The lights in the diner were bright.

They'd booked into a nearby hotel for their stay. It was comfortable and run by a local family. Joe was tired, but in no hurry to head back. Once they went back to their rooms he wouldn't see Lien again until the morning. This was the first time they'd had to sit down properly all day. Regan had made his way over to the kids' corner and was playing with a garage, dinosaurs and a pirate ship. Joe watched him for a few moments then turned to Lien. Since the moment he'd got here, he'd found her to be the person he wanted to talk to most—particularly when it came to Regan.

'I got a report from Regan's nursery teacher just before we headed down here.'

'Really? What did she say?'

He played with the cutlery in front of him. 'She said he's been doing great and has settled in well.'

She tilted her head to the side. That was the thing about Lien. She seemed to be able to read him so well. 'So why the long face?'

He leaned his head on one arm. 'They said that sometimes he takes himself off into the quiet room and just lies down.'

'The quiet room?'

'It's a space they keep in the nursery to allow kids to have some time out. It's got a library, and some cushions. The lights can also be dimmed and it has planets and stars painted on the walls.'

'What's bad about that?' Her question was reasonable. She made it sound so simple. But it didn't relieve the knot that had been churning in his stomach since the nursery teacher had talked to him.

He swallowed, his fingers drumming on the table. 'Regan told the teacher that he goes in there to speak to one of the stars because it's his mum.'

Her stomach flipped over.

'Oh.' She hadn't expected that. In all the time she'd been around Regan he hadn't mentioned his mum, and she hadn't wanted to bring it up.

His gaze met hers. 'Yes. Oh.'

She wasn't quite sure what to say. 'Is there a reason that he thinks his mum's a star?'

Joe nodded. 'I told him a story a few years ago, about how someone had bought us a star to name after Mummy, and that she would always be up there to talk to.'

Lien shifted a little in her seat. 'That's nice. And it seems a good explanation for a kid as young as Regan. So, what's wrong? Is this unusual for him?'

Joe's eyes looked sad. He interlinked his fingers and Lien got the distinct impression he was wringing them together. She could sense his low mood and frustration. 'He's never done this before. At least, he's never told *me* he does this. But he told his nursery teacher. What does that mean?'

Lien glanced at the happy little boy playing in the corner of the restaurant. He was currently involved in a great battle between dinosaurs and pirates, complete with sound effects. She reached her hand out to Joe's. 'It means he's a four-year-old boy who still wants to talk to his mum.' The truth was, she knew nothing about any of this. But she could try to think about this rationally.

'Now Regan's at nursery he probably sees other kids being dropped off by their mums and their dads. Maybe it's left him feeling a bit lonely. Maybe taking that time to go into the quiet room and talk to his mum, the way he sees the other kids doing, makes him feel less different.'

She put her hand between his and intertwined her fingers with his. 'I know this is hard, Joe. I'm not an expert in kids—I'm not a parent. I can only tell you what I think it might be. Most kids don't want to be different from each other, even though they are in a million ways. I bet if you think back to your childhood or teenage years you can remember doing something that stopped you feeling different from others.'

Her heart squeezed inside her chest. For her, it had been in her late teens. It had been realising just how poor her family were, and all the different ways she'd tried to hide it from her friends. She'd tried to fit in every way she could. She had been pretty. And smart. Well mannered. When people had found out where she'd really come from—one of the most deprived suburbs in Hanoi—she'd seen them wrinkle their noses. And that was before all the stuff with her ex-boyfriend. He'd told her so many times how perfect she was—until he'd found out where she came from.

It had taken qualifying as a doctor and adulthood before she'd realised she should be proud of her upbringing, her parents, and what she'd learned in life.

Assumptions around poverty were made all over the world. Dang Van Lien made it her job to challenge them at every turn. She wasn't stupid. She wasn't dirty.

Yes, she'd been hungry at times. Yes, the house she'd been brought up in would have seemed like a slum to others. Her clothes had mainly been second-hand, most of her school books had been borrowed, and she'd spent her whole childhood finding ways not to require money. But she'd been brought up in a simple, tidy house filled with love. Her parents were proud people. Even though she'd offered to help them move, they didn't want to. They'd told her on lots of occasions they had what they needed.

That didn't stop her buying gifts that were gratefully received. She'd replaced most of the household appliances and pieces of furniture as they'd broken down or had got to the stage where they couldn't be repaired. Every birthday and Christmas she bought her parents brand-new sets of clothes and a pile of books. Two years ago, her father had even accepted his first mobile phone.

She wanted to do more. She understood where the line was, and that by trying to do more she would insult them. Lien would never do that.

She squeezed Joe's fingers. 'Regan is a smart kid. And kids are more resilient than we think they are. He knows he has you. He knows he has his grandparents who love him. He also knows that his family is a little different from some of the other kids around him.'

She saw him blink and recognised the unshed tears in his eyes. Every instinct told her that Joe didn't normally let anyone see him cry. She could bet he'd shed a million tears over the loss of his wife, but Joe was the kind of guy to do that in private. His face for the outside world would be stoic. He was revealing parts of himself that he wouldn't normally.

Maybe it was being in a different country with unfamiliar people that was amplifying things for him. Or maybe he felt the connection between them that she tried her best not to think about.

She spoke quietly. 'Joe, I know this is hard. And I

know there will always be dates, or occasions, in the future that will hit hard too.' She was thinking of special birthdays or Christmases. 'But I just want to tell you I think you're doing a great job. And Regan? He's a great kid. Smart, cheeky, with a big heart. You can't ask for more.'

Joe sucked in a deep breath and the expression on his face softened. The deep lines on his forehead smoothed out. He untangled their fingers and turned her palm over, tracing little circles with one of his fingers.

It was soothing. It was comforting. But it also sent a whole host of little zings up her arm.

Those green eyes met hers under heavy lids. 'How did I get so lucky?' he asked.

'With Regan?'

He shook his head. 'No.' His gaze was steady. 'With a colleague like you.' He lowered his gaze now. 'I don't like to wobble. I hate to feel that I can't be everything that my kid needs. On the few occasions I wobbled back home, my mum and dad helped paper over the cracks. We didn't talk about it. I'd just get up the next day to find my mother had crept in overnight and left a big pot of soup on the stove, or had done the mountain of ironing that I'd left. Or I'd get home from work and find my dad had mown the lawn that had been in danger of turning into a jungle.'

She gave a little laugh. The heat was spreading up her arm.

'Well,' she said softly, 'I certainly don't have—what do you call it, green fingers?'

He nodded and she continued. 'Neither am I particularly great with ironing. But I can tell you where all the best restaurants and stores are. I can find a thousand ways to amuse a kid without spending any money, and I can loan you another thousand bedtime stories.'

Joe sighed, and his finger kept tracing circles in her palm. 'I feel so weird about all this.'

'Why?'

He looked up, straight into her eyes. 'Us.'

Her back automatically straightened. Her mouth almost asked the question, *Is there an us?* But Joe started talking again.

'I feel as if I was meant to meet you. Meant to come here.'

She laughed. 'Your mother bought you the tickets.' She was doing her best to make light of this conversation because she was nervous. Nervous about what he might be about to say, or ask.

'She might have. But this time, this place...' He looked around and held out his hand. 'A crazy diner in the middle of Vietnam...it just feels...' he took a breath before the next word as their gazes meshed '...right.'

It was as if something unfurled inside her, like a flower bud opening to blossom. She could feel the heat spread out through her abdomen. She hadn't expected this. She hadn't expected anything. But she couldn't deny the crazy connection she was feeling.

She took a deep breath. 'You mentioned Scotland—'

She didn't get a chance to continue because Joe's eyes lit up and he started talking straight away. 'Yes. Think about it. Why not give it a try? The scenery is just as good as Vietnam.' He smiled. 'Maybe not the temperature. But there's so much to do. So much to see. Even I can't believe the similarities I see between Glasgow and Hanoi.' He reached over and grabbed her hand. 'I'd love to show you around Glasgow, just like you've done for me and Regan here. Who knows, you might even want to stay.' His eyes sparkled as he said those words and her heart sank like a stone. 'You can stay with us—we have plenty of room.'

She swallowed, her mouth dry. A few seconds ago their connection had felt stronger than ever as he'd told her about his worries about Regan. He'd confided in her enough to tell her that. She could see he was brimming with enthusiasm now and she couldn't find the right words. Their cultural and social backgrounds didn't just feel different at this moment, they felt like a vast abyss. She would never realistically leave Hanoi again—not for anything other than a holiday. Her heart rested here. With the people who needed her most.

She licked her lips. 'Thanks for the offer,' she said as casually as she could. 'Lots to think about.' She stopped there. She didn't feel up to this conversation going any further.

The waitress appeared with a bright smile and put the plates on the table with a loud clunk. Both of them looked up sharply and Lien pulled her hand back. Regan had obviously spotted the food because he appeared at their side. 'Is that my burger?'

'Sure is, buddy.' Joe pulled him up into the booth with them and shot her a quick smile.

She nodded back. This conversation had to be over for now. But as she picked up her knife and fork the turbulent feelings inside her stayed, and somehow she knew as she tried to sleep tonight her brain would be awash with a million other thoughts.

It was the first time he'd been openly affectionate towards her. It was the first time he'd looked at her and said the word 'us'. In just a few months he'd be going back to Scotland—with an expectation that she might want to go too.

And even though there was only a few inches between them, she'd never felt further away.

CHAPTER NINE

'I DON'T WANT you to get too excited, but today we get a day off.' Lien appeared at their hotel room door just before seven a.m. She was smiling, standing in the doorway wearing a loose bright orange top and a pair of white linen trousers. Her hair was in a ponytail tied up high on her head.

Joe opened the door rubbing his eyes, but at her words he automatically perked up. 'What? Really?'

Lien nodded. 'We're just down here to cover for holidays. Plus, we're only about fifty kilometres from one of the most beautiful places on the planet—it's even a world heritage site.'

He wrinkled his nose. He was still waking up and his brain was playing catch-up. 'Where's that?'

'Hạ Long Bay. I feel kind of obliged to take you there and show it to you. Nobody should come to Vietnam and not see it. Plus there are some gorgeous hotels to stay in overnight, and watching the sunset there at night is just magical.'

He gave her a curious stare. For some strange reason he felt a sweep of jealousy. 'How often have you done that?'

She tapped the side of her nose. 'More often than

you need to know about.' She was teasing, he knew
that, but it was strange how his brain was working.
That sharp twinge of jealousy remained, along with a
lot of curiosity.

'Can we go, Daddy?' Regan had appeared beside
him and was instantly excited. 'Is there swimming?'

Lien walked over and bent down beside him. 'Sure
there's swimming. Want me to take you in?'

Regan was already excited, jumping around. 'Yeah!
Find my swimming trunks, Daddy. Let's go!'

Joe couldn't help but smile as he watched her bending
down with his son. It was still playing on his mind—
persuading her to think about coming to Scotland with
him and Regan. Maybe today would be the perfect opportunity. Lien had a large brown paper bag in her hand.
'What's that?' he asked.

'Aha.' She gave them both a wide smile and opened
the bag, letting the aroma of fresh Vietnamese bread
spread throughout the room. 'This is breakfast. We can't
start a day without snacks, can we?'

They piled into the car after finishing their breakfast and headed down towards the coast. Even though
he offered to drive, Lien waved him off. 'Let me, I'm
familiar with this road. It gets a bit twisty later on.'

She was right, of course, and while the busy traffic
of the city wasn't quite replicated on these roads, there
were still numerous motorcycles that seemed to dodge
in and out of the sometimes stationary cars.

As they moved towards the coast the traffic built up
again. Lien turned to them both. 'Okay, I have to warn
you. This is an absolute tourist hotspot. This place will
be busy.' She shot over her shoulder, 'Regan, you always
need to hold someone's hand.'

'We have a few of these in Scotland too. Not World Heritage sights,' he said quickly. 'I mean tourist hotspots. The castle in Edinburgh practically buzzes with people. As do the Christmas markets.' He gave her a smile, as he could see them in his head, bright lights, decorations and the smells of chestnuts and wine. 'I think you'd like them.'

Lien pursed her lips. It was almost as if she hadn't heard those words. She, instead, continued their previous conversation.

She nodded ahead. 'The good thing is, you're here with me. I've booked us into a hotel just a little way up the coast that sits practically on the beach.'

'Doesn't it get overrun with tourists too?'

She smiled and raised an eyebrow. 'They don't take international bookings. They're not on any website to speak of. They don't need to. You can only book by phone and you have to speak Vietnamese to book.'

Joe pulled a face. 'Then how did we manage to get in?'

She patted her hand on her chest. 'Because you guys are with me. Plus they know Khiem and Hoa. Our doctors regularly have a night or two down here.'

She wound her way through some back streets and pulled up outside a hotel that was set on stilts like the hospital. Except this building looked very modern—it was white with large glass windows. They parked at the back and checked in at Reception.

'Don't look out of your bedroom window, you two, just get changed into your trunks, keep a T-shirt on, and I'll meet you back down here in five.'

Joe resisted the temptation to pull back the large white curtain from the glass doors in the room, and changed quickly, taking a few minutes to cover both him and Regan in sunscreen with mosquito repellent. He didn't want to take any chances, so he also threw some light long-sleeved tops and trousers into their beach bag.

Lien was waiting for them near the top of a flight of stairs. 'Are you ready?'

She was smiling as she waved them up. 'Take a look at what I think is one of the wonders of the world.' She smiled.

Joe stepped out. In front of them were hundreds of little islets in a bay of bright green water. Some of them were topped with thick jungle growth and a whole host of them were dotted all along the expanse of the bay. Further down, there were numerous boats, motor cruisers, Vietnamese junks and smaller fishing boats. A few rowing boats were bobbing underneath them along a wooden pier. 'Wow,' he whispered.

Lien's arms brushed against his as she leaned on the wooden railing alongside him. 'Yep—wow.' She pointed to the islets in front of them. 'There are more than sixteen hundred islets. They're made of limestone and they're all different sizes. Some big enough to have their own lakes, and a large number of them are hollow inside with gorgeous caves.' She sighed as she looked out across the bay. 'This beauty is the result of five hundred million years of tropical downpours.'

They stood for a moment just admiring the expansive view.

Lien nudged him. 'There are lots of tours and special cruises that go around the caves—particularly at night. Some of the caves are lit up in spectacular colours, oranges, purples, pinks. There are also lots of tours where you can go diving in the middle of the bay.'

She looked up out of dark eyes.

'Anywhere you can do that in Scotland?' There was the glimmer of a faint smile on her lips, even though it looked a little sad.

Joe shuddered. 'Only thing like this in Scotland is what we call the "stacks". Stacks of rock in the sea up and down the coastline of Scotland. Most are around the Highlands, and you definitely wouldn't want to swim in the sea there.'

Lien shuddered. This time her face brightened a little more. 'Let's stick to Vietnam, then.'

They stood watching as one of the sleek white cruisers, packed with people, prepared to head into one of the sets of caves in the distance.

'What are we going to do, Lien?' asked Regan, practically bouncing on his toes.

She bent down to speak to him. 'We are going to go down and take one of the rowing boats. See those islets out there? We can row over to any of them and explore. You pick.'

'Really?' Regan's head whipped one way and then the next. 'I can choose?'

'You can choose.' She beamed at him.

Joe's heart swelled at how sweet she was with Regan. And it came naturally to her, it wasn't forced at all. He could see that, and it made it more special.

He looked down at the array of boats. 'Have you done this before?'

'Of course. Lots of times. It's the best way to explore the bay.'

She held out her hands, one to Joe and one to Regan,

and led them down the narrow path from the hotel to the bay. They climbed into the boat they chose, Regan laughing nervously as it rocked, and donned the life jackets inside. Lien leaned back for a second, closed her eyes and just breathed.

Regan shot Joe a questioning look.

Joe couldn't help but keep his eyes on Lien. It was almost like he was witnessing her little ritual. A wide smile spread across her face before she opened her eyes again.

Now it was all business. The business of fun.

She clapped her hands together. 'Okay, so we're at the quieter end of the bay. Like I told you, hardly anyone knows about this hotel in the fishing village. There are around seven hundred and seventy-five formations in a space of just three hundred kilometres in the main hub of the bay.' She turned to Regan. 'It's almost like a baker stood above it and sprinkled it with chocolate chips.'

He let out a laugh. 'Want to sit next to me and help me row?' she asked.

'Can I?' Joe could see the excitement gleaming in his eyes.

'Sure,' he said as he took his position at the other oar. Together they pulled away from where the rowing boats were moored and made their way across the perfect green sea.

'It doesn't seem real,' Joe murmured as their boat cut across the water.

It only took a few minutes for Regan to frown and say, 'This is hard work.'

Joe laughed. 'You think?'

Regan pointed to the nearest stack of limestone covered with thick green foliage. 'I pick this one.'

Both Joe and Lien laughed. She shook her head. 'Lazybones. There's another one, just a bit further out. It's got a cave we can take the boat inside. It's like a private lagoon. I think you'll like it more.' She leaned forward and whispered in his ear. 'Maybe we'll spot some pirates!'

Regan gasped, a gleam appearing in his eyes. 'Row faster!' he exclaimed.

Around them other boats appeared. A party of around twenty kayaks glided past them, gathering at the bottom of one of the more impressive tall islets. 'It's a rock-climbing tour,' said Lien as they kept rowing.

'People are going to climb that?' asked Regan, his eyes wide as he tilted his head back and stared at the towering stack.

'Every day people climb that.' She nodded. 'This place is really popular with rock-climbers.' She paused and shipped her oar. 'Want to watch for a bit?'

Regan nodded and they shipped the other oar and leaned back in the boat, watching the intricacies of people attempting to climb a stack in the middle of the bay.

It took the climbers a while, and Joe reapplied their sunscreen and mosquito protection as they watched. Lien let him finish, then smiled. 'How about we take a dip in the water while we wait?'

Joe leaned over. The emerald-green water was clear, but he had no idea how deep the bay was. Lien must have read his thoughts. She tapped the life jacket she was wearing. 'Let's just keep these on,' she said. 'There are no currents around here, so we have nothing to worry about.' She turned to Regan. 'Will I go first, then you can jump in and join me?'

Regan nodded enthusiastically, so Lien positioned herself at the side of the boat, let out a yell, pulled up her legs and jumped.

It was a perfect dive bomb. Not at all what he was expecting. In his head he'd pictured her diving into the bay in one smooth move, but of course she was wearing a life jacket, and diving properly into the bay wouldn't work.

He already knew that Lien didn't need the life jacket—neither did he—but she'd wanted to make sure that Regan would be happy to keep his on, which was why she'd mentioned it out loud.

'Can I do that, Daddy?' asked Regan straight away as Lien pushed her wet hair back from her face and bobbed, laughing, just in front of them.

She held out her hands towards him. 'Come on, kid,' she said, her eyes sparkling.

Regan didn't hesitate. He let out a yell and copied Lien's dive bomb, flying through the air and splashing into the green water.

Joe automatically held his breath, waiting for the second when Regan would bob back up.

He sighed as Regan burst back up, coughing and spluttering. There was always just that moment when his irrational brain kicked in—fearing that something had happened to his son.

He knew it was ridiculous. He'd had to check himself a few times to stop himself from wrapping Regan in cotton wool. It was so hard. He'd already lost his wife, he couldn't bear it if something happened to his son.

But he didn't have time to think about that because Lien and Regan were shouting for him to jump in too.

'Come on, Daddy!'

'Let's go, slowcoach!' shouted Lien. 'What's up? Scared?'

She was laughing. He knew she was joking but, in a split second, his brain was interpreting the question in an entirely different way. Was he scared? Of course he was—but not of the water, not of the bay.

But of what was inside it.

Lien and Regan were splashing each other, carrying on, and having the time of their lives. He couldn't remember when he'd ever seen Regan interact with another woman like this.

He sent up a silent prayer. Thank goodness for this place. Thank goodness his mother had given him the push to step on the plane. Being in Scotland had left him feeling hemmed in. Here he was just Joe, the doctor. Joe, Regan's dad. Joe…the man who might actually consider looking at another woman, spending time with another woman.

His skin prickled. These thoughts had been dancing through his brain since he'd got here. But they'd only been dancing in the direction of one woman. A woman he'd already invited to visit Scotland with them. But Lien didn't seem quite so keen. Was he reading this all wrong? It had been so long for him that he wasn't quite sure how to do this any more. He took a breath and shook his head. It was time to stop.

He didn't let himself think any longer. He just jumped.

They splashed about in the water for a while, eventually tugging themselves back into the boat. Lien managed easily—she'd done it before. Regan scrambled up Joe's back as he held onto the side of the row boat. And Joe?

Joe's attempt to get back into the boat led to hysterical laughter from Regan and Lien with no help whatsoever. He kept getting one leg up, before the boat would tip towards him and deposit him straight back in the bay.

Eventually he ordered them both to the opposite side of the boat as a counterbalance before he finally, inelegantly, flopped into the boat, not quite sure that his dignity was still intact.

'Looks much easier on TV,' he muttered.

Regan was still laughing so hard that Joe started laughing too. It was infectious. Seeing his son so happy and at ease.

When they finally recovered from their laughing fit, Joe helped Lien row over to an islet a bit further away. As they circled around the back they saw the large cave, which was hidden from view from the small beach. It was still daylight, but the streams of sunlight reflecting into the cave gave the place a magical green glow.

Regan's eyes were wide as Joe guided the boat inside. Lien had slipped her arm around Regan's shoulder in a reassuring way. She bent down and started speaking in a low voice. 'This is the pirates' lair,' she said.

Regan's head flicked from side to side as if he actually believed there could be pirates lurking within the cave. 'I don't see them,' he whispered back, his fists clenched in his lap.

Lien kept up the atmosphere as the boat bobbed further inside. 'They come here at night. Look at the groove in the wall. That's where they moor their pirate ship.'

'Their pirate ship fits in here?'

Lien nodded. 'It's magic. It gets to the entrance and squeezes down just enough so it can fit inside the cave and let them unload their treasure.'

'There's treasure in here?' Regan's voice rose in pitch.

'Oh, yes.' Lien nodded as she shot Joe a conspiratorial glance. 'Sometimes if you touch the inside of the cave, part of it will disappear and show you the pirate chest with all its gold and jewels.'

'Can we touch the cave?'

Lien smiled and nodded as she guided the boat over to one of the walls. 'Have a go,' she encouraged.

Regan stood up in the wobbly boat and pressed his hand against the wall, moving it in a few different directions. 'It's not working,' he moaned after a few minutes. He scrunched up his nose and pointed. 'Can we try the other side?'

Lien nodded again and this time Joe guided the boat to the other side of the cave so Regan could press his hands against the wall.

After a while Regan let out a sigh of exasperation and flopped back down in the boat. 'I can't find the treasure chest,' he said.

Lien nodded solemnly. She folded her arms. 'You know, there is a rule, but it's special. It's only for kids.'

Regan sat back up. Joe felt a little burn somewhere inside his chest. Regan was hanging on her every word.

He felt captured in this little world in the green-lit cave. In here he could forget about everything else. He could forget about everything that had gone before, the pain and the sorrow. In here, he could take pleasure in the connection that his son had made with Lien without wondering about what came next. Watching them together warmed his heart and his soul. If he could take this moment in time and put it in a bottle somewhere and keep it, he would. In a heartbeat.

'What is it?' Regan asked in wonder.

She put her hand on her chin. 'Well, it's said that if you can't find the magic treasure chest, and you're a kid, you get to make a wish.'

'What kind of wish?'

'A good wish. A lucky wish. Something to look forward to. Something that only you will know.'

Regan frowned. Joe could practically hear the whirring in his brain. He held up one hand, glancing between Joe and Lien. 'I've got it.' He looked really excited. 'How do I do it? How do I get my wish?'

Lien seemed to relish his excitement. 'It's easy,' she said. 'Lean forward and put both hands in the water. Once they're there, just say the wish inside your head. It's that simple.'

There was a swelling in Joe's heart. If only wishes were this simple. This easy. Regan stuck his hands into the water and closed his eyes. Joe could see him mouthing silent words over and over, but couldn't work out what they were. This place did seem almost magical. Joe wanted to believe that wishes came true in here too.

After a few tries, Regan sat back in the boat, looking pleased with himself. He nodded at Joe and Lien, then folded his arms across his chest. 'It's done.'

Lien was smiling, her gaze connected with Joe's. 'Then our work in here is done.' She pulled up the bag she'd brought with them. 'So, who's for some lunch before we go back out into the sun?'

The response was unanimous. They ate a leisurely

lunch before spending a few more hours rowing across the bay and watching the various sights.

As they headed back to the wooden pier, Joe's hand closed over hers. He couldn't not say something. 'Thank you for today,' he said quietly. 'You made it really magical.' He paused for a second, then added the words that seemed to just spill out. 'For both of us.'

Her dark eyes were watching him carefully. 'Of course,' she said softly. 'Anytime.'

The buzz spread through him. It felt like pieces of a jigsaw puzzle were slotting into place in his brain—and he was finally getting to see the way the world should be, and all he could concentrate on was what he wanted to do next.

She'd had the best day. And she couldn't even begin to sort out why. If someone had told her last year that one of the best days of her life would be spent with a Scottish doctor and his son, she probably would have wrinkled her nose and said, *'What?'*

But there was something else. It was the way their gazes occasionally meshed, and in those few moments of silence it felt like a million unspoken messages were passing between them. She'd quickly learned to trust him at work. He did a good job, and queried anything he wasn't sure of.

After their tour of the bay, they went back to their rooms and rested for an hour, before dressing for dinner and dining in the hotel restaurant. Regan had been a relentless ball of energy all day, so it was inevitable that he would almost fall asleep in his dinner. So once they were finished, Joe carried him up to their room, got him settled, and then they met downstairs in the bar for a glass of wine.

The wide doors of the bar were open above the bay, letting the warm winds sweep in, and it was too tempting not to move outside and sit on the little beach just outside the glass doors of the hotel.

From this position they were almost directly beneath Joe's room. The windows and doors were firmly shut to keep out any mosquitoes but if Regan woke and flicked the light on, they would see it instantly.

All day today had been a bit strange.

Lien could almost feel the invisible cord pulling them both together. It was like a constant tug. If she ignored the little voices telling her that, socially, they were a million miles apart, she could easily let that tug take over.

Joe had started to look at her oddly at times. Almost as if he wanted to ask a question but was stopping himself from doing so.

She felt the same. How did you ask someone these days if they wanted to date? Was it even called that any more? Was she crazy to think about something like that?

They settled on the sand, her wine glass beside her and his beer bottle in one hand. For a while they just sat in comfortable silence. The bay was still dotted with little boats, and the green water gleamed in a variety of colours from the lights within some of the caves where people were still diving. It looked like something that should be on a postcard. After a few minutes of companionable silence Joe cleared his throat. 'Can I ask you something?'

Her stomach flip-flopped, wondering what came next. 'Of course you can,' she said as casually as she could.

'What do you want out of life?' The question was like a bit of a bolt from the blue. It wasn't exactly where she'd thought their conversation would go.

She pulled her knees up to her chest and stared out at the lapping water. 'I want to be happy. I want to be a good doctor.'

'Is that all?'

The words kind of stung. 'What do you mean, is that all?' Her brow furrowed. 'Is there a wrong answer to that kind of question?'

He closed his eyes for a second, and when he opened them again he looked at her in a way that sent tingles down her spine. 'What I meant was, is that enough?' There was almost an ache in his eyes.

'Why wouldn't it be?' Her voice was a little shaky now. She was treading so carefully. Fearful of taking a misstep. She hadn't been on the same journey that Joe had been on.

His fingers trailed along in the sand. 'I just wondered...'

'Wondered what?'

He didn't answer. He left those words hanging in the air between them.

The setting was beautiful. The sun was dipping in the sky, sending streaks of silver and lavender across the glittering ocean.

She couldn't help the pang in her heart right now. She'd never been this attracted to a colleague before. Something between them felt like it had just clicked. Her heart was currently ignoring the fact he was a mass of complications. He was a widower, who said he was trying to move on, but she wasn't entirely convinced. From what she could gather, his wealth was at the other end of the spectrum from her own family's. He was only here for a short time, and he'd already mentioned his intention to go back to Scotland. He was a single parent to a little boy. They seemed a perfectly contained little unit. There was no future here for either of them.

She and Joe seemed like they were a million miles apart in lots of ways. But she couldn't ignore the little stars that in her head were currently sparkling all around them—even if it was just her crazy imagination. Because that was how it felt, deep inside, like something bright and sparkly.

She actually wanted to laugh out loud. Her brain was obviously having a throwback to teenage hormones. This wasn't normal for her. Not at all. She'd guarded her heart very fiercely since the last time. She had no intention of letting herself be hurt again.

But as her brain filled with crazy thoughts, something else happened.

'I just wondered—' his voice was husky '—if it was enough. If you wanted more.' He put his hand up to his chest. 'From me, I meant. I wondered if your heart skipped beats the same way mine does whenever we're together, and if sometimes you think about me, the way I think about you?'

She couldn't breathe. She couldn't even gulp.

His green gaze met hers. Both of them were bathed in the dimming light. This could be a scene from a movie, and before she could think any further, Joe reached over and swept a bit of hair back from her face. The lightest touch of his fingertips made her lick her lips.

That was it. That was all it took. It was like a current flowing between them both and binding them together. She could see the same hunger in his eyes that was currently sweeping her body. In an instant, his head bent and his lips met hers. Her hand reached up automatically, her fingers threading through his thick hair. It made it real. This wasn't her imagination. This was really happening.

He wasn't gentle. There was a craving to his kiss. It felt like a test. One that she was determined to ace.

Her other hand reached up around his neck and he pulled her towards him. All of a sudden they weren't side by side on the beach any more. Her leg moved automatically so she was sitting astride him, letting her chest press against his.

His unshaven face scraped against her jaw, but it didn't make her pull back. Instead, it just seemed to light up her senses even more. His hands slid to her waist, one finger resting at the tiny break between her shirt and trousers, contacting her bare skin. It made her catch her breath.

She should stop now. She knew she should.

But she didn't want to.

She didn't want to be sensible. She didn't want to think about the trouble with mixing work and pleasure. All she wanted to think about was the here and now.

She'd thought about this. She'd imagined it. But her imagination hadn't even got close to how good the reality was. She could feel all her senses ignite. She pressed closer to him, wishing they were skin against skin. Her hands had gone from his hair and were now tracing down the broad muscles across his back. Her fingers itched to pull the shirt over his head.

As his hands slid up the bare skin at her back she let out a little gasp and tipped her head back. His lips went to her neck. To that tiny spot just below her ear where even the barest whisper of contact made her crazy. For a moment she was lost in the sensation. Lost in what might happen next.

'Whoa.' She put both hands on his chest and pushed back.

He stopped immediately. 'Lien?'

She let herself catch her breath. Her heart was thudding unevenly in her chest. His hands left her skin and went back to the sand. The first thing that struck her was how much she'd wanted them to stay where they were.

She gave a slow nod. 'I just need a moment,' she said huskily, gulping to try and let some more air in, to still her speeding heart.

'Sure.' He leaned back a little, giving her more space. She left her hands on his chest, letting the heat from his body permeate through her palms. She liked it. She could feel the energy, feel the buzz. This could be addictive. *He* could be addictive. Her own heart was racing in her chest and she could feel his doing exactly the same beneath her palms.

Her brain was trying to tell her to slow down and think. But she was tired of the voices in her head constantly reminding her how far apart she and Joe really were. She didn't care they were from different continents. She didn't care about their pasts. She didn't care how both families were at opposite ends of the financial spectrum. All she cared about was this buzz between them—this feeling.

She took a moment, breathing slowly, relishing what came next.

She let her fingers tap his chest before she lifted her

head and gave him a smile. At any moment she knew she could stand up and walk away, but she didn't want to.

'Okay,' she murmured, tracing a line down his forehead and nose, pausing at his lips.

His face was serious. 'Okay…what?'

He was a workmate. She'd never mixed business with pleasure before. Every rational part of her brain told her to stop this now and walk away. But her thighs were practically clamped around his hips right now. It didn't matter what her brain said, her body had different ideas.

'It's fine,' he said softly, his accent broad. 'We can forget this ever happened. Write it off to two grown-ups getting carried away with the setting and the moment.' The hoarseness of that voice was setting pings off all over her body.

She shook her head firmly and twisted one finger through his hair. 'What if I don't want to forget it?' she said. She couldn't hide her teasing tone.

He straightened again, his hands leaving the sand and resting on her hips. 'You don't?'

Their gazes meshed. She could almost swear she could hear her heartbeat above the crashing waves behind them. 'What if my heartbeat races just as much as yours, and I think about you until I drive myself a crazy?'

A smile danced across his lips. 'You're sure?' he reiterated.

She said the words with complete conviction, 'I'm sure,' before leaning forward and pressing her lips to his.

CHAPTER TEN

'DR LIEN, THERE's an emergency!' The banging at her door woke her out of the perfect dream she'd been having of wearing red sparkly shoes and dancing down the yellow brick road. Joe had been there too, laughing and waving. Where on earth had that come from?

She rubbed her eyes as she strode over to the door and yanked it open. Her eyes caught the clock. Six a.m.

One of the nurses was at her door. 'What's wrong, Tan?' she asked.

'I'm sorry for waking you, but one of the kids that came in last night—he's taken a bad turn.'

Lien was already walking back to her bedroom to grab some clothes. 'Tell me more.'

'He's seven. Khiem admitted him with a type of malaria. His temperature had been really high and he had some infected bites. We started him on IV fluids and IV antibiotics. For a few hours we thought he was picking up.'

She'd finished pulling on her trousers and blouse. Her stomach had that sinking feeling as she quickly brushed her teeth. Over the last couple of years she'd managed to get dressed and out of the house within two minutes. As she crossed the grounds towards the hospital she twisted her hair up and fastened it with a clip.

A range of things was shooting through her mind. Japanese encephalitis? It could progress out of nowhere really quickly.

She'd only just made it onto the ward when Joe joined her. He was wearing jeans and a red shirt. Her stomach twisted. It was the one he liked to wear in bed.

'Where did you come from?' she asked.

He gave her a soft smile. 'Haven't you realised I've got a built-in radar when it comes to you?'

She returned his smile. Since coming back from the other hospital their relationship had blossomed quickly, and no one seemed surprised.

They never slept overnight in the same house but she often joined Joe and Regan for dinner, and frequently told Regan a bedtime story. It was always the small hours of the morning when she made her way back to her own house. They'd never really discussed it. There had been plenty of times when Joe had hugged her tighter and asked her to stay. But for Lien it didn't feel right. She didn't want Regan to wake up early one morning and find her in Joe's bed when he wasn't expecting it. She liked the way their relationship had been a slow burn.

It made it feel more real. More valuable. She'd got to know both Joe and Regan over months before anything had happened. They were friends first. He respected her. Getting to know him felt like peeling back layers. The big Scot was so much more vulnerable than anyone really knew—she suspected even his mum and dad. He hid it well. But the fact that he exposed little bits of it to her made her appreciate how close they were becoming.

There were still parts of herself that she kept locked up—she continually tried to avoid thinking about the differences in their backgrounds. So she couldn't really expect him to tell her everything at once.

Esther's name was barely mentioned. Lien didn't like to ask questions. What she knew and what she'd learned had mainly been through casual conversations about something else, or from the little snippets that Regan occasionally blurted out.

His family were so welcoming. She'd already had an open invitation to visit Scotland from his mum and dad, and while that was lovely, it only made her feel more self-conscious. Could she really visit and be around people so obviously wealthy? She hadn't fitted in before, and she'd vowed never to feel like that again.

Joe touched her arm and smiled at her. There was an intensity to the gaze between them now, an intimacy, and every time he looked at her that way her mouth automatically responded. 'Tell me about our patient,' he said.

Tan appeared with the notes and gestured them both over to the room where the small child lay. She spoke quickly. 'This is Chinh. He was admitted last night with a fever and infected bites. He has malaria and has been on IV fluids and IV antibiotics with little effect so far. His heart rate has increased, and his blood pressure has dropped in the last twenty minutes.'

Lien went to step forward but Joe got there first. He touched the little boy's hand and his head shot round, his gaze fixing on hers. She could tell immediately he was concerned. 'What?' she mouthed.

Joe bent over the little boy and started saying a few words in Vietnamese to him, asking him how he felt, and if he could tell him his name, with little response.

He ran his hands over the little boy's arms, lifting the sheet to look at his leg. Two of the bites on his lower leg looked particularly angry. One had a nasty thin red trail tracking just underneath the skin.

'Sepsis,' said Joe quietly, his head flicked to Tan. 'Do we have a sepsis trolley?'

Lien shook her head. 'No.'

He turned to face her. 'We have a history of skin infection, he's tachycardic, his breathing is shallow, he's confused and it looks like one of the bites is tracking. His hands are cold and clammy and his colour is poor.' He pulled his stethoscope from his pocket and listened to the little boy's chest. 'Shallow breathing,' he murmured.

He shot her a nod of acknowledgement. 'For me, this has to be sepsis.'

He gave her a few seconds. Her brain was racing. It had been a while since she'd seen a child with sepsis. Their deterioration could be very rapid as the infection raced through the blood, and the body's own overwhelming response could lead to tissue damage, organ failure and death.

She reached up and turned the IV bag around. 'These antibiotics clearly aren't working. Let's give him something else. Let's do something about that blood pressure too.'

'He needs an ICU,' said Joe in a hushed voice. 'Is there one nearby we can transfer him to?'

'Let me try and arrange it,' she said, tears pricking at the back of her eyes.

Sepsis could rarely be predicted but sometimes, if it was recognised early enough, action could be taken to stop it being fatal. Lien was praying that Tan had called them quickly enough to try and have some kind of effect.

She picked up the phone. Transferring a patient from their hospital to the nearby ICU would be costly. May Mắn Hospital would be expected to pick up the cost as the referring hospital. The truth was, Lien didn't care about things like that. But life at the hospital meant making a decision that could affect everyone who worked here. It could mean fewer supplies, fewer facilities for the large population of people that they served. She could stop and wake up Khiem and Hoa to consult with them. But they trusted her. And she knew the decision had to be made.

She started speaking to the ICU, arranging the admission by speaking to the receiving physician, then booking an ambulance to transfer the little boy. Tan had already spoken to the parents—but they hadn't arrived yet.

Joe moved about, making up a new set of IV antibiotics and starting their administration. He monitored the little boy alongside Tan, charting everything carefully.

He was meticulous, and she was grateful for that, because she could feel herself starting to feel overwhelmed at the speed with which the little boy's condition was deteriorating.

The ambulance arrived and they helped with the transfer. The little boy's parents appeared just in time to climb in the back of the ambulance and kiss him before the transfer. By now Khiem and Hoa had appeared, with Hoa offering to drive the parents to the other hospital.

Lien waited until everything was done and the ambulance had disappeared in the distance before she felt her shoulders start to shake.

Joe exchanged a glance with Tan as he slung an arm around Lien's shoulders. 'Is there anything else that needs to be done right now?'

Tan shook her head and Joe nodded gratefully. 'I'm taking Lien for a break.'

He walked her back across the gardens to his house, settling her on the sofa while he woke Regan, got him dressed and fed him breakfast in extra quick time.

Regan was his usual chatty self and didn't seem to notice that anything was wrong.

Joe bent down and whispered in her ear. 'Do you want to wait here while I drop Regan at school?'

She shook her head. Her stomach was in such knots that she just wanted to get some air. 'I'll come with you. The walk will do me good.'

She still felt jittery. She couldn't stop thinking about the little boy. It didn't matter that Hoa had admitted him the night before. Lien had been on call last night. Maybe she should have gone over to the ward in the middle of the night just to double-check on the patients. Instead, she'd been in Joe's house—in Joe's bed—for a few hours before finally stealing back to her house in the early hours of the morning.

Tan had come for her this morning, but if Lien had been there, would she have picked up any deterioration earlier?

Joe held her hand the whole way to the nursery, and had his arm around her as they walked back, guiding her into one of the local coffee houses and sitting her at a table. She didn't even need to say what she wanted. An iced coffee and a bar of her favourite Vietnamese chocolate.

She'd expected him to sit opposite her, but he didn't. He sat next to her, putting his arm around her waist.

As she reached for her coffee she realised her hands were shaking.

'We need to give it a few hours,' Joe said. 'I'll phone to find out how he's doing. You know things will be hectic while they try to stabilise Chinh.'

It was almost as if he'd flicked a switch and turned on a tap in her. All her emotions bubbled to the surface. 'What if I missed it? What if I could have picked this up hours ago?'

Joe shook his head. 'It's sepsis. It's one of the most missed conditions in the world. It's only now that hospitals are really getting a handle on the signs and symptoms.'

She put her head in her hands. 'It was you who picked it up, not me.'

Joe shook his head. 'Only because I ended up a few steps in front of you. I've seen this. I've seen this before. Twice. As soon as I touched his cold hands my gut instinct just kicked in. You would have got this, Lien. I know you would have.'

She turned to face him, her emotions more raw than ever. 'But would I have? I should have gone back over last night. But instead I was distracted. I was with you.'

'What?'

Joe's face had fallen. He shook his head. 'We were together, Lien. You were still available at a moment's notice. You were still there if you were needed.'

She knew his words made perfect sense. But right now she just couldn't think straight. All she could think about was the little boy. She'd never seen a case of sepsis before. She knew it was worst in children and in the elderly, but she'd never seen a patient deteriorate so quickly.

She put her head back in her hands. 'It almost feels like I could see his organs failing, one by one, right before my eyes.'

Joe's arm tightened at her waist. 'It's a horrible condition. It seems to come out of nowhere and it's vicious.'

He was still here. He was still supporting her, with his arms around her.

Even though she'd lashed out. Even though she'd almost blamed him for keeping her from her work.

Guilt flooded through her. If she'd been alone last night in her house, would she really have got up in the middle of the night, uncalled for, to check on the patients?

She reached out and put her hand over his on the table. She couldn't hide the fact her hands were still trembling.

Joe's voice was steady. 'Maybe you need a break. You work so hard. You're completely dedicated to the hospital. Maybe you need some time away.'

She felt instantly wounded by those words. 'Why would I want to be away from the place I love?'

Joe adjusted in his seat. He spoke softly. 'What I meant to say was maybe you'd like a holiday. A chance to be somewhere entirely different. Like…Scotland, with me.'

She froze. The tiny hairs on her skin prickled. Her brain felt as if it was spinning. This again. The conversation she kept trying to avoid. She shook her head. 'Scotland.'

It must have been the way the words came out but in her confusion she could see the wave of regret on his face. He looked down at the table. 'Maybe you need a change. I'd love you to join us. I can't stop thinking about this. I'd love you to come with us, Lien. Every time I bring it up you seem to avoid the conversation.' He pressed a hand to his chest. 'Tell me, Lien, am I reading this all wrong? I want to be with you. I can see a life for us together. You, me and Regan. Can't you see it too?'

She blinked. He was inviting her to visit in Scotland. The conversation that neither of them had actually had. But it felt all wrong.

'But you're going back. You're going back to put Regan in school. It's not a holiday, Joe. It's a relocation.'

He sighed and ran his hands through his hair. 'My time at the hospital will be up shortly. I'm sure that Khiem and Hoa have already recruited someone for this job. I need to go back home. Regan needs a chance to spend some time with his grandparents again.' He let out a long slow breath. 'I just wondered if you wanted to see a little of Scotland.'

Her insides were churning. Part of her had wanted this conversation to take place. She'd half dreaded that he might just step back on the plane back to Scotland and wave goodbye.

What she really wanted to do was throw her hands around his neck and try to keep him with her.

But life didn't work like that. He had a job back home. A house. A house that someone like her would never belong in. It didn't matter how welcoming his parents were. After a while they'd enquire about her, where she came from, and what her own parents were like.

Lien didn't want to leave them. She didn't want to live in a different country from them. How could she keep them safe if she wasn't here? How could she try to keep them healthy?

'You're going home, Joe. You're going back to your job, and your life. If I came—then what? You show me around Scotland for a few weeks then I come back here?'

'I guess that depends on you,' he replied. His gaze was steady, and she just wasn't sure if he was nervous about making any more suggestions.

She shook her head. 'I don't understand what you're saying.' Frustration swept over her.

Joe squeezed her hand. 'I guess I'm wondering what you'll think when you get there.' He gave a kind of hopeful smile. 'Maybe you'll love Scotland as much as I love Vietnam. Maybe you'll decide you want to stay with me and Regan. Work there.'

She could feel all her automatic defences slide into place. 'Because that's the only way we'll work—if I give up my life and come to Scotland with you and Regan? Scotland. A place I've never been, and know nothing about.'

He pulled back from her, grasping his hands together on the table and wringing them together. 'I don't know, Lien. I don't know how any of this will work. I'm trying to make sense of everything in my head. I'm trying to think of a way that this—us—doesn't actually end.'

Again her skin prickled and she took a deep breath. He was telling her that he didn't want this to end. Part of her heart wanted to sing. But it couldn't. Because in all his ramblings she hadn't heard any solution that would work for her.

Try as she may, she couldn't put the picture of his

home out of her head. How many times over could
her own parents' home fit into Joe's? Tears pricked at
the corner of her eyes. She hated this. She hated those
deep-down thoughts of not being good enough. It didn't
matter how much she tried to shake them off, the adver-
sity of poverty was ingrained within her. She'd learned
to accept those feelings were there. She put her hands
flat on the table, as if she was trying to steady herself.
'You know that I adore Regan,' she said steadily. 'And
I would love it if you both stayed. But...' she shook her
head slowly and willed herself not to cry '...I'm not sure
that coming to Scotland is a good idea.'

'Why?'

'Because I can't stay, Joe. I won't stay. My life is
here, in Hanoi. I've worked in a few other places for six
months at a time. But I wasn't in either of those places
to put down permanent ties. I always knew my permanent ties were here at the hospital. If I go to Scotland
and stay with you and Regan, even for a few weeks...'
she swallowed '...it gives him an unrealistic expectation of what happens next. He's a kid, Joe. He'll think
we're playing happy families, and if I pack my case a
few weeks later to leave again, what does that do to
him? To his little brain? He's already got around losing
someone he loved. How cruel would it be to walk away
from him? I'm telling you upfront that I can't stay, but
you're asking me to come without thinking about what
message that sends to Regan.'

Joe bristled next to her. She'd never accused him of
not paying attention to Regan's needs before, and this
had obviously set him on edge. He went to open his
mouth but Lien turned directly towards him and held
her hand in front of his mouth. 'Would you want to tell

your son that I don't love him enough to stay?' Tears spilled down her cheeks. She couldn't stop them.

Whatever words had been on Joe's lips seemed to die in the air between them.

His phone buzzed. A text from the hospital. But she wasn't interested in the text. She was interested in the fact that a few months on, his screen shot hadn't changed. It was still Esther.

It seemed so petty to complain about a photo of his dead wife. But it made her stomach ache in a horrible twisty way.

Joe seemed oblivious to it. He didn't even notice it any more.

But she did.

He reached up to brush away her tears but she shook her head and pulled back out of his reach. 'Don't.'

She couldn't bear him to touch her right now. Touching him would evoke all the memories that would make her crumble. His touch was proving addictive to her, and she couldn't go there right now. Not when she was trying so hard to be strong.

Joe's face looked broken. His voice came out of nowhere. 'Don't you love him enough to stay? Don't you love *me* enough to stay?'

Rage flooded over her like a tidal wave. 'How can you say that to me? How can you ask if I love you both enough to give up my whole life for you, when you wouldn't consider it for me?'

She pushed herself up from the chair. 'You're not playing fair. Why should I do this? Why should I be prepared to give up everything, go to Scotland and get my own heart broken when I have to leave?'

She leaned forward and willed herself not to breathe

in. Not to inhale his familiar scent. 'What's so good about Scotland, Joe? What is it you need to go home to? Is it the memories—are you really ready to leave the past behind?'

She could sense he wanted to speak. But she didn't want to give him the chance. She couldn't listen to him right now.

The thought of not seeing Joe and Regan every day was already niggling away at her. It wasn't a reality. Not yet.

But soon enough it would be, and she hated how much that pained her. She'd allowed herself to get too attached to them both.

She should have stayed away. Right at the beginning when she'd had that first little flutter of attraction, she should have pushed all thoughts from her mind. Instead, she'd let that attraction between them grow. She got more and more attached to that gorgeous little boy who looked at her with pure admiration and filled her days with joy. She'd allowed every flicker of a glance between her and Joe to build momentum. She'd reached the point where she ached for his touch. Even though he'd told her since he'd first arrived that he was only staying for six months, now it felt like a betrayal.

She knew it was irrational. She knew it was ridiculous. But her heart was overruling her head at every turn.

Part of her still wanted to jump at his invitation to go to Scotland. But every cell in her body knew it wasn't the right thing to do.

The ache at the bottom of her stomach sat like a stone. He still had a picture of his wife on his phone.

He'd told her he'd come here to give himself and Regan a chance to move on. But his wife's picture was still there.

How would things be back in Scotland? She would be going into a home he'd shared with his wife. Scotland would be full of memories for him at every twist and turn. How on earth could she compete with those?

She shook her head. She didn't want to compete.

Here, Joe felt more like hers. Here, all the memories were theirs. No one else's.

It didn't matter that she'd always known he would leave. She'd stopped trying to think about it. Put it in a box somewhere in her head that she just didn't open.

But now it was here. It was the elephant in the room. Maybe this was why they'd both been avoiding this conversation.

She took a shuddery breath. Her hands wouldn't stop trembling. The tears were forming again.

'I can't do this,' she said rapidly as she pushed herself up and stepped away from the table.

'Lien, don't—' Joe was on his feet in an instant.

She shook her head. 'Don't. Leave me.' All the words just came tumbling out. 'I can't do this. I just can't. I don't fit in your world. You don't know me—not really. I can't go to Scotland and live in your castle with you. It's not me. It's not where I fit. And you don't have room for me in your life, Joe. You think you do—you tell yourself that—but the truth is you don't, you're not ready. I need some space.'

She wiped one final tear from her face. He looked aghast—as if he couldn't believe or understand what she'd just said to him—but she turned and fled the coffee shop before he could follow.

* * *

For a few seconds he felt as if he couldn't breathe. Had that really just happened?

He stared at his hands for a few moments, wondering how things could have gone so, so wrong. Every instinct in his body told him to get up and run after her. But she'd asked him not to. She'd asked him for space.

He had to respect that—even if he didn't want to.

He'd been nervous. His heart knew what he wanted. He wanted Lien. Every day he spent with her just reinforced that more and more.

He'd thought inviting her to Scotland was the perfect solution. The perfect solution for him and Regan.

He couldn't think about anyone but her. Her smile, her laugh, her fingers on his skin. The way she interacted with Regan.

Regan.

Part of the reason she'd said no.

He hated the way his guts were twisting right now. Being a single parent was hard. Asking someone else to come into your life meant they had to understand you were part of a partnership. Lien had sensed that right from the beginning. Most of the times they'd done something together she'd included Regan. She thought about him all the time, they had a connection together. One that had warmed his very soul.

But now?

She'd been clear. Part of the reason she wouldn't join them was because she loved Regan. She loved him. She'd said coming to Scotland and then leaving Regan would break her heart.

He took a deep breath. He'd been selfish. Somehow, because he'd told her from the first day they'd met that he was going back to Scotland in six months, he'd just assumed she wouldn't expect that to change.

He had already enrolled Regan in the local primary school back home. As the relationship between Lien and him had progressed he'd hoped she would consider joining them—that she would love them both enough to want to come.

But now he realised just how selfish that was. It was clear she loved working here and was dedicated to the people that she served.

He'd made an assumption. He'd made the assumption that because she'd worked in some other places before, she would be prepared to do it again. For him. For Regan.

He shook his head and put his head in his hands. He hadn't even asked her—not properly—not until now, and then he'd handled it in such a clumsy manner. No wonder she was upset with him.

He hadn't even got the chance to take her hand in his and tell her how he loved her, and how much spending time with her had made his world seem whole again.

Something sparked in his brain. When she'd been upset, she'd told him he didn't really know her. What did that mean?

He couldn't even begin to imagine. He knew so much about her already. The way she drummed her fingers on her hip bone when she was impatient, the fact she lost a hair clip practically every day. She only liked one brand of jasmine tea, and she needed just the right amount of ice in her iced coffee.

The fact she loved it when he traced his fingers lightly over her back, or that her most sensitive part was just behind her ear.

How could she say that he didn't know her?

All he knew was that he loved every part of her.

He leaned his head back and closed his eyes. His fists clenched on the table in front of him. He had to find a way back from this.

He had to find a way to win the woman he loved.

CHAPTER ELEVEN

THE LAST WEEK had been a miserable nightmare. Joe had tried to talk to Lien on more than one occasion, but had respected her wishes each time she'd just shaken her head and said no.

They had talked about hospital work and duties, but nothing more.

The dark circles under his eyes looked even worse than the dark circles under hers.

Regan had, at first, seemed oblivious and was still a little ball of energy around her. But even he'd noticed the change and wandered over one night and tugged her trouser leg. 'Why don't you come and tell me bedtime stories now?' he asked.

Lien crouched down to speak to him. 'I'm sorry, honey, I've just been really busy at work.'

Regan shook his head, his face solemn. 'No. That's not it.' He tipped his head to one side, his bottom lip trembling. 'Have I done something naughty?'

She shook her head and leaned forward to give him a hug. 'Of course not. You are the best boy that I know.' Her heart felt as if it were tearing in two. The last thing she wanted to do was upset the young boy who'd stolen a little part of her. She touched his cheek. 'Sometimes adults have to do other things.'

He wrinkled his brow. 'But if you can't do the bedtime story, you could still come and have dinner with us.'

She flinched. Everything was so easy when you were four years old.

Joe appeared at the door. 'Sorry,' he said quickly, holding his hand out towards Regan. 'I turned my back for a minute and he disappeared.'

'It's fine,' Lien said quickly, not quite meeting his sad eyes.

'But, Daddy—'

'Let's go, Regan,' Joe said firmly. 'Lien has work to do. You'll see her some other time.'

He led Regan back out and she watched as they walked back across the grounds to their house. She couldn't tear her eyes away. It wouldn't be long before they walked away for ever. How would it feel to be here and know that she wouldn't catch the familiar scent of his aftershave or hear the rough burr of his voice? She'd got so used to being around them, so comfortable.

But as they walked away, the void between them seemed wider than ever. Reuben appeared at her side, clutching some paperwork to add to the pile on the desk. 'Hey, Lien,' he said simply, shuffling the papers in his hands. He gave her a sideways glance. 'I meant to ask, how are your parents keeping? They live around here somewhere, don't they?'

Her skin prickled, her defences automatically on edge. It was a simple question. But one that she struggled to answer. Just that simple question flooded her brain with a whole host of thoughts about the differences in health between the richest and the poorest in Hanoi. It was likely he didn't mean it that way, but it sent a surge through her. She turned on him. 'Reuben, have you made a decision about what happens next?'

He seemed confused by the sudden question. 'What do you mean?'

She folded her arms across her chest. 'Long term. You said you'd work here for a few months. That time is nearly up.' She pointed to the piles of paperwork. 'There's still so many patients that could do with your services.'

He sighed and ran his hand through his hair. 'I know that. It's just the timing issue. I have other responsibilities, other priorities…'

She held up one hand. 'Shouldn't your main priority be about keeping your clinic licence?' She gave a casual shrug of her shoulders. 'If you're not working here— or somewhere similar—you're not really serving the needs of our population, and therefore not continually meeting your licence requirements.' She met his gaze steadily. 'Wouldn't you rather continue to have good publicity than bad?'

She hadn't said the words. She hadn't said she would report him or speak to the papers. But the unspoken implication hung in the air between them.

'You've got a good set-up here,' she continued. 'A good theatre and competent staff.'

Silence, then he took a deep breath, and let out a long sigh. His gaze met hers. 'It's nice to contribute to the health and well-being of the less fortunate,' he said smoothly. He paused. 'Maybe…two sessions a month on a permanent basis?'

'Two sessions a month would be excellent, Reuben.'

She dipped her head. 'The May Mắn clinic thanks you for your services to its patients.'

Her heart swelled in her chest as he walked out the door. Standing up to him had made her feel proud. A few years ago she could never have done this, but she'd already seen the differences his surgery had made to the lives of some of their long-term patients. This wasn't about her. And it wasn't about him. It was about the people who came here looking for help. The population she wanted to continue to serve.

She stared at the pile of paperwork on her desk. Referral letters, prescriptions to write and a few patients to review. Enough work to keep her here for the next few hours. At least then she wouldn't be sitting in her house, wondering what was happening in the house next door.

Her phone rang. She frowned at the number that flashed up on her screen. Her father. He rarely used the phone. It only took her a few minutes to realise something was wrong.

It wasn't her father that had phoned—it was her mother, and she was upset and babbling, talking so quickly that Lien could barely make out the words.

'What's wrong? Is it you, is it Dad?'

She tried to keep calm as she stood up and made a grab for her coat, the phone balanced at her ear.

'Yes, okay, does he have a temperature? Is he conscious? Can he hear you?' Her footsteps slowed a little. 'How long has he been sick? Why didn't you phone me sooner?' She grabbed her stethoscope.

Her heart was clamouring inside her chest. She kept walking. There was no point blaming her mother. She knew exactly what her dad was like. He didn't want to see any doctor—let alone his daughter.

He didn't ever want to admit that anything was wrong with him. It was just his nature and, no matter how hard she had tried over the years, there was no changing him.

'Mum, don't panic. I'm on my way. I'll be there as soon as I can.'

Tan frowned as she saw Lien rushing towards her. She raised her eyebrows in question, without getting a chance to say a word.

'I have to go. Emergency. I have to go and see…' She paused, not wanting to say the words out loud. 'A patient.'

'Which patient? Which area?' Tan started to walk alongside her. She grabbed hold of Lien's arm.

But Lien wasn't going to let anyone slow her down. She quickly gave her mum and dad's address as she bolted out of the door. 'Get someone to cover the hospital!' she added as she headed outside, looking up as lightning shot across the sky and the dark clouds opened above her.

Joe fought against the lashing rain that seemed determined to distort his vision. He was trying his best to use the app on his phone to direct him to the house that Lien had gone to.

He still couldn't get his head around this. She'd pointedly told him that they didn't make home visits, no matter what his objection. But she'd left the clinic without a word to him, and the only clue he had to her whereabouts was the note Tan had scribbled for him that had the address on it.

The streets here were narrow. Forgotten washing hung between the cramped rows, dripping enormous amounts of rain on him. Garbage cans were piled up all along the street, some overflowing.

Joe squinted again at a doorway just as someone pulled open the door and almost stumbled into him. The small man was clearly taken aback at someone nearly on his doorstep and started shouting at him angrily.

Joe took a few apologetic steps back with his hands raised. As the man continued Joe decided to take a chance and thrust the now damp piece of paper in his hand towards the man. He couldn't pretend he was anything other than hopelessly lost right now. The man looked at it for a few seconds and pointed to the other end of the street, continuing his rapid tirade.

After a few moments the man seemed to take pity on Joe's confused expression and switched to English. 'Last house, black door,' he said, before throwing something in a nearby garbage can, then pulling up his collar and hurrying down the street.

Joe sighed in relief and hurried down towards the black door. He lifted his hand to knock, and then paused. He wasn't even sure what to say. His Vietnamese was still sadly lacking, even though he'd tried his best to master the basics. He hadn't caught a word of what the other man had been saying to him.

A shadow moved further along the street. Another man, staring at him quizzically. Joe lifted his hand again and knocked sharply. Joe's stomach plummeted. He had no idea what this area was like. He'd sped out after Lien without a thought to his own safety. Lien's expression the last time he'd done this swam in front of his eyes—when she'd asked him if he would risk leaving Regan with no parent. He tightened his grip on the doctor's bag in his hand, wishing he'd taken the time to bring something less conspicuous. Trouble was, as soon as he'd heard that Lien had rushed out of the clinic alone, he hadn't hesitated to follow. There was no way he was going to leave her alone with an emergency. He knocked again. 'Hello, it's the doctor from the May Mắn hospital. Is Dr Lien here?'

Lien froze. She'd just finished sounding her father's chest. His colour was terrible and his lips distinctly tinged with blue. It had to be pneumonia. She had to get him to hospital.

She was already cold from the pouring rain, but the familiar voice made every tiny hair on her body stand on end.

Her mother looked at her and frowned at the strange voice. Before Lien had a chance to stop her, her mother's petite figure had crossed the room and pulled the door open.

Joe stood in the doorway. There were only two rooms in the house so he could see Lien tending to her father as he still stood outside. He bowed to her mother and stepped inside. He had a large bag with him. 'What do you need?' he asked quickly.

She watched as he unloaded things he'd clearly brought from the hospital. A small oxygen tank, a pulse oximeter, along with an IV giving set, saline and a variety of antibiotics.

She blinked. She hadn't thought to pick up anything when she'd left. She'd been so panicked by the phone call all she had was the stethoscope around her neck and her phone in her hand.

Her hands started shaking as her father had another coughing fit. Joe took one glance. 'Is it pneumonia?'

She nodded. 'I think so.'

'Which antibiotics do you want to use?' he said.

She pointed to one with a trembling finger. Joe noticed, but didn't mention it. 'Why don't you let me set up the line while you tell the patient what's happening?'

He took a look around the simple home. She could almost hear his thoughts. Small, cramped. It was relatively tidy but the furnishings were worn.

He mixed the antibiotics, injected them into the saline bag, then ran the fluid through the giving set. She watched as he inserted a cannula into her father and quickly connected the bag, starting the process of delivering the IV antibiotics.

Her mother watched everything with wide eyes before finally starting to talk rapidly, gesturing towards Joe.

Joe's eyes were taking everything in. He still hadn't asked her any questions. He'd just come in and tried to assist. She watched as his gaze settled on a photograph in the corner. It was her. Dressed in her cap and gown when she'd graduated from university.

She saw him stiffen, the jigsaw pieces falling into place in his mind. He turned towards her, his mouth slightly open and his eyes wide. 'Are these your parents, Lien?' he whispered.

She automatically bristled becoming defensive. 'Yes, this is my mother and father.'

He reached into his bag and pulled out a tympanic thermometer. He held it up. 'Will you let your father know what I'm going to do?'

Tears pooled at the sides of her eyes. She had been

so busy with the hospital the last few days she hadn't had time to see her parents. When her mother had phoned in a panic to say her father was unwell she'd just run from the hospital. She knelt beside her father's fragile body on the lumpy sofa and spoke quietly to him, before nodding to Joe to put the thermometer in his ear. It beeped a few seconds later and Joe turned to let her see the reading.

As suspected, her father's temperature was high. She'd already heard the crackling and wheezing in his lungs. The pulse oximeter showed his saturation level was low. Joe turned the oxygen tank on, and gently placed a filtered mask over her father's face.

'How soon can we get him to the hospital?' he asked.

She smiled tightly, mirroring the feeling in her chest. 'He won't go.' She let out a sharp laugh. 'He hates hospitals. He always refuses to come. I treat him at home for just about everything.'

She gestured to Joe's bag. 'I'd probably have had to go back to the hospital to collect some supplies.' She took a breath. 'Thank you for bringing them.'

Joe gave a nod. He pulled out some paperwork. 'Well, I guess you shouldn't really be prescribing anything for your father, so let me write the prescriptions.' He automatically started charting things on the paperwork. She watched the chamber on the IV drip, drip, drip the antibiotics into her father's vein, praying that this medicine would make a difference to him.

He was dangerously stubborn—always had been. He meant it when he said he didn't want to go into hospital. Any other person with an infection like this who refused to be admitted for treatment would probably die. She was pulling out all the stops for her father. Of course she was. But so was Joe.

The unlikely doctor from Scotland had made his way through the back streets of Hanoi to help her. To be by her side.

She wanted to believe that this meant something. She wanted to believe he wasn't just being a good colleague. The one part of her life she'd kept hidden. Now, for all her polite conversations, he could see exactly where she came from. But what if, deep down, he was just like Reuben and the thought of spending time with someone from such a poor background made him turn and run in the other direction?

Everything she knew about him said that wouldn't happen.

Every patient interaction, the way he responded to his son, his ideas for taking medicine to the people who needed it. It all told her he was an entirely different man from the one she'd spent time with before.

But those nagging self-doubts always persisted. It was like a tiny, insidious voice, whispering away inside her brain. No matter how much she tried to rationalise and push them away, they remained.

She hated them. She hated the fact they were there. She hated the fact that something that had happened years ago still had an impact on her life today. She was brighter than that. She knew so much better than that.

Reuben wasn't even a shadowy memory any more. He was a real, live, breathing person who she saw every week. She'd faced him down. She'd spoken to him. She'd even put him in his place. But still those horrible feelings of inadequacy persisted.

Would she ever get away from this? Would she ever be able to shake this off?

Joe continued to work away quietly, watching the monitors and her father's condition. He nodded gratefully when Lien's mother brought him some jasmine tea that she'd made.

He didn't even look at her, and the tiny hairs on her arms stood on end. Was he embarrassed by her background?

She looked at her watch. Time was ticking past and it was close to midnight. 'Maybe you should get back to the hospital,' she said quietly. Then her head flicked up. 'What about Regan? Who's looking after Regan?'

'Hoa,' he replied swiftly, 'and Khiem is taking care of the patients.'

He looked up and met her gaze. 'Everything is under control, Lien. This is where you need to be, and I'll stay as long as you want me to.' His voice was steady, soothing, like a warm blanket spreading over her shoulders.

He'd been asking to speak to her all week. Even now, he was letting her know that she was still in charge, and he'd only stay as long as she wanted.

He hadn't even tried to argue, or persuade her father about the admission to hospital that was clearly needed. She could tell from his face he didn't think this was the best idea, but it was clear he was going to respect her father's wishes and, in turn, hers.

With the storm raging outside, the temperature in the room had dipped. Lien's mother pulled out some blankets, tucking one around her father, then handed one to Lien and one to Joe.

She looked at Joe curiously and asked him his name.

It was one of the few phrases that Joe had managed to conquer while in Vietnam. He gave Lien's mother a tired smile. 'Joe,' he replied as he shook her hand.

Lien's mother cast her eyes back to Lien as she shook her head, putting both her hands over his. 'Joe,' she repeated thoughtfully. 'Ah, Joe…and Regan?'

There was no point pretending that her mother didn't recognise the name. Lien looked hurriedly at Joe. 'I've mentioned you,' she explained.

'You have?' He seemed shocked and she couldn't be surprised about it.

'I wish you'd brought us to meet them,' he added. 'We would have liked that.'

He said the words without a hint of criticism but with some disappointment. His gaze stayed on hers.

He didn't understand. He truly didn't understand her reservations and worries. He just looked hurt. As if she hadn't wanted to introduce him to her parents because there was something wrong with *him*, not with her.

Her father groaned and she moved quickly back to his side. 'Rest easy, Dad,' she said. 'It's going to be a long night.'

She pulled the blanket up around her shoulders and settled on the chair next to him, kicking off her shoes.

The rain thudded against the fragile window frame, already a few drops leaking in around the edges.

Joe stretched out his legs in front of him.

'Do you want to leave?' she asked, her stomach clenching.

He shook his head. 'Regan will be fine with Hoa.' He gestured towards her father. 'My patient is here. This is where I'm staying.' He raised a weary eyebrow at her. 'Unless I get thrown out.'

She wanted to smile. She wanted to smile because at one of the worst moments of her life he was here, and he was by her side.

But as she listened to the gurgling from her father's chest she knew the last thing she could do right now was smile.

It was going to be a long, long night.

CHAPTER TWELVE

IT TOOK DAYS for Lien's father to get better. Pneumonia wasn't easy for anyone to shake off, let alone a patient with an existing chest condition with no real reserves.

Joe made arrangements with Lien so that both of them checked on him morning and night. At first she'd been surprised. But Joe could see the strain she'd put herself under. He wouldn't let any colleague do something like this alone. So between them they ensured the IV antibiotics were given, his observations checked, and they kept his oxygen supply topped up.

Joe had managed to exchange a few short conversations with Lien's mother. The woman was delightful, and seemed amused by his determination to conduct some of their conversations in Vietnamese.

By the end of the fifth day, Lien's father finally started to look a little better. His eyes fixed on Joe in a curious manner, and he managed to ask a few questions between coughs. All were signs of improvement.

He liked them. It was clear they didn't live in the best part of town. Their house was small, with most of their possessions showing signs of wear and tear. But they were a proud couple—particularly of their daughter. They spoke of her frequently when she wasn't there.

He could feel a real sense of determination about them. Somehow he already knew that any offer of help their daughter made would usually be refused. He learned that her father had worked in a factory for years but had been paid off when his health had failed. Her mother worked shifts in another place and frequently came home looking tired.

Joe knew better than to comment. His heart ached for Lien. If these were his parents, he would want to help too. But, he knew, in the same set of circumstances, his own parents would be equally proud.

It was a bitter-sweet cycle. They'd worked hard to support their daughter when they could, but wouldn't accept anything in return.

After five days he went to find Lien at the clinic. He needed that final chance to talk to her. He'd given her space like she'd asked, but he didn't want to leave Vietnam without telling her how much she meant to him and Regan, how much they both loved her.

One of the nurses gave him a wave. 'She's with a patient. She's putting in a chest drain. Why don't you take a seat in the office and I'll tell her you need to see her when she's finished.'

Joe nodded and sat in the office, his brain churning over what to say. He'd got it so wrong the last time. He couldn't afford to do that again.

He pulled his phone from his pocket and looked at the screensaver. Esther. He smiled. It had been there so long—for the last four years. He'd thought he would always want to look at it, to remind himself of the woman that he loved.

Yes, he would always love Esther. But he loved someone else now too. Moving on was done in lots of little stages. He thought back to the day at the lake. They'd asked someone to take a picture of the three of them on the red bridge. The first picture had them all standing smiling. The second picture that had been snapped had been much more impromptu, and had caught them laughing when he had pretended something had jumped from the water.

It was a moment in time. And it was his favourite picture he had of them all.

It was time for a replacement. That was the picture he wanted to look at every day. Life, love and laughter.

She felt jittery. She had to do this. She'd known this for the last five days. He'd been good enough to help with her father, and the least she could do was thank him for his assistance. But it was so much more than that.

The thing she was dreading. This was goodbye and her heart was already breaking.

She paused at the doorway, trying to steady her breathing before she went in. Joe was looking at his phone. Looking at the picture of his wife.

All the sadness and wistfulness rushed from her body. If she'd had any hope that this was going to be anything other than goodbye, it dashed out of the room like a bullet train.

Her insides coiled. This man she loved. This man who had stolen her heart and asked her to go to Scotland with him was still looking at a picture of his dead wife. Before, she'd tried to rationalise things. The time for that was over. Now she was just *mad*.

'What do you want, Joe?' she asked coldly as she strode into the room.

He turned, appearing surprised by her tone, and placed his phone on the desk.

'I wanted to talk to you. We leave in a few days and I can't go like this. I just can't.'

She folded her arms across her chest. 'Why?'

'Why?' He held out his hands and looked confused. 'Why? Because I love you, Lien, and I don't want to go home without telling you that.' He put his hand on his heart. 'Regan and I, we love you. You feel like part of us. Walking away from this feels awful. I can't imagine not seeing you every day. I can't imagine not working with you every day. I hate how things are between us right now. Tell me what I can do. Tell me what I can do to make things right. To make things better.' He stepped closer and reached out to touch her. 'Please, Lien. Tell me what to do. You're breaking my heart.'

It was all too much. All the things that had been nagging away inside her just bubbled to the surface, erupting before she could stop herself. All she could feel right now was rage. A few moments ago he'd been looking at his dead wife, and now he was telling her that he loved her. Lien just couldn't think straight.

'I won't do this,' she said, her voice shaking. She shook her head. 'I don't even really mean those words. But I won't be anyone's second best. I can't be with someone who still belongs with someone else.'

Now she'd started she couldn't stop. 'I don't want a bit of you, Joe. I want all of you. Yes, I'm selfish. No, I'm not prepared to share you with your dead wife and that sounds much more insensitive than I mean it to. You had a life. You had a child together. I respect that.

I respect the memories that you have, and want you to share those with your son.

'But I can't be holding your hand, kissing your lips or sharing your bed and thinking for a second that your mind is with someone else.'

She pressed her hand over her heart. 'You told me you were ready. Ready to move on. But are you? Are you really ready? Because you're saying the words, but it's as if your heart isn't quite there yet.' She shook her head. 'I was a fool. I wanted this. Even though it took me by surprise.'

He looked stunned by her words—as if she'd swept his legs out from under him.

She took a deep breath. 'In a way—not just this—other things have helped me make up my mind. Your life back home. It's totally different from my life here.'

'What do you mean?' He still looked stunned.

She shifted uncomfortably. 'The house, the place your parents live, the place where you live. It's obvious—' she tried to choose the right words '—that you've all done well.'

Joe frowned. 'What are you talking about?'

She sighed. She couldn't look at him right now. She didn't want to see *that* look on his face. That one of quiet revulsion. That one of not being good enough.

'You don't get it. You've lived a comfortable life. Not everyone does that.'

He frowned. 'I know that. I work in one of the worst areas of Glasgow city centre. Deprivation levels are high. Poverty is everywhere. What is it you're trying to say to me, Lien? That I don't know? That I don't understand? Every time I see a sick kid in my practice I have to take in all the things that affect them. A damp house. The chaotic lifestyle of a parent.' He stopped and shook his head. It was as if something had clicked inside his head. 'No, no way. This is about your parents' house? Where you were brought up?'

She stepped forward and lowered her voice. 'It's not my past, Joe. It's my present. It's every part of me, and part of them. I've already experienced people rejecting me because they thought I wasn't good enough. And it's impossible to shake that off. My heritage is in my DNA. My childhood will shape the future of my adulthood. We know that now. We know that poverty and malnutrition in early childhood impacts on the health of adults. Even if I have money now, and do well, my body remembers. I don't know what's around the corner for me.' She shook her head. 'You don't get it. You just don't get it.'

The furrows in his brow were deep. His face was incredulous. 'You want us not to be together because of your upbringing? Where does this come from, Lien? Why on earth would you think that matters to me? Because I look as if I have a *posh* house back home? Because my mum and dad have one?'

He shook his head and stepped forward. 'I have a "posh" house because Esther and I had life insurance. When she died, I decided to put some money away for Regan's future and use the rest to buy the biggest house I could find. Something that didn't remind me of her at every turn. It doesn't *mean* anything, Lien.

'How on earth could you think I'd care about where you lived? Your mum and dad are two of the nicest people I've ever met. They are so, so proud of you, but they're also proud of themselves. I get it, Lien. I do. I know you want to help them more than they'll let you. But the most important thing was what struck me the moment I stepped through the door of their house. Maybe there wasn't money when you were a kid. Maybe you were hungry, and I'm sorry about that, but you had two parents who clearly adore you.

'We both know that for a child's health it's the most important thing. A loving, stable environment is the one thing that supports a child's brain development. Research shows it's the biggest thing that counts and you have that in spades. But if you didn't? That wouldn't matter to me either, because I love *you*, Lien, I know *you*. I don't care about everything else. I care about the fact that I want us to be together.'

She was holding her breath. He'd jumped all over the fears she'd held for most of her adult life. He didn't care. He didn't care about wealth and money.

Something passed across his eyes. 'Reuben.' He looked her in the eye. 'This is about that pompous ass, Reuben, isn't it? He treated you like that. He did that to you.' Joe started pacing. 'I never liked that guy. I heard the whispers, I knew he was your ex, and anyone can see that you don't want to be in the same room as him. That's why.' He shook his head again. 'Why didn't you just tell me the truth, Lien? Why did you think you had to hide your background from me? Why on earth would you think I would care about something like that?'

He lowered his voice almost to a whisper and looked up at her from under hooded lids. 'Is that really the kind of guy you think I am?' He looked wounded.

Her heart twisted inside her chest. She was confused. What he was saying to her confused her. As she stared into those green eyes she felt as if she could see right down into his soul. He'd told her the part of herself she'd thought she had to hide from so many people, and it didn't matter to him. And for that part she believed him.

But her heart still ached. While he might say he loved her, he'd still been looking at Esther's picture. She might know now that the house back in Scotland didn't hold memories of another woman, but she still felt she was in her shadow. She still felt as if Joe weren't truly hers. She might ache to have a life with him and Regan, but it still didn't feel right. Not really. Not when her heart was still here.

She shook her head. 'I love you, Joe, and I'll miss you. But I can't come with you to Scotland. There isn't a place for me there.' She put her hand to her chest. 'Not in here. Not where it matters most.'

Tears slid down her cheeks. 'Please don't make this any harder than I'm already finding it. I'd like to see Regan. I'd like a chance to spend some time with him over the next few days.' She gave a soft smile. 'I want him to take happy memories of Vietnam home with him.'

She tried very hard not to let her voice shake. 'And that's what I want for you too, Joe. I want you to take away happy memories of your work here, your time here. Because we've loved having you. You've played a huge part in the hospital over the last six months and we'll miss you when you're gone.'

She wiped a tear from her cheek and straightened her shoulders. 'Goodbye,' she whispered, then she turned away and walked on shaking legs out of the room.

CHAPTER THIRTEEN

HE UNDERSTOOD EVERYTHING that she'd just said to him.

Alongside Regan, she was the first person he thought about every day. Somehow, when he blinked he saw her perfect skin, straight, shiny hair and cheeky smile, as if they were ingrained somewhere deep in his soul.

He hadn't come here looking for someone, but that was what he'd found. And he couldn't pretend it hadn't happened.

Home for him had always been Scotland. For the last four years he'd never looked any further. He'd never wanted to. But what if home could actually be somewhere else?

His life had turned upside down in so many ways. What if home wasn't the country he'd always lived in but instead where his heart lay?

Vietnam, and the woman in it, had captured him in so many ways. She'd woken him up in ways he hadn't expected.

When he'd got on the plane to come here, he'd fully expected to turn around in six months and head back to the home he owned, and the job he'd postponed back in Scotland. He hadn't really considered anything else.

And the truth was part of him was scared.

Could he live his life in another country?

Could he change his future plans for himself and his son?

He hadn't considered those things as part of his future. But now, discovering how much he loved one woman was making him reconsider his future in so many ways.

Part of the little seed of doubt inside him depended on a conversation he needed to have with his parents. He loved them both dearly. They expected Regan and him to fly back to Scotland and start anew.

Both of them were getting older. He wanted to be there for them, just like they had been there for him when he'd needed them most.

But his world had changed.

Places that had been smoky around the edges had sparked to life in a rainbow of colours he wanted to embrace.

And the person holding the key to those changes was Lien.

Of course she would have doubts. He hadn't even asked her the real question yet. Did she have room in her future for a Scotsman and his son?

All he knew for sure was that he loved her. Any plan that formulated in his head from here on included her.

Vietnam was a land of discovery for him. He wanted to stay here. He wanted to spend the rest of his life here.

And that realisation was everything.

It was the one option he hadn't given her. That they would stay here, with her. He smacked his hand to his head. Was he really that dumb?

He'd been asking her to upend her life for him when he hadn't offered to do the same for her. He knew that in her heart she felt she had so much work to do here. If he loved her, why on earth would he ask her to leave?

Lien was scared to trust him with her heart. He couldn't take back what he'd already lost to her.

He understood those fears. He understood that her whole future might look different from what she'd planned. Would she really be willing to share her future with him and Regan?

The fog that had enveloped him for so long had finally lifted. He wanted to reach out and grab the future, for himself, for Regan and for her. He just had to hope that her future looked a lot like his.

He pressed a button on the computer in front of him. He had to be honest and it started here.

Her legs were still shaking even though she'd lain down on her bed half an hour ago, curling up into a ball.

So much of her wanted to turn back and just say yes.

Joe and Regan made her happy. She was being selfish. One person couldn't have everything their way. She'd found love and family, maybe it was reasonable to have to sacrifice some of her career ambitions. But even just the thought of that made her stomach churn.

The knock at the door was something she truly wanted to ignore. She was always ready to work at the drop of a hat, but why today couldn't they find someone else?

The knocking continued, more insistently this time.

She rubbed her face, wondering if she should wash it before answering. But just as she swung her legs from the bed she heard the door open.

The footsteps were pensive.

'Lien?'

Her heart jumped.

Joe stood in the middle of the room with his hands at his sides.

'What are you doing?' she asked, staying at the doorway of her bedroom. 'I don't think my heart can take much more of this.'

'Neither can mine,' he said softly.

This time when he moved towards her she didn't object when he reached out to cradle her cheek in his hand.

'I'm sorry,' he whispered. 'I'm sorry that it's taken a broken heart for me to realise what was the first thing I should do.'

She frowned. 'What do you mean?'

She could tell he was nervous. His thumb brushed underneath her eye. 'I thought home was Scotland,' he said. 'I had never considered anything else. And I should have. Of course I should have. I don't want us to be apart. I want to spend my life creating happy memories with you, Lien. With you, me and Regan. If you'll have us.'

She shook her head. 'I don't get it.'

He smiled softly. 'Neither did I. But I do now. If we leave now, I leave my heart behind in Vietnam. I don't want to do that. This place?' He held up both hands. 'It's opened up a whole new world for me and Regan. We love it. The place, the people, the work, and—' he met her gaze '—one very special lady.'

His voice trembled. 'I don't want to go back to Scotland, because Scotland doesn't feel like home any more. Here, with you, feels like home.'

She held her breath. This was different. This was different from what he'd said before.

'If you'll have us—' his voice was still shaking and there were tears in his eyes '—we'd like to stay. For good.'

She let out a gasp. 'What do you mean? I thought you had to take Regan home for school? What about your mum and dad?'

He nodded thoughtfully. 'Regan can stay in school here. He's learned so much already at the international school and he loves it. I'd be foolish to take him out now. As for my mum and dad...' He paused for a second, then reached up and cradled her cheek again. 'They told me to grab love with both hands and hold on tight. They love you already, Lien, and can't wait to meet you. They're probably booking flights as we speak.'

She blinked, tears flooding down her cheeks. 'But your job, your house...'

He shook his head. 'My house can be sold. I've rented it to the doctor and his wife who've been covering for me at the GP practice. It could be that they want my old job and my old house on a permanent basis.'

'You'd sell everything?'

He nodded. 'What do I have to go back for? We can visit my mum and dad whenever we choose.' He took her hand and put it on his chest. 'I want my life to be here, with you.'

'But...'

He pressed his lips together for a second. 'Maybe I'm reading all this wrong. Because if you don't want me to stay, I won't. I'm not trying to push things on you. But somehow I think that you love us, just as much as we love you.'

'You want to stay?' She almost couldn't believe her ears. Her heart felt as if it was swelling in her chest. 'You really want to stay?'

He nodded, and now a smile formed on his lips. 'Of course, Lien. We want to stay with you.'

Her hands started to shake. It was like the pieces of her life, and her heart, were finally falling into place.

'You're sure?'

He put both hands around her waist. 'You don't need to ask me that. I'm sure. Surer than I've been of anything. I won't change my mind. You don't need to worry about this. I love you, Lien. I asked Hoa and Khiem if I could stay. You know what they said? They asked when the wedding was.'

Her mouth opened. 'They, what?' She was shocked. It seemed like her colleagues knew her better than she did.

He moved a little closer. The solid warmth of his body was reaching out to hers. She wrapped her arms around his neck. 'So, what did you say?'

He smiled. 'I said it was all up to you. Pick a date.'

The love that she'd tried to fight for in the last few days finally bubbled over. She could love this man, and his son, all on her own terms.

She leaned her forehead against his, trying not to let her emotions overwhelm her.

'I'm sorry,' he whispered. 'I'm sorry you thought I was still living my old life. You caught me changing the picture on my phone that night—but didn't give me a chance to tell you that.' He pulled his phone from his back pocket and turned it around so she could see the screensaver. Her breath hitched. It was them, on the bridge at Hoàn Kiếm lake, laughing and joking together. 'This is how I hope we'll be for the next fifty years,' he said huskily.

She looked up into those green eyes. 'Just fifty?' she teased.

He closed his eyes for a second. 'However many we're blessed with.'

Now it was her turn to get it. And she did. He was accepting they'd take whatever time they had. Through his health or hers.

She ran her finger down his cheek, feeling his stubble under her fingertip. 'So…' she smiled '…about this date, how soon do you think your mum and dad will get here?'

'Dad!' Regan shot through the door, making them spring apart, laughing.

'Ooh!' he said, looking at them both, then putting his hands on his hips. 'Dad, were you kissing the girl?'

Joe laughed and swept Regan up into his arms. 'I was trying to. What's going on?'

Regan looked serious, as if he was trying to be grown up. 'I have a message. You missed Grandma and Papa video-calling. They said to let you know that they'd be here in three days and you need to find them somewhere to stay.'

Joe turned to Lien and raised his eyebrows. 'Three days?'

She wrapped her arms around them both. 'Sounds perfect to me.' And she kissed him, keeping her arms around the family that she loved.

* * * * *

JUST FRIENDS
TO JUST MARRIED?

SCARLET WILSON

MILLS & BOON

This book is dedicated to all my best boys:
Noah Dickson, Lleyton Hyndman and Luca Dickson.
Love you guys!

CHAPTER ONE

THE SHRILL OF the phone cut through the dark night.

Vivienne Kerr fought her way free of the tangled sheets, her brain desperately trying to make sense of the noise. Was she on call? Was this a home delivery?

By the time she reached for the phone she was shaking her head. No. Definitely not on call. Not tonight. She'd been on call for the last three nights in a row. This was her first night off.

Or maybe it was morning. Maybe she'd slept for more than twenty-four hours and was late for her next shift…

Her eyes glanced at the green lights of her clock. Three thirty-seven. Her heart sank. Nope. She definitely wasn't late, and no normal person would phone at this time of night—not unless it was bad news.

She picked up the phone, sucking in a breath as if, in some way, it would protect her from what would come next.

She was practically praying that this would be a wrong number. Someone looking for a taxi, or someone with crazy middle-of-the-night hunger pangs that could only be filled with some kind of takeaway food, or even a drunken call from some guy she'd previously given her number to. She'd take any of the above.

'Hello?'

For a few seconds there wasn't really a reply.

Every tiny hair on her bare arms stood on end. She swung her legs from the bed and sat bolt upright. All her instincts were on edge. Her stomach clenched.

'Hello?' she tried again.

There was a noise at the end of the phone. She couldn't quite work out if it was a sob or a choke. 'Viv.'

The voice stopped, as if it had taken all their effort just to say her name. She'd recognise that voice anywhere.

'Duc?' Panic gripped her. Her best friend. Where was he working now—Washington? Philadelphia? She moved into work mode. The way she acted when everything that could go wrong at a delivery did go wrong.

Take charge.

'Duc? What's wrong? Where are you? Are you okay?'

Every tiny fragment of patience that she'd ever had had just flown out of the window. Duc. As she squeezed her eyes shut, she could see his floppy brown hair and soft brown eyes in her head. Duc. They'd met at a teaching hospital in London while she'd been a midwifery student and he'd been a medical student. No one could have predicted how much the crazy, rootless Scottish girl would click with the ever cheerful, laughing Vietnamese boy.

It was fate. It was…kind of magic.

A clinical emergency had floored them both. A young mother with an undiagnosed placenta praevia. Both had only been in the room to observe. Both had

had no experience of a situation like this before. The mother had haemorrhaged rapidly, leading to the delivery of a very blue baby. Both Vivienne and Duc had ended up at either side of the bed, squeezing in emergency units of blood at almost the same rate as it appeared to be coming back out of the poor mother. It seemed that every rule in the book had gone out of the window in the attempt to save both baby and mum.

By the time things had come to a conclusion with mum rushed to emergency surgery, and baby rushed to the NICU, Duc and Vivienne had been left in the remnants of the room, with almost every surface, them included, splattered with blood.

Vivienne had done her best to hold it together. And she'd managed it. Almost.

Right until she'd reached the sluice room to dispose of aprons and gloves. Then she'd started to shake and cry. When the slim but strong arms had slid around her waist without a word, and Duc had rested his head on her shoulder, she'd realised that he had been shaking too. He'd known not to try and speak to her. He'd known not to ask her if she wanted a hug. He'd just acted, and they'd stood there, undisturbed, for nearly five minutes, cementing their friendship for ever.

But now? Fear gripped her chest. Duc hadn't answered.

Worst-case scenarios started shooting through her brain. He was sick. He was injured. Something terrible had happened to him.

'Duc? Talk to me, please. I need to know how you are. I need to know that you're okay.'

'I…I…I need you.'

She was on her feet in an instant, looking frantically

around her room. She clenched the phone between the crook of her neck and her ear as she fell to her knees and pulled a bag from the bottom of her cupboard.

'I'll be there.' She'd never been surer of anything in her life. 'Where are you? What's wrong?'

'It's...*mẹ va cha.*'

She recognised the Vietnamese words instantly. 'Your mum and dad? Duc, what's happened? Are they hurt?'

Her stomach clenched. She'd met Khiem and Hoa on a few occasions. They were a charming couple, completely devoted to the hospitals they ran in Hanoi and two other outlying areas in Vietnam.

Silence filled her ears and an ache spread across her chest. Experience told her that silence usually meant the worst possible case.

'Duc,' she stumbled. 'No.'

She couldn't keep the emotion out of her voice or the tears from pooling in her eyes.

She heard him suck in a deep breath, it was almost like he'd flicked a switch somehow. 'I need you,' he repeated. 'There was a car accident. I've had to fly back to Hanoi. We don't have another obstetrician, and I don't have any midwives. I can't do this, Viv. I can't do any of this. I need someone with me. I need someone to help me. Can you come?'

So many questions crowded her brain. She knew there were good, reliable medics who worked at the hospitals. Khiem and Hoa were meticulous about who they hired. But she also knew that, right now, that wasn't what Duc needed to hear.

Officially, she should give notice to her current employer. She hated to be thought of as unreliable. But this was an emergency. A family emergency, because Duc felt like family to her.

'I'll sort it. I'll get there.' As she started pushing random clothes into a bag her heart ached for him. Last time they'd spoken, a few weeks ago, he'd been full of enthusiasm. He'd started a new job a month before—a surgical and teaching fellowship in one of big cities in the US. She'd almost been a tiny bit jealous about how happy he'd sounded. Duc had a charm about him, he was friendly and good at his job. No matter where they'd worked together in the past, she'd always ridden a little on his coattails. Duc was the one who made friends and got them invites to dinner and parties. Viv was just his plus one. It was like he'd realised early on that she struggled with forming relationships, and he would do that part for her.

'Thank you,' his voice croaked.

It halted her in her tracks and she dropped back down onto her knees.

'Of course,' she said without question. 'I'll go to the airport. I'll find a flight. I'll text you once I have the details.'

She wanted to wrap her hands around his neck right now and give him the biggest bear hug. She wanted to breathe in the, oh, so familiar aftershave that always drifted into her senses when they were close. She hated to think of her friend in pain.

'Duc?' she whispered, before she hung up. She looked at the crooked little finger on her right hand. Years ago they'd adopted a quirky move from a kids movie where they intertwined their pinkies and said the phrase, 'Friends for life.' It had become a long-standing joke between them. She licked her lips. 'Friends for life,' she said huskily, then her voice broke.

There was a muted pause for a few seconds. This time he sounded a little stronger. 'Friends for life,' he repeated, before she hung up the phone.

CHAPTER TWO

DESPITE LEAVING LONDON three days ago, Vivienne still wasn't here.

It could only happen to her. There had been no direct flights available, so she'd taken a whole host of journeys that had bounced her halfway around the globe in order to reach him. She'd had delays, cancellations, engine failure and then an air traffic control strike to contend with. Duc stared at his watch, his eyes flicking back to the arrivals doors at Hanoi airport. Each text had seemed just a little more frantic than the one before.

His stomach was clenched in an uncomfortable knot. It had been this way since he'd got the initial news about his mother and father. He could barely remember packing up his rented apartment, or his flight from Philadelphia to Hanoi. By the time he'd reached the May Mắn Hospital and Lien and her new husband had rushed out to meet him, he had been numb.

There had been a string of traditions and rites around the funeral to take care of. So many people had visited that Duc felt as if he'd worn his white funeral clothes for three days straight. He knew it was because people wanted to pay their respects but keeping his expression in place had been hard.

In the meantime, the hospital had to be kept running. The staff were distraught. The leaders and motivators that they'd worked with for years were gone, and he could see everyone look at him with wariness in their eyes.

By the time he'd buried his mother and father he'd been exhausted. What he really wanted to do was climb back onto a plane and forget anything like this had ever happened. He'd spent the last week hoping someone would pinch him in an on-call room and this whole thing would just have been some kind of monumental nightmare.

Something flickered at the side of his vision. Then a sound. It started as a tinkling laugh that grew into something much deeper and heartier.

His heart gave a little leap. There was only one person who had a laugh like that.

Even though he was tall, he stood on tiptoe to try and catch his first glimpse of her in amongst the exiting crowds.

There. Vivienne was talking animatedly to a rather frail, elderly gentleman, her arm interlinked through his. Her red curls were tumbling down her back in loose waves, a white shirt knotted at her waist and a pair of cut-off denim shorts showing off her long legs.

The original pretty woman. It was what everyone said as soon as they looked at her. Only her Scottish accent betrayed her similarities to the famous actress.

He could see heads turn as she sauntered past. Her casual grace was always noticeable. There weren't too many people here who looked like Viv.

Duc watched as she guided the man over towards his family, walking easily with him as if she had known him all her life. She was in nurse mode. He could tell. People watching would think it was a grandfather and granddaughter, not just some random Scots girl who'd befriended the elderly man on the flight to make sure he was okay. Duc couldn't help the smile that tugged at the edges of his lips—the first time he'd smiled in days. Only Vivienne. He watched as she brought the man safely to his family, shaking hands with them all, before turning around and scanning the crowd until finally catching Duc's gaze.

She didn't hesitate. Her face lit up. She dropped her bags at her feet and ran over to him, jumping up and winding her legs around him. She didn't even say a word. She just buried her face deep into his neck and held on tight.

He could see the amused glances from people close by—as if they were witnessing a pair of lovers reunited. But somehow Duc didn't feel the urge to explain. Just the press of her body against his felt good.

He closed his eyes for a second too and just held her there, letting the heat from her body sink into his. His senses were flooded as the familiar aroma of orange blossom from her shampoo drifted around him.

For an instant in time he was in an entirely different place. One where he hadn't received the call about his parents when he was about to walk into surgery. One where he hadn't had to come here and bury the mother and father he'd unrealistically thought would probably live for ever. One where his current career plans weren't up in the air as he was left with a number of hospitals to run.

Nope. He was in a bubble. A Vivienne-sized bubble. The things he'd craved in the last few days swept over him. Reassurance. Safety. The ability to just be Duc, instead of the bereaved son putting on a brave face— that was the range of feelings that overwhelmed him. Viv was here. She would help him. She would help him sort all this out and get back to the life he truly wanted.

He blinked back the tears that flooded into his eyes. He'd waited days to do this. To feel his friend in his arms and know that someone would have his back. Part of him wished they could teleport out of this airport and straight back to his room so he could crumple on the sofa.

His back was stiff and every muscle in his body ached from keeping it together. He'd nodded his head so many times it was now almost on autopilot. He'd shaken hands with so many old and familiar faces. But for some reason it hadn't brought the comfort he'd thought it would.

This was what he needed. That was what he'd craved.

She pulled her head up, her pale blue eyes just inches from his. 'I stink,' she whispered. 'I've been wearing the same clothes for three days.' She jumped down.

Instantly, his bubble was gone.

'I've smelled worse.' He smiled as he grabbed one of her cases and she slid her arm through his.

As soon as they stepped outside into the warm humid air of Hanoi, Viv started fanning herself. Her brow creased. 'Was it this hot the last time we came here?'

'Hotter,' he replied. He had a car waiting for them outside the airport building and he opened the door for her and waited until she slid inside. He bent his head inside. 'And we need to discuss your clothing.' He winked and pointed at her long bare legs. 'Those? They're a banquet for the mosquitos around here.'

He closed the door and walked around to the other side, climbing in, closing the door and letting her lean back against the cool leather seats. The air-conditioning was on full blast.

'Wait until you get to the hospital. There's a new guy. He was a GP from Scotland. You two will be able to cackle away to each other in Glaswegian, and no one else will have a clue what you're saying.'

She turned her head and raised one eyebrow—a move Viv had perfected years before. 'Cackle?'

He laughed, something that came from deep inside him. But the release of the laugh made his shoulders shake in a way he couldn't quite work out, then his arms and his hands.

It was almost as if a switch had been flicked somewhere deep down inside. By the time the tears started to fall down his cheeks, Viv had slid across the leather and wrapped her arms around his neck. 'Oh, Duc,' she said quietly, 'what am I going to do with you?'

It wasn't really a question. And he knew that—and was glad, because he couldn't possibly answer it. All the emotions he'd bottled up from the last few days just seemed to come tumbling out.

The frustration. The anger. The grief. All while Vivienne held him and the city sped past outside.

This wasn't what he'd wanted. It had been years since she'd visited Hanoi. He'd expected to point out some of the sights to her, and then talk to her about the current issues at the hospital. He couldn't do that when he was struggling to even breathe.

It was like she read his mind.

'Count to ten,' she whispered in his ear. 'We'll do it together.'

Her voice was slow and steady. 'One, two, three, four, five, six, seven, eight, nine, ten.'

She did it again. Then again.

Each time she slowed her speech down more, making his breaths longer and smoother. One of her hands rubbed his back while the other intertwined her fingers with his.

By the time he realised that the car had stopped outside the May Mǎn Hospital he felt as if he was back to normal—or as normal as he could feel.

He ran one hand through his hair and shook his head, almost embarrassed to look Viv in the eye. This was the last thing he wanted to do.

'I'm sorry,' he said hoarsely.

'Why?' she said simply, as she moved back over to the other side of the car and picked up her bag. 'I'm your best friend. If you can't be like this with me, then who can you be like this with?'

She opened the door before he had a chance to say anything else, stretching out her back and facing the pale yellow hospital. 'Now,' she said loudly in her no-nonsense Scottish accent, 'before anything else—can you show me where the shower is?'

And for the first time in days things finally felt as if they might be a bit better.

CHAPTER THREE

SHE'D SPENT THE last three nights sleeping on chairs or airport floors. Every bone and muscle in her body ached.

The hospital was eerily quiet. The staff she'd met had shaken hands with her politely and looked at Duc with wary eyes. She could sense everyone tiptoeing around him.

She'd always loved this place on the times they'd visited. Even the name May Mắn, which translated to 'good luck' in English and that was what she always called it in her head. The Good Luck Hospital. The place had an upbeat vibe and served one of the poorest populations in Hanoi. But somehow now, as they passed through the corridors, the vibe felt very different.

Once they'd walked through to the grounds at the back, he took her to one of the three white cottages built on the land the hospital owned. It had a pale yellow door. Khiem and Hoa's house.

For some strange reason she hadn't thought he would be staying in his parents' home and it made her catch her breath.

She blinked. Unexpected tears formed in her eyes. She'd met Khiem and Hoa on a few occasions. They had been lovely, warm people, dedicated to their work, and to the people they'd served.

She'd been able to tell from a few glances just how proud they had been of their son. But more than that, they'd been welcoming, interested in the lonely Scottish girl that Duc had invited into their home. They'd never made her feel as if she'd outstayed her welcome, or that she couldn't come back whenever she wanted. Hoa had emailed on a few occasions when vacancies had arisen at the hospital—almost giving Viv first refusal. It had been considerate, and kind, and she'd appreciated the gesture, even though she'd only ever visited with Duc.

Now she was back in their home, without really having had time to mourn the passing of her friends. She'd missed the funeral and just walking through the front door sent her senses into overload.

She glanced nervously at Duc, wondering what this must be doing to him. Today was the first time in their friendship that she'd ever seen him break down.

Of course he would. He'd just lost his mum and dad in some random crazy car accident. And deep inside she knew that it had killed him to do that in front of her. But this was why she'd come. This was why she hadn't hesitated to jump on a plane to get here.

Duc had played this role in her life over and over again. By the time they'd met, her adoptive parents had already died. He'd supported her when she'd searched for her birth parents—and had been there when both of them had turned out to be less than she'd hoped for. He'd wrapped her in his arms when she'd had her heart broken twice. And when she'd had a cruel diagnosis a few years ago that had messed with her head.

Of course she would be here for him. Her heart was

breaking for him—but she wouldn't let him see that. Here, she had to be the strong one. Duc had played the role for her time and time again, and this time she would do it for him.

Even if everything in this quaint house reminded her in every way of both his parents.

She breathed deeply. She could even smell them here—the jasmine tea they always drank, the sandalwood cologne his father always wore, and the rose-scented spray his mother used in the rooms. Vivienne blinked. The truth was that she expected them to walk through the door at any moment. And if she felt like that, she could only imagine how Duc was feeling.

She reached over and grabbed his hand. 'Duc, are you sure about staying here? About being here?'

On a table was a framed picture of Duc and his parents together. In another corner was a pile of books that one of his parents must have been reading. A popular fiction novel, a historical romance, a book about alternative therapies and a research journal about obstetrics.

He turned around to look at her, leaving her case in the middle of the sitting room. For the first time she realised just how tired he looked. 'Where else can I go? I've have to cover shifts at the hospital.' He looked almost apologetic. 'And so do you.'

She nodded. 'Of course. I'm ready to start tomorrow. Just tell me what you need me to do.' She gave him a careful stare. 'There isn't anywhere else you can stay but here?'

He looked around and held out his hands. 'Here,' he said. 'It's home. It's not my home,' he said quickly, 'but it's theirs. And I can't stay anywhere else.'

He stepped forward and tugged her case. 'I've put

you in here. I changed the beds…' He pulled a face. 'Actually, that's not true. Mai Ahn, our interpreter, came in and did everything. I think she just wanted to help and, to be honest, I'm really glad she did.'

He was accepting help. Good. Duc could be stubborn sometimes, his intense pride getting in the way of things. She wasn't sure quite what kind of relationship he had with the people who worked here, but at least he wasn't shutting everyone out.

Viv moved towards the room. It only took an instant to realise the room had belonged to Khiem and Hoa. Their belongings were still scattered at various points around the place. A pair of shoes neatly tucked under a chair. Another book on the bedside table. A notepad with some scribbles next to the phone in the room. She gulped, feeling a little overwhelmed. Of course she could object—but Duc was obviously using the other room. Objecting would just make things more difficult for him.

She pressed her lips together for a second then turned and gave him a bright smile. 'Okay, let me get showered, then we can talk.'

There was the briefest of pauses. Talking was the last thing Duc clearly wanted to do. But she wasn't going to be put off. She was here to help, and she couldn't do that by not talking. Duc knew her better than that anyhow.

She walked back over and stood underneath his nose. 'No, I'm not too tired. No, I don't want to do anything else first. Find me some food, and I'm all yours.' She nudged him with her elbow. 'No excuses.'

He let out a sigh. It was clear she'd won this battle. 'No excuses,' he agreed as he strode through to the kitchen and started opening cupboards.

* * *

He hadn't eaten properly in the last three days. He hadn't been hungry, and it had been the last thing on his mind. But as he pulled some food from the cupboards and fridge, splashed some oil into the wok, his stomach let out an involuntary rumble.

He heard the sound of the running shower, closely followed by the blast of the hairdryer. Vivienne was quick, opening the door with her hair in a red cloud around her head and wearing a pair of soft white cotton pyjamas. She glanced towards the table and tiled floor, then moved across to the sofa and sagged down on the comfortable cushions, pulling her feet up. Duc was already serving up into two bowls. He handed her the chicken and noodle mixture then sat down next to her on the sofa.

She warily sniffed her dish. 'Okay, is this edible?'

He smiled. 'What are you trying to say about my cooking?'

'I say that for as long as I've known you, your cooking has always involved a takeout menu.'

He pretended to look hurt. 'Try it. It's one of my mother's recipes.'

The words came out of nowhere, quickly followed by the tumbleweed that seemed to blow across the room in front of him.

Viv's hand reached over and gave his knee a quick squeeze. 'I'm sure it's fine,' she said quietly, as she started to eat.

Every spoonful was an unconscious reminder. He'd used the spices and oils from his mother's cupboards. The pangs of hunger he'd felt for a few moments instantly vanished. Now he understood why grieving friends lost weight. It was so easy to be distracted—to be put off.

Vivienne was different—she ate hungrily, emptying the bowl in five minutes. She stood up and walked over to the fridge, examining the contents before pulling out a bottle of spring water. 'This wasn't what I had in mind,' she said as she held it up, 'but I'll make do.'

He watched as she rested one hand on the chair. Her white cotton pyjamas might cover every part of her, but they still highlighted every curve. Curves he'd never really paid any attention to before—and he was currently asking himself why.

The lines between him and Vivienne had been clear from the beginning. They were friends—best friends. He'd held her hair back while she'd been sick, she'd put him up when his roommate had wrecked their apartment and they'd been flung out. From the word *go*, they'd felt comfortable around each other. They'd had countless conversations over the years about Viv's disastrous relationships. She was smart. She was gorgeous. She was sassy. And she had appalling taste in men.

Every no-good layabout, sob-story-carrying wastrel seemed to cross her path. Each one breaking her heart more than the one before.

Viv had also cast her eyes over Duc's partners over the years. Some she'd been grudgingly approving of, others had been dismissed with a wave of a hand and a few perceptive words. *Gold-digger. Stalker. Needs a backbone. Self-obsessed.*

He, in turn, grudgingly admitted that on most occasions those few words had turned out to be uncannily accurate. He'd started to call her the fortune teller and tease her to pick their lottery numbers.

But she hadn't seen this coming.

The door rattled behind them and Lien burst through the door. 'Good, you're here. I need you.'

Lien's eyes went hastily to Vivienne and she gave a little start.

Duc stepped forward. 'Lien, this is Vivienne Kerr, my friend, the midwife that I told you about.'

Lien gave a quick nod of her head. 'Perfect timing.' She didn't ask why Vivienne was standing in Duc's house in her pyjamas. Instead she turned back to the door. 'Get changed quickly—you're needed.'

Everything happened in the blink of an eye. One minute Viv was contemplating sitting down with her friend and finding out exactly how she could help him best.

The next second she was stripping off her comfortable PJs and yanking on a pair of the burgundy-coloured scrubs she kept in the top of her rucksack. She grabbed her matching soft shoes and ran across the grass, back towards the hospital.

Even though it was the middle of the night, every corridor was brightly lit. Vivienne followed the others. Lien was talking rapidly in Vietnamese and Duc was nodding. She tried to focus. She'd worked here a few times and had picked up a few phrases in Vietnamese. For a midwife they mainly comprised of 'push', 'stop' and 'breathe', but her brain was struggling to remember them right now.

Duc walked through to another room. Viv tried to keep track. She hadn't familiarised herself completely with this place again. Between that, the jet-lag, and the overwhelming sweep of tiredness, she wasn't firing on all cylinders. Thank goodness she'd had time to eat.

Her hands caught her hair and coiled it at the back of her neck, twisting it back on itself until it was anchored in place. Lien's gaze caught hers. 'Neat trick.' She gave Viv an anxious smile.

Viv shrugged. 'Years of people stealing my hair elastics. Had to improvise.'

The anxiousness of Lien's smile made Viv's stomach clench. Last time Viv had been here she'd been impressed by the relaxed nature of most of the deliveries at May Mắn Hospital. Hoa had very much believed in letting the woman take the lead for her labour—much like most of the midwife-led units back home—and Viv shared this philosophy. But right now? When there was a clinical emergency? Things were different. Now it was the job of the professionals to guide the woman and baby to the safest possible conclusion, and from the look on Lien's face it was up to Viv to take the lead.

Duc pulled his T-shirt over his head, swapping it for a pale blue scrub top that he grabbed from the pile on a rack on the wall. Viv tried not to stare. But it had been a long time since she'd seen Duc in a state of semi-undress. His chiselled abs weren't lost on her. She wasn't blind. She pulled her eyes away just as Lien moved closer. 'Do you want to come and meet our patient, Viv?'

Viv nodded. 'Of course.'

Lien gave her a small smile as she pushed open a door. 'I'll introduce you.'

Lien gestured to the woman in the bed. There was another man with light brown hair by her bed. 'This is Resta. She's thirty-nine weeks, or thereabouts. Presented in labour with what appears to be shoulder dystocia. We have no prenatal history.'

Viv nodded. Because she'd worked here before with Duc she knew it wasn't entirely unusual for women not to present for prenatal care.

Lien pointed to the other guy in the room. 'My husband, Dr Joe Lennox.'

Joe was in position at the bottom of the bed, one hand cradling part of the baby's head. He gave a quick glance up. 'I hope you're the cavalry,' he said in a hushed voice, keeping his expression neutral, 'because I'm no obstetrician and I'm out of options.' His Glasgow accent was thick, and Viv immediately recognised the stress in his voice.

Viv drew in a breath. Shoulder dystocia. Every midwife and obstetrician's nightmare. A baby whose shoulder got stuck and stopped the baby being delivered safely.

Viv looked around the room quickly, locating some gloves. 'Would you like me to take a look?'

Joe nodded gratefully. 'Please.' Lien turned to the woman on the bed and spoke to her in Vietnamese, introducing Vivienne to her. There was no getting away from it, the woman looked exhausted and terrified. No wonder. Shoulder dystocia could rarely be predicted. Women typically got to the end of a long labour and once they'd delivered their baby's head thought it was only a matter of minutes until it was all over.

Vivienne glanced around the room again, quickly taking note of the equipment available to her.

She took a deep breath. Lien and Joe were both doing their best to keep their faces neutral, but Joe had already told her this wasn't his field. From what she'd gathered from Duc, this was nobody's field right now at May Mắn Hospital.

Hoa was dead, and the other obstetrician who normally helped out was off sick, having just been diagnosed with breast cancer.

It looked like Vivienne was the total of midwifery and obstetric knowledge here.

She could see the baby's head tight against the perineum. This wasn't the first time she'd dealt with a shoulder dystocia. But usually a diagnosis was followed by hitting the emergency buzzer, with two other midwives, an anaesthetist and an obstetrician all rushing to assist.

Those people weren't here now. It was her. It was just her.

Deep inside, part of her wanted to scream for this poor woman. She'd worked with Duc over the years, and she knew he was a good doctor. The absolute worst-case scenario here would be the Zavanelli manoeuvre, where they had to try and put the baby's head back into the vagina and perform an emergency caesarean section. Duc was the only surgeon here. She doubted if he'd performed a caesarean section before but, if need be, she could talk him through it.

She pushed that thought away and tried not to think about it, taking a note of the time on the clock on the wall.

Viv moved automatically into midwife mode, reassuring her patient, even though she didn't speak the language, and letting Lien or Duc take time to translate everything she said.

It was a stressful situation for everyone in the room. Joe and Lien were calm influences, moving smoothly and easily. They seemed to foresee each other's actions. It was interesting to watch them work together.

Vivienne took charge. Assessing her patient. Directing her not to push. She attached a monitor to the baby that would alert her to any signs of distress.

'Okay, folks,' she said calmly. 'We're going to try a change of position. It's called the McRoberts manoeuvre and it's used in this condition to try and release the shoulder. What we really want to do is create some space in the pelvis, and we need to move mum and, sometimes, baby to do that.'

She gave Lien a nod, waiting for her to explain to Resta that they were going to help her to lie on her back and move her legs outwards and up towards her chest. As this was a delivery room there was no end on the bed and Vivienne could move easily to try and assist.

She kept her face completely neutral. 'This entirely depends on the baby's position. If it's the anterior shoulder caught under the symphysis pubis, this tends to work.'

'And if it's not?' Duc's dark eyes met hers. He'd moved behind the patient, supporting her position.

Vivienne kept her voice calm and low. 'If it's both shoulders, they'll be stuck under the pelvis brim and this won't help. But this is where we start.'

She kept calm. Running through the mental checklist in her head. Waiting to see if the change of position would have any effect on the baby's ability to be delivered. She was lucky. This baby wasn't showing signs of distress. Yet.

After a few minutes she shifted to the side of the bed, giving Duc a nod. 'I'm going to press on the abdomen just above the pubic bone to try and release the shoulder. Can someone explain to Resta and keep re-assuring her?'

Duc nodded and spoke in a deep, low voice, his hand gently on the woman's arm. She could tell that the woman seemed to trust what he was telling her, even though she was clearly exhausted. Viv understood that at this stage all any woman wanted was to deliver her baby and have it safely in her arms.

It was interesting. She was in a room with three doctors, who were all perfectly willing to allow her to take the lead. There were no power struggles in here. Everyone just wanted this baby out safely.

Vivienne kept a careful eye on the clock and the baby monitor. Timing was crucial.

'Okay, time to try something else, I'm going to do something called the Rubin manoeuvre to try and release the baby's shoulders.'

She explained carefully, then slid fingers in on either side of the baby's head, trying a number of techniques, without success.

The baby's heart rate started to slow. Both mum and baby were tired, and the baby was starting to get distressed.

She was calm and methodical, secretly glad that the heart monitor wasn't on her instead of the baby because, despite everything, panic was definitely setting in. She wasn't quite sure how long it would take them to set up a theatre if need be.

'Okay,' she said. The baby's head was still wedged tightly, with very little room for a blade to make an episiotomy. 'Let's try mum around on all fours. Let's see if a further change of position lets things move on.'

In another few minutes she would need to attempt

to deliver one of the baby's arms or give Duc the nod that they needed to head to Theatre. She was running out of options.

Lien explained in a reassuring manner to Resta what they wanted her to try, just as Vivienne sent a little prayer skyward. Joe and Duc helped mum around and baby let out a little grumble at the change of position.

But within a few seconds it was clear it was the right move. Resta was on all fours on the bed. Viv hated the fact she no longer had eye contact with mum, but this was a case of needs must.

Almost instantly she could see a change. 'Give me a second,' she said to the others. The baby's face looked a little more relaxed. 'I think the shoulder's been dislodged. Tell Resta to give me a push on her next contraction.'

One minute later the little bundle slid out into her arms. After a few seconds of shocked silence the baby started screaming. Vivienne did a few quick checks. Colour was good. Baby was breathing.

Joe appeared at her side and held out his hands for the baby. Duc helped her clamp and cut the cord, then they helped Resta turn back around to deliver the placenta. Viv caught Joe's eye. He gave a hopeful nod. When shoulder dystocia had a complicated delivery there could be injuries to the baby's shoulders and nerves. The baby would need to be observed. But for now he brought the baby over to let mum have a cuddle. *'Đó là một cô gái,'* he said.

A girl. She recognised the word. Mum looked thrilled. The relief in the room was palpable, all the professionals exchanging glances. Duc shot her a smile and gave a grateful nod of his head as he walked back

towards her. 'Thank goodness you were here,' he whispered.

Viv looked around the room as she started to tidy up.
'I'm sure you would have all got there.' The clenching
in her stomach was only just starting to ease.

Lien came over and rubbed Viv's arm. 'Thanks so
much.' She glanced at her husband. 'Sorry for the rude
introduction earlier. Joe and I can take it from here. You
must be exhausted.'

Viv nodded. 'I am, but let me finish the notes and
a few final checks on mum.' It didn't matter how tired
she was. She would always make sure her clinical work
and her paperwork were completed.

One of the aides brought in some jasmine tea, and
Joe did some more checks on the baby. As Vivienne
made sure she was satisfied that mum and baby were
settled and well cared for, Duc slung an arm around
her shoulders.

'You look as if you haven't slept in a week. Let's go.
Those jammies are still waiting.'

They walked back out into the cooler night air. Viv
stopped for a moment, putting her hands on her hips
and arching her aching back.

'Okay?' He was right next to her, the warmth from
his body crossing the minuscule space between them.

She looked up into his dark eyes. 'You weren't joking, were you—when you said you'd no one for obstetrics?'

His dark eyes clouded. He shook his head. 'No. No
one. I don't know when, or if, our other doctor will be
back. This was an area that my mother always took
care of—was always on top of. The last few days...'

he looked up the dark night sky '...I guess we've just been lucky.'

'You can't rely on luck, Duc,' she said quickly. 'That's not fair on the staff, or the patients.'

He sighed, and she could literally see the energy sagging out of his body. He'd come into that situation tonight, knowing that performing an unfamiliar surgery could be the difference between life and death for that mum and baby. She hadn't seen him halt or contemplate refusing. He'd been there. Ready to perform if required.

She turned to face him, their bodies almost touching. 'What would have happened if you'd needed to do a section?'

He paused for only a second. 'Then I would have done a section.' He looked down at her. 'I'm sure you could have talked me through it.'

Viv's skin prickled—and not in a good way. 'But that puts horrible pressure on you, and me.' She shook her head. 'This can't happen again.'

He stepped back and ran his hands through his hair. 'You think I don't know that?' He threw his hands upwards. 'You think I wasn't in there absolutely crapping myself?' He turned his back and took a few steps away from her, his momentary flare of anger starting to dissipate. 'You think I want any of this, Viv?'

His voice broke and she stepped forward and took his hands in hers. He kept talking. 'Of course I don't. But tonight would have been considered emergency surgery. Whether obstetrics is my area or not, I'm still a general surgeon. I would still be expected to perform emergency surgery as and when required.'

His hands were shaking, and she realised just how scared he had actually been.

'I don't want to be here, Viv. I don't want any of this. But what can I do? The worst part about all this—I don't even feel myself right now. I can't be myself. I need to be Khiem and Hoa's son.' He had a bit of a wild, panicked look in his eyes. 'The one who will sort out the hospitals and make sure the patients are looked after. The one who will make sure everything keeps running exactly as it did before—supplying all the same services for patients, even though we're two doctors down. Maybe I just wave my magic wand and whip them out of thin air? I tried to place an advert and begin the recruitment process yesterday—but apparently there's some red tape and I need to meet with the lawyer first. How can a hospital run with no doctors?'

He put his hands on his hips and took a few deep breaths, his head downcast. Now she understood the pressure he was truly under. Before, she'd just been thinking about the grief of losing his parents. But it seemed she really should have paid much more attention to his panicked phone call. He raised his head and met her gaze, pressing a hand to his chest. 'I can't just be Duc Nguyen, surgeon from Philadelphia. The guy who was just about to sign on a house he's spent the last six months looking for. The guy who had been tipped that he was going to be offered the next slot on the team at the teaching hospital. I'd even been told to start thinking about recruiting my own team.' He threw up his hands. 'This is just not where I thought I would be.'

She reached over and put her hand on his arm, gently bringing it back down. Part of her had always envied Duc and his lovely family life. But now she could see how much pain it had unlocked for him. Maybe her detached way of life was actually easier.

She hadn't known about the house, or the potential to become a permanent member of the team in Philadelphia. That was huge. He must have done so well. It was clear they were impressed by him. Now she understood exactly how much being here was costing him.

He closed his eyes and spoke quietly. 'The reading of the will is in a few days and then I'll find out what my parents' plans were for this place.' His face crumpled. 'They always mentioned they wanted me to take over—and I always told them my heart was in surgery. But we never had a truly serious conversation—not one with plans and lawyers. Our half-hearted discussions took place at the dinner table or between seeing patients when I came back and helped out during the holidays. Now I'm realising how much I don't know. I guess we just never imagined that something like this would happen.'

He shook his head. 'Until it did.' He held out his hands for a few seconds, before walking closer and resting them down on her shoulders.

His head dipped towards hers. And they stood there for a few seconds in the moonlight with their foreheads touching. 'I'm just glad you're here, Viv. I couldn't cope with any of this without you.'

She had so much she wanted to say right now—about the hospital, the responsibilities, the issues that needed to be sorted out straight away. But it wasn't the time. He didn't need that right now. What Duc needed right now was his friend.

She reached up and put her hand over his, giving it a squeeze. 'And you don't need to.'

They stood for a few more moments, before Duc

slung his arm back around her shoulders and they walked back to the bungalow.

As he pushed open the door, he gave her a half-smile. 'Hey, Viv?'

She was already eyeing her discarded white pyjamas, dying to jump straight back into them. She glanced back at him. 'What?'

He gave her a weary smile. 'Welcome to Hanoi.'

CHAPTER FOUR

VIVIENNE HAD WORKED in a lot of places. She generally lasted between six months and a year before moving on. She made friends superficially at each new workplace. She was good at her job and generally had a good feel for people—she naturally knew who to avoid and who to trust. Her instincts had always been sound—except, of course, when it came to men.

Viv seemed to have an inbuilt ability to find the worst man in the room—no matter where she was. Her love life had been one disaster after another. The only guy that had been half-good was Archie, an electrician she'd met when she'd worked in Bristol. Archie had been too good, too nice—even Duc had liked him. But Archie had got too close. He'd tried to support her when she'd tried to trace her birth mum and then found out she was dead. His sympathy had felt overwhelming. His questions about how she was feeling had probed into emotions she wasn't ready to deal with. It was almost like he had been trying to 'fix her'—and Viv didn't need to be fixed by anyone.

So she'd done what she did best, and retreated quickly. Instead, seeking out men who were their own natural disasters, and emotionally unavailable to her, made her life simpler. It made it easier to keep the shell she'd constructed around herself unbroken. Duc was the only person who'd ever been allowed to tap at the surface—the only man she'd ever really trusted. Which was why she was here, trying to get her head around her role within this hospital.

By day three she'd begun to get a feel for the place again. May Măn Hospital had always been a little different. She'd only been here for short spells, but there was something about this place—it had a little buzz around it that she couldn't explain. Before, she'd just imagined it was because of the connection to Duc. His parents had always been the heart and soul of the place.

Walking through the corridors, she could almost sense the echo of them. She half expected to turn a corner and walk into either one of them.

Trouble was, the staff had relied on them so much for, well, everything.

Lien seemed to have a good head on her shoulders for the day-to-day running of the hospital. For the general medical patients she was the go-to clinician. But she didn't know anything about rotas, ordering supplies, or maintenance of the building. Her husband, Joe, helped out at some of the antenatal clinics. He'd worked as a GP back in Scotland, and could do general antenatal care, as well as regular hospital duties. But what was most interesting was the fact he seemed to have a real panache for working with the kids. They seemed to gravitate towards him—even though he still struggled with the language barrier, much the same as she did. It probably helped that he had a young son of his own, but watching her colleagues gave Viv a chance to understand the skills of those around her.

While all that was well and good, she hadn't found anyone who had the skills she needed as an obstetrician. There was a visiting plastic surgeon, there was Duc, and there was a whole host of part-time nurses working within the hospital.

Trouble was that between Hoa and the other obstetrician there really had been no one else to look after the steady stream of pregnant women who came to the hospital. Viv had learned quickly that not all women in Hanoi presented early enough in their pregnancy to have any kind of antenatal screening.

Viv was lucky. One of her jobs had been on a Scottish island and had required her to have further training in carrying out sonograms. This meant she found herself doing routine sonograms on a whole range of women at different gestations, coming up against a whole host of potential issues.

The truth was, she couldn't do this on her own. She was a midwife. Not a consultant.

She wandered through the corridors in the midst of another busy day. Duc was sitting at the desk in her father's office, his head resting on one hand.

'Knock, knock,' she said as she walked in.

He looked up. There were dark circles under his eyes. Even though she knew he went to bed at night, it was clear he wasn't sleeping.

He started to stand up but she shook her head as she sat in the chair opposite him. 'Don't. There's no emergency. But we need to talk.'

His brow creased. 'Just don't tell me you're leaving.'

She gave a weak smile. 'Not yet. But you know me. I never hang my hat anywhere for long.'

He opened his mouth as if he was about to respond, then shook his head and held out one hand. 'So, what's up?'

She nodded. This was business. It had to be. She could see gaps that she wasn't comfortable working around.

'Things need to be clearer. At any other hospital I've worked at, we have protocols. A strict set of guidelines that everyone follows for certain events, certain conditions.' She gave him a weak smile. 'Thing is, at May Mắn? The protocols were your mum—literally. She knew everything, and everyone just went on her say-so. While that was fine when she was here...'

Duc winced and she cringed at her choice of words, but Viv kept going, this was too important. 'Now... she's not. Staff need guidelines to work to. Written-down guidelines. Maybe even stuck-to-the-wall guidelines. Your mother and Dr Tan were their safety net. Not all the nurses are midwives here. Some of them don't know the first thing about dealing with maternity patients. In lots of cases the care isn't difficult. They just need specifics. What to do, what to look out for, when to raise the alarm.' She paused for a second, letting her words sink in.

Part of her was amazed at herself. She never really stayed anywhere long enough to look at procedures and protocols. Last time she'd been here, she'd been just as guilty of using Hoa as her sounding board. But Hoa wasn't here now, and staff were unsure.

'This could be relatively simple. There are protocols and guidelines for most things in hospitals the world over. We can choose the ones that work here, and you can get someone to help me translate them. The staff can do short training sessions, and we can put the most important ones in easy, visible places as reminders.'

Duc put his head in his hands. He was shaking it. 'I can't believe something so basic isn't in place.' He glanced back up, an incredulous look on his face. 'How come this wasn't done before?'

Viv pressed her lips together. It wasn't up to her to judge. She'd no right to. She was just an outsider here. All she knew was that some of the staff were out of their depth and dealing with cases that stretched their abilities. They didn't have the back-up that was normally in place.

'We need some safeguards.' She put her hand on her chest. 'And I need some safeguards. Have you thought about getting another obstetrician, or at least another midwife?'

Duc sighed. 'Of course. But my hands have been tied with red tape that I don't understand. I am so out of my depth I don't even know which way to turn.' He held up both hands. 'This?' He looked around. 'This was just a place to come and help out. Do a few ward rounds, prescribe some antibiotics, help with the occasional clinic. Cover the on-call so my mum and dad could have a few nights together.' He leaned back in his chair. 'What I know about obstetrics I could write on the back of a postage stamp. I've spent the last two days panic-reading about emergency caesarean sections just in case it happens in the next few days.'

He shook his head. 'Have you any idea how long it takes to advertise a post, check someone's credentials, then wait for them to give notice at a previous post?'

Vivienne leaned across the desk towards him, put

her head on her hand and raised one eyebrow, obviously waiting for the penny to drop.

After the briefest of seconds Duc realised what he'd said. 'Yeah, sorry about that. Did I wreck your chances of ever getting another job with that health authority?'

Vivienne sat back and gave a half-hearted shrug. Truth was, she'd quite liked the place where she'd been working. The staff were pleasant enough, and she'd managed to rent a flat in a nice area. A flat that was now currently empty. Maybe she was getting old. It was the first time she'd ever really thought like that. 'You know me,' she answered flippantly. 'Only take one job per health authority then I move on.'

'Keep that up and you'll eventually run out,' said Duc. He was watching her carefully.

'That's why every now and then I throw a whole different country into the mix.' She leaned right back and put her feet up on the table. 'I was contemplating Ireland next. Probably Dublin. Anyway, I told my boss it was an unexpected family emergency. I might have left them in the lurch a little, but I'd just finished two weeks on call—and that's definitely not allowed. I'd bent over backwards to help them cover shifts, and I worked hard.'

Duc's eyes clouded a little. 'Family,' he said softly.

Vivienne gulped. 'That's what we are,' she said simply. 'At least, that's what I think we are.'

She meant it. Getting into midwifery college at seventeen had been a blessing. A year later her adoptive parents had died and when she'd tried to track down her birth parents it hadn't exactly been good news. Her birth mother had died from cancer years earlier and her father had spent his life in and out of prison. She didn't have any idea where he was right now. When she'd qualified at age twenty, she'd taken every opportunity that had come her way.

Her salary was enough to rent somewhere reasonable in whatever city she took a job—some of the hospitals even had staff accommodation at reduced rates. Duc had been the one reliable, relatable friend she'd made along the way. Her ground level. The person she spoke to most. The person she always connected to.

It was odd. Although they'd visited before, she was now seeing Duc in a completely new light. It was clear he'd never seen himself as an integral part of May Mắn hospital. His career aspirations had never been here. He'd always been focused on being a surgeon.

But now? With his parents dead, she did wonder if he might reconsider.

Duc gave her a sad smile. 'Family. Yeah. It's just you and me now. Maybe you should reconsider, I don't know if I'm that lucky right now.'

He stood up, pushing his chair back, and headed for the door. As he reached the doorway he paused and looked back at her. The circles under his eyes were so dark. He was still hurting. Of course he was. She was supposed to be here to take some of the burden. Instead, she'd just come in and heaped a whole lot of trouble on top of him. What kind of a friend was she really?

'After the will reading tomorrow,' he said slowly, 'I'll get to some of this stuff. I will. I promise.'

He looked as though the weight of the world was on his shoulders. Tears brimmed in her eyes. She gave a stiff nod.

He'd just lost both parents. How on earth could she expect him to think straight? If she really wanted to be a friend, she was going to have to step up.

CHAPTER FIVE

THE LAWYER'S OFFICE was unfamiliar. It took three attempts to find the correct street. By the time he got there, his shirt was already sticking to his back.

Vivienne had agreed to come with him. She was wearing a thin, pale green long-sleeved blouse and dark skirt and heels—not her normal attire.

As she stepped out of the car, her long red curls swinging, he could see heads turn in her direction. There was something different about a woman's walk when she wore heels. Viv didn't walk. She strode. Every step accentuated the cinch of her waist, the swing of her hips and the curves of her breasts.

His footsteps hesitated and he pushed the thoughts from his head. Nerves. That was what this was. He didn't think about Viv like this.

She moved to his side, fingers touching his arm and her orange blossom scent dancing through the air towards him. 'Are you okay with this?' Her voice was laced with concern.

He sucked in a breath. 'I have to be. What other choice do I have? We just…never had the chance to talk about anything like this.' His feet were rooted to the pavement. The air around him felt oppressive.

Viv moved her hand and interlocked their pinkies in their old trade-mark move. She gave him a soft smile. 'Friends for life,' she whispered.

He nodded, finding her words reassuring. 'Friends for life,' he repeated, and they walked up the stairs to the lawyer's office.

The man was waiting for them. 'Pleasure to meet you, Dr Nguyen. I am just sorry it's under such sad circumstances. I knew your mother and father for many years. I am Henry Quang.'

He had a slight twang of an American accent. 'Have you always worked here in Hanoi?' asked Duc.

He shook his head. 'I have offices in Washington, New York and Hanoi.' Duc nodded. Now he understood why Quang's name seemed Westernised. In normal circumstances he would have introduced himself slightly differently but, as Duc had found himself, constantly explaining why in Vietnam surnames, middles names and forenames came in a different order quickly became wearing.

The man gestured towards the seats across his desk. 'Please, take a seat.'

Duc's stomach gave an uncomfortable flip. This all felt so final. He'd spent most of the last week living in a weird kind of bubble. He kept expecting his parents to walk back through the door. His father to be sitting in his office. His mother to come beaming down the corridor to tell him about a delivery. Or either one of them to be sitting in the kitchen in the bungalow, sorting out medical cover for one of the other hospitals.

Now, sitting in their lawyer's office, he knew things were finally coming to a head. This was it. This was where he had to stop playing make-believe.

'I have to let you know that my mother and father and I never really had a chance to talk about their...plans.'

Quang gave a solemn nod. 'Believe it or not, Mr Nguyen, that isn't unusual. In a way, you're lucky.' He realised what he'd said and lifted one hand, rapidly shaking his head. 'No, I didn't mean it that way at all. What I mean is that your mother and father planned ahead. Because they had responsibility for three different hospitals, they put plans in place.'

Part of him felt relieved. Maybe he'd been wrong to worry about things.

'Okay.'

Viv gave him a kind of forced smile. It seemed he wasn't the only one nervous in here.

The lawyer spread some papers across his desk, spinning them around to face Duc.

'There are a number of properties. The three bungalows in the grounds of May Mắn hospital, the hospital itself. The second hospital in Trà Bồng and the third in Uong Bi. They also have several other properties. An apartment near May Mắn Hospital. A small house in the south of France and an apartment at Canary Wharf in London.'

Duc gave a nod. He knew about all these places.

'Naturally, the ownership of all these properties passes to you, Duc.'

'All of them?' He blinked.

'Yes, as Khiem and Hoa's son and heir, you are the only person named in their will.'

Duc gulped. 'But what about the running of the hospitals? The arrangements? They must have put some provision in place.'

Mr Quang gave a tight-lipped nod. He pulled out a

folder from under his desk. 'Yes, they did leave a number of instructions. Mainly about practical things. Supplies, deliveries, bank accounts. Payroll arrangements and details of their accountant.' He gave a sympathetic smile. 'It is all rather complicated.'

Duc leaned forward, trying to drown out the roaring that was currently in his ears. 'But the hospitals. There has to be some other arrangements. I assumed...' he ran a hand through his hair '...that they'd made some kind of provision—a long term plan. Arrangements for a board of some sort, or an oversight committee.'

Quang shook his head. 'Maybe they hoped you'd change your mind? Or, as you said, they hadn't quite foreseen anything like this happening and assumed they would have plenty of time to put those kinds of arrangements in place.' Quang gave him an almost impertinent look.

'When I said they'd made arrangements, I was talking about the fact they'd even got around to making a will. Have you any idea how many people don't get that far?' He didn't even wait for an answer to that question before continuing, holding up the folder. 'This contains most of the essential information you'll need for the safe running of the hospitals. In most instances this could take months to find.'

He leaned back in his chair but left his hands clasped together on the desk. 'The legalities of everything, the transfer of rights, et cetera, will, inevitably, take some time. Probably a minimum of six months. You won't be able to make any major changes or...' he raised one eyebrow as he looked straight at Duc '...or sales until that point.'

A chill passed over Duc. This really wasn't happening. It just couldn't be.

'But what about staffing? I have no obstetrician. If rights don't pass to me, I'm assuming I can't advertise posts for staff? And what about the bank accounts and payroll—are the staff supposed to work without getting paid?'

The lawyer gave a smile, shook his head and shuffled some papers. 'No, no, of course not. There are legal provisions for situations such as these—when there are hospital or medical facilities involved. Your parents had an agreement with the Vietnamese government about providing medical facilities within areas of greatest need. That allows some…' he pulled a face '…flexibility, in order to allow the service to continue. It falls under…' he lifted his fingers '…"emergency service" remit.'

Duc tried to breathe in—even though it felt as if a clamp had just fastened around his chest. 'That makes sense,' he muttered. He'd heard about similar arrangements in the past.

The lawyer pulled out some other papers. 'You can recruit staff in order to maintain service provision.'

Duc shook his head, waiting to see if Mr Quang would say anything else. But silence filled the space. 'That's it? Six months until the paperwork is sorted out?' He knew his voice was rising in pitch, but he couldn't help it. 'I can't stay here. I have a job—responsibilities. I've currently left a teaching hospital in Philadelphia without a resident surgeon. I'm part of a programme. A programme I worked very hard to be part of. Backing out now would virtually get me blacklisted from every other programme that exists.' Panic gripped his chest.

The lawyer seemed nonplussed. 'I'm sure other staff

have family situations that have to be dealt with. If you let them know what's happened, I think you'll find they will be quite understanding. And there will be other residencies—other surgical programmes.'

'Spoken like a true lawyer with no understanding of the medical profession and just how competitive things actually are,' Duc snapped.

Quang acted as though he hadn't heard. He pushed a few pieces of paper towards Duc and held a pen towards him. 'I need your signature on a few items.'

Duc stiffened. Hostility sweeping through him. A hand came over and squeezed his knee. He glanced sideways. He could see the tension in the muscles at the bottom of Viv's neck. She was trying very, very hard to stay quiet right now. 'What if I refuse?'

Quang's eyebrow moved a few millimetres upwards. 'Your staff won't get paid. Deliveries of supplies to the hospital will cease, and there will be no budget to pay for all the tests you send to the labs.'

He had him. Of course he did.

Duc snatched the pen from his hand and scribbled his signature on the three pieces of paper. The air in the office was stifling. He had to get out of there. He walked out without another word and strode back down the stairs. He could hear Vivienne's light footsteps running behind him.

But as he burst out into the bright sunlight, he knew immediately the error of his ways. The heat outside was every bit as warm as in the office. He couldn't seem to catch a cool breath.

'Duc!' Vivienne's voice was loud behind him and she clamped down her hand on his arm. 'What on earth just happened in there?'

The heat was starting to get to her hair. It was getting a little frizzy around the edges. And, from the look of Vivienne, she was getting a little frizzy around the edges too. Her mouth was set in a harsh line.

'My career just divebombed out the window,' he replied. He glanced around them. 'Come with me.' He grabbed hold of her hand and led her across the street to a franchise of a popular coffee chain. The air-conditioning blasted them as soon as they walked through the door. It only took a few moments to order some coffee and cake and take a seat in one of the booths.

Duc could feel the sweat that had emerged on his skin instantly cooling. He undid the button on his collar and pulled his tie down. Viv undid the button on her collar too. Her thin gold chain was nestled against her skin.

Before he could think, his fingers had reached across the table. 'You still wear that?'

On anyone else, this would be an intrusive move, but with Viv it felt entirely natural. His fingers rested on the chain and gave it a little tug upwards, revealing the gold butterfly with pale blue tourmaline stones in its wings.

Her hand came up and caught the pendant. 'Of course I still wear it,' she said sharply.

He'd bought it for her a few years ago for her birthday. It had been an entirely spur-of-the-moment purchase. He'd been walking through a shopping arcade in one of the more prestigious parts of Chicago when it had caught his eye in a window display.

Viv had joked the year before that no man had ever bought her jewellery, but as soon as he'd seen the pale blue in the butterfly's wings it had reminded him of the blue of her eyes. He'd bought and shipped it that day. It had gone clean out of his head until this very second.

He dropped his hand and gave her a smile. 'You told me no man had ever bought you jewellery.'

She stared at him for a few seconds. He was well aware of the fact he was avoiding the elephant in the room, and he didn't doubt for a second that Viv knew it too.

She leaned her head on one hand and dropped the pendant, letting it dangle between the curves of her breasts outlined by her shirt. She lifted her spoon and stirred her cappuccino round and round.

'No man has.' Her lips quipped upwards.

He didn't take the bait. Just stared at the random cakes he'd just bought sitting on the plates in front of them.

Her fingers drummed on the table. 'I guess this wasn't exactly what you expected,' she said softly.

'Nope.' The anger was still thrumming through his body. He'd loved his parents dearly, but he'd never expressed any interest in taking over from them at the community hospitals. They'd always known his plan was to be a surgeon. Why on earth would they not have made better plans?

His hands clenched into fists. 'This is a mess. A complete and utter mess. I shouldn't be here. I shouldn't be doing *this*.' The last word was said through gritted teeth.

Silence encompassed them.

Viv wasn't normally the type to keep quiet. Whilst she always had a good manner with patients, Duc had seen her stand up to arrogant colleagues, wipe the floor with rude medical students, and question incompetent methods at every turn. One question. That was all she'd asked. He glanced at his watch. They'd been in here more than ten minutes. The fact she'd been this quiet this long wasn't a good sign.

'Spit it out, Viv. I feel like I'm dangling from the cliff edge already. Just spit it out.'

Her shoulders went down, and her chin tilted up. He still couldn't get away from the businesswoman look she was sporting today. He'd always known Viv wasn't someone to mess with, but today, with the smart skirt, shirt and heels, she looked like she was about to wipe out a whole boardroom.

Or him, at the very least.

She clasped her hands on the table and looked him straight in the eye. 'I love you, Duc, but it's time to get a grip on things.'

The words hit him like a punch to the stomach. He opened his mouth to object, but this new ultra-calm incarnation of Vivienne wasn't finished with him yet.

'What happened to your mum and dad is awful. Absolutely awful. I admired them, and I know you did too. But they've left behind something that matters, Duc. That really *matters* and if you don't get a grip, you're going to ruin everything.'

He knew that. Of course he knew that. But he couldn't help how he felt deep down inside. He let out a huge sigh. 'But this was their dream, Viv. Not mine.' Even the words felt weary.

She shot him a look of impatience. 'It wasn't just their dream. This is their *legacy*, Duc. They've done so much good—not just at May Mắn Hospital, but at the other two hospitals as well. Think of all the patients who wouldn't have had treatment. Diseases picked up, infections prevented by immunisations. Can you imagine what would have happened to all those people if your mum and dad hadn't dreamed big?'

She was doing the big-picture stuff. The stuff that made him realise how selfish he was being right now. But was it really selfish to work your guts out for ten years to become a surgeon, only to have it whipped away because of a terrible accident and a pile of legalities?

She took another breath and gave her head a small shake. 'You don't have the same drive and passion for the hospital that they had. That Lien has. Maybe that's just because you've never seen it in your plans or your future, but…' she took a breath '…plans change. People have to adjust their plans all the time, and now it's time to adjust yours.'

This was her no-argument voice. He'd heard it before.

'May Mắn Hospital is an essential part of the community. Starting tomorrow, things are changing. This afternoon we draw up adverts for another midwife, an obstetrician, and for some admin support. You need someone to keep on top of the paperwork for you.' She put her hand to her chest. '*I* need some assurance that staff are working safely. I'm going to download all the procedures and protocols from the last place I worked. We'll adapt them.' She looked him right in the eye. 'Together. This is your inheritance, Duc. Your responsibility.'

She was right. He knew she was right. She reached over and grabbed a bit of cake from under his nose and took a bite.

He spoke quietly. 'They inspire me, Viv. Just like they inspire everyone who works with them.' He grimaced, realising he was still using present tense for his parents. He couldn't help it.

He kept going. 'It's a lot to live up to. What if I'm not as good as them? What if this really isn't the job for me? I guess—at the back of my mind—I always thought that if I did come back here, I'd be a fully qualified surgeon. I'd have fulfilled my career ambitions. I'd come back here with a whole lot more experience than I currently have. You said yourself—between them—look at the host of things they covered. Not many doctors have the skill set to do that. Medical issues, infectious diseases, surgery, obstetrics, paediatrics. These are all specialist fields.'

He took a deep breath. 'People who come to work here have heard the reputation. They expect to be inspired by the Nguyens.' He put his hand on his chest. 'What if they don't get that from me?'

She stared out of the window. Her voice was a little wistful, with a tang of slight envy. 'You don't get it. You have something. You really have something. Something that can make a difference. Do you know what I inherited from my parents? Probably cancer genes from one and an addictive personality from the other.'

Another punch to the stomach. He got it. He did.

He'd had a family. He'd had years of love and support from his parents. Viv had never experienced anything like that. No wonder she was calling him out.

He hung his head, watching his career in surgery waving goodbye for the time being.

Her voice cut into his thoughts again. Her hand brushed against his. 'And why won't people be inspired by you, Duc? I am. Always have been.' She let the words hang between them for a few seconds. He didn't really even have time to process them before she started again. 'And you can't be miserable.'

'What?' Now he frowned.

She pointed a finger. 'You can't act as if this is the last place you want to be. You have to be positive. You have to try and get the staff to embrace the changes. If you walk around with a long face, either Lien will end up punching you or I will. This can only work if *you* make it work.' She spoke quietly. 'The staff need you right now—not just the patients. They're bereaved too. Your mum and dad were reliable and loyal to their staff. They knew everything about them. You need to fill that gap.'

Nothing like piling on the pressure. But in a way he needed this. Only Viv knew when he needed a kick up the backside, and she was exactly the person to do it. And it wasn't just that. It was the fire and determination in her eyes as she said it. It sent endorphins flooding through his system in the weirdest possible way. Was this the way Viv looked in the bedroom?

Where had that thought come from? He gave himself a shake. If it were possible, he'd just shocked even himself.

It was almost like he could feel a gentle smoke settle around him, resting on his shoulders and making him try and clear his thoughts.

Behaving like a kid and shouting, 'This isn't fair!' in between grieving for his parents wouldn't do any good at all. Mixing it up with weird thoughts about Viv made it even more confusing.

He had to get his head back into the game. He pulled his eyes away from that pendant dangling down her neck and resting on her curves.

He would ask for a temporary suspension from the surgical programme. He would have a meeting with all the staff at the hospital to tell them they all had to try and work together to do business as usual.

He'd get to the job adverts. He'd let Viv take the lead on the midwifery protocols. His head was already forming a list of admin tasks for the new assistant, not least finding some computer software that could help with the rota systems of three separate hospitals.

Viv's blue eyes met his. He was ready for a whole new onslaught but she seemed to realise that in this case less was more. She pushed the remaining doughnut towards him. 'Eat up.' She gave him an easy smile. 'Somehow I think you're going to need it.'

CHAPTER SIX

FOR THE FIRST week she wondered if she'd been too harsh. As she replayed the shock on Duc's face in the lawyer's office, and then again once they'd got outside, she wondered if she'd almost crossed the line into being a little mean.

Part of her got it. He was literally watching his career dreams slip through his fingers like grains of sand on the beach. He hadn't been joking when he'd told the lawyer that the competition for positions was tough. He'd now requested a temporary suspension. Who knew if the hospital board would look on his request kindly or not?

Viv had downloaded a whole heap of maternity protocols and Mai Ahn, the translator, had helped her translate them into Vietnamese. She now had folders with protocols in both languages, with the most important laminated and put up in the non-clinical areas as visual reminders.

The job adverts had been written and placed. The schedule had been juggled amongst the existing doctors. The antenatal clinics were busy. There were a few patients giving them cause for concern, and Vivienne had arranged a few case conference calls with an obstetrician in the main city hospital to get some professional expertise and to put plans in place.

Whilst there was a first flurry of activity, she quickly learned that within May Mắn hospital it paid to be adaptable.

The antenatal clinics only ran two days a week. The rest of the time, if there wasn't a woman currently in labour, she had a little time on her hands. Yes, she could put plans in place for different ways of doing things, service enhancements and a review of all equipment, but most of all Viv was conscious of how much she was currently treading water.

The staff was still getting used to Khiem and Hoa not being around. Every now and then someone would mention them as if they were still there, or Viv would catch a wistful look from a staff member lost in their own thoughts.

It wouldn't do to try and change too much at once. Not until she'd really had a chance to see what was best for the staff and patients around here. She'd experienced many areas where a new staff member or manager had charged in, full of enthusiastic plans, without taking stock of where they were, or the population they served. Just because something worked wonderfully well in a city landscape, it didn't mean it would work well in a rural one. She'd seen too many past disasters to create one of her own.

So Viv had learned to be a willing pair of hands. She dressed wounds, helped with some of the elderly patients, assisted with patient procedures, and even helped out in Theatre when Reuben, the plastic surgeon, visited. She hadn't quite got to the bottom of what the story was about him. But as soon as he'd heard her accent he'd queried if she was a relative of Joe's. She'd met his question with amusement. 'Scotland's a pretty big place. There is more than one family.' He'd kept his questions to a minimum after that.

She liked helping out. Although her first love was midwifery, she enjoyed using her nursing skills elsewhere when it was appropriate and it also helped her get to know all the staff a little better. She still had some challenges with the language, but she was trying hard, and the patients and staff seemed to appreciate it.

There was something about this place. She normally adapted well to new places. But Hanoi just felt different. A more vibrant community. A more international place. She was quickly learning the places to shop, the street markets to go to and the best places to eat.

She'd even picked up Lien and Joe's son a few times from nursery when they'd both been busy at work. Regan was a cute little guy. Whenever she was with him, it was like both their Scottish accents got stronger and stronger. By the time they'd walked the street back to the hospital only Joe could understand them both.

But she liked it. The staff here welcomed her, included her in things. She'd been for drinks to celebrate a secret wedding, a thirtieth birthday party and a buffet party at someone's house. It was nice to feel included. With the exception of being around Duc, it had been a long time since she'd felt like that.

She turned the corner to the offices and saw Duc sitting behind his father's desk. Even she still thought of it as Khiem's, so how must he feel?

She stopped in the doorway and folded her arms. 'Hey,' she said softly.

He looked up, his eyes tired. 'Hey, yourself.' He

pushed away the laptop in front of him. 'How many did you deliver today?'

She smiled. 'Just the one. And she was very obliging and perfect in every way.'

She crossed the room and stood next to him. 'When was the last time you ate?'

He didn't really meet her gaze. For the last few weeks they'd been like ships passing in the night, both of them so busy that there hadn't been time to sit down together, let alone to eat.

She cracked a smile. 'I don't know, you invite a girl here, get her to work, cover all the shifts, and you can't even buy her dinner?'

He met her gaze. He knew she was teasing him. She gave him a nudge. 'Come on, Mr Cool. Lien and Joe are covering tonight. Joe might have suggested we get out of here for a bit.'

'He did?'

She nodded. 'I think they worry. Come on, there must be somewhere good around here you can take me. Can't remember the last time I had a good dinner.'

For the briefest second she thought he might try and make some kind of excuse. But he shook his head and stood up, lifting his jacket from the back of the chair. 'Tell me what you want to eat.'

She closed her eyes for a second, imagining her dream dinner. 'Fish. Sea bass if it's available anywhere around here.'

He looked at her burgundy scrubs. 'I know just the place, but you'd better get changed.'

She wrinkled her nose and stretched out the leg of her scrubs. 'What, you don't like the colour?'

He shook his head. 'Come on.' He glanced at his

watch. 'I'll call and make us a reservation. Can you be ready in half an hour?'

'Race you.' There was a glint in her eye. He wanted to laugh out loud. Whenever they'd worked together it had been a standing joke that you didn't want to be in Viv's way when she was racing to the hospital canteen. It seemed that nothing had changed. He smiled. There was something about the familiarity that spread a warm feeling throughout him. Viv was the last real person he had a connection to—a connection that felt as if it counted. As he turned to close the door to the office the paperwork on the desk caught his eye.

Out of nowhere a thought shot into his head. Routine hospital paperwork included the patient giving their next of kin. His skin prickled. He'd only had a few hospital admissions his entire life. A few stitches as a kid. A broken wrist. It didn't matter that he'd been an adult for years and had never needed to name a next of kin. But if he needed to, who would he name now?

Vivienne. Her name washed through him. Now his next of kin would be Vivienne. There was no one else. As he pulled the door closed another thought crossed his mind—one he'd never considered before. For as long as he'd known her, Vivienne had had no close relations. So who did she name?

She stepped out of the bedroom after pulling the sides of her hair back with a delicate clasp that Lien had loaned her.

Duc made a noise just to her left. She spun around and looked down. 'What? Is there a mark on it?'

He had a strange expression on his face. She'd grabbed one of the few nicer pieces in her wardrobe.

She'd only ever worn it once before. A red knee-length, off-the-shoulder fitted dress. It hugged her curves, the thick red lace bonded over a perfectly matched lining.

She slid her feet into her heels. The only jewellery she was wearing was her butterfly pendant. Her fingers went to her neck. She knew it didn't really match, but she didn't like to take it off.

Duc was still staring at her. He'd changed into dark trousers, a white shirt and a matching dark jacket. 'What's this?' she joked. 'The James Bond look?'

His eyes were wide. She'd moved over right next to him. She glanced down again self-consciously. 'What is it?' She twisted from side to side, trying to see if there was a split in one of her side seams.

It was almost as if Duc had been in a trance. He blinked and shook his head, a smile dancing at the edges of his lips. 'I've never really seen you in real party gear. It suits you. You should wear it more often. Just like the business look the other day—you almost scared me.'

She lifted her eyebrows. 'The business look? Duc, those are my interview clothes.' She gave a half-shrug, then a little nod of her head. 'To be honest, they've been pretty lucky. I've got every job I've ever gone for in that outfit.'

He laughed. 'You'd get every job in that red dress too. Where have you been hiding that?'

She ran her hands across her stomach, smoothing down the fabric. 'I saw it in a shop window, walked in and bought it. I never even tried it on—to be honest, I'm lucky that it fitted.' She gave a sigh. 'I bought it out of spite really.'

'Spite?' Now he was intrigued. 'What do you mean?'

She held up one hand to her hair. 'I'm a redhead,

you might have noticed, and I spent my entire child-hood with people telling me I couldn't wear red—no matter how much I liked the colour—that it just didn't suit me. So, I saw the dress, had just been paid, and de-cided I was buying it.'

He gave her a soft smile. 'Well, from where I'm standing, it was a good decision. A great decision.' He lifted a hand a tugged a little strand of her hair forward. 'Your hair's a dark red, it's dramatic. It suits it perfectly.'

She looked up into his dark eyes. Duc didn't nor-mally give her compliments—they were more the type of friends to constantly spar with each other. This felt... different. For the first time she wasn't quite sure what to say.

He tilted his elbow out towards her. 'Shall we?'

She grinned. 'I'd love to.'

As they reached the door, he grabbed her coat. 'Did you put on your mosquito repellent?'

She rolled her eyes at him. 'Of course I did.'

He gave a nod. 'Still, better cover up. Your dress is gorgeous, but for the mosquitos you show too much skin.'

She sighed and slipped her hands into the coat, fas-tening it up to the neck. 'By the time we reach the res-taurant I will be a humid mess.'

He shook his head. 'Don't worry, it's not far.'

They walked across the grass, through the hospital, and out into the main street.

There was something nice about getting away from the hospital. They'd rarely left the premises together since they'd got here.

Duc pointed out some of the local places to Viv. 'It's been five years since you were last here. This is the place the food cart stops during the day. It has the best noodle soups, like *hủ tiếu*—the pork base with noodles—and *bún riêu*—the crab and tomato broth—which are the nicest. Then there's *bánh mì*, with freshly baked baguettes that just melt in your mouth. But remember, most street food vendors here change their menu every day. Try and make it when the *chả giò*—the crispy spring rolls—are on.'

Vivienne was rapidly trying to store all the words in her brain. 'You know I have been walking around here, finding my own favourite places.'

'You have?' He looked surprised.

'Of course I have.' She laughed. 'I'm a big girl. I get out and about. I've lived in ten different cities. I've learned to find the best food.' She laughed again. 'You know food's my priority. It's almost like I have an in-built antenna. But I might need to make a few notes in my phone.'

Duc gave her an appreciative stare, as if he hadn't quite realised she had been finding her own feet. He pointed at a building across the street with bright blue shutters. 'And that's the shop where they sell those candies that you like.'

Her footsteps faltered. 'You remember that?'

He rolled his eyes. 'How can I forget? I had to keep asking my mum to ship me some so I could send them to you.'

A wave of sadness flashed across his eyes at the memory and she tugged him a little closer without saying anything. She didn't need to. She just looked around her. 'I'd forgotten how much I love this place,' she sighed.

He looked surprised. 'You do?'

She nodded slowly as they strolled down the brightly lit street. 'Look at the buildings up ahead.' She pointed to the row of shops with red, blue and yellow awnings. Packed above and looking kind of squished together was a multitude of flats—all entirely individual. There was one column in pink brick with a balcony on each level, the next column was white, with plants trailing down to the awning beneath, then came the thinnest column of flats that Viv had ever seen. One had a balcony packed with a dining table and chairs. The one above was crowded with a whole array of children's toys. The one nearest the top had given over the entire balcony to green foliage, with dashes of brightly coloured flowers.

Viv smiled and hugged Duc's arm. 'This place is just packed with character. That's what I love about it. Where else would you see such a great array of colours?' She took a deep breath. 'And smell such a fabulous aroma of food.' Her eyes were gleaming. 'This place had better be close, or you're gonna get crazy low blood sugar, Viv, and we both know that isn't good.'

He laughed and led her to a black door in one of the side streets, revealing a glass-fronted elegant-looking restaurant.

Viv frowned and did a double-take. 'Is this place a secret? It looks a little out of place.'

He tapped the side of his nose. 'It's a closely guarded secret. The food in here is brilliant. You asked for sea bass and you won't find better.'

He opened the door and they were greeted by a head waiter who took Viv's jacket and led them to a pristine table, covered in a white linen tablecloth. He took their drinks order then left them with menus and Viv leaned across the table towards Duc. 'Uh-oh, I look at a tablecloth like this and want to take bets on how long it will take me to spill something on it.'

He shook his head. 'Well, you look the part, now you just have to act the part.'

Her eyes widened in mock horror. 'How dare you?'

He shrugged. 'It's payback. You told me to man up a few weeks ago.'

She smiled. This was them. This was the way they always had been, and she instantly felt relaxed again. The last few weeks had been…odd.

She knew Duc was under enormous strain, but there had something weird in the air between them too. Something she couldn't quite put her finger on. It was moments like this that made her realise just how deep their friendship was cemented and that filled her with relief.

The waiter arrived with their drinks then took their order. Viv glanced around. The restaurant was busy, but it wasn't noisy. There was kind of a quiet ambience, people spoke and laughed quietly, giving the place an intimacy that wasn't apparent from the glass frontage. It was clear just from looking around that the clientele were wealthy. Hanoi was a real mixed bag, with pockets of real wealth and real poverty, and Viv wondered if she really fitted in here.

She lifted her glass of wine to Duc. 'Let's have a toast.'

He nodded and picked up his glass too. 'What are we drinking to?'

She grinned. 'Well, last time around we were in a beach bar, with bottles of—quite possibly—the worst beer we'd ever tasted.' She blinked and pressed her lips together. 'I think we toasted new beginnings then.'

He sucked in a breath. He'd been due to start at the

Philadelphia hospital, and she'd just got a new job in London at that point. They'd met for a crazy week in Ibiza, which was blurry around the edges.

She gave a sigh. 'I think I spent most of that week in those denim shorts.'

He rolled his eyes. 'Or that black bikini. Did it finally die a death due to overuse?'

She laughed again. 'It went where all my clothes go to die—the tumble dryer!'

He held up his wine and mimicked her Scottish accent. 'If it cannae go in the tumble dryer there's no point havin' it!'

She was still holding her glass up. 'Is that going to be our toast?'

He shook his head, the laughter leaving his eyes. 'No. I guess we should stick to the original. New beginnings. It seems kind of apt, in an entirely different way.'

She swallowed and nodded her head. He looked serious now for the first time since they'd got in here. She wished she could take away the black cloud that seemed to have settled around Duc's shoulders from the first instant she'd arrived. She'd wanted to steal back a moment of the old Duc. The one who made her laugh until her sides ached. Who was happy to stay up until three in the morning discussing the latest sci-fi series and where it had all gone wrong.

Would she ever get that back? Her insides ached at the thought. Bereavement changed people. Of course it did. She knew that. She'd never been the same girl after her own adoptive parents had died. But witnessing her best friend being so out of his depth was hard. Duc had always been capable and more than competent. Ambitious and dedicated, with an edge of fun.

Right now, only glimmers of the real Duc were shining through. She knew he was there. She just had to try and bring him back.

She lifted her glass and clinked it against his. 'To new beginnings. For both of us.'

His smile didn't quite reach his eyes as he lifted his glass to his lips.

The waiter appeared and sat down their plates in front of them. Sea bass with sizzled ginger, chilli and spring onions on a bed of noodles for Viv, and Vietnamese marinated flank steak for Duc. He closed his eyes for a few seconds while he was eating and let out a moan. 'Mmm… I'd forgotten just how good this place was.'

'You come here a lot?' The sea bass was delicious, tasting just as good as its succulent aroma.

He nodded. 'Every time I've been back.' He never added anything else and a wave of something washed over her.

'With your mum and dad?'

He gave a slow nod. She could see that memories were filling his head. He gave a visible shake and picked up his glass again. 'And with friends, sometimes visiting doctors, trying to tempt them to stay.'

Viv looked around with a smile. 'Ah, so this is the charm machine.'

'The what?' He looked amused.

She held out her hands. 'The place where you do all your schmoozing.' She looked around again with an appreciative nod then frowned and looked back at him. 'Should I be offended this is the first time you've brought me? I've visited you here more than once.'

Duc pulled a face, realising he was in trouble. 'I've

never needed to schmooze you before. Because...' he paused for a second '...you're Viv.'

She took another bite of her fish. 'I'm not sure whether to be offended or complimented.'

She held her cutlery at either side of her plate. 'I feel cheated. Others have been wined and dined. I've been bought the occasional beer.'

'Uh-oh. Are you about to renegotiate your contract?'

'You need to give me one first,' she quipped. 'And this fish...' she pointed her fork down at the plate '...has to be a compulsory part of it. A restaurant visit on a weekly basis will have to be part of my contract.' She raised one eyebrow, pausing for a second as their gazes connected. 'If you still want me to stay, that is.'

She wasn't quite sure where it had come from. Or why she would say it now. But she'd dropped everything to be here for Duc. And the truth was she had no real job security. No guarantee. She'd learned early on in life to be self-sufficient. For Viv, that always meant dotting the i's and crossing the t's. Every lease was double-checked. Contracts were in her hand before she gave notice at the last job. Insurance was always in place. She'd more or less thrown all that out of the window to be here for Duc.

But something else was unsettling her. It had been since she'd got here—but she hadn't quite been able to put her finger on it. They'd always been so easy around each other. So comfortable. She'd put the strange feeling down to Duc being upset at losing his parents. But the more she was around him, she realised it wasn't just him. It was her too. Things just felt different between them. And the truth was it scared her. Running away was what she did best—but she'd never run from Duc before.

Duc froze. 'Of course I want you to stay. Why would you say that?'

She lowered her gaze and started pushing her food around the plate. 'I don't know. You've seen the lawyer now. You know what lies ahead. We've made some plans. Maybe you think you can take things forward yourself?'

He put his cutlery down and leaned towards her. 'Are you crazy? Why on earth do you think I don't need you? I need you more than ever.'

She gave a slow nod. Some reassurance swept through her, along with an unexpected squeeze of her heart. Everything just felt so unsettled right now.

His gaze narrowed but his voice was laced with anxiety. 'You've only been here a few weeks. You can't be ready to move on already. You just told me that you love this place.'

She bit her lip. 'I do. But you know me, I never stay anywhere for long.'

'Most places you give at least six months.' He wrinkled his nose. 'The other place—the one you were working at. Do they expect you back?' The worry on his face was evident.

She almost choked on her fish. 'Are you kidding? I think I've burnt my bridges there. Leaving without giving proper notice?'

He rested his hands on the table. 'Then why are you in such a hurry to leave here, to leave me?'

The words wouldn't really form in her brain. She couldn't really explain where the question had come from. It had just happened like that. Sometimes she was at a place, and just got an overwhelming sensation that it might be time to move on. Granted, it never usually took just a few weeks, but all her of senses felt out of alignment right now—and she couldn't fathom why.

She let out a long slow breath. 'Oh, you know me. I always have a wobble.'

'Is it me?' His dark eyes were staring right at her, sucking her in. Making her feel completely self-conscious. He ran his fingers through his hair. 'Darn it. I'm not myself right now. I know I'm not.'

Maybe she was going crazy. Maybe this was all her in head. But her automatic reaction to feelings she couldn't explain was to run in the opposite direction. *That* was where the question had come from.

Because the thought of staying here, with Duc, for any longer was doing strange things to her mind.

'Stay, give me the six months that you normally give everywhere else. By then, plans should be in place. There should be some new, permanent staff. I can't do this without you. You know I can't.'

His hand reached across the table and his fingers intertwined with hers. A jolt of heat shot up her arm. Maybe it was the wine. She was on her second glass. But for some reason she didn't want to let go.

'Six months,' she said softly. 'Six months and then we both go back to where we belong?'

Her stomach was clenched, because even as she said the words she wasn't sure if she could do it.

And she didn't want to make promises she couldn't keep.

Especially to Duc.

But his smile broadened and he gave a nod. 'Six

months. We'll have it all worked out by then. I promise you.'

She hesitantly lifted her glass and clinked it against the one he offered while her stomach tumbled over and over.

Because for the first time another thought entered her head. Was six months really enough? Or would it turn out to be too long?

Maybe she wasn't the only one making promises she couldn't keep…

CHAPTER SEVEN

HE WAS FINALLY starting to get to grips with things. The new administrator was fabulous. Sen had worked as a PA at a Fortune 500 company and decided to take early retirement. Working for a place like May Mắn Hospital was exactly what she wanted. She'd sat across the desk from Duc at her interview and, after five minutes, had sighed and written him a list of all the things he needed to get in order. She'd started work after he'd taken her for coffee and cake across the road.

For the first time since he'd got here it felt like a little part of the weight was off his shoulders. Sen regularly had a stacked pile on his desk awaiting signature, then would wave him off with her favourite comment. 'Go, be a doctor!'

Today he was covering partly in one of the drop-in clinics and partly on the wards.

One of the nurses called him in to assess a man with a leg ulcer. Lots of older patients had poor circulation, which caused slow healing of any injuries. Duc checked the man's notes. This leg ulcer had been there for more than eight months. Whilst some ulcers never healed, with correct treatment most could heal in three to four months.

He peeled back the bandages, taking care not to damage any of the surrounding skin. The ulcer was smothered in a thick gel and covered with a non-adherent dressing. As soon as he started cleaning it, he noticed a slight discharge and a strange aroma. He asked a few questions, then leaned back.

He walked over to the cupboards and came back with some new products. Viv appeared at his side. 'What are you doing?'

'Leg ulcer.'

Her nose wrinkled. 'Okay, new skill. It's time to learn.'

He gave her a smile. 'What, midwives don't deal with leg ulcers?'

'Debrided wounds, yes. Leg ulcers? No. Thankfully, most of my patients are in a slightly younger age range. But in the future, who knows?'

Duc nodded as he picked up a wound swab and sterile bag. 'Well, it's one of the common things you'll see in the outpatient clinics. Might as well get used to them.'

She moved over and introduced herself to the patient in stilted Vietnamese. She was getting better. He was impressed.

Duc acted as translator as he swabbed the wound. He'd already decided to prescribe some antibiotics. 'Look at the edges of the wound, there's some redness and swelling, add in the discharge and slight odour and...' He let his voice tail off.

'You have an infection,' replied Vivienne. She moved a little closer to study the edges and depth of the ulcer.

Duc nodded. 'I think it's likely. A lot of venous ulcers that don't heal have an underlying bacterial infection.'

Viv shot him a curious glance as she looked at the

dressings on the sterile tray. 'So, do you put the same thing back on, or do you try something else?'

He waggled his hand. 'Actually, a bit of both. We'll keep using the alginate gel. There's lots of good research on its effectiveness. But I'm also going to add in a silver-based wound dressing that helps combat infections.'

Vivienne gave a smile. 'A two-pronged attack.'

Duc nodded as he spoke to the patient and finished dressing the wound. 'Let's make it a three-pronged attack. Compression bandage to finish to help keep swelling down. This has gone on long enough.'

Vivienne automatically stood to help with the tidying up as Lien appeared at the door. 'Oh, good, you're both here. Can I grab you once you're finished?'

Duc gave the patient the antibiotics, along with some instructions and a return appointment. He followed Viv into the next room where Lien was standing with her arms folded.

'What's wrong? You look worried.'

Lien nodded. 'I am. You know that Joe gets these ideas in his head.'

Vivienne's brow creased and Duc realised she'd no idea what they were talking about.

He put his hand on Viv's shoulder. 'Joe's from your neck of the woods. He likes to try and do home visits. Set up more community clinics.'

'Is that bad?' Viv held up her hands. 'That's just normal.'

Lien shot her a look. 'I have a hard enough time getting my husband to toe the line. Don't you encourage him.'

'What's the problem, then?' Viv had mirrored Lien's position and folded her arms across her chest.

It was almost like they were in direct competition with each other.

Lien turned her attention to Duc. 'We've had a few patients with unusual symptoms and Joe decided to investigate.' She looked sideways at Viv. 'Two of the women are pregnant.'

Viv instantly straightened. 'Where are they?'

Lien pressed her lips together. 'Everyone in the family is sick. They all stay in a building a few streets away. At a guess, there are eight family members. Two elderly parents, a son and daughter who are both married with a child of their own.'

'They can't get in to the clinic?' Duc asked—even though he could already guess the answer.

Lien shook her head. 'All of them have fevers, muscle and joint pain—so severe they can hardly get of bed. Throw in some nausea, vomiting and other GI symptoms.'

Duc let out a long slow breath. 'It could virtually be anything from norovirus to dengue fever, zika or chikungunya. Even food poisoning, or a weird strain of malaria.'

He nodded slowly. 'Okay, Lien, you know I've been working in Surgical lately. But I still remember all the basics.' He turned to Viv. 'I'll need to brief you on a few of these as they might not be too familiar.' He nodded again, decision made. 'Lien, call Joe. Tell him that we'll join him at the address in around an hour. Are you okay to cover the hospital?'

She nodded and he paused for a second. 'Lien, can you organise some supplies to take with us, and I'll brief Viv and arrange some transport for us.'

Lien's tight shoulders dropped, as if some of the tension had just left her body. It was clear she was relieved that Joe wasn't going to be left in that situation alone.

Duc hurried down the corridor with Viv close behind him. 'I'm going to give you some crib sheets.'

'What?'

He smiled and reached for a folder above the desk. 'Sen found a whole pile of things randomly filed by my dad. It seemed he made crib sheets for some of the international doctors on conditions that crop up in Vietnam that aren't so well known in other countries. Just to give them some first line information. She's duplicated and filed them all in here.' He raised his eyebrows. 'Apparently, in future we're going to have induction packs for staff. Maybe even send the information beforehand to let them study it.'

Viv looked around the office and smiled. 'This place looks a whole lot tidier.'

Duc paused and gave a thoughtful nod. 'It is. My parents loved being doctors too much to worry about the paperwork. Sen has been a blessing. She's gone through this place with military precision. I think half the contents ended up shredded because they were out of date or not important any more. She's scanned some things for electronic filing and cleared out the filing cabinets and reorganised the rest.' He gestured to the seat behind the desk. 'I can actually pull the chair in now, instead of having to dodge the boxes under the desk.'

He pulled out the sheets for Viv. 'And watch out. She's got her eye on how we deal with patient records. Apparently, she's also getting us a quote about electronic prescribing.'

Viv nodded as she stared down at the crib sheets.

For the first time since she'd got here she looked a little swamped.

Duc put his hand on her shoulder. 'Don't worry. Lien and I will talk you through anything.'

Viv shook her head. 'Zika. I heard news reports about it, but I just never had a patient who'd been exposed.' She pulled a face. 'So I didn't really read up on it. Now I'm feeling like a prize idiot.'

Duc squeezed her shoulder. 'You're never an idiot. This is an entirely new place. Look at what you did a couple of hours after you arrived.' His face grew serious. 'And you have no idea how relieved I am that you were here.'

He waited for a few seconds, giving her time to get over the little burst of nerves. 'Now, let me talk to Sen and organise the transport. Sit down for ten minutes and give yourself the chance to read the basics. I'll shout for you when we're ready to go.'

Duc walked back down the corridor, giving some instructions to Sen and then pulling his phone out of his pocket and calling Joe's number. 'Hello, crazy Scot number two, tell me what you've got.'

It was the first time since she'd got here that she felt nervous about her clinical skills. She'd always known that there were diseases endemic to Vietnam, and if this had been a job she'd applied for, she would have researched them completely. But there hadn't been time, and she'd just been so caught up in getting to Duc that she hadn't really thought about the job properly.

Her first experience had thrown her in at the deep end. She'd quickly taken stock of the fact there was no functioning obstetrician and had taken steps to try and put safety measures in place.

But all her running around and organising had left her at a disadvantage. How could she really serve as an efficient and competent midwife or nurse if she didn't know the basics about the population? She was letting them down, and she was letting the hospital down. A single bead of sweat trailed down her back and she shifted uncomfortably. It was unbearably hot today.

She tried to memorise everything on the sheets— then pulled out her phone to search for specific effects on pregnant women. The conversation between Duc and Lien seemed accurate. At first glance, any of these conditions could be mistaken for each other—but all had different results. It was important to diagnose correctly.

Lien appeared at the door. 'Are you ready?' she asked.

Viv nodded and stood, but Lien pointed at the table. 'Put on some more mosquito repellent before we go.' She handed Viv a lightweight long-sleeved jacket. 'Just to be safe,' she added.

The journey only took ten minutes. Duc, Viv and Mai Ahn were packed into a four-by-four with a pile of equipment.

Viv watched out the window as they turned into a street on the outskirts of Hanoi. The street was cluttered with bikes, mopeds and trash cans. A number of washing lines hung between the tightly packed buildings.

She climbed out the car and watched as Joe opened a door nearby and gave them all a wave.

His brow was creased as they approached. 'Eight people. Most dehydrated and likely requiring some IV fluids. One of them is elderly, two are pregnant and two are kids.'

'Then we'll deal with them first,' said Duc. 'What about the rest of them?'

Joe handed over a notebook where he'd scribbled some notes. 'Most of them are pyrexial. Some are also hypotensive.'

Duc looked around and split the patients between them all. Viv found herself with the two pregnant women. Mai Ahn stayed by her side.

Vivienne looked around. The house was clearly in disarray—but when every member of the household was sick, that was no surprise. During her variety of jobs as a midwife she'd often worked in people's homes both during delivery and post-delivery.

Her first woman was paler than could be reasonable and was lying in bed, her breathing shallow. Vivienne sat down at the bedside and introduced herself, asking her name and for permission to check the woman over.

'This is Mai-Lyn. She's twenty-four, and sixteen weeks pregnant.' Mai Ahn pulled a sympathetic face. 'She didn't realise she was sick at first. She thought maybe she just had late symptoms of early morning sickness. She'd been fine up until that point.'

It only took Vivienne five minutes to do some general checks. Mai-Lyn was very dehydrated. She had marks on her skin that looked like infected mosquito bites. Her blood pressure was low and her temperature high and a quick finger-prick blood test also revealed low blood sugar. Vivienne asked some pregnancy-related questions. Mai-Lyn had been having severe stomach cramps, but there had been no bleeding.

Vivienne pulled out her portable sonogram machine,

and smeared some gel on Mai-Lyn's abdomen, breathing a sigh of relief when the rapid noise of a heartbeat could be heard.

Duc appeared at Viv's side. 'What have you got?'

'Are we moving these people to hospital or treating them here?'

He looked around and sighed. 'They could all do with hospitalisation, but there is still a chance this could be infectious. For now, we'll treat them here.'

Viv nodded and stood up. 'In that case I need to set up some IV fluids, including some dextrose. I also want to administer some antipyretic for her temperature. She needs fluids quickly in the first instance. I think she's got some infected mosquito bites. What the mosquitos might have carried?' She looked up into his dark eyes. 'I'll let you experts get to the bottom of that. It could be anyone of the three conditions you showed me earlier.'

Duc nodded. 'Let's treat the symptoms and put the pieces together once we know all the patients are stable.' He handed her some blood bottles. 'Get some samples when you set up the IV.'

Vivienne nodded and got to work, quickly taking the sample and then setting up an IV, then moved on to the other pregnant woman. Her symptoms were almost identical but her history of mosquito bites went back a few days earlier.

She treated her patient and made her way back through to Duc, who was conferring with Joe.

'I'm concerned by just how much joint pain both my ladies have. They've been bed bound for the last few days. One has a particularly nasty rash too. Is there anything safe to give them for the mosquito bites? A cream perhaps, as well as the antibiotics? I'm worried they'll end up breaking the skin they're both scratching so much.'

Joe pulled out a medical bag and rummaged through it, pulling out a mild steroid cream. 'This should stop the itching and inflammation.' He gave her a look. 'If we were back home, I'd recommend a bath with porridge oats.'

She smiled. 'The well-known remedy for itchy chicken pox. I remember it well.' It was like a blast from the past. 'But, considering I wouldn't trust either of my pregnant women in a bath right now, I'll stick with the cream, thanks.'

She looked around the room. Most of the others had IVs running. She'd basically never seen such a dehydrated bunch of patients in her life.

'This has hit really hard and fast,' she said. 'What on earth does this?'

'We're just deciding,' said Duc. 'It's crucial we get this right. Particularly for Zika—because that could have real implications for your pregnant women.'

Inside the pocket in her scrubs Vivienne secretly crossed her fingers. They still had to recruit another obstetrician. And if Zika was the diagnosis they needed one quickly.

Joe frowned. 'Most of the symptoms fitted with being unwell days after being bitten by mosquitos. The sudden fever, muscle and joint pains all fitted. Some have had headaches, fatigue and nausea. A few have GI symptoms—and most have the nasty rash.'

Duc turned to him. 'You're thinking chikungunya?' He gave a considered nod.

Joe nodded. 'For me it's the joint pains being so intense and prolific. Other than that, the symptoms could literally be interchangeable.' He turned to Duc. 'What do you think?'

Duc was weighing everything up. 'It's just unusual. For some people chikungunya is symptomless,' he explained to Vivienne. 'But this has hit this family so hard and so fast it must be some kind of vicious strain.'

Viv wrinkled her nose. 'What does that mean? They've all been bitten by the same mosquito?'

Duc shook his head. 'No. One person usually gets bitten and becomes infectious. If they then get bitten by another mosquito, it can pass the virus to another person. Literally, the virus could have passed between them all in a matter of days.'

'Is there a cure? A treatment?' Viv asked hopefully. She hadn't got that far in the crib sheet yet—there just hadn't been time.

She liked the way they were discussing the case. They were all comparing notes, looking for the most likely cause.

Duc shook his head again. 'No cure. No vaccine. Just treatment. Those with underlying conditions, the young, and the elderly are most at risk of developing complications.'

'But if we keep our eye on this family over the next few days,' Joe said, 'by this time next week, they could all be on the road to recovery.'

Joe pulled some sample bottles from one of the bags. 'Okay, folks. Is there anyone we haven't taken blood from yet? We need to get samples and get them to the lab.'

Duc pointed to the two people who hadn't quite required IVs. 'Just these guys. I'll do it if you want.'

'I'm going to keep an eye on my ladies,' said Viv.

'One of them is having stomach cramps that I hope don't turn into anything else. I'm sure it's just a symptom of the disease but I'm going to keep an eye on her in case I need to recheck things.'

Joe pulled out some paperwork. 'Okay, let's get this up to date for each patient and make sure everything is charted and prescribed.' He raised his eyebrows. 'Then we'll have a chat about how we're going to manage this situation for the next few days.'

Viv put her hand up straight away. 'I'm happy to cover a few nights. I know I'm really a midwife, but general observations, IVs and antibiotics are all things I can cover—just as long as I'm not needed at the hospital.'

'How many patients do you have due right now?'

Viv pulled out the work phone that Sen had given to her that morning. 'Well, thanks to our wonder admin assistant I'll be able to tell you. Let me check. Yip. Twelve due this month. Seven have already delivered and we've had one from next month deliver already.' She gave them all a big smile. 'I actually don't have anyone due this week.'

Joe laughed. 'You know that means nothing. Let's hope you didn't just curse yourself by saying those words out loud.'

Vivienne laughed too. She liked how well everyone worked together. Teamwork was essential in any hospital, and the way that everyone had been willing to pack up and come out here had impressed her. Could they really have found ambulances to ferry all these people back to May Mắn? She simply wasn't sure.

She went back to check on her patients, turning up the speed on one of the IVs. Duc appeared and slung an arm around her shoulder. 'How do you feel about us both covering the night shift so we can send Joe home to his son?'

Viv nodded. 'Fine with me.'

Duc handed her a bottle of cream. 'First job for us to make sure everyone—including us—is covered from head to toe in mosquito repellent. There could still be virus-laden mosquitos hanging around. We don't want to be the next victims.'

Vivienne shuddered. 'You say the nicest things. Can I barter for another dinner for this?'

His eyes twinkled. 'I think I can manage another dinner.'

They worked comfortably together, settling down on the sofa in the main room once everyone had been tended to. Mai Ahn had come back with some extra bags of IV fluids and some food for them both.

It was dark outside now. Throughout the house they could hear the sounds of deep breathing. All the patients were sleeping.

Viv put her head on Duc's shoulder. 'I think I'm too tired to eat right now,' she murmured.

'You did good,' he said.

Her hand moved over to his arm. 'So did you. We all did. Let's just pray it's the right diagnosis.'

There was a long pause. Viv gazed at the dark sky speckled with stars outside the window.

'I'd forgotten about this part,' Duc said, his voice sounding a little strange.

She lifted her head. 'What?'

He made a sad kind of sound. 'The being a doctor and not just a surgeon part.' He held up one hand to gesture to the room they were sitting in. 'I would never do this, haven't done it in my whole career. I spend my life in a hospital setting, seeing patients in clinics, wards or Theatre.'

Viv smiled. 'Ah…a home visit virgin. Well, welcome to the world of community nursing. Every home opens a whole new world. You've no idea what you're stepping into.'

He looked at her and she continued. 'I've been in houses where they have giant birthing pools in their living rooms. Some where I've had to step over the passed-out drunk person as I step inside. Houses where my feet stick to the carpet and I'm afraid to take my coat off. Then there's the family pet who snarls and growls at me, looking as if they want to eat me, and there's the inevitable shout, "Don't worry, hen, he'll no' touch you!" Then…' she wagged her finger '…there's the pristine houses that are miles cleaner than the hospital and you feel positively shabby as soon as you cross the threshold.' She rolled her eyes. 'I've been asked to take my shoes off at the door or put those blue coveralls on my feet.'

He shook his head as he smiled back, his brown eyes looking at her fondly.

'Looking after people in their own environment is a privilege, Duc. I never forget that. And it makes you better at your job. You don't have a team to back you up. You can't press an emergency buzzer and a whole team appears in under two minutes. It's you. You're it. You have to improvise and make do. It makes a more experienced practitioner, and a more resilient one.'

He gave a slow nod of his head at her words. 'You love it, don't you?'

He pressed his lips together as she nodded. 'And I've taken you away from that.'

She squeezed his arm. 'There's lots of ways to look after a community, Duc. According to Lien, she's practically had to put a tracker on Joe because he's so used to home visiting because he worked as a GP. Maybe there's a way to look at more outreach work. Or...' she held out her hand '...when it's needed, taking services to the patients. You did okay this time around.'

He leaned back against the sofa and Viv looked at the expression on his face. She saw something that hadn't been there before—curiosity.

'Every job can be a challenge. Sometimes the challenge is what gives you the enthusiasm to keep going.'

She wanted to say more. She wanted him to take a look around and realise just how important the work here was.

He'd risen to the challenge today. But his long-term plans weren't for working at May Mắn Hospital.

Her stomach gave a little twist. What were her own long-term plans? She'd never had any before. Just living from one six-month contract to the next.

But Hanoi was a wonderful city. Bright, exuberant and filled with special people. She could see a fantastic role here. One that she couldn't possibly even begin to tackle in six months.

She licked her lips, mouth suddenly dry. This was the first time ever she'd had thoughts like this. And what would be the point in thinking of staying here longer if Duc was going back to the US?

She leaned her head back on his shoulder and murmured, 'Okay, I bags first sleep. Wake me up in an hour.'

She settled down as he slung his arm around her shoulders again and let her snuggle against him. She'd think about all this later…

CHAPTER EIGHT

THE WEEKS PASSED QUICKLY. Vivienne started to become more familiar with the particular conditions that could affect the pregnant women around Hanoi.

Several of her patients had HIV and tuberculosis. They still didn't have a permanent obstetrician, but Joe had an interest in tuberculosis and helped her out with the complicated prescription regimes for her patients.

She was completing the paperwork for a new patient when Lien wandered into the treatment room.

'Hey.' She smiled as she started loading up a trolley for a chest drain.

'Hey. Oh, who needs a chest drain?'

'The tourist, Mr Hom. We've just done a chest X-ray.'

'Do you need a hand?' Viv couldn't help herself. She always offered to help.

Lien shook her head then leaned against the wall. 'No, I'm good, thanks. But how's things? How are you finding it?'

Viv was a little surprised by the question. 'It's great. I'm loving it.' She gave a shrug of her shoulders. 'Obviously it will be better when there's a permanent obstetrician. But the closing date has passed, and Duc said he'll look at the applications tonight.'

'Yeah, Duc.' Lien kept smiling, her eyes fixed on Vivienne. 'How long have you two been friends exactly?'

There was something about the way she said the word *exactly* that made Vivienne straighten up a little.

'Since he was a medical student.' She waved her hand. 'Not quite as long as you two, but I met Duc in his last year when he was on one of his placements in England.' She almost bit her tongue in an attempt to stop her babbling. What was wrong with her?

'Were you always so tactile?'

The question took her unawares. 'What do you mean?'

'You and Duc, you link arms, you hug, you hold pinkies.' She smiled and wagged her finger at Viv. 'It seems so natural to you both. Don't think I haven't noticed.'

Viv frowned. 'It is. It always has been.'

Lien gave a careful nod. She bit her bottom lip. 'You've never thought about doing anything more? Becoming anything more?'

Viv leaned back. It wasn't like people hadn't asked questions about their closeness before. But she'd always laughed it off with a wave of her hand. And being asked about it in the middle of the treatment room seemed odd.

'He's my best friend,' she stumbled.

Lien had the most careful expression on her face. Vivienne knew that her and Joe had recently married. They were a perfect match. Maybe she was one of those people that just tried to match up all those around her?

But even as she had that thought, somehow, Vivienne knew Lien was nothing like that.

Lien kept pressing. 'Do you ever think it was meant to be more than that?'

Her dark eyes met Vivienne's gaze steadily.

It was like a ripple of breeze from the sea back home had just jumped across the ocean to prickle her skin. She wasn't quite sure how to answer that question. But Lien's gaze was unwavering. It seemed that not answering wasn't an option.

Viv knew she wasn't jealous. Lien had her own husband and her own ready-made family. But she'd gone to medical school with Duc and had worked with his parents. Of course she would be protective of him.

Maybe she was worried that Duc was vulnerable right now. Maybe, if the shoe were on the other foot, Viv would be the one asking the questions.

Her stomach rolled over. The fleeting imaginary thought of Duc and Lien didn't sit comfortably with her at all. Even if it wasn't remotely possible. What on earth was wrong with her?

A bead of sweat seemed to form instantly between her shoulder blades and snake its way down her back. 'Once you take that step,' she said throatily, her voice shaking just a little, 'you can't go back.'

Lien licked her lips. Her gaze felt like some kind of laser beam cutting into Viv's brain, exposing all the mixed-up thoughts and feelings she'd had for the last few weeks. 'No,' she said carefully. 'You can't.' Her voice was clipped. She nodded her head at Viv, then put her hands on the trolley and turned and walked out.

Duc sifted through the application forms. Sen had written some notes on the top corner of each. She'd double-checked their résumés and their references. He couldn't help but wonder who his mother would have picked to work alongside, who would have met her seal of approval.

He sighed and leaned back. His mother had had things down to a fine art. She'd never offered someone a job then changed her mind when she'd actually met them. It was like she'd had a sixth sense for who would be a good fit for May Mắn. And Duc just didn't have that.

He didn't want to make a mistake. This was a crucial post. It was essential he get this right.

He needed someone else's opinion on this. Someone who was grounded. Who could see past the padding on a CV. He smiled. There was one person he knew who could always cut to the heart of the matter.

He looked out of the window. Viv wasn't working today. She'd gone shopping to the local market, offering to buy them both something for dinner. He got up and walked over to the bungalow, quickly changing into a loose, long-sleeved top and a pair of jeans.

He wandered through the streets, searching above the milling heads. There. A flash of the telltale red.

She was haggling with the fish seller. The old man was looking at her in complete amusement as she spoke Vietnamese with a very Scottish accent. She was gesturing with her hands, and he could tell the seller was, in part, mesmerised by her. Just like a few others round about.

Viv was wearing skinny jeans and a white long-sleeved tunic top. Her hair was loose around her shoulders, reminding him of a picture of Guinevere from a childhood storybook.

She finally pulled some money from her pocket,

shaking hands with the man with a broad smile on her face.

'I take it you just used your Scottish charm?'

She jumped at the sound of his voice. 'Where did you spring from?' But before he got a chance to answer, she raised her eyebrows. 'And, no, I didn't use my Scottish charm. I decided to just be crazy Scot number one—that is what you've been calling me, isn't it?' She planted one hand on her hip.

The man behind her started to laugh, shooting a look at Duc as he handed over her fish wrapped in paper.

Duc pulled a face, cringing. 'Okay, busted. But, hey…' he held up his hands in defence '…at least I made you number one instead of number two.'

She shook her head and put the fish in the bag that she carried. He leaned in for a closer look. She'd managed to find some fresh vegetables and spices too.

'Looks great. What's for dinner?'

'Aha.' She smiled. 'It's a secret recipe.' They started walking back down the crowded street.

Duc was definitely surprised. 'You have secret recipes?'

'You know.' She shrugged. 'It's a secret to me too. I'm just going to bung it all in the wok and hope for the best.'

'How about some wine?' He steered her into a nearby store. 'Or some beer?'

Viv gave a shrug. 'Whatever.'

Duc grabbed a bottle of wine and a few bottles of beer. As he paid for them, he noticed Viv watching him, biting her bottom lip. 'Something wrong?'

She jerked, as if she'd been caught doing something she shouldn't. 'What? No.'

He shook the strange feeling off and joined her back in the street. 'I was wondering if I could ask a favour?'

She groaned. 'You want me to do the night shift again.'

He shook his head. 'No. And thank you for the night shifts you did do.' Not only had she helped with the large sick family—who had all recovered well—she was also more or less on call every night in case a woman arrived in labour. He spent most days just relieved that she was there. 'What I was actually wondering was if you wanted to interview with me for the new obstetrician.'

Her footsteps faltered. She stared at him. 'What? Me?'

He nodded. 'Who else knows exactly what we need? I've got two potential candidates that we can interview via a video call. Will you help me?'

She paused, and he could see her biting the inside of her cheek. 'What's a consultant obstetrician going to think about being interviewed by a midwife?'

Duc shrugged. 'Who cares? He or she needs to know that we are a team here. The normal hierarchy doesn't apply.'

She gave him a stunned smile, then gave an appreciative nod of her head. 'Actually, I'd love it. Can I prepare some questions?'

'You can prepare *all* the questions.'

She nodded: 'Okay, then, let's find May Mắn an obstetrician.'

She'd changed back into her denim shorts and had thrown all the food into the wok, where it was currently sizzling. Nothing had turned black yet so it seemed as though dinner might actually be a success. Duc had appeared and was watching her with unguarded amusement. He'd changed into a fitted black T-shirt and jeans. The clothes seemed to hug his frame, highlighting his broad shoulders and the planes of his chest. She couldn't help but notice the way the jeans moulded to his thighs and heat flooded her cheeks as she realised what she was thinking.

She tugged at the bottom of her own denim shorts. Maybe they were too short? She was so used to being casual and comfortable around Duc that she hadn't really given the clothes she wore much thought.

'Is this the first thing you've managed to cook without burning?' he teased.

She shot him an indignant look. 'I can burn it anytime. Just say the word. In fact...' she waved her hand '...make yourself useful and get me a beer.'

He cracked open the beer bottles and watched as she put the food into two bowls and carried them over to the table. It was odd. She was so conscious of his eyes on her. It wasn't like Duc hadn't looked at her before, but something in the air had changed between them. It was like someone had found a dial and turned it up a few notches.

She grabbed for her beer as soon as she sat down, folding one knee underneath her. Lien's words were still banging around in her head. She'd always laughed off any comment that anyone made to her about her and Duc. But this time she didn't want to laugh it off. Because it had made her brain spin.

She pushed a sheet of paper in front of him. 'Here, some sample questions. I wrote them while you were in the shower.'

He ran his eyes over them, elbows leaning on the

table, a beer in one hand and a fork in the other. He took a bite of the stir-fry and looked up.

'What?' She hadn't tried it yet.

Duc stood up silently and walked to the cupboard, grabbing some spices and some soy sauce. He added some to both of their dishes, gave them a stir and sat back down. This time, when he lifted the fork to his mouth, he didn't baulk in the same way. He gave her a smile. 'It was fine.' He smiled, clearly hiding the fact he wanted to laugh. 'Just missing some taste.'

Viv bent forward. It did smell more appetising now. She took a bite, and bit her tongue on the snarky reply she'd planned. This was good.

'I've arranged another call tomorrow with Ron Jung, our advising obstetrician. It will give you a chance to review some of the patients with concerns again. He's been so good, but we can't keep relying on him permanently. We need to appoint someone soon.'

'Yeah.' Viv leaned her head on one hand and started twiddling a bit of loose hair. 'What do you think of him?'

Duc looked up, a little surprised. 'Ron? He's fine. Worked with my mother years ago. She spoke highly of him.'

Viv looked thoughtful. 'Have you ever thought of poaching him?'

'What?' Now he just looked confused.

'Poaching. Stealing a doctor from elsewhere. Happens all the time.'

Duc put his fork down. 'You want to steal Ron? Why? He's worked at the national hospital for years. He's never expressed any interest in working somewhere smaller—much smaller. He has a whole department and a salary to match. Anyhow, what's wrong with the two candidates we have for interview? I thought they looked quite good.'

Viv leaned back, stretching her arms across the table. As she stretched, her short loose top crept higher and she only realised when she saw his eyes staring and lingering. She pulled them back with a bump. 'Yeah, about them…'

'About them, what?'

'The first one will never stay. Just from the application form they've applied on a whim. Plus, he seems to go from job to job, never really staying anywhere.'

Duc's eyebrows rose. 'Sounds like someone else I know.'

Viv shot him a glance but ignored him. 'That's not what May Mắn needs right now. Not the staff and not the patients. They need an obstetrician who's here for the long haul.'

'And the other candidate?'

'Doesn't have any special knowledge about the issues in Vietnam.' She put her hand on her chest. 'A bit like me. We can't rely on Lien or you to tell us about the most prevalent conditions all the time. We really need someone that knows about malaria, TB, dengue fever, Zika and chikungunya.'

Duc looked her straight in the eye. 'Someone like Ron?'

She took a sip of her beer. 'Someone like Ron.'

'But what makes you think he might even be interested?'

Viv leaned back and smile. 'My intuition. Managing a big department isn't all it's cracked up to be.'

Now Duc smiled. He loved the way the Scottish words and expressions were scattered throughout her language.

She kept going. 'He has a huge team. Twelve consultants—twelve egos to manage. He's getting older. He's just had his first grandchild. He's already told me he wishes he could spend more time at home.'

Duc stirred at his food with his fork. It was clear he was thinking about what she was saying.

She opened her hands out. 'Why does anyone want to be a doctor? To help people. To make a difference. What if we could offer Ron a chance to finish off his career, with a bit more time at home, along with caring for those who need it most?'

Duc shook his head. 'It would be a huge salary drop.'

'You're telling me that Ron doesn't already have his pension plans sorted out?'

Duc pulled a face. 'True. Knowing Ron, he's had that sorted out since he was twenty.'

Viv leaned forward. 'I just get a feeling when I talk to him. He's been consulting with us free. But he's genuinely interested in the work that we do here. He's been so enthusiastic about some of the cases—both the ordinary ones and the complicated ones.' She played her trump card. 'His mother grew up in the same street as Lien's parents.'

Duc's eyes widened. 'Really?'

She leaned forward even further. 'Really. I think he has a vested interest in this area. How about we both do the consultation tomorrow? We could sound him out?'

For a second he said nothing and after a moment she realised just how far forward she had leaned, and that Duc had a clear uninterrupted view of her cleavage. Her automatic reaction was to pull back, but something stopped her.

Duc hadn't looked away.

Her skin prickled. Under normal circumstances both of them would have moved and thought nothing else about it. But Duc's eyes were firmly fixed on the result of her folding her arms across her chest and leaning forward, allowing her V-neck top to dip a little lower than it should.

A crazy surge went through her.

She winked. 'And see if I'm just crazy Scot number one or not.'

Duc's hand jerked at her voice, knocking the bottle of beer she was holding loosely, sending the whole thing tipping towards her.

Viv jumped up, but not before the pale amber liquid was halfway down her top and shorts.

'Sorry!' he said quickly, standing up and following her as she ran over towards the kitchen sink, grabbing a tea towel to try to wipe away some of the damage. He lifted his hands automatically to help, grabbing a roll of kitchen paper towel.

As she lifted the tea towel away it was clear her top was sodden and was clinging to her like a second skin.

Duc started patting her down with the paper towel. He started at her waist and abdomen, and then moving up to her breasts. He seemed to be on autopilot, trying to right his mistake without thinking too much about his further actions.

As his hands brushed against her breasts, she stopped breathing. He was only inches away from her.

His hands seemed to freeze in mid-air. Almost as if he'd just realised what he was doing.

She looked at him. His dark eyes were wide.

Silence filled the air between them, but the air wasn't silent—it sizzled and crackled, brimming with sexual tension.

'Surgeons aren't supposed to be clumsy.' Her voice was barely a whisper, her eyes focusing on the hands that had just touched her.

Duc's voice was lower and throatier than she'd ever heard it before. 'Haven't you heard? I'm not a surgeon any more.'

Her eyes fixed on his lips. Her tongue came out and traced along the edges of her own, instantly dry, lips.

Her move was like a magnet towards him.

He moved forward. Just an inch. Close enough she could feel the heat from his skin. It was torture.

This time it was she who moved. Her hands automatically reached out and ran up his bare arms to his shoulders. He let out a little groan as her palms and fingertips touched his skin, and it was her undoing.

She closed the space between them, pressing her damp body next to his.

Duc reacted instantly, one hand sliding around her waist and pulling her even harder into him. There was no question what was going to happen next. No doubt at all.

And for all the shooting thoughts that fired through her head, there was one that overwhelmed all the others. *Now.*

His lips met hers greedily.

It was like a million little explosions going off in her body at once. His other hand slid through her hair, anchoring her head.

She'd never wondered what kind of lover Duc might

be. But all of a sudden in a few moves she knew. Masterful. Decisive.

Her legs were shaking as she responded to his every move, matching him all the way.

Her hands slid under his T-shirt, sending shudders of desire through her as she felt the hard planes of muscle and the dark hairs on his chest. At the same time one of his hands slipped under her top and he ran his fingers up her spine.

The move set every nerve firing under her skin, and her breath caught somewhere in her throat.

He bumped her back against the sink and she pushed herself upwards, making room for him to step forward and letting her wrap her legs around his waist.

Her brain was completely lost in the moment, lost in the part frustration, part desire that had erupted from inside.

She wasn't sure what had triggered the change in them both, but from the moment she'd set eyes on him at Hanoi airport she'd just known something was different between them.

For a few days she'd told herself it was his sadness and the obvious grief that was overwhelming him, but it hadn't taken long to realise that there was something else—something underlying—no matter how much they both tried to ignore it.

But she didn't want to ignore it any more—she didn't want to pretend this connection wasn't there.

Her hands tugged at his thick hair as his lips trailed a path down the side of her neck. She could see the pulse at the base of his throat racing just as much as her own.

She tipped her head back and let out a groan as the sensations started to overwhelm her, then Duc froze.

She sensed it automatically. His muscles tensing, his lips lifting from her skin.

She opened the eyes she'd just closed. 'Wh-what is it?' she breathed. She didn't want this to stop.

Duc was still frozen, his lips just inches from her neck and his hands on her skin.

He lifted his head, his dark eyes locking with hers. 'Vivienne, what are we doing?' The huskiness was still there, but now there was a sense of something else—a sense of panic. A sense of removal.

It was like a cool breeze dancing over her skin. It would be so easy to continue. So easy just to let the heat of the moment take them and carry them on to the next place.

Right now, that was exactly what she wanted.

All her words were lost somewhere in her throat. She didn't know how to answer that question.

Her pause made him step back, taking his hands from her skin. His eyes were shot with worry and confusion.

'I'm sorry,' he said. He could barely look at her. 'I don't know what came over me. You're the best friend I've got. The last thing I want to do is anything that will affect our friendship.' His hand came up and ran through his hair—the hair that moments ago she had tangled through her own fingers.

He took another step back, his voice racked with emotion. 'You're it for me, Viv. You're all I've got left. I can't mess this up.'

'Of course.' She could barely get the words out, rejection stinging harder than she'd thought possible.

She jumped down from the sink edge and walked

back over to the table. 'Let's just write it off to a moment of madness.'

His tight shoulders sagged, and his sigh of relief
made her stomach twist and turn. Tears threatened,
gathering in her eyes.

She turned away so she wasn't facing him. 'I need
to dry off,' she said, her hands leaving the plates she'd
been about to lift from the table.

He reached a hand out towards her and she flinched
away. 'I don't want this to spoil things between us.
You're too important to me.'

She didn't feel important. She felt like the giant elephant in the room.

She waved her hand as she headed towards her
room. 'Forget it.' She waved the hand over her shoulder. 'Tomorrow is a brand-new day.'

She closed the door behind her before he had a
chance to respond. Every nerve ending was on fire.

Every part of her body was calling out to be touched
by his.

Instead, she was left alone. Her knees buckled and
she slid down the door, wrapping her arms around herself.

She pulled her knees up to her chest and rested her
head on them, letting the tears fall down her face.

Part of what he'd said was true. Duc was the closest
thing she had to family. The only difference was she'd
never really told him how important he was to her. Duc
had still had his mum and dad. She'd always just imagined she didn't feature quite as highly in his life as
he did in hers. Best friend had been comfortable. Best
friend had been manageable—at least she'd thought so.

But everything had changed. How could she forget

about a kiss like that? How could she pretend it'd never happened?

She wiped the tears from her face, realising that her hands were shaking. No, her whole body was shaking. She stood up on trembling legs and ducked under the mosquito net to wrap herself in the blankets on her bed.

The air around her was clammy but she couldn't seem to retain any heat. She rested her head on the pillow.

She'd started this. She'd initiated this. She'd been the one to step forward and slide her hands up to his shoulders.

She could have brushed off the damp shirt. She could have ignored his apologetic actions. Instead, she'd moved. She'd acted.

She'd reached out to grab the connection that had blossomed before her. A connection she rarely ever made.

Or had she ever made it?

Vivienne was very used to being alone. Very used to looking after herself. From the age of seventeen she'd never relied on another person. Living a life like that was isolating. It also meant she erected a shield to protect herself from being hurt. It made it easier to move around. Moving around, she wasn't anywhere long enough to get too attached to people or to places.

Duc was the only person she'd ever let penetrate that shield—just a little.

And right now she was regretting even that. His friendship had been the one thing she'd reached out and grabbed onto.

She couldn't tell him how she was really feeling. She couldn't tell him that from the moment she'd set eyes on him at the airport and hugged him it had felt like coming home. Home. A thing she'd never really had. A word she'd never really found a place for.

May Mắn Hospital was exquisite. The problems were sortable. The staff were welcoming. The thought of getting the chance to cover at one of the other hospitals wasn't exactly too shabby either. How could she explain that for the first time ever she felt a buzz of excitement about a place. Just walking through the corridors made her smile.

And the realisation was that a huge, huge part of that was Duc.

But now?

Emptiness rolled around her in waves.

The truth was she'd never felt so lonely in her entire life.

And that made her sadder than ever.

CHAPTER NINE

DUC WAS WALKING on eggshells and they were all of his own making. For the past two weeks Vivienne had had a grin plastered to her face as if it had been painted on there.

He'd screwed up. He'd screwed up big time.

Joe had started shooting him funny glances and Lien was being down right off with him.

In the meantime, Vivienne had been true to her word. The conversation with Ron had gone well, even though both of them had been shuffling in their seats uncomfortably. Ron had asked for a few weeks to think about things, whilst still agreeing to consult on difficult cases.

Vivienne had read him well. Duc would never have imagined asking Ron to consider a position at May Mắn. But he'd smiled when asked, nodded, and hadn't seemed at all surprised. Duc's complete dread had been the thought that Ron might be insulted at being asked to give up his position for what most people would consider a less prestigious job.

But Ron had revealed that he was ready to think about some changes in his life, and that he liked the possibility of working at May Mắn. He'd mentioned a few community outreach projects that could be developed and had asked some questions that seemed to check if he and Duc were on the same page.

Vivienne had been enthusiastic, chipping in with projects she'd been involved with in other areas, and their success rate and transferability to Hanoi.

Duc hated the atmosphere in the house between them both right now, and his biggest dread was that she might go back on her promise to stay the full six months.

They'd arranged interviews this week with another midwife. But whoever they employed wouldn't be able to replace the intensity that Vivienne felt for her job and her patients.

Duc had to try and sort things out.

Viv was finishing up in an outpatient clinic when he found her.

'Do you have a minute?'

She looked up from some notes. 'Yeah. What's up?'

He could tell she immediately thought he wanted to talk to her about a patient.

'Do you want to go somewhere this afternoon?'

The pause was agonising. It felt like asking a girl at school on a date and seeing all the reasons that she wanted to say no flit behind her eyes.

'I think we should try to get back to normal,' he said quickly.

She flinched at those words, but it was too late to pull them back. He wasn't about to tell her he'd spent the last two weeks unable to sleep because of the whole 'what if' scenarios drifting through his head.

It was like being a kid with one of those books where you got to choose what happened next.

Except…none of his choices had seemed right, even in his imagination.

'Let me take you on a tour of the city. Or a drive further out. Whatever you like. I've been a poor host.'

She was going to say no. It was written all over her face.

He watched as she bit her bottom lip. 'Or let's take some time to do what we normally do. We can catch a movie. Find a bar.'

He was getting desperate and he didn't care if she knew it.

She blinked. 'I'd rather just go for a walk around the city, towards the park maybe.'

Relief flooded through him. 'Great. Why don't we get changed and I'll meet you out front.'

He turned quickly before she changed her mind, finishing up a few things with patients, then heading back to the house to change into jeans and a light shirt.

It took nearly an hour for Viv to come and meet him. He'd started to pace outside the front of the hospital. She appeared wearing skinny jeans and a long-sleeved white top with a simple bag over her shoulder and a pair of sunglasses nestled in her hair.

'You came.'

'I came,' she sighed. He could tell she wasn't exactly happy, and he wasn't used to Vivienne being like this. Normally things were so easy between them. They got to be themselves, without any need for other faces.

He wanted to reach out and touch her. But every molecule in his body told him not to. Told him that reaching for Viv again could set off a catastrophic chain of reactions that his body would want to react to.

'Let's go this way,' he said quickly. 'It takes us through the Hoàn Kiếm district and will lead us down towards the lake.'

She started walking. He was sure he should actually be leading, but Viv's long strides made him wonder who exactly was leading who here.

He kept up and started pointing out part of the city. 'This is the local school. There are more than four hundred pupils. This is where Lien and I went to school together.'

Her head turned towards him. 'You went to school together? I thought you met at medical school?'

He shook his head. 'We did both. You know Lien's parents stay just a few streets away?'

She nodded and he continued. 'They've always lived there. My parents and I originally stayed in an apartment further into Hanoi. They didn't build the bungalows until after they took over the hospital.'

They wandered through the streets. The walk from the hospital to the lake took around an hour.

Duc kept talking, partly because he couldn't stand any silence between them. It was easy to chat as the area on the way to the lake was full of shops.

Duc pointed down various streets. 'Things get a little quirky around here with each street having specific kinds of stores. Look, this street is mainly book stores. The one to the left, that's all shoe stores.'

Viv nodded and stopped to look in a few windows. She picked up something with an international brand. He nudged her and shook his head. 'This is a tourist area. That's not likely to be real.' She gave a little shrug of her shoulders. 'But it's right in my price range.' So he waited while she pulled some money from her jeans pocket and paid.

As they moved along there were vendors at various street corners selling fresh fruit and they stopped to pick some up.

The traffic was chaotic, the streets packed with cars and mopeds, and it took an age to cross some of the roads en route to the lake. As they walked down one street they saw a bride getting her picture taken on the steps of a grand hotel. Duc smiled. 'That's one of the most luxurious hotels in Hanoi.'

'It certainly looks grand,' murmured Vivienne as she stopped to watch the bride and groom posing together. Duc didn't want to hurry her along, so he waited while photographer posed the couple on the steps. Even from here, he could tell just by the way they looked at each other that they were totally in love.

An uncomfortable prickle ran down his spine. Viv had stopped watching them and was staring at her feet. Images shot into his brain. He could remember exactly the expression in her blue eyes that night, and if he closed his eyes he could remember exactly how much his heart had thudded in his chest and exactly how much he'd wanted things to go further.

Was he a fool?

She was quite simply the best person he knew. But there was no way he could have a fling with Viv and still retain the closeness of their friendship. Even now, he'd probably gone some way to ruining it.

Everything he did now had to try and pull things back.

He gave a tug at her elbow. 'Let's go around the corner. There's some gorgeous architecture. The Hanoi Opera House is there.'

They walked to the opera house and he noticed Viv tugging at her top. The temperature was rising, and he could see her hair sticking to her neck.

'Let's stop for a minute and get a drink before we

head to the park.' He ducked into a doorway and led her to an elevator that took them four floors above the streets. 'Café hopping is almost a trend here.' He led her to a table in a café overlooking the streets below, with a view of the lake. He handed her a menu, which she handed back with her eyebrows raised.

'Sorry.' He shook his head as he realised it was in Vietnamese. 'What would you like?'

'Frozen mango smoothie,' she said promptly, and when the waiter approached, he ordered two.

He pointed down at the busy road and crossing beneath them. 'This is Hanoi's answer to Times Square or Shibuya Crossing. I could people-watch up here for hours.'

Viv leaned back in her chair. Her gaze had narrowed. 'So, are we going to talk about things or are we just going to ignore them?'

He started. He hadn't expected her to say anything quite so blunt, but this was Viv and he should have known better.

His cheeks flushed and he shook his head. 'I'm sorry. I feel as if I took advantage of you. You've came here, given up a job and everything to help me out, and then… that happens.' He ran his fingers through his hair. 'I meant it when I said you're family to me. I crossed a line. I don't know what I was thinking of.'

For the first time since it had happened her face didn't seem quite so annoyed. She raised an eyebrow. 'I know what you were thinking of.'

The waiter placed the frozen glasses down in front of them and they both jumped.

He rolled his eyes. 'Yeah…that.' He looked up and met her gaze. 'But why? Why now? How many times have you and I got drunk together—shared a bed even—and nothing like that has ever happened?'

A sad kind of smile appeared on her face. 'Who knows? Timing? Hormones? Change of venue?' Her voice dropped. 'Change of circumstances?'

He reached across the table and grabbed her hand. 'I'm sorry. This is what I hate. I'm scared to touch you now. Scared that something that was so easy between us is now just...'

He let his voice tail off. His thumb was unconsciously making little circles in the palm of her hand.

'The last two weeks have been hard,' she said simply, and he could tell she was trying to keep her voice steady. 'I wanted to go home.'

His head shot up. 'No.'

A tear slid down her cheek. 'But I realised I don't know where home is. I don't even really have one.'

He didn't hesitate. Duc stood up and moved around the table, wrapping her in his arms. 'Home is with me, Viv. We're family.'

She was shaking now, and he hated every bit of himself for doing this to her. 'You should have told me. You should have shouted at me—yelled at me. You should have told me you wanted to leave. I am so, so sorry. I had no idea you were feeling like that.'

She gave a nervous laugh and pushed him back a little. 'How could I do that? I was the one that kissed you first.'

His breath caught somewhere in his chest. She was right. She had kissed him first. She'd responded to his every touch. Every moment of that night was seared on his brain. But he'd wanted to take all the responsibility, all the blame for what had happened.

He could tell that right now she was struggling to keep her emotions in check, and he couldn't get past the first words she'd said—that she didn't know where home was, that she didn't have one.

It pained him that she felt like that. That sweet, sunny Viv didn't have anywhere to call home in her heart.

'We reacted,' he said firmly. 'We reacted to...' he smiled and flicked his fingers '...let's just call it something in the air.' His hands went back to her shoulders. 'But we can't let this come between us, Viv. We just can't.'

She reached up and touched the side of his cheek. It was the lightest of touches and for a split second he was taken back to that night and the feel of her fingertips on his skin. Their gazes meshed. 'No, we can't,' she whispered. For an instant he thought he could read a world in her eyes—a world of loneliness. His heart twisted for her. He wanted to fix things. He wanted her to be happy.

He could feel hormones surging through him. He wanted to sweep her into her arms and tell her that everything would be fine, that home could be here for them both. But how could he do that when he still hadn't figured out where he wanted to stay or what he wanted to do next?

The waiter appeared with a loaded tray and Duc moved to let him past, going back to his seat and putting his hands around the frozen drink. Maybe it would chill some of the heat in his blood?

The mood had changed. The strain was starting to gradually lift between them. It wasn't entirely natural, but he could sense they both wanted to make a concerted effort to fix this. They finished their smoothies and went back out onto the busy street, dodging the mopeds and finally entering the park.

As they moved inside Duc turned towards her. 'Hoàn Kiem Lake really is the centre of everything around here. The lake and temple are probably the most famous places in Hanoi city. People come here to rest, enjoy the view, and have a chance to sit back and watch the rest of the world.'

Viv looked around. 'Or get away from the traffic,' she quipped sarcastically with a big smile. She was right, of course. The noise of the constant traffic could be wearing.

The park was dotted with people. It was busy but with enough space for everyone. 'The streets in Hanoi are always busy with motorbikes and cars,' Duc agreed. 'It's nice to get a break from it. And to see a bit of green.' He gave her a smile. 'You kind of forget you're in the middle of the city in here.'

They walked amongst the dog walkers, people sitting on benches, families having picnics on blankets and tourists snapping photographs.

'That's Jade Island.' Duc pointed to the structure in the middle of the lake. 'The red bridge is called the Rising Sun Bridge and there's a pagoda on the island. Want to visit?'

Viv shook her head. 'It looks too busy. Too crowded with tourists. Let's just walk through the park and go out the other side.'

He hesitated a second then slung his arm around her shoulders, holding his breath. But Viv just leaned into him, letting her arm rest around his waist as they walked.

They didn't talk through the rest of the park. Each

step seemed to give him more confidence. Hopefully the tension in the house would lighten. What he wanted more than anything was for things between them to get back to normal.

At least, that was what he should want. But there was a tiny little voice in his head that was out on a limb here. A tiny part of his brain that wondered, *What if?*

For the last few years he'd been so focused on being a surgeon he hadn't made room in his life for anything else. Sure, he'd had girlfriends. But only for a few months at a time. His mind was always on a million other things.

But in these last few weeks when he'd been with Viv? In any second that he hadn't been thinking about the hospital, his mind had been on her. There wasn't space for anything else. Viv had captured every part of his attention. Every cell in his body had responded to her actions. He couldn't remember ever feeling a rush of emotions like that, a connection like that. Now he was agreeing to lock all that away—to put it back in the box it had erupted out of, and not think about it any more. Could he actually do that?

The words that she'd said echoed in his head again. *I don't know where home is. I don't even really have one.*

His gut twisted with the memory that Viv felt that way. He'd been so lucky. He'd had something that she'd never experienced—a happy home life with interested and loving parents. He straightened up as they walked. It didn't matter what his confusion was. It didn't matter that every time she brushed against him, his cells exploded. It didn't matter that since that kiss he'd wanted to do it again and again and again. He had so much uncertainty in his life right now, so much he needed to sort out. Did he want to go back to surgery? Should he try and make things work at May Mắn? Could he offer her anything other than a few weeks of hot and heavy fun that could ruin the friendship for both of them?

He couldn't do that to Viv. He had to put her needs first. She needed family. She needed a friend. That was his job here.

'Want to do some sightseeing?' he asked as they emerged from one of the other park entrances.

She looked around the busy streets. 'What're my options?'

A whole host of inappropriate thoughts flashed through his head. He gave his head a shake but couldn't help but smile. He pointed in one direction. 'A few blocks west is St Joseph's Cathedral.' He looked her up and down.

'What?' she asked, putting her hands on her hips.

'You have to be dressed appropriately to get in. But you'll do. No photos inside, though.'

Viv wrinkled her nose. 'What are the rest of my options?'

Duc looked around, racking his brain. It was weird. The place he'd lived a good part of his life—and everything had just gone out of his head. Maybe it was because of the way Viv had tilted her head and was looking up at him?

He waved one hand. 'There are other historical touristy places. There's Hoa Lo Prison, the Vietnamese Women's Museum and the Thang Long Water Puppet Theatre.'

She folded her arm across her chest. 'You want to take me to a prison?'

He gave a shrug. 'Only part of it exists as a museum any more. What about the puppet theatre, then?'

Viv blew a dark red strand of hair from her eyes. 'Actually, let's get something else to drink. I can't believe I've only walked across a park and I feel as if I'm ready to keel over again.'

Duc shot her a sideways glance. 'Coffee or wine?'

She looked at her watch just as his phone rang. He pulled it from his pocket and couldn't help his surprise. He turned to screen towards Viv so she could see the name as he answered.

'Ron, it's good to hear from you.'

He waited, flicking it to speaker so Viv could hear too, expecting Ron to ask about a patient, but he didn't. Instead he spoke slowly. 'Duc, thank you for your offer. I wanted to call to let you know that I'll accept. I've spoken to my family over the last few days and we all agreed there needs to be a work-life balance. I also want something that will challenge me again and let me feel as if I can make a difference. May Mǎn will do that for me. I can give you three days a week. And you had better keep that sparky Scottish midwife on duty. I like her. She has passion for her job and her patients. If you're happy with those terms, I'll hand in my notice today.'

Duc's mouth was hanging open. He literally couldn't believe it. Viv had moved over, leaning over the phone but pressing against his side so she could hear part of the conversation. She tried to hide her squeal as she jumped up and down.

'What was that?' asked Ron.

Duc smiled. It felt like an enormous weight had lifted off his chest. 'That was your sparky Scottish midwife.'

He kept grinning as Viv gave him a wink and then turned a cartwheel on the pavement, much to the amusement of some passers-by.

'Ah, good,' said Ron, oblivious to the sight that Duc was currently seeing. 'I look forward to keeping working with you both. Email me the contract.'

Duc agreed as Ron rang off, then he turned and grabbed Viv around the waist and spun her around. 'We've got an obstetrician!' he shouted.

'We've got Ron!' she shouted back, laughing.

Duc shook his head. 'I can't believe it. I can't believe he's accepted and he's giving up his other job.'

Viv's eyes twinkled. 'I told you he was ready for a change.'

'How on earth did you know?'

She kept laughing. 'Let's just call it women's intuition, which means that you had no chance of sensing it. Now, weren't we going to get a drink?'

'Hold on,' said Duc as he grabbed his phone again and spoke to Sen for a few moments. 'Right, contract on its way. Let's hold him to it before he changes his mind.'

'Why would he change his mind? He's getting to keep doing a job he loves, without the pressure of running a department and managing a dozen other doctors. And...' she put her hand on her chest '...he gets to work with me.'

'He does,' Duc agreed. 'Lucky him.'

He slung his arm back around her shoulders. 'All of a sudden this day seems a whole lot brighter. I've got my best friend back, and I've got an obstetrician that we know and we can trust.'

Viv's hand came up and interlinked with his hand on her shoulder. He pretended to ignore the tingle that shot across his skin.

'Didn't you promise me wine?'

He laughed. 'Oh, so it's wine now? The coffee is out the window?'

Her face looked slightly more serious. 'I think we should celebrate,' she said.

She was saying the words, but he could see something else going on behind her eyes.

Home. Those words were still echoing in his head. She'd never really had a home. She'd never staying anywhere long enough to let that happen.

Something stirred inside. She'd already told him she liked it here. She'd just persuaded a top obstetrician to work for May Mắn permanently, and Ron wanted to work with *her*.

Viv might be Scottish, but was there any reason she couldn't make a home in Hanoi?

The seed started to sprout in his brain. He gave her hand a squeeze. 'Wine it is. Let's go.'

CHAPTER TEN

THE TENSION IN the house had lifted and Vivienne finally felt as if she could concentrate on her job and enjoy it. She was learning as much as she could about the health of the people in Hanoi and getting more in tune with the specific conditions here that could affect pregnant women.

Duc had started humming again. That meant he was more relaxed.

She should be happy. She should be delighted. She should be able to write off what had happened between them as just a blip.

But somewhere deep inside it felt like so much more.

One kiss had stoked a whole lot of illicit thoughts about her best friend that she was trying really hard to lock away in a box somewhere.

Every now and then they would brush against each other or she would find herself looking at him in a different way. And either of those things would send a whole host of tingles down her spine. It was as if someone had just flicked a switch in her body.

Before, Duc had stayed safely in the 'friend' category.

Could she really ever feel that way about him again?

Part of her was hurt that he clearly hadn't wanted things to proceed between them. No. Strike that. Part of her was devastated.

It hurt to know that he'd been the one to stop. He'd been the one to reject her.

She couldn't even explain it to herself. But the fact that it had been Duc who had pushed away. It hurt more than ever.

With the rest of the guys she'd been involved with, there had been no real expectations. Sure, she'd thought she'd had her heart broken a few times, but the truth was there had been no promises. No happy-ever-afters. All the break-ups had been inevitable. She'd gone into the relationships knowing none of these were the guy to capture her heart.

But Duc? That was different. That was a whole host of emotions and hormones for a guy she already loved and respected. A guy she laughed with. A guy she didn't hesitate to throw her arms around. This wasn't some random pick up in a club. This was Duc. The one solid relationship she actually had with a man.

And he'd kissed her then backed away.

She was trying so hard to put on a brave front and pretend that her heart didn't feel as if it had been ripped clean out of her chest.

But in order to keep things in check, she pushed all those thoughts away and jammed them in a box in her head, somewhere out of reach. She'd learned to live like this a long time ago. When her adoptive parents had gently tried to push her in certain directions. When they'd both died in quick succession and the rest of her adoptive family had kind of faded into the background.

When she'd tracked down her birth parents and realised there were no happy endings. Not for her anyway.

For the most part, she tilted her chin up and smiled.

She had to. She had a job to do. The staff here were some of the nicest she'd ever worked with. She was slowly but surely tackling the language barrier. Some nights she asked Duc to speak to her purely in Vietnamese so she could practise.

She'd become familiar with the surrounding area, the restaurants, the shops, the shopkeepers, the local transport.

The city was bright, colourful and vibrant and she felt surprisingly safe for a foreign girl in a strange place.

Some things didn't change, of course. She still burned everything she attempted to cook.

Duc still laughed at her regularly as she set off the smoke alarm in the house and had to open the doors and windows to let the smoke out.

Three months, that was how long she'd been here now.

Ron had served his notice at the obstetric hospital and had started with a bang. It had taken him five minutes to get on board with some of Joe's ideas about community clinics, and she'd found herself screening pregnant women alongside school-age children who were coming for vaccinations and older people getting treated for long-term health conditions.

He'd agreed with all the protocols she'd started within the hospital and helped oversee staff training.

She'd just gathered some notes for the clinic this afternoon when Sen appeared at the door with some letters in her hands. 'Oh, sorry, I was looking for Duc.'

'He's gone to see a patient. Someone with suspected appendicitis, I think.'

Sen gave a nod. 'I printed out the emails he asked for. I'll just leave them on the desk.'

She disappeared and Vivienne glanced at the pile of papers. Something caught her eye and she froze.

She didn't mean to read a private email—but it was just sitting there and Sen had already seen it.

It was formal, thanking Duc for his enquiry, with a string of dates and steps he'd have to take if he chose to go back to his surgical position.

He hadn't mentioned a single thing. Not once.

She looked further down the page. Duc had only sent the original email a few days before.

She gulped. He was planning to go back to his job. It was hardly a surprise. He'd always said he didn't want to stay at May Mắn permanently, and this would only ever be a temporary solution.

Her mouth was dry. But he hadn't mentioned it to her. He hadn't said anything at all.

She took a deep breath. She had a job to do. She had to get on.

She'd only taken a few steps when she heard a screech and a loud bang outside. She didn't hesitate but turned and dropped the notes back onto the main desk and ran down the corridor. Two of the nurses were already at the main entrance.

Viv ran up behind them and stared at the disaster outside.

A lorry was on its side. The front of the lorry looked as if it had hit the side of a crumpled car. The traffic outside the hospital had come to a complete halt with only a few mopeds snaking past.

She ran outside with Lien and the two nurses hot on her heels. She dropped to her knees on the road, bending down to look through the broken glass at the driver. His leg was twisted at an ugly angle and he was unconscious. She put her hand under her scrub top and punched out some of the shards of glass, so she could reach inside and feel for a pulse and check for breathing. He had one, and his breathing seemed steady.

Lien shouted over to her, 'I've got a heavily pregnant woman here. Do you want to swap?'

Viv nodded but as she turned to move away a flash of red caught her eye. Her heart rate stuttered. She knew what she was seeing. A small leg under the wheel of the truck.

'Lien!' she screamed. 'I think there's a kid under here.'

Duc appeared at her back, closely followed by Joe. They exchanged glances and Duc dropped to his knees and partially disappeared beneath the twisted metal. He looked up and spoke a few whispered words to Joe.

The nurses had run back inside to grab some supplies, and they reappeared, one with a mobile trolley and one with a wheelchair.

Joe's face was serious. 'Viv, you swap with Lien. Shout for me if you need a hand. Duc and I will take care of this.'

Her heart twisted in her chest. She knew they were trying to protect her, and a grateful part of her brain kicked in. She was primarily a midwife. She wasn't a children's nurse. Could she even be useful to them anyway?

Lien was still at the other car. She gave Vivienne a nod and they both ran, swapping places.

The little red trouser leg had imprinted itself on her brain and it took all her strength to focus on the woman in the car in front of her. She wasn't just pregnant. She was *very* pregnant.

Viv spoke in her best broken Vietnamese. 'I'm Viv. I'm a midwife at the May Mắn Hospital. How many weeks are you?'

The woman had both hands on her stomach and tears running down her face. 'Thirty-nine,' she breathed. 'But my waters have broken.'

Viv looked further into the car. There was a damp patch on the front seat between the woman's legs. Viv turned to one of the nurses. 'Can I have a BP monitor and a stethoscope? And a portable Doppler.' The woman had the window down in her car, and Viv reached her hand in to release the door. The worst impact had been on the other side, so thankfully the door opened with a couple of tugs.

She bent down next to the car so she was down at the woman's level. 'What's your name?'

The woman winced for a second.

'Labour pain?' Viv asked.

The woman nodded, her face contorting for a few seconds. 'Tho,' she breathed. 'My name is Tho.'

Viv nodded as one of the nurses ran over with the equipment. 'Okay, Tho, I'm going to check you over before we move you from the car. First thing…' She struggled, trying to find the words she needed, then catching sight of Mai Ahn waved her over. 'Sorry,' she apologised. 'Can you ask if she has any pain or numbness, in her neck or back or legs—apart from her labour pains, I mean?'

Mai Ahn looked startled by the last remark but collected herself and asked the question.

Viv grabbed hold of one of the other nurse's arms. 'Can you get me a neck collar from the orthopaedic clinic?' It wouldn't be as good as the ones that paramedics normally had in their ambulances, but hopefully it would immobilise Tho's neck enough for them to safely move her. She could hardly give birth in a car.

Mai Ahn turned back. 'No unexpected back pain, and she can move her legs and hands with no problems.'

'Thank you,' Viv breathed. She wound the BP cuff around Tho's arm and slipped a probe on her finger to check her pulse. Both were a little faster and higher than she'd expect—but then again, Tho had just been in a car accident.

'What happened to the child?' Tho asked. Tears were still falling down her face.

Viv glanced over her shoulder. Lien was dealing with the man in the upturned lorry, and both Joe and Duc were practically underneath the wheel arch, blocking her view completely.

Tho started babbling and Viv lost track of her words. Mai Ahn saw the distress and looked at Viv, asking for permission to come back over. Viv nodded, mouthing the word *please* at her.

Viv lifted the portable Doppler and waited a few moments until Tho had finished speaking to Mai Ahn.

Mai Ahn kept her face neutral. 'A little kid ran in front of first her car, and then the lorry. They both swerved to avoid him. She wants to know how he is.'

Impatient horns started to sound around them. Viv glanced up. The traffic was tailing back in every direction. She ignored it and nodded. 'Can you tell her that our doctors are looking after him, and that I'm going to listen to her baby now?'

She was always going to check on the health of the baby, but right now she was glad of the distraction for Tho.

Tho nodded and pulled her top up slightly. It only took Viv ten seconds to locate a heartbeat. She gave Tho a reassuring smile. 'It sounds good. But let's get you into the hospital, then we can contact your family.'

Tho looked relieved and Mai Ahn added another few words.

One of the nurses came over with a wheelchair. 'One minute,' said Viv.

She ran over to Lien. 'I want to move my pregnant woman. She's in active labour, her waters have broken but she's stable and I have a neck collar on her. But I'm not an expert on spinal injuries. Can you do a quick check before I move her?'

Lien nodded. 'Absolutely.'

The truck juddered and tilted towards them for a second and they both jumped. 'Sorry,' came the muffled shout underneath them.

Viv bent around the side and looked over the side of the overturned truck. Joe had his feet rooted on the ground and his back straining against the truck, giving it just a few inches of movement and allowing Duc to gently pull out the small child from under the wheel arch. Viv held her breath. The small boy was clearly unconscious, but his body and face seemed virtually unmarked. She'd been terrified about what might have been.

Sweat was coating them all. The heat outside was oppressive and as Viv turned, she saw an ice-juice cart at the corner of the street. Had that been what the little boy had been running towards?

Joe released the truck and immediately bent down next to Duc, checking the child's breathing and pulse. 'We're taking the trolley,' Duc said, waiting for Joe to come around and put his hands on either side of the child's face to stabilise his neck. Duc looked up at Lien. 'We'll send it back out for your man.'

Lien nodded and turned to Viv. 'Stay here. Give me two minutes and I'll check your woman.'

Viv gave a scared nod. Road traffic accidents weren't her thing at all. Her natural reaction had been to help. But she still felt out of her depth. She spoke a few words quietly to the man still behind the wheel. Keeping her fingers on his pulse and watching the rise and fall of his chest.

Lien was back in the promised two minutes. 'I've secured the collar and she seems stable to move. Mai Ahn will help you. Meet you back inside once I've got my man out of the truck.'

In the distance Viv could hear sirens. It was probably police. As soon as the traffic stopped in Hanoi, people called the police.

It took a few moments to help Tho into the wheel-chair, with Viv inconspicuously checking there was no sign of blood on the car seat or between her legs.

It was a relief to push her back into the air-conditioned hospital.

Sen met her at the door with a phone in her hand. 'Ron said to give him a rundown. He's about an hour away.'

Viv wasn't sure whether to be relieved or offended.

Sen had obviously decided to give their new obstetrician a call in case he was needed.

She was mindful of the fact this was one of his days off this week. But Ron had said he would always be flexible around his working hours—if there was an emergency, day or night, he wanted staff to feel as if they could call.

She hadn't had to do that—yet.

She let Mai Ahn take the lead with the wheelchair. 'Ron, I've got a lady at thirty-nine weeks with ruptured membranes and contractions who's just been in involved in a car accident outside the hospital. I've not had a chance to do a proper assessment. Blood pressure and pulse both slightly high, no other obvious injuries, and no sign of bleeding. Can I call you back if I have any concerns?'

She didn't want to be rude but was anxious to make a proper assessment of Tho. 'You've got it,' said Ron smoothly, as if he could read her mind. 'I'm sure you can handle things.'

'Thank you.' She smiled as she switched the phone off. It was good to know there was back-up if she required it.

It didn't take long to check Tho over. Yes, her waters had broken. Yes, she was in labour, which had started before she'd got into the car to drive to another hospital. Tho didn't stay in this area but worked in an office a few streets away. She was familiar with May Mắn Hospital and was just relieved to be somewhere that could look after her.

Viv set her up on a foetal monitor. Her blood pressure and pulse rate were slowly but surely coming down—in between contractions, of course.

Sen gave a knock at the door and Viv went out to speak to her. 'Tho's husband returned the call you made. He's stuck in the traffic jam. Might take a while to get here.'

Viv nodded. She had to admire the woman's ruthless efficiency.

One of the other nurses came to join her, wheeling in a cradle for the imminent arrival.

Viv relayed the message to Tho, then quickly took a maternal history. There was nothing that concerned her. She spent the next five minutes doing a basic examination of Tho's body to check for any other apparent injury. Tho tugged at the collar. Under normal circumstances patients involved in an accident should have an X-ray to make sure there were no neck or spinal injuries. But X-rays weren't easy for a woman in labour.

Viv took her hand. 'I need to get one of the doctors to recheck you before the collar can come off. I'm sorry, but it's best to be safe.'

Tho pulled a face but nodded. 'Let me finish another few checks,' said Viv.

'Can you find out how the little boy is?'

Viv gave a careful nod. 'I'll let you know as soon as I can.'

It only took a few minutes to confirm that labour was indeed established and Tho was five centimetres dilated. Viv made her as comfortable as possible and, because she was unfamiliar with Tho's plans for her birth, had Mai Ahn assist in the discussion.

One of the other nurses came into to relieve her for a few minutes and Viv gave Tho's hand a squeeze. 'I'll find out what I can and see if I can find out where your husband is.'

She hurried down the corridor, searching the rooms for Joe and Duc. As she turned one of the corners she almost walked straight into Lien. 'Oh, good, the little boy, how is he?'

Lien went to answer, then put a hand to her mouth and dashed into the nearest bathroom. Oh, no. Was it bad news?

Vivienne stood for a few moments then wrinkled her nose. Her spider sense was tingling. She stuck her head around the bathroom door. 'Lien,' she asked quietly, 'is there something you want to tell me?'

Lien spun around, a paper towel at her mouth and her eyes wide.

She didn't even make any attempt to deny it. She just moved over to Vivienne. 'Please, don't say anything. Joe and I want to keep things quiet for the first few months. We've still to tell our parents, and Regan.'

Vivienne smiled and shook her head. 'Lien, your secret is safe with me.' She reached out and gave her a huge hug. 'Congratulations, I'm so happy for you all.'

Something tugged inside. She'd spent her life congratulating friends and colleagues on being pregnant. She was a midwife. Of course she loved babies. But she'd never really thought about having one herself.

Of course, at some point in the future she'd always pictured herself eventually having a family. But it had always seemed so far away.

So why now—for the first time—did she feel a pang of something else? She didn't want to acknowledge it, because then she would need to admit it was a pang of envy, something she really didn't want to admit to.

Lien nodded gratefully. 'Sorry, I think it was just the shock of the accident and the heat outside.'

'Can I do anything for you?' asked Viv.

Lien shook her head. 'No, I just want to carry on as normal. I'll grab something to drink in the kitchen.'

Now it was Viv's turn to shake her head. She took Lien's hand and led her into the kitchen and sat her down at the small table, grabbing something from the fridge, filling two glasses, then adding ice.

She sat down opposite her. 'So, we're just two members of staff who've been involved in something scary, in searing heat, who are taking a five-minute break to get something to drink.'

Lien was watching her carefully. 'What is this?' she asked cautiously as she eyed the contents of the glass.

Viv smiled. 'You can read a million potential cures for nausea online. I always recommend this one to my mums. Apple juice, ice cold. Give it a try.'

Lien took a tentative sip, gave a nod and sat back a little in her chair. She gave a little sigh and then smiled at Vivienne. 'It feels good to finally have told someone.'

Viv raised her eyebrows. 'You didn't technically tell me. I guessed.' She scratched at an itch on her shoulder.

Lien waved her hand. 'Whatever.'

'Have you seen anyone yet? Have you had a scan?'

Lien's cheeks tinged pink. 'Not officially. But Joe and I might have sneaked over the other night.'

Viv laughed. 'Well, I can complete your booking paperwork and take your bloods whenever you like. And, I can do a proper scan.' She raised her hand. 'But it's entirely up to you to decide when you want that.' She looked at Lien carefully, she seemed a little more relaxed. 'And you know Ron will see you whenever you're ready.'

'I know.' She nodded. 'Just give us a little longer.'

She gave a dreamy kind of smile. 'There's something so nice about it still feeling like our little secret.'

The look on her face said it all—the connection between her and Joe. The love. Vivienne swallowed. All of a sudden her independent streak didn't seem quite so cool. All it made her feel was well and truly alone.

She gave herself a shake. 'You feeling okay?'

Lien nodded and took another sip of the apple juice. 'There might be something in your theory.'

Viv smiled then looked around. The clinic around them was surprisingly quiet. 'Where is everyone?'

'Oh, Duc is in Theatre.'

Viv straightened. 'With the kid?'

Lien shook her head. 'With my man—the guy from the truck. He had an open fractured tib and fib. Duc's taken him in to repair it.'

'So, what happened to the little boy?'

Lien's face was serious. 'Joe's taken him in an ambulance to one of the bigger hospitals—he needs a CT scan. He had no visible injuries apart from a few scrapes. But he still hadn't woken up.'

'Oh.' Viv sagged back in her chair. 'Tho, my pregnant woman, has been asking. She's upset. She wanted an update.'

Lien frowned. 'I'm not sure that either of the drivers hit him. I think they just skidded and hit each other because they swerved to avoid him.'

'So why's he unconscious?'

Lien shook her head. 'Joe and I suspect he got a fright, fell over and hit his head. Even then, there wasn't a big lump or anything on his head. We did the Glasgow coma scale on him and he had reactions to pain. He just didn't wake up.'

Viv put her hand up to her chest. 'I'll need to find a way to tell her something. Maybe just that he's been taken to another hospital, but I couldn't see any big injuries.'

Lien nodded. 'She'll just stress otherwise. You need to keep her calm. It's hardly an ideal start to her labour.'

Viv stood up and pulled her burgundy scrub top away from her body, scratching her bare arm again. 'I think I'll just change quickly before I go back in. Still feel a bit icky.' She gave Lien a smile. 'And I've got a baby to deliver. Tell Duc to come and see me when he's out of Theatre, would you?'

Lien gave a nod and Viv grabbed her juice glass and ducked back into the locker room. She ended up taking a quick two-minute shower and pulling on a fresh pair of scrubs, tying her hair up and tucking it away.

Just as she arrived back at the delivery room Tho's husband rushed along the corridor to meet her. Viv held up her hand. 'Slow down, everything's fine.' His anxious expression instantly changed to one of relief. She smiled and held the door open for him. 'Come in. In a few hours you'll meet your baby.'

Duc pulled his theatre cap from his head. He was a general surgeon, not an orthopaedic surgeon, but the open fracture had compromised some of the man's blood vessels. If he hadn't operated, the man could have ended up losing his leg.

He made his way down to the delivery room to check on the pregnant woman. The room was buzzing. He arrived just as Vivienne was handing the newborn baby to mum. She had a glow in her eyes. It was clear that she loved this part of her job.

He stayed silent for a few moments, watching her interactions with the new parents, as a little fire came to life somewhere inside him. He couldn't help the smile that appeared on his lips.

A thought burst across his brain. He could watch her all day.

Maybe he shouldn't be thinking like this, but he couldn't help it. He'd asked her to come here and help him—and she'd done that. Now he was contemplating trying to get his old job back. The appointment of Ron was a huge factor. Ron was a safe pair of hands—someone he could trust. The new midwife from Australia would start in a few weeks too. At that point, it seemed it might be time to recruit a new doctor and get his old life back.

But even though he'd sent the emails and received a semi-positive response, something was holding him back.

And the longer he stood here, the longer he thought that thing was Viv.

All of a sudden he wasn't thinking about work any more. It would be easy to list all the ways she'd helped around here—how adaptable she'd been—not least today.

But he was thinking of all the little things, the personal things she did. The way he sometimes caught her looking at him. The way he knew he sometimes looked at her.

There it was again. The flare of attraction he kept trying to temper down. The one he constantly tried to ignore.

Just at that moment she threw back her head and laughed as the baby started to make a whole load of noises, almost as if it was having a conversation.

His stomach clenched as her gaze connected with his. For a second it looked as though she caught her breath. Then she pasted on a smile and waved him in. 'Come and meet our latest arrival.' She gestured to the parents. 'This is Duc. He owns the hospital. And this…' she smiled down at the baby '…is Tho and Jin's beautiful baby daughter.' She winked at them both. 'Can't give you a name as yet, because they were convinced they were having a boy.'

He owns the hospital. The statement made his footsteps falter.

He pushed the uncomfortable thought from his head and went over to admire the baby. He spoke in a low voice to Vivienne. 'Do you need me to do anything for you?'

She gave a shake of her head. 'Lien said we should take a precautionary X-ray once Tho had delivered, but apart from that, everything seems good.'

She lowered her voice. 'Have you heard how the little guy is?'

He nodded and gave a smile of relief. 'He woke up around an hour ago. He's developed bruises to his back and hips and an egg on his head, but he's conscious and talking.'

Her smile spread across her face and right up into her eyes. 'Oh, thank goodness. Best news I've heard.'

'Busy tonight?' The words came out before he could stop them.

'Eh…no,' she said with a wrinkle across her brow.

'Good,' he said. 'In that case, we have plans.'

He gave her a smile. Right now he had no idea what those plans might be, but he would think of something.

CHAPTER ELEVEN

'WHERE ARE WE GOING?'

'Dancing.'

'What?' Viv's face was a picture. 'You don't dance.'

'I do. Well, I do now. Let's go.'

Duc was waiting for her by the door. Her eyes ran up and down his frame. 'Are these your dancing clothes?'

He looked down at his black shirt and blue jeans and held out his hands. 'Why, something wrong with them?'

He glanced back at her. She was wearing a pair of jeans and a black shirt tied at her waist. 'Hey—we look like a matching pair!'

She pulled a face and ducked back into her room, emerging one minute later with a bright green top scattered with some sequins.

She walked over to him as she grabbed her jacket near the door. For a second he saw her biting her lip.

'What's up?'

For the briefest of seconds his gaze meshed with hers. He thought she was going to say something deep, but she just shook her head and slung her bag over her shoulder. 'A horrible accident and three, no, four patients that are all doing okay. I think our hospital might have had some good luck today.' She winked at him. 'Maybe there's some magic to the name of this place. Okay, Mr Good Luck, it's time to take Crazy Scot number one dancing.' She shot him a glance as she bopped out of the door in front of him. 'Show me your moves!'

And as she shimmied away onto the grass he thought this might have been the best idea he'd ever had.

So far, they'd been to a bar that served American burgers, then hit three different bars and had a cocktail in every one of them.

By the time they reached the club she'd was ready to move on to water. They climbed the stairs of the club. Music was thumping, it felt like the walls around them reverberated with every beat.

The club was busy and the dance floor was packed.

She stared around at the bodies jumping up and down on the floor. 'I feel old,' she said, watching the synchronised vibe around her.

Duc bent down, his lips brushing against her ear. 'What?' he shouted.

'I feel old!' she yelled in his ear.

He laughed and grabbed her hand, pulling her towards the bar, which was packed three people deep. They jostled through the crowd as the music changed to a nineties rave tune and a scream went up around them.

It seemed the old-style tunes were the favourites.

Duc's broad shoulders took him to the front of the pack at the bar and he pulled her in tight behind him, spinning around and putting a hand on the back of her waist as he bent to talk to her.

'What do you want?' His lips touched her ear again. It couldn't be helped—but neither could her reaction to his touch. Every cell in her body seemed to spring to life.

'Just water,' she said.

'What?' His brow furrowed, the music was booming around them. This time as he pulled her even closer, her whole body was pressed against his.

It was like the crowd had just moved around them, giving her no room to step backwards. As she breathed in, her senses were assaulted by the smell of him. His aftershave, the scent of his shampoo, the laundry detergent from his clothes.

One hand went automatically to his shoulder. She stood on tiptoe, reversing positions so it was she who was talking in his ear.

The cocktails were still in her system: a strawberry daiquiri, a mimosa and a sex on the beach had made her bold and a little cheeky. This time it was her lips that brushed against his ear. How would his body react? Would he react the same way that she had?

He might try to hide it, but she felt him stiffen for the briefest of seconds. It made her smile. 'Just water,' she said in his ear, lingering longer than she needed to.

Part of her was annoyed. She'd seen that email today—even though she'd no intention of mentioning it. He wanted to leave. He wanted to go back to being a surgeon.

She should be happy for him, but the truth was it annoyed her. Couldn't he see how good it was here? Couldn't he see the wonderful opportunities he had at the tips of his fingers?

Part of her was irritated by that. Duc was a smart guy—at least she'd always thought of him that way.

He'd inherited not only a legacy but something he could make his own.

Viv had never had opportunities like this. The only thing she'd inherited from her birth mother was her hair colour. She didn't even know if her father was dead or alive. She had no intention of trying to find out.

As Duc's large brown eyes stared down into hers, she thought about how life might have been if their situations had been reversed. Would she be trying to run away from ownership of three hospitals, along with the responsibility and the staff?

Maybe she would. Maybe she didn't really understand. There was no career conflict for her here. She could do the job she loved every day here—along with opportunities to learn new skills.

There was no downside.

Duc narrowed his gaze and she realised she hadn't moved. Her face was only inches from his. The last time they'd been this close...

She could see the flicker of recognition in his eyes and she quickly turned away. Last time Duc had pulled away. She wouldn't give him a chance to do that to her again.

He turned back to the bar and she pushed her way free of the crowd, standing to the side. She'd only been there a few seconds when a tall blond guy approached her. He'd had a few drinks and was in a good mood, talking closely in her ear—it was the only way to do it in the noisy club—and asking her if she wanted to dance.

She shook her head. But he didn't want to take no for an answer.

He nodded towards the dance floor as the music

changed to another old tune. One that she liked. He held out a hand towards her, and after a few seconds' hesitation she took it. Why not? The electricity between Duc and her was close to setting her on fire. She had to expend her energy somewhere.

This guy was just her type. A bit merry, obviously a tourist, with no expectations of her—just like she would have none of him. Duc was planning on leaving. Why shouldn't she have a little fun?

The dance floor was busy, but not enough that she was crushed. The guy was from New Zealand. And he could dance.

Being here, in the middle of the dance floor, she could feel the energy all around her. It was electric. The guy was funny, a little drunk and he could move. She matched him, laughing away as they jumped up and down to the beat.

She couldn't remember the last time she'd been to a club and had fun like this. He grabbed one arm and spun her around, first one way and then the next.

It was fun. She was having fun. And all of a sudden she forgot about everything else.

Duc fought his way back from the crowded bar and looked around, scanning the crowd to see where Viv had gone.

He frowned, looking for her distinctive red hair. He thought she might have moved away from the claustrophobic bar and took a few steps nearer the dance floor.

He could feel the floor under his feet bounce with the movement of the people on the dance floor. Hands were in the air as everyone jumped up and down in time with a song that was distant memory from his student days. Even then, the song had been fifteen years old.

Then he saw it. The red hair swinging out wildly as Viv danced freely in the middle of the floor. She was dancing with someone. A guy with broad shoulders and blond hair. Duc felt an instant flare of jealousy.

She was laughing, the sequins on her top catching the lights in the club. It made her sparkle in the middle of the floor.

He couldn't take his eyes off her, mesmerised by the swing of her hips, the way he could see the skin at her waist as she punched her hands in the air. It had been years since he'd seen her like this. Free, laughing, enjoying life.

It was the way he loved her most.

That thought hit him like a spear through the heart.

The bottle of water nearly slipped from his hand.

It was as if all the little pieces of the jigsaw puzzle had just slotted into place in his brain.

He gave a shiver but kept watching. The guy grabbed Viv's hand and spun her round. She laughed and spun back the other way as the guy swayed with his movements.

Duc could feel his hackles rise. The guy was clearly drunk. It took every ounce of self-control not to storm over there and yank her away from him.

But what right did he have to do that? None. And Viv would eat him for breakfast.

He shook his head. He'd watched her a million times before, flirting or laughing with some guy, at times ending up in their arms—just like she'd watched him before with other girls.

Never once had it ground away so deeply in his stomach like it did tonight.

Viv twirled away, her arms in the air, sequins still sparkling. She sidled through the crowd, jigging in time to the music, back towards the bar. She spotted Duc and yelled, waving at him. The guy behind her was forgotten.

She was still dancing as she reached him, pressing both her hands on his chest. 'Come on, you promised to take me dancing!' She gave him a saucy look. 'You haven't shown me your moves yet!'

He handed her the bottle of the water. Part of him was relieved, but every cell in his body was still bristling. If Viv had put her hands around that guy's neck and started kissing him…

He put his hand around her waist. 'Think you can keep up?' he said throatily in her ear.

Her eyes were glistening. She grabbed his hands and pulled him back to the dance floor. The beat changed again, it was still fast paced—but not one of the old-type dance tunes. This was more eighties pop.

'Yeah!' Viv jumped up and down, happy with the beat. It maybe wasn't his first choice, but Duc had enough moves to match hers.

Her skin brushed against his as she twisted and turned. One kind of tension left his body, to be replaced entirely by another.

He had to keep his hands off, no matter how much they itched to touch her. They'd both had a few drinks. She was his best friend. The words continued to echo through his head.

Viv turned her back to him, lifted her arms once again and sidled backwards, still moving to the beat.

As her body came into full contact with his, his hand automatically slid around to the front of her stomach. As she continued to dance, the bare skin beneath his fingers felt on fire.

He was dancing in time with her. Their bodies moving together. And he knew he should step back. He knew he *had* to step back.

But then Viv spun around and put her hands around his neck, the whole length of her body up against his. She stood on tiptoe to talk in his ear. 'Okay, so I guess you can keep up. But take me home—I'm tired.'

As her lips moved from his ear they brushed against the side of his face.

He moved. The action was automatic—he couldn't help it.

Their lips locked. Her sweet taste against him. It didn't have the same urgency as their kiss the last time. This one was different. Like a little bubble had formed around them in the crowded club—like an old-fashioned snow globe—holding them in a time and space that was just their own.

Last time it had been him that pulled away, but this time it was Viv.

Her eyes were wide, but she seemed calm. She pressed her lips together and gestured with her head towards the door.

He followed her as she pushed through the club, heading for the stairs. His brain was rushing ahead of itself, wondering what came next.

But as soon as they hit the muggy air outside, she spun around and pointed to a cart across the street. 'I'm hungry, let's get some food.'

The streets were quieter in the early hours of the

morning and she darted across the road ahead of him. His heart was pounding in his chest. He couldn't read her at all.

He crossed the street and pulled some cash from his pocket, paying for the food she'd just ordered. Viv walked down the street, chatting as she ate. It was almost like nothing had happened between them.

But it had. He'd felt it. Every cell of his body was on permanent alert right now. Crying out to be next to her again.

It took him a few minutes to realise it was entirely deliberate. She was talking without talking. About the shops, the clubs, the people they worked with.

He took a few long, slow breaths. His brain was spinning. Watching her tonight had been like someone flicking a switch in his brain.

Why had they been such good friends all these years? Why had it never been more?

The swamp of caveman feelings he'd experienced in the club would never go down well with a free spirit like Viv. Truth was, he'd never felt them before—for anyone. So he was having a hard time figuring them out himself.

All he knew was that he had to speak to her.

The buzz was there. The attraction was there. He'd never wanted anything more.

She was still talking. Still filling the air between them with constant chatter.

He wanted to silence her with a kiss.

After some time they reached the outside of the hospital. She put her litter in the nearest trash can on the street and fell silent as they walked through the hospital. One of the nurses glanced at them both and gave them a knowing smile.

Did everyone see what was happening between them?

The silence echoed around them as they crossed the grass towards the bungalow. As Viv pushed open the door he started to speak. 'Viv...'

She turned and held up her hand. 'Don't.'

She walked inside and his chest tightened.

As he closed the door behind him she stood in the middle of the main room. 'Don't,' she repeated. 'We're friends. That was all. It was just a moment of madness.' Her eyes went downwards. '*Another* moment of madness.'

She stopped for a second then tilted her chin in a determined way towards him. 'It stops now. If we want to preserve our friendship, it stops now. You have one life to lead and I have another.'

Her voice shook a little at those last words then she turned, walked into her room, and closed the door.

Duc tried to breathe in. Last time he'd done this. Last time he'd been the one to step back.

But he'd stepped back without realising exactly how much his feelings for Vivienne had changed. Now they were front and centre to everything.

The closed door in front of his eyes hurt in a way he'd never imagined. He'd wanted a chance to speak to her, to tell how things had changed for him. He hadn't expected her to stop him dead. Because that was not how Viv functioned.

He wanted to throw open the door and demand that they talk this out.

But there had been something else in Viv's eyes. He'd known her too long not to see it.

She'd been happy tonight. Laughing and carefree with that other anonymous guy. When she'd come back to him, her eyes had been glistening with mischief and flirtation and he'd lapped it up, reacting to it in an instinctive way.

Because he didn't have a single doubt about what he wanted to happen next.

But Viv had looked hurt when she'd backed away. Why? This was what she wanted—and he would always respect her decision.

He breathed out, walking back over to the kitchen and pulling a beer from the fridge. As he looked around the house, he noticed things for the first time.

The shoes on the little stand in the corner of the room. The cupboard door ajar with coats hanging inside. The litter of things on the mantelpiece and side tables that were all items belonging to his parents.

For a few seconds he hung his head. He hadn't dealt with all this. And now it was time. Their clothes were still in the bedroom wardrobe. Those shoes and coats were his parents'. It was time to clear out and move on.

Viv's words about the lives they had to live echoed in his head. It had been a few months. Maybe he couldn't have faced this at first. But now it was time.

Now it was time for lots of things. And he had to make a new start.

CHAPTER TWELVE

VIV HELD LIEN'S hair back while she vomited in the sink. After a minute or so she grabbed a paper towel and wiped her mouth, straightening up with a huge sigh.

'I'm sorry,' she breathed. 'It just came out of nowhere.'

Viv had kicked the treatment-room door closed so they wouldn't be disturbed. 'How often has this been happening?'

Tears formed in Lien's eyes. 'Constantly. All day and most of the night too.'

Viv frowned. 'Please, don't tell me that you've been like this since the last time I caught you being sick?'

Lien gave a sorry nod.

'And you haven't told anyone? That's been more than two weeks!' Viv sighed and shook her head. 'What does Joe say?'

Lien wiped her eyes. 'He has no idea it's this bad. I don't want him to fuss.'

Viv rolled her eyes. 'Oh, I can guarantee he'll fuss. There's a name for this, Lien. Hyperemesis gravidarum. Let me take some bloods and hook you up to an IV.' She gave a sympathetic smile and wrapped her arm around Lien's shoulders. 'You can't hide this any more. Let me take care of you.' She winked at her. 'I'm the big bad midwife. You might not know it yet, but I'm actually the boss around here.'

Lien leaned against the wall, giving another sigh. 'We've told Regan. We've told our parents. But I haven't told any of the other doctors—or the nurses.' Tears still brimmed in her eyes. 'I haven't even told Duc yet. He needs all his doctors. We're still one down.'

Viv shook her head and took Lien's hand. 'Okay, this is the point you stop being a doctor and I start being your midwife. I'm going to phone Ron. I'm going to get him to order you to stop working, get some rest, and get started on an IV. You're dehydrated, Lien. We need to get this under control.'

Lien's eyes were glassy now, but she nodded and Viv understood. She'd needed someone to take the decision away from her, otherwise she'd just keep working until she finally collapsed.

Viv opened the treatment-room door and led her through to a single side room, grabbing a sick bowl on the way. 'Have a seat on the bed and I'll get things organised. And,' she said slowly, 'I'll go and grab Joe, and tell Duc he needs to come in and see you.'

Lien nodded. She already looked secretly relieved. Then she held up her hands. 'Take my bloods first, otherwise that pair will try and do it. I'd prefer it if it was you.'

'Of course.' Fifteen minutes later the bloods were taken, Ron had consulted with them over the phone, insisting he'd be in that evening to see Lien, and the IV was in situ.

Viv walked down the corridor to Theatre and shook off the headache she was having. Last night had been

weird. She'd had chills, actual chills, and had woken
up sweating so badly she'd had to change her pyjamas.
When she'd checked her temperature it had been high.
Truth was she'd felt kind of weird the last few days.
She'd hoped she wasn't coming down with something
so she'd taken some paracetamol then, and a few more
this morning. She still wasn't feeling a hundred per
cent, but she had a job to do. There wasn't time to be
sick. She pushed open the door to where Duc and Joe
had just finished and were changing into clean scrubs.

'Hey, guys,' she said, as the door banged open.

Both looked up, surprised. It wasn't that she hadn't
seen either of them in a state of undress before—the
theatre changing room was shared. It was just unusual
for her to come in unannounced.

'Something wrong?' Joe asked immediately.

She gave him a nod. 'I have a new patient in room
seven. Hyperemesis gravidarum. Eleven weeks. Dehydrated and hooked up to an IV.'

Joe let out an expletive and walked straight out the
door.

Duc was clearly confused. 'What am I missing? Is
Ron not available?'

It was clear he was thinking about the patient and
symptoms. This wasn't usually the kind of patient Viv
would bring to him.

His frown deepened as he processed Joe's reaction,
then she could see recognition forming in his brain. She
nodded. 'It's Lien. I said I'd come and get you both.'

He finished pulling a fresh scrub top over his head.
She couldn't miss the broad shoulders and abs, but she
was telling herself not to look at them, just to focus on
his face because that was safer. But was it?

Ever since that second kiss, she'd had dreams every night that were filled with Duc. Every morning she woke up angry with her subconscious for letting him in. He would be leaving soon. She had to stop associating this place with him. Particularly when she liked this place so much.

The previous fleeting thoughts about this place feeling like home had been pushed from her head. She'd recognised that she'd started to associate Duc with feeling like home. That wouldn't happen. She'd been crazy to even think about things for a second. It was a waste of time and energy, and if she focused on the angry part, she could try and forget the hurt part.

Because if she thought about it too much, it played havoc with her senses. Her brain was so glad she didn't have to contemplate the thought of Duc not wanting to leave, because where would that leave her? She'd have to face up to how much her feelings towards him had changed, and what that was doing to her. Even at the club, that guy who'd asked her to dance had been her 'safe' option. The type she always chose. Because there was no attachment, no relationship potential. She could keep that shell around herself perfectly in place. But if it was Duc...

She was trying hard to keep things on an even keel between them.

Things had been awkwardly casual. It was the way it had to be.

She appreciated that he hadn't pressed her on what had happened between them. But it meant that once again there was a tension in the air between them, both of them finishing conversations as quickly as possible and moving on.

He still hadn't told her about returning to his surgical position, and she almost understood that. The old ease between them had gone. Previously she would have expected him to tell her almost everything. But now? Would he be the first person she would tell about any life-changing plans? Probably not.

Now he gave her a half-scowl. 'Why didn't you tell me Lien was pregnant? Why didn't you tell me she was sick?'

He'd started down the corridor with long strides and she had to run to keep up. She grabbed his hand, making him stop. 'If I have to explain patient confidentiality to you, Duc, it's a bad day between us.'

There was a flash of fury in his eyes. She almost expected him to spit out, 'Isn't that normal for us now?'

Instead, she watched him take a deep breath. 'I thought we practically had a shared brain, Viv. You tell me, I tell you. It doesn't go any further.'

She met his gaze head on as a surge of anger pulsed through her. She could so easily spit out that she'd seen his email. But she didn't. She just shook her head. 'So did I,' she said instead, and walked past him into Lien's room.

Joe was sitting on the bed next to her with his arm around Lien's shoulders.

He looked at Viv straight away. 'Did Ron give you a time?'

She nodded. 'He just sent me a text. He'll be here at five-thirty.'

Duc walked around her and bent to kiss Lien on the side of the cheek. 'Congratulations, Mumma. Now, what can I do to help you?'

Lien laid her exhausted head back on the pillow.

'Cover her shifts,' Viv answered for her. 'Lien needs some time out. Sometimes this passes—sometimes it can last a whole pregnancy, and right now we have no way of knowing.'

Duc nodded. 'Fine. I had some enquiries the other day. A doctor who worked here with my mother and father wondered about coming back for a spell.'

Joe looked up. 'That would be ideal. You know that your mum and dad will already have checked them out. It would save the time of having to advertise and interview for a job.'

Duc nodded. 'I'll get Sen to pull out their file. Unless there's anything to give concern, I'll see when they can start.'

Lien's brow furrowed. 'Do you have a name? I might have been here when they worked here before.'

Duc nodded and pulled his phone from his pocket checking his emails. 'Yip, here it is. A French guy, Emile Dupont?'

Lien smiled as she closed her eyes. 'Ah, I remember him. He's in his fifties. He's a great doctor, very lyrical.'

Viv frowned. 'What do you mean?'

Lien kept her eyes closed. 'He's like a walking poet. His grasp of the language is good, and he can talk to patients for hours. They get almost mesmerised by him.' She opened her eyes for a second and met Duc's gaze. 'He's a good fit. He'll do well. I hope he can make it.'

'Consider it done.' Duc sounded determined. Viv could see the worry on his face as he looked at his friend.

She liked that about him. Part of her felt a little guilty for not telling him about Lien, but her professional head reassured her she'd done the right thing. The good thing was she was confident he would do anything he could to help Lien—as would the rest of the staff.

She gave a nod. Joe was stroking Lien's hair and she could tell they needed a little time alone. 'Hey, guys, can I pick up Regan for you at nursery?'

Joe shot her a grateful look. 'That would be great. I'll call and tell them you'll be there. Thanks so much.'

'No problem.' Viv checked Lien's IV one more time, filling in her charts before leaving the room and giving a quick handover to the nurse in charge.

Duc followed her out of the room. 'Viv.' She turned, thinking he was going to complain, but instead he gave her a grateful glance. 'Thanks for looking after Lien. I'm sorry I snapped at you. Of course you couldn't tell me, and I know she's in safe hands with you and Ron.'

She breathed a sigh of relief. 'Don't worry, Duc. If I need to consult at some point, I will.'

He nodded, reassured, then paused, and she could tell he was going to say something else. Her stomach clenched as she waited.

'Could you give me a hand with something later?'

'Sure,' she said cautiously, wondering what on earth she'd just got herself into. That headache was still nagging away at her.

'I need to have a clearout—for the goodwill store. I should have done it earlier, but I guess—' his brown eyes met hers '—I wasn't ready yet.'

She understood instantly. She knew the cupboards were still stuffed with his parents' clothes and possessions. She'd never said anything because it wasn't her issue to push. She gave a nod. 'Let me pick up Regan and I'll help you when I get back.' She turned to leave then gave a little smile. 'Stick around for a bit in case Lien needs anything prescribed.'

She knew he was frustrated about his friend and letting him feel valuable would help them both. Joe shouldn't really prescribe anything for his wife, so until Ron arrived, Duc would be in charge.

'Sure.' He nodded and took a seat behind the desk at the nurses' station. Somehow Viv knew he would still be sitting there when she got back.

Duc was feeling odd. He supposed it wasn't unusual. He'd collected a host of boxes and bags. Viv appeared at the bedroom door, looking looked a little paler than normal. 'Let's be methodical about this,' she said. She'd changed into a pair of old joggers and an oversized T-shirt, her hair tied up high on her head. He was glad. She knew exactly how big a job this was going to be.

She went to one of the kitchen drawers, found a black marker and started writing on a few of the boxes. The word *Goodwill* adorned a few, *Keep* adorned another, and at the last second she paused, finally writing *Completed* on it.

'Okay,' she breathed. 'We'll start with the clothes. Anything that's in good or reasonable condition goes to goodwill, anything you want to keep for yourself goes in the keep box, and the rest of things, like underwear, et cetera, we'll put in the completed box.'

Now he understood. She hadn't wanted to write *Garbage* or *Disposal* on it. *Completed* was a nicer way to label all the things he'd have to take to the dump.

He nodded. She grabbed her phone and set it on the speakers. He wondered what she was doing, but then a familiar playlist filled his ears. It was songs they'd

listened to across the span of their friendship. Most
of them had a memory attached. But it was a memory
of Viv and Duc—usually fun and light-hearted. Feel-
good sorts of songs. Something to distract them while
they worked. She pulled out a bowl and filled it with
the chocolate they always ate in the UK.

'Where did you get them?' he asked.

She smiled. 'I had them stashed. Seemed like a good
time to share.'

He leaned over and gave her a hug, not letting it
mean anything more than it should. She was doing this
for him.

It was harder than he'd thought. Every now and then
a flash of his mum or dad's clothing would give him
a flashback—a memory from the past. Several times
he had to stop and just breathe. Viv watched quietly.

She was methodical, folding his mother's clothes
into piles neatly in the appropriate box. He hesitated
over a familiar shirt of his father's. He eventually shook
his head and put it in the goodwill box along with the
others.

Books were next, with him keeping a few. Then
shoes which were all bagged up for goodwill too. The
photograph albums he left in a cupboard. They could
be done another day. Viv helped him wrap some older
ornaments in tissue paper and pack them away. A few
were sentimental but some could go.

He watched as she sighed as she wrapped things in
tissue paper, her hands pausing. Her voice was quiet.
'Last time I did this was for my mum.'

She glanced up at him. He could see the hidden tears
in her eyes. 'My adoptive mum,' she clarified. 'You

think that you're ready but packing up the house is hard. It hits your gut in places you just don't expect it to.'

He reached over and laid his hand over hers for a second. He'd expected this to be hard, but he'd forgotten that this would bring up memories for Viv too.

'You don't need to help.' His voice was hoarse.

Her eyes met his. 'Yes,' she said clearly. 'I do.'

She stood and walked through to the bedroom, coming out a few moments later with his mother's jewellery box in her hands. 'What about this?' she asked tentatively. 'Will we just put it somewhere safe?'

He shook his head and held his hands out. 'Bring it here. My mum had a vast collection of jewellery, most of it just decorative. There are only a few things that are special.'

She sat next to him on the sofa and set the wooden box on his knees. Duc paused for a moment, noticing his hands were shaking. This should be routine. There were millions of people around the world who'd had to do this. He wasn't the first person to pack up the belongings of his mother and father.

He opened the box and lifted out the first item, a black jewelled necklace. It was something his mother had worn frequently because it had gone with lots of her clothes. He passed it to Viv without a word. A long silver chain followed, then a necklace with a large red charm. There were a number of bracelets and bangles. Some he didn't recognise at all, and he passed them one by one to Viv. He stopped at a tri-gold bangle, the three colour strands twisted together. He put that back in the box. It had been an anniversary present from his father.

Then there was a gold locket. He turned it over in his hands. It was followed by an emerald-and-diamond ring.

His mother and father had been buried wearing their wedding rings. He hadn't thought to question where his mother's engagement ring was. He hadn't thought about it until now.

A sound caught in his throat.

Viv's hand came next to his. She intertwined their pinkies but didn't say the words. She didn't have to. The warm feeling spread through his skin.

'Of course,' he said softly. 'She wouldn't wear her engagement ring at work. Infection control.' His finger ran across the face of the emerald with diamonds set on either side.

Viv spoke quietly. 'It's nice, you know. That you have something to cherish that belonged to your parents. Something you can keep and remember them by.' Her voice had a strange tone to it. 'I remember your mother wearing that ring on occasion. She loved it. It meant so much to her.'

He looked up to catch the expression on her face. It made him catch his breath.

The look in her eyes was distant. It wasn't envy, it was sorrow. It struck straight to his heart.

This was the second time he'd realised what he had in comparison to her. How not everyone grew up with happy memories and safe lives.

He took the last things from the box, leaving just the bangle, the locket and the ring. His eyes fell on the packed boxes covering the floor. 'I think this is enough for today.'

She nodded and pressed her lips together. 'Sometimes I wonder if you know what you've got here, Duc.'

He looked up sharply. 'What do you mean?'

She took a deep breath. 'I mean, I like this place. It's

already wonderful, and you could make it even better. I haven't even seen the other two hospitals. I have no idea of the potential there.'

He was surprised. 'Viv, you almost sound like you don't want to move on.'

She stood up quickly, not wanting to get into any conversations like this. 'You know me,' she said breezily. 'I don't put down roots.' But when she swallowed there was a lump in her throat. Even though they were sorting through Duc's parents' things, it was hitting her hard. It was bringing home to her just how isolated an existence she led. Who would do this for her one day? She couldn't even bear to think about it.

She'd spent so long being self-sufficient, not giving any part of herself to someone else, because she didn't trust anyone with her heart, and her life.

She blinked away the tears that formed in her eyes. Even Duc. She'd pushed away the one person who'd managed to break through her barriers a little.

Now it was her turn to have shaky hands. She'd seen the relationship between Lien and Joe. It actually made her stomach ache she envied it so much—the togetherness. The 'us against the world' mentality of it all. Joe had lost his first wife. How hard had it been for him to reach out again?

She sucked in a breath through her teeth, willing it to steady her hands and her heart rate. Tiny parts of Hanoi had been tugging away at her heart this past few months.

She loved the people, she loved the buzz of the streets, she loved the work. It was the first time in a job where she hadn't started automatically looking for something else a few months in.

But Duc was a huge, huge part of this.

Would she want to stay if he wasn't here?

His voice was quiet. 'But you can't be like that for ever. At some point, in some place, you might find a place that you don't want to leave six months later. Do you think this could be the place?'

It was almost like he was reading her mind.

She looked up at him, her eyes wide. 'How can it be the place, Duc? It's yours. It belongs to you—and you don't even want to be here.'

She could feel the anger rise in her chest. 'I've told you before to look around you—look at what you potentially have. But you don't want it.' She shook her head. 'I just don't get it. Everything handed to you on a plate and you want to walk away.' Now she really was shaking all over. 'I saw the email. You didn't even tell me about it—but I know you're going back to the surgical programme. So what's the point of asking me if I want to stay when you want to run away?'

She could have asked about this earlier—she'd wanted to. But part of it had been pride. She'd wanted him to tell her himself. And the other part? That was being afraid of his answer. The reasons why he wanted to go back. She didn't need to hear that she just wasn't enough for him to consider staying.

Duc flinched. 'You think I'm running away? And you think all this came on a plate?' He flung out his hands. 'I got this because my parents are dead, Viv. Not because I chose it.' He was mad and he couldn't hide it.

But Viv didn't back down, she was too riled up. She leaned towards him. 'Well, you should. You should choose it. You should want it. Because I do.'

The words came out of nowhere from a place deep

inside her and they both stopped talking and stared at each other for a few silent seconds.

Duc reached up and touched her shoulder. 'You want to stay?' His touch seemed to still her trembling body.

Panic gripped her. She'd said that out loud. She hadn't meant to, and Duc was looking at her in the strangest way…

'No,' she shot back quickly, trying to find a way to retreat. 'Of course not.'

'You do.' He shook his head. 'Admit it. You like it here. You want to stay.'

It felt as if her throat was closing over. No words would come out. She felt exposed. As if he could see inside her. She didn't like that—she wasn't ready for it.

Her head was pounding again. She stood up and walked over to the cupboard to find some more paracetamol. Duc followed her. 'We need to talk about this.'

'No,' she said determinedly. 'We don't. What difference does it make anyway? You want to leave. I want to stay. What's there to talk about?'

She popped some paracetamol from the foil and grabbed some water. Duc's eyes went to the medicine. 'What's wrong?'

She shook her head. She didn't want to discuss this with him either. But before she had a chance to respond his brow furrowed. 'Who said I was going back to surgery? I might have made a few queries, but I haven't decided that.'

She was starting to see spots in front of her eyes. 'If you're not going back, why ask the question?'

Her stomach cramped as a wave of nausea swept

over her. All of a sudden she knew she needed to lie down. Maybe if she did, this headache would go away.

Duc glanced at her, a worried expression on his face as he moved closer. He sighed. 'I was keeping my options open. But the longer I stay here, the more I realise what I can do. You're right, there's a world of opportunity here. It's just taken me a while to see it. I was so set on being a surgeon that I didn't really take the time to consider other options. But now...' He let his voice tail off.

He blurred. Either that or he moved a supersonic speed. Or maybe he didn't. She was going to be sick. The tiny spots that had appeared at the edges of her vision threatened to take over.

Then all of a sudden everything went black.

The last thing she felt was Duc's arms around her as the world slipped away.

CHAPTER THIRTEEN

'WHAT ON EARTH HAPPENED?'

Joe met him in the corridor as he carried the collapsed Viv in his arms over to the hospital. His arms were starting to shake as Joe took part of the weight and they carried her over to a trolley.

'She had a headache. She felt sick, then she just went.'

He was as confused as Joe, trying to put the pieces together.

Joe moved straight into doctor mode—he wasn't blinded by the emotion that encompassed Duc.

'Let me check her over.' He turned, giving Duc a look that told him he expected him to leave the room, as one of the nurses rushed in to assist.

'Viv!' She gave a strangled little cry as she realised who it was, and her reaction made Duc aware of just how much the staff here loved Viv.

He took a few steps out to the corridor, staring down the hallway. The irony. Joe's wife was in a room just up the hall and officially Joe shouldn't treat her. Now Viv was in this room, and Duc knew deep down that the same rules should apply.

Joe shouted out to him, 'Go and check back in the

bungalow and see if you find any clues. Any medications. Anything that could cause this.'

Duc shivered. Did Joe think this was deliberate? No way. He ran back across the grass to the bungalow, throwing open the door to Viv's room and looking around. There was nothing. Nothing to give him cause for concern. He tripped over a pile of pyjamas on the floor and bent down to pick them up, and then he froze. They were damp. Just a little. But the temperature in here was warm, meaning they had much damper when they'd been taken off.

Had Viv had a temperature last night? Sweats? Why hadn't she mentioned it? She'd just got up and gone straight to work this morning.

Something sparked in his brain. Those paracetamol had been sitting out earlier. It was he who had put them back in the cupboard while making breakfast. She'd either had a temperature last night or a headache.

He dashed back across the grass, stopping at the door of the examination room. 'Paracetamol,' he said quickly to Joe. 'She's been taking them since the middle of the night. She said she had a headache just before she collapsed but I think she's had a temperature too as she changed in the middle of the night.'

Joe looked up, his face grave. He was at the far side of Viv. But before he got a chance to speak one of the nurses rushed down from Lien's room. 'Lien said to check her over. She said at the accident scene a few weeks ago Viv rushed out to help wearing just her short-sleeved scrubs. Could she have been bitten by a mosquito? Lien thinks she remembers seeing her scratching a few times.'

They all exchanged glances and Duc felt sick to his

stomach. He'd been there too and hadn't even considered the dangers for Viv. They'd all been too focused on the accident. Had he noticed her scratching since then?

'But I always remind her about wearing repellent. She's good at it.'

'Has she been shaking at all?'

Duc felt cold. The list of symptoms were forming in his head. 'She was trembling earlier.'

Joe pulled a face. 'There's a mosquito bite here. Right around the back of her upper arm. Impossible for her to see properly, but still somewhere she could scratch.'

He gave some instructions to the nurse. 'Get me some blood bottles and a cannula I need some ACT and a glucose drip.'

Duc couldn't help himself. 'Let me help.'

Joe looked up. 'No.'

'If it was Lien, would you take no for an answer?'

Joe paused for just a second, then waved his hand. 'You draw up the drugs while I take the bloods.'

Duc was shaking his head as he drew up the broad-spectrum antibiotic. 'How can it be malaria? It's supposed to be virtually eradicated in city areas. She's been taking her medication. I don't get it—I just don't get it.' He couldn't stop the frustration bubbling inside him.

'Virtually eradicated,' said Joe carefully. 'Not completely. And we have to treat what we see.' He finished inserting the cannula and attached the glucose drip. 'What I do see is an infected mosquito bite. Maybe she missed a dose of her medication. Maybe she's part of the ten per cent it isn't completely effective for.'

As Viv gave a few twitches on the bed, Joe kept his voice steady and calm. 'I think we have signs of cerebral oedema. You know how we need to treat this. We can't waste time fighting about it. Time is too important.'

A chill spread over Duc's body. He knew Joe was right, but he hated him right now for saying the words out loud. Duc couldn't remember the last time he'd seen a fatal malaria case—but he'd spent the last few years in the US.

He'd brought her here. He'd asked her to come. She would never have set foot in Hanoi if it hadn't been for him. This was all his fault. If anything happened to Viv, he would never forgive himself.

Her onset had seemed quick. She could have been bitten up to two weeks ago, but her actual symptoms only seemed to have been emerging over the last day or so. Just how virulent was this parasite?

'What's her blood sugar?'

Joe looked up as he pulled up a chair to the bed and turned a chart around.

Duc gulped. It was low. Malaria caused hypoglycaemia. The glucose drip should bring it up, but if she still remained unconscious once her blood sugar was corrected it meant that cerebral malaria had taken hold—and that could be fatal.

He handed over the other drugs to Joe, who started to administer them slowly. If Joe noticed his shaking hands he didn't say anything.

Maybe he should go and spend time with Lien while Joe was here, but the truth was he just couldn't leave Viv's side.

Joe caught his gaze. It was almost like he could read his mind. 'Lien's sleeping right now. The vomiting has really taken it out of her. She needs some rest.'

Duc nodded, his hand reaching across the sheet to

intertwine with Viv's. She was deathly pale. It was amazing. The whole time Viv had been here her skin had seemed kind of sun-kissed. But maybe it just seemed that way because she was normally so full of life. Right now, she was paler than he'd ever known her.

His eyes fixed on the thin gold chain around her neck leading to the butterfly pendant. The one he'd bought. The one she always wore.

Her hand twitched in his. He was back on his feet in an instant.

Then her arm twitched, then her whole body started convulsing. Duc pulled her over onto her side, trying his best to get her into the recovery position. Ron appeared at the door and took one look, sizing up the scene in seconds.

'What drugs do you need?' he asked Joe.

Joe rattled them off and Ron reappeared in the blink of an eye. 'Let me help,' he said. Joe was trying to support Viv's airway as Duc kept a firm hold of her twitching body. He'd glanced at the clock as she'd started and was praying this wouldn't last more than a minute. His head was close to her hair and the orange scent of her shampoo was filling his senses. He felt panicked. He'd only just realised that he loved her, and he hadn't had a chance to tell her yet. To tell her that he'd been thinking about nothing else.

He'd thought there was time. He'd thought there was plenty time. He'd been figuring out about the job—and she'd challenged him in that too. Viv seemed to know his life before he did.

He'd just decided to turn down the position he'd been offered. He could still be a surgeon and work here. But he could also be a doctor. A person who worked with the most disadvantaged population on a daily basis.

The thing that had driven him to go to medical school. He'd forgotten about it for a while, getting caught up in the bright lights and competitiveness of the surgical rotations. It had taken all this for him to realise he should take another breath, reassess.

All the things that Viv had said to him.

Viv, the woman he was holding in his arms. The woman that he loved. Maybe he'd always loved her and had just been afraid to say it out loud. Or maybe it was just the change of time and conditions for them both.

Whatever it was, it was here. It was now. And, as his gaze flickered to Joe and he could see the worry in his colleague's eyes, his heart plummeted.

He could only pray he'd get a chance to tell her.

Ron came around and held her arm firmly to access the cannula and insert the drugs. Worry streaked across his forehead. 'When did Viv become ill?' he asked.

'In the last hour,' said Duc, his voice cracking. 'We think she may have been bitten when she helped at the RTA the other week. But she only complained of a headache today.'

'That's all?' Ron's brow remained creased.

'I think she was having night sweats too and just didn't say anything. I found her nightclothes back in the bungalow.'

Ron winced. 'A sudden onset, then.' The words struck them all, and they exchanged glances. They all knew exactly how serious that could be.

'Has she been taking anti-malarials?'

Duc nodded. 'Religiously.'

'Could be a resistant strain or a new one?' said Ron

thoughtfully. Viv's body started to cease twitching, the movements becoming smaller and less pronounced.

There was a collective sigh of relief.

'Did you take bloods?' Ron queried.

Joe nodded.

Ron straightened. 'Let me follow them up. I have connections at the city lab. I can get them fast-tracked and see if there is anything else we can start her on.'

As he headed to the door he stopped and put a hand on Joe's shoulder. 'Give me five minutes and I'm all yours. We'll get Lien sorted too.' He gave him a smile. 'Congratulations.'

Duc felt numb. Of course. He should be celebrating his friends' good news. But somehow that had gone completely out of his head. One of the nurses appeared at the door with a cardiac monitor and BP cuff on a portable trolley. Duc rolled Viv onto her back and let the nurse attach them. 'I'll stay with her,' she said.

But Duc shook his head. 'No. I will.' He sat down by her bed and took her hand again, raising his gaze to Joe. 'Thank you.'

Joe nodded. 'I'm just down the corridor. Shout for me anytime.'

'Me too,' reiterated the nurse.

They both left, leaving the only noise in the room the sound of the monitor and Viv breathing.

Duc leaned forward and brushed a strand of her hair from her face. He couldn't believe this had happened. All his fault. If he'd never asked her to come here, she would be back in England somewhere—somewhere safe.

Her skin was soft to his touch. 'Wake up, Viv,' he

whispered. 'Please, wake up. Wake up and I'll do anything you want. I'll give you anything you want.'

Her breathing continued, steady and calm. He'd thought the worst day of his life had been the phone call about his parents, but now? This was a close rival.

He intertwined his fingers with hers. 'I can't lose you, I just can't.'

Nothing mattered more to him right now. Nothing at all. The pulse of attraction that had buzzed between them. The kisses they'd shared. The fights. All he wanted was his Viv back.

But as he looked at her lying on the bed, so pale she practically matched the sheets, his guts twisted.

There might be chance that wouldn't happen.

He adjusted their hands so their pinkies intertwined. 'Friends for ever,' he whispered.

CHAPTER FOURTEEN

HE STAYED THERE for two days and two nights, terrified that if he left something else might happen.

Her blood-sugar readings came back to normal relatively quickly. But still she didn't wake up.

The staff was great. He still had a job to do, so they would bring him charts to sign along with cups of tea and snacks. Joe brought him in a towel and a fresh pair of scrubs with a pointed nod, so he used the shower in the bathroom attached to Viv's room so he wasn't too far away.

Lien was still unwell too. It was unlikely she'd be able to resume duties anytime soon. That didn't stop her wheeling her IV down the corridor and coming in to speak to them both, clutching a sick bowl in one hand.

Ron had been as good as his word. Viv's bloods had been fast-tracked and after a quick consultation with another expert they'd started her on an alternative medication. Right now, Duc would try anything.

It was late at night. Duc had pulled in a more comfortable chair so he could sleep next to her bed. It was the kind that could recline and even though the nurses could do it in the blink of an eye, it always took him about five minutes to figure it out.

Just as he finally managed to push it back there was a little moan from the bed.

He froze. And spun around.

It was the first sign of anything from Viv in two days.

He leaned forward, grasping her hand again. 'Viv, it's Duc. Can you hear me?'

Nothing. His eyes went to the monitor, willing the heart rate to speed up to give him some kind of sign that she was listening, that she was hearing him.

But it just continued to blip along.

Frustration gripped him and all the while he told himself to remain calm. It was *something*.

After hovering over her bed for an age, he finally settled down into the chair beside her bed. 'I'm here, Viv,' he said quietly. 'Whenever you need me, I'm here.'

Sleep finally claimed him but he woke in the early hours of the morning. He sat straight up, wondering what had woken him. It was dark outside with only a smattering of stars in the sky. He frowned, straining to hear any noise in the corridor outside. Had it been one of the nurses? A phone perhaps?

He pushed the chair forward, planting his feet on the floor.

There was a noise, a groan again and he was instantly on high alert. 'Viv?'

Her nose was wrinkled. 'Headache,' she croaked.

'Brilliant!' he shouted, leaning over and gathering her up in his arms. Her body was still weak, and she didn't return the hug. He pressed the nurse call button.

'You have no idea how worried we've all been,' he breathed. 'I am so, so sorry.'

It was almost like she wasn't really processing his

words. 'Headache,' she repeated as she sagged back into the pillows.

The nurse appeared at the door, her eyes wide. 'She's awake?'

He nodded. 'Just. Can you get Viv something for a headache?'

The nurse nodded and disappeared, coming back a minute later with a glass of water with a straw and a couple of pills.

'Let's try these first.'

Duc wound the bed up and helped Viv adjust her position so she could take a tiny sip of water. She coughed and spluttered. She still hadn't really opened her eyes.

He tried to move into doctor mode and ask a few standard questions, but her replies were distinctly groggy.

He knew her body was hydrated because of her IV, but she still hadn't drunk any fluids in two days.

After a minute or so she held out her hand for the tablets and swallowed them awkwardly. Her eyes closed immediately.

Duc wanted to shake her, to make her try and talk again, to see what else he could do. But the nurse shot him a warning look. 'Our patient needs rest. Take it from someone who's had malaria.'

He pushed himself to give her a smile. She was right. He knew she was right. But so much was bubbling inside him right now.

She headed for the door. 'I don't suppose there's any point in me trying to persuade you to spend the night in your own bed now that she's woken up?'

He shook his head. 'None at all.'

She shook her head too, giving him an amused smile. 'Didn't think so.'

* * *

Her head was fuzzy. And not a good kind of fuzzy. Somehow this felt like the worst hangover on the planet; in fact, she'd never actually had a hangover this bad.

And she was tired. Really, really tired. This didn't feel normal.

She turned around in her bed, wondering why she couldn't get comfortable. The sheets were stiff. So was the pillow. Had Duc changed her bedding?

Her eyelids flickered open. White. Everywhere. That wasn't right. She'd grown used to the pleasant washed-out red of the walls in Duc's house.

If she had the energy she'd sit up. But she didn't.

Then she saw Duc in a chair next to her. Why would he be sitting by her bed? He looked terrible.

She didn't even need to speak because his eyelids flickered open and he jerked then leaned forward, grabbing her hand. 'Viv, you're awake. How are you feeling?'

Now she really couldn't make sense of things at all. 'Wh-what?' was all that came out.

Her joints ached. She looked down. These weren't her PJs. She wrinkled her nose as she realised she was wearing a hospital gown. She pulled it away from her body. 'What?' she asked again.

'You haven't been well,' Duc said quickly, his face grave. 'You have malaria. We think you got bitten while helping at the accident—you had short sleeves that day.'

Malaria? 'But I take the meds…'

His hand was still touching hers. It was almost like he didn't want to let go.

'I know,' he said, then shook his head. 'But for some

reason they've not worked. They're doing some special bloodwork to find out more.'

He looked at her seriously. 'Why didn't you tell me you weren't feeling well? The night sweats? The headaches? Was there anything else?'

She honestly couldn't remember right now. Plus, right now this felt like a bit of a lecture.

'I need to sleep,' she said firmly, closing her eyes and curling on her side again. Next time she woke up she'd complain about these sheets and the hospital gown…

It was four days before Viv was anything like normal again. She was cranky, and constantly tired. It had to be expected. She still couldn't seem to get her head around the fact she'd contracted malaria.

All the hospital staff kept popping in. Joe was a constant, as was Duc, with an occasional visit from Lien, who was still suffering from her hyperemesis gravidarum. Ron had even dropped in on a few occasions, bringing tea and sitting down to chat.

She still couldn't believe this had happened to her. Now, in hindsight, she remembered having an itch on the back of her arm. But she'd never even thought to look at it in the mirror. She'd been too busy. There had been too much else going on.

Too much Duc…

Today she'd managed to persuade him to let her go back and sleep in her own bed. At least, that was how she still thought of it. But he'd insisted on carrying her the whole way.

She hadn't been amused.

She'd also had to promise that people could come in

and 'check' on her. It seemed no one was listening when she insisted she was a nurse and could look after herself.

The bungalow was a lot tidier since the last time she'd been here. 'What happened to all the boxes?' she asked as Duc carried her through the main room.

He had the good grace to look sheepish. 'Mai Ahn. When you collapsed, I took you straight across to the hospital and stayed with you. I kind of forgot we'd been in the middle of things. But Mai Ahn came and asked if she could do anything to help and offered to take the boxes to goodwill for me.'

Of course. They'd been in the middle of emptying out his parents' things. She remembered the emotions on his face. How final it all must have seemed to him.

'Sorry,' she muttered.

'What?' he looked surprised. 'What have you got to be sorry for?'

She waved her hand. She couldn't look at him right now. It seemed that now she'd woken up, all the emotions she'd kept locked away these past few months were fighting to get out now. It seemed that being sick had used up all the firm reserves she normally had.

If she looked at Duc, with his floppy hair and soft brown eyes, she would crumble.

'I think I need to leave,' were the words that came out.

'As soon as I feel better. I think I need to leave.'

'What?' His voice was incredulous.

She concentrated on her hands. 'This isn't working out—not for me, Duc.'

'But I thought you liked it here?'

'I do. I mean I did.'

Her hands had never looked so interesting.

'Viv, talk to me. Tell me what you mean?'

How could she do that? How could she tell her best friend that their relationship could never be the same again—at least, not for her?

From the instant she'd stepped off the plane and seen him again, things had changed between them.

It was nobody's fault.

Neither of them understood the change, but they'd crossed a line for Viv. No matter how hard she tried, she couldn't ignore the spark of attraction she felt for Duc now.

She'd never felt so connected to a person, or a place.

'I can't st-stay. Not here. Not now.'

He thumped down on the bed next to her. She closed her eyes. She could smell him. The familiar scents she associated with Duc. The laundry detergent he used for his clothes. How many times had she cuddled him, or lain with her head against his shoulder breathing that in?

He swung his legs up on to the bed so he was sitting parallel with her. She could almost hear his brain spinning, trying to find words. She knew him. Sometimes she thought she knew him better than he knew himself.

She took a deep breath. 'You've done well, Duc. This place is great. You've sorted things out. You can go back now. You can go back and be the surgeon you've always wanted to be.'

There was a long pause. 'You think that's what I want to do?'

'I know that's what you want to do. You should live the life you want.' Her voice started to shake a little. 'You should be happy.'

'What if I told you that's not what makes me happy?'

She jerked, and automatically turned to face him, cursing herself for letting down her guard.

His brown eyes were fixed straight on her. Sincere.

'Viv, what if I told you that it might have taken me a number of years to figure out, but the thing that makes me happy is you.'

She felt herself start to shake. She shook her head. 'No. No, it's not, Duc.'

His voice was steady. He reached over and intertwined his pinkie with hers. She wanted to pull her hand away, but the warmth from his skin seemed to hold her there.

'Viv, I'm sorry. I never really tried to walk in your shoes. I never really understood what your life must be like. You always seemed so independent, so self-sufficient, as if it was what you wanted, what you needed. I just didn't think any further than that. I didn't look deep enough when I should have.'

She didn't know quite where this conversation was going. 'What do you mean?'

He ran his other hand through his hair. 'I thought we told each other everything. I thought we were best friends. But when I look back, I've not been the friend that I should have.' This time it was his gaze that dropped to their intertwined pinkies. 'I let you down. I should have realised—I should have understood.'

She could feel herself starting to panic—she couldn't quite follow where he was going with this. 'What do you mean?'

'All those bad boyfriends. All the no-hopers and rat-bags. The one guy you went out with who was actually nice—Archie? Remember him?'

She felt herself shudder. She still couldn't under-

stand what this conversation was about. Archie. Yes,
of course she remembered him. The electrician from
Bristol. A lovely guy, good-natured, hard-working and
hopelessly devoted with a good sense of humour. She'd
dumped him after a few months. Archie had been nice.
Archie had been safe. Archie would have looked after
her. There wasn't a single bad thing she could say about
him.

She nodded without speaking.

'You ran, Viv. You ran so fast you practically
sprinted. Because Archie could have offered you an
attachment. Love.' He bit his bottom lip. 'A home. But
you couldn't do it. You couldn't cope. And everyone
you picked after that? They could offer none of those
things. I didn't see it at the time. I didn't understand.
But you deliberately went for guys like that because
they would never make you form an attachment. You
didn't need to invest your heart in them. It was like you
predetermined every relationship. And I think you did
it without even realising why.'

Her skin prickled as he spoke. There was something
so achingly familiar about some of the things he was
saying. She actually felt nauseous. She wanted to be
indignant. She wanted to automatically shout and deny
every part of this. But too much of it was making her
feel uncomfortable. Too much of it sounded so close to
the truth that it made her stomach hurt.

And it seemed that Duc didn't know when to stop.
'You run, Viv. You run because it's easier than stopping to find out if love and home are actually worth
the heartache.'

Now she snapped and snatched her hand away from
his. 'Not all of us had the life you did, Duc. Not all of

us had Khiem and Hoa.' It was cruel to bring them up when only a few months before they'd been snatched away from their son, but it seemed like now it was time for no holds barred.

'But when do you stop running, Viv? When do you stop and catch your breath? When do you take the time to look around and decide if someone and somewhere might actually be worth the risk?'

She could almost hear his heart in those words. There was a pleading tone to his voice.

'I could have lost you. I invited you here. You contracted a disease that's endemic to my country. I invited you to a place that could have killed you. I've spent the last few days scared to breathe, Viv. Scared that every breath might be the last one with you by my side. I had no idea. No idea what I had. And every idea about what I might lose.'

Her heart gave a little flip. Where was this going? She wanted to speak. She wanted to say something. But all the words were just gummed up in her mouth.

'You taught me about here. You let me learn to love being a doctor again. Not a surgeon, a *doctor*. You made me realise just what I've got here. Not just a building, but the people too. I can't imagine leaving. I can't imagine ever working anywhere else.' He took a deep breath. 'But I will. If you want me to.'

She frowned. 'What?'

He took a few moments. 'I want you to be happy, Viv. And if staying here isn't something you can contemplate, then tell me where you want to go, and I'll come too.'

She shook her head. 'What are you talking about?'

He pointed to his chest. 'Me.' Then pointed at hers.

'You. We have to give this a chance. We have to give us a chance. We have to see if this, us, is meant to be.' He reached over and gently touched her cheek. 'Let me show you what home can be.'

Maybe it was the way he said the words. Or maybe it was some of the stuff he'd said before, but every hackle went up at the back of her neck.

Her stomach plummeted. This was so not what she wanted to hear. He felt sorry for her. It was like he was still in doctor mode. 'You can't fix me, Duc.' She shook her head and tried to stop the tears forming in her eyes. 'Even if all the stuff you think about me is true, I'm scared to form relationships, I'm scared to take a chance on a home. I'm not your charity project. You don't get to feel sorry for me. And what you never get to do is...' she lifted her fingers in the air '...fix me.'

The very thought repulsed her. This wasn't what she wanted. In every tiny splintered dream she'd imagined what they could become to each other, and this wasn't it.

Duc gave a bewildered smile and shook his head. 'I don't want to fix you, Viv. That's not why I'm here. You don't need fixing. You're perfect just the way you are.'

'So what are you trying to say?'

He fixed his deep brown eyes on hers. 'What I'm asking for is permission to love you.'

She froze. Was that really just what he'd said?

'But...but you pulled away. You didn't want us to go down that path. You pulled away as if it was the worst thing you'd ever thought of. As if kissing me was the worst thing you'd ever done. Then you made an excuse about us just staying friends.'

He let out a wry laugh. 'Really? You thought I didn't

like kissing you?' He looked incredulous. 'Viv, when you're wrong, you're *so* wrong it's scary.'

She scowled as he used one of her own expressions, mimicking her Scottish accent.

'Viv, I've thought about kissing you from practically the moment you stepped off that plane in those denim shorts and that tied-up shirt. From the second you wrapped your arms around me at the airport something changed. At least, for me it did. Every casual hug or brush of your hand just seems to set me crazy—in a good way. I spend my life sniffing for that orange-blossom scent from your shampoo, wondering where you are. You sent my blood pressure skyrocketing in your "interview" outfit. As for that red dress?' He shook his head again, his smile reaching his twinkling eyes.

'I have no idea why we didn't go down this road before. Maybe we just both weren't ready. Maybe we weren't at that point in our lives. Maybe we needed to both find our feet a little. But now? Now, Viv? I'm ready if you are. Just say the word. Because I want to love you, Viv. I do. I want us to try and be together. More than anything in this world. More than this place. More than the other hospitals. I want to try with me and you. So, just say the word. Say that you'll give us a chance. It can be anywhere in the world. I'll follow you anywhere you want to go, Viv. Just tell me that you think we're worth a chance.'

She was stunned. This conversation had started in a very different way. She wasn't quite sure how after all this time Duc had just managed to say a million things at once.

'You have no idea—' his voice was lower, more gravelly '—what it felt like to see you collapse. To see you lying in that hospital bed. I lost my mum and dad this year, Viv. The thought of losing you too? I couldn't handle that. I can't handle losing the person I need most. I'm not crazy. I know I'm not crazy. But things have changed between us. We both know that. So let's take this, let's grab it with both hands and see where it takes us. We've got to be worth a try, surely, Viv.' He lowered his voice even more. 'I know I want to, with all my heart.'

A single tear slid down her cheek. She looked over at him. Now she saw it. Now she saw the fact he hadn't slept properly in days. The lines around his eyes.

She took a deep breath. 'It's not your fault I got sick. That's life. I was taking precautions, but I did go out to the accident in short sleeves. I didn't think about it—and I didn't notice any mosquito bite. That's my fault, not yours. But—' she locked gazes with him '—you haven't really told me how you feel about me, Duc. You say you want to try—but why do you want to try?'

He looked confused for a moment.

She held out her hands. 'This place is…different too. For me, that is. Maybe it is an age and stage thing, but I finally feel as if I've found a place I can fit in. I can be me. I like the people. I like the patients. The only thing that stops me wanting to stay here is you.'

He looked shocked. 'Why?'

She shook her head. 'You can't stay because it seems like a good idea. You can't stay because you think I want to. You dreamed of being a surgeon. Is that dream still there? Because if it is, in a few months you'll start to be miserable and unhappy. You won't want to be here, and it will affect everyone around you.'

He shook his head. He looked out the window across

to the hospital. 'I'd never taken the time I've had here to look at things. You know what surgical teams are like? It's a back-stabbing competitive world. I thought that was how I wanted to live my life. But after a while I realised just how much more of a doctor I can be here. I'm still adjusting. But there's so much work to be done that I don't want to stand still. I want to keep this place moving and make sure we're doing all we can. This is a job of a lifetime, Viv—at least, for me. I know you've moved about. I know you might still want to. You asked me how I really feel about you? I love you. I think I might always have loved you. If this place doesn't make you happy…' he put his hand to his chest '…and I don't make you happy, then I want you to know that I will always love you, I will always be here, I will always be your best friend. And…' he slowed down '…you will always have a home here, with me.'

She started to sob. She couldn't help it, and Duc moved, wrapping one arm around her shoulders and pulling her close.

'I love this place,' she said between sniffs as she laid her hand on his chest. 'But I love this place because it's got you in it. It is you. Everywhere I look I'm reminded of you. I couldn't be here if you weren't. You drive me crazy, do you know that? You kissed me in the kitchen and then pulled away. Do you know what that did to me? What that did to my heart? I thought it might break in two.'

He kissed her head. 'I'm sorry, Viv. I was mixed up. I thought I'd crossed a line and ruined everything between us. I thought you'd hate me.'

Her hand thumped against his chest. 'How can I hate you when I love you, stupid? The guy who's been my everything for the last ten years. The one person I'm honest with and tell all my dark family secrets.' She fingered the chain at her throat.

'The one man to buy me jewellery just because it matched my eyes. And when you kissed me...you turned my world upside down. A kiss between friends isn't supposed to feel like *that*. Isn't supposed to steal the breath from your throat and turn your legs to jelly. Isn't supposed to leave your heart racing so much you can't sleep at night.' Her fingers were brushing the skin at the base of his neck. He looked down at her with those dark eyes. She could see the sparkle. Feel the sizzle in the air between them again.

She moved her fingers more slowly. 'And this? This electricity that constantly buzzes between us? How are we ever supposed to get any work done in future? How will any patients ever get seen if we both work here?'

She couldn't help the teasing tone in her voice. Her heart was so full she couldn't breathe again. Duc loved her. He said he loved her. Could the world ever be this perfect?

He changed position, tilting her chin up to his. 'So, this is us. This is really us.'

It was like he was just making sure.

She nodded.

But he kept going as a sexy smile appeared on his face. 'No pulling back. No changing minds?'

'No pulling back, no changing minds,' she repeated with a smile on her face, then she sighed as he jumped off the bed and headed to the doorway. 'Duc, are you ever going to kiss me? Or am I going to have to die waiting?'

'Oh, I'm going to kiss you, I'm just making sure we'll

not be disturbed.' He smiled as he turned the lock on the door and joined her back on the bed. He slid his arms around her waist. 'Now, where were we?'

'Right here,' she said as her lips touched his.

CHAPTER FIFTEEN

Six months later

'PUSH, LIEN. PUSH!'

It was the middle of the night. But no one at May Mắn hospital currently cared what time of day it was.

The corridor outside the delivery room was practically full. This was their first official May Mắn baby, created by two doctors who worked there, delivered by staff who loved them both.

Duc was pacing outside. Lien's parents were sitting impatiently on two chairs, watching for every swing of the door. Several of the nurses had lined the corridor. Two of the visiting doctors who were officially on duty tonight were watching the whole scene with amusement.

They'd even started to serve snacks while they waited.

Every now and then Viv stuck her head outside with an instruction for someone and they all held their breaths, letting them go in frustration when she still didn't bring the news they were all waiting for.

Ron was the most amused of all. There was a coloured chart at the nurses' station with guesses for date, time, sex, birth weight and name. 'Is it always going to be this much fun?' he said as he walked past.

For a few minutes there was silence. Then came a loud cry.

A cheer erupted from outside as Baby Lennox announced her arrival to the world. Viv cleaned off her face, did a few quick checks and placed baby on Lien's chest.

Lien wrinkled her nose as she lay back against the pillows, exhausted. 'Tell me they aren't high-fiving out there.'

Viv and Ron laughed together. 'It's been a closely fought contest. Three staff were watching the clock, hoping they'd win the bet.'

Lien shook her head as she stared at her brand-new daughter. 'Wow,' she breathed. Then she looked at Joe. He hadn't taken his eyes off his daughter from the second she'd been born. 'I'm not doing that again.'

Viv and Ron looked at each other. 'That's what they all say,' they said in unison.

Lien smiled. 'I mean it.'

Viv nodded. 'So do they. It doesn't mean that in two years' time I won't see you again.'

Ron grinned. 'Well, I'm delighted. Do we have a name for our latest arrival?'

Joe sighed. 'Nope. We both agreed we would give Regan the final say, and since we didn't know if it was a boy or a girl, he said he was keeping his name a secret.'

Ron let out the biggest laugh of all. 'Yes! I can't wait.' He stood up. 'We were talking about his favourite superhero the other day so hold on, folks, who knows what we'll get?'

Five minutes later Lien and the baby were settled, and Viv had cleaned up the room for visitors, meaning the rest of the hospital could visit.

Duc shook hands with Joe and gave Lien a kiss on the cheek after admiring the baby, and waved to Viv to come outside.

Viv left things in the hands of Melody, the other midwife, and walked outside with him to sit on the grass for five minutes.

It was cooler outside, and once he'd wrapped an arm around her shoulder she leaned against him.

'Ooh, I'm knackered. You need to make me some tea.'

His breathing was slow and steady. She could actually stay in this position all night. They sometimes sat outside for a short spell at night, just to watch the stars.

It took her a few moments to notice something unusual. 'Hey? What's happened to the trees?'

'What do you mean?'

She sat upright. 'What's with the twinkling lights?'

Someone had strung little white lights between the trees to the left of the bungalows. They'd put a memorial bench under the trees a few months ago for Khiem and Hoa.

'Oh, *those* lights,' said Duc, as he stood up and held his hand out towards her.

She smiled but wrinkled her brow in curiosity as he led her towards the bench. They watched as Joe crossed the grass behind them, ducking into his own bungalow to collect Regan and let him meet his new sister.

Viv sat down on the bench and looked up at the lights. 'They really do add a little magic to the place, don't they? We should have thought of these before.

And maybe, at Christmastime, we can change them for another colour?'

She looked to her right, expecting Duc to be beside her, but he'd vanished.

'Duc?'

'Right here.'

He was kneeling on the grass in front of her.

She let out a little gasp and pulled both hands up to her mouth.

He smiled. 'Timing is everything.'

He took her hands in his. 'Viv, the last six months have been the best of my life. You're my partner in crime and the love of my life. I can't imagine spending a minute of this life without having you by my side. I can't imagine a day when you don't shout at me in your crazy Scottish accent or fight me for a bit of chocolate. Let's not wait. It's been too long already.'

He pulled out the glittering emerald-and-diamond ring that had belonged to his mother. 'You know that my mum and dad loved you.' He glanced upwards. 'Somehow I know that right now they're up there, smiling down on us and telling me to hurry up.' He shot her a wary look. 'If you want something else, I'll buy you something else. But my mum always told me she hoped I'd find someone to love, like she loved Dad. And maybe she already knew who that would be. So, what do you say, Vivienne Kerr, crazy Scot number one, will you be my wife, for ever and ever?'

Her hands were shaking, but that didn't stop her holding out her finger so he could slip the emerald-and-diamond ring onto it. She touched his cheek. 'Duc Nguyen, I got so lucky the day I met you. I can't imagine what might have happened if you hadn't been there to give me a hug in the sluice that day. You've stolen my heart, and you've given me something I couldn't ever have found without you—a home. And the ring? I love it. I'm honoured. So, yes! Tell the world that, yes, I'll be your wife.'

Duc swept her up into his arms and spun her around but when her feet touched the ground she took a step back for a second until she found his hand.

She linked their pinkies together and looked up into his eyes. 'For ever,' she whispered.

'For ever,' he repeated as he bent to kiss her.

* * * * *

COMING SOON!

We really hope you enjoyed reading this book. If you're looking for more romance, be sure to head to the shops when new books are available on

Thursday 3rd October

To see which titles are coming soon, please visit

millsandboon.co.uk/nextmonth

MILLS & BOON

Coming next month

FROM HEARTACHE TO FOREVER
Caroline Anderson

'I wasn't brave, Ry, not at all. I was just doing what had to be done, and then once it was done I just felt empty.'

'I shouldn't have left you.'

She took his hand and kissed it, then held it in her hands, warm and firm and kind, Beth all over.

'I sent you away, Ryan. I couldn't deal with your grief as well as mine, and that was wrong. We should have grieved together for our daughter, but we didn't know each other well enough. We still don't, but we're learning, day by day, and we'll get there.'

He nodded slowly. 'Yeah, I suppose so.' He glanced at his phone and sighed. 'Beth, I'm sorry, I need to go.'

She chuckled softly. 'You need to get to bed. You've had a hectic few days, you must be exhausted.'

'I am. I tell you what, that bed had better be comfortable,' he said wryly. 'Did you try it?'

'No, I didn't have time, but if it isn't there's always the sofa.' She cocked her head on one side, her eyes searching his. 'Are you all right, Ry?'

He laughed softly and nodded. 'Yes, Beth. I'm all right. You?'

Her smile was sad. 'I'm all right. I'm used to it now. It's the new normal.'

He nodded, then got to his feet, pulled her up and into his arms and hugged her gently.

'Thank you, for everything. You've been amazing, ever since I got here. You've always been amazing.'

'Don't be silly.'

'I'm not. I mean it. You're the strongest person I know, Beth, and the kindest, and I don't deserve you. Thank you.'

She hugged him back, then let him go. 'You're welcome. I hope you sleep well.'

He laughed. 'I'm sure I will.'

She walked him to the door and he turned and kissed her, just the slightest brush of his lips on hers, and let himself out and drove home, then paused a moment on the drive, staring up at the stars twinkling in the clear, dark night.

He loved the stars. They never changed, untouched by all the madness around him, the one constant in a changing world.

He let himself in, checked his email and looked at the bed—his new bed, carefully put together by Beth to save him the trouble because that was the kind of person she was—and felt another wave of guilt for leaving her alone when she'd been so sad and lost and torn with grief.

She would never have left him. He knew that, but at the time she'd been adamant that she didn't need him. Only now it turned out she had, but she'd been unable to cope with his grief, too, because they didn't know each other well enough to grieve together.

Well enough to make a baby, but not well enough to lose one. Maybe, given time, they would find that closeness and with it some closure. He hoped so.

Continue reading
FROM HEARTACHE TO FOREVER
Caroline Anderson

Available next month
www.millsandboon.co.uk

LET'S TALK

Romance

For exclusive extracts, competitions
and special offers, find us online:

f facebook.com/millsandboon

🐦 @MillsandBoon

📷 @MillsandBoonUK

Get in touch on 01413 063232